WRECK and ORDER

[a novel]

HANNAH TENNANT-MOORE

HOGARTH
London / New York

Published in the United States by Hogarth, an imprint of the Crown Publishing
Group, a division of Penguin Random House LLC, New York.
www.crownpublishing.com

HOGARTH is a trademark of the Random House Group Limited, and
the H colophon is a trademark of Penguin Random House LLC.

Library of Congress Cataloging-in-Publication Data
Tennant-Moore, Hannah.
Wreck and Order : a novel / Hannah Tennant-Moore. —First Edition.
pages cm
1. Young women—Fiction. 2. Voyages and travels—Fiction.
3. Self-realization in women—Fiction. I. Title.
PS3620.E554W74 2016
813'.6—dc23   2015018862

ISBN 978-1-101-90326-1
eBook ISBN 978-1-101-90327-8

Printed in the United States of America

Book design by Lauren Dong
Jacket design by Elena Giavaldi
Jacket illustration by Leah Goren

10 9 8 7 6 5 4 3 2 1

First Edition

For Wyatt—true reader, true love, true friend—
and for W. L. E., with admiration and gratitude

WRECK and ORDER

[one]

CARPINTERIA

My father inherited a small fortune when his mother died, and on my twenty-first birthday he handed me a card with a check inside. I spent a year in Paris after high school and had been living with Dad since then, working at a pottery store and reading my way through a box of moldy French novels and partying at the local bar with college students who wore American-flag bandannas and U.S. Army pants even though they went to a liberal arts school in New England. "Do you dress like that because you support the wars?" I asked one of these boys, after we'd slept together. He laughed with his nose. "Whatever," he said. I was glad I'd decided not to go to college. Better to use my father's money to travel than to sit in class with a bunch of morons. And now I had enough money that I didn't need to make decisions at all. My father beamed as I gazed in astonishment at the four zeroes on his check, proud of his ability to provide for his child. I started driving around the country with a tent and sleeping bag in the back of my car, settling in whatever town could hold my interest for a few months, sometimes doing business transcription or working in coffee shops. I lived frugally to make money that wasn't mine last. So I was shocked to find myself penniless one day, unable to pay for my sandwich at a deli in Carpinteria. I called my father, and he provided me with a few more years of choicelessness.

It was nearly dark when I hung up the phone. I'd have to spend the night in this maybe seedy, maybe idyllic coastal California town. I went to a bar to find out about campgrounds in the area. A guy looked me up and down when I walked in. Then he started a game of pool. He had thick arms and goldfish tattoos on each wrist; pale, pockmarked cheeks; a dainty nose. His jeans were too short and his legs were stubby. I was not attracted to his appearance. But I was attracted to him. I drank three pints of Guinness and watched him win four games. His brown eyes were open wide, so he could watch his shot and stare at me at the same time. His look reduced me, not unpleasantly, to sex. When I got up from my stool to walk to the bathroom, I felt the cotton of my underpants shifting over my buttocks, my asshole tingling and contracting as if I were lying facedown in the sun after swimming in icy water.

When he walked to the back patio, I followed him out and asked for a cigarette. The arbor above our heads was interlaced with broken Christmas lights. They flickered dizzyingly as he lit a Camel for me. I hoped he wouldn't notice that I winced with each inhale; tobacco is one of the few drugs I hate. "You know you're sexy, thank god," he said. "So we don't need to talk about it all night." I was wearing a short skirt with ripped black panty hose and a tight tank top with a ladybug embroidered over my left nipple. My breasts are small and my legs are short, but I have a perky ass and symmetrical features. Jared was right. I love my body. I like my face, too. It's not that I'm a knockout, but you don't have to be a knockout to be desired. My appearance is one thing I don't worry about. "I don't like talking, anyway," I said. Jared dipped a key into a small baggie, held the white powder under my nose.

After the bar closed, I hopped on the handlebars of his bike. Jared stopped short in front of a turning car and I flew forward. The heels of my boots weren't sturdy enough to support the impact of my fall. My ankles twisted as I spiraled to the ground, landing on my back with my feet crossed. Jared grinned as he helped me up. "Took yourself a tumble, didn't ya darlin'?" I touched my face. Smooth, dry. I straddled the front wheel and hopped back onto the handlebars. His breath warmed my neck as he raised himself off the bike seat to hurtle us through a thicket of fog-softened headlights. When I woke up in his bed the next morning, it looked like someone had sewn a piece of midnight blue fabric onto my hip with yellow thread. Jared shook his pillow out of its case, filled the case with ice and held it to my side. "I like you so much," he whispered in my ear. He caught the back of my neck in his teeth. Icy waves lapped at my hip. His teeth tickled my skin. I got dizzy, free of thought.

I stayed with Jared for the next few days. We stumbled into a stranger's party and danced until dawn, and skinny-dipped in the ocean under a huge orange moon, and set out on bikes with beer and sandwiches, riding equestrian trails through woods that led to sea cliffs, taking breaks to have sex in eucalyptus groves. Here was an answer to the question of what to do with my life.

I found a room for rent in a tiny, lopsided cottage occupied by a forty-year-old bachelor who had blown off his right hand in a drunken fireworks accident. Our bedrooms shared a thin wall. I wondered if Ron was always sheepish or if the accident had made him that way. The rent was negligible. I got the impression he wanted someone around, just in case. A week after I moved in, I peeked into the garage that we were not allowed to use. Piles and piles of lace-up shoes. Ron only wore slip-ons. The accident had happened years ago, but maybe he was still hoping to learn. Or to find someone to do the tying for him. In any case, I wasn't worried about getting a job anytime soon. The money I had left from my dad felt like a lot to someone who had never really thought about money.

So when I wasn't with Jared, I had plenty of time to indulge my recent obsession: the torture of so-called terror suspects, meaning mostly poor Muslim men whom corrupt warlords handed over to the United States in exchange for bounties. Not that you could talk like that in public or people would think you were not sufficiently distressed over 9/11. A handful of lunatics succeeded in changing the way regular people thought about sadistic violence. Torture was now acceptable. You needed a measured rationale to justify being against it—it was ineffective; it was a recruiting tool for the terrorists; it made it more likely that captured American soldiers would be mistreated. I learned these reasons because I had to. If I said, even at a bar in a liberal town in Southern California, that my opposition to torture was based on a *feeling*—the feeling that it's wrong for one human being to inflict as much pain as possible on another human being—then I was pitied for being idealistic and sentimental. But if the problem with sentimentality is that it wastes our need to feel on false, trivial tropes—a Nazi who weeps at the opera but is unmoved at the gas chamber—then wouldn't the solution be for us to feel strongly about real stuff instead, for pure, uncomplicated emotion to be aroused not by baby animals on YouTube but by ordinary people in pain?

The first act of sadistic violence I witnessed was a crow pecking a baby bat to death in my backyard. I gave the bat a funeral at which I read a memorial poem ("I will never forget you little bat / It was so mean of the crow to do that") and then had to stay home from school for two days because I couldn't stop crying. I was probably six. My mother was worried; my father was proud. It was from him that I learned to anguish over mass suffering I could do nothing about. Throughout my childhood, he spent several hours a day reading terrible news stories, which he would talk about throughout dinners, rides to and from school, trips to the grocery store. My mother would tell him not to disturb a child; my father would say privileged people not wanting to be disturbed was the cause of the problem. Since my father never did anything with his knowledge except get angry and then depressed, I thought my mother might have a point. But after she abandoned us for a pretty dimwit, I sided with Dad: My mother was frivolous; my father's angst was purposeful and important. I filled my adolescence with books about slavery, the Holocaust, the Stasi, the Gulag, the Chinese oppression of Tibet, the Gaza Strip. I used to wonder what I would do if I lived in a country that imprisoned people in massive, indiscriminate sweeps (Rumsfeld's leaflets "falling like snow" over Afghanistan, promising "wealth and power beyond your dreams" in exchange for turning in supposed enemy combatants) and tortured them without ever charging them with crimes (the legal memos with graphic descriptions of waterboarding, stress positions, beatings to inflict maximum distress without causing organ failure or death). After Abu Ghraib and Bagram and Guantánamo, I knew what I would do: feel rage, shame, disgust, loneliness, helplessness, sorrow, despair, great and debilitating hatred for everyone who did not also feel these things.

A young woman from PeaceByPeace knocked on my door in Carpinteria one afternoon, asking if I had a minute for peace. What she really wanted was money, but at least she was out doing something. So I tried canvassing, too. But I hated asking strangers for money that I wasn't even convinced helped all that much. PeaceByPeace lobbied politicians to support their initiatives. I had no faith in politics; the first presidential election I voted in was decided by a single American who happened to be on the Supreme

Court. And even at PeaceByPeace human rights was not a popular cause. The fastest way to get people to give—other canvassers advised me—was to make an economic argument against Bush's policies, something I couldn't have done even if I wanted to. You had to slip in the human rights stuff later, once you'd hooked them—the same way that, if you were writing a novel, you wouldn't want to start off with a diatribe against torture and indefinite detention or you could turn off a lot of potential readers. Maybe you could slip the political stuff in later, after you'd made a particular Muslim character really sympathetic, perhaps in an unlikely feminist way, like he collected bits of charcoal to make rudimentary writing implements for poor, oppressed schoolgirls. Then you could have him detained and tortured and readers might care.

I understood the method. I just couldn't abide it. After the twentieth door was slammed in my face as soon as I mentioned humane treatment for so-called enemy combatants, I quit. Reading the news alone was less depressing than trying to do something about it.

I met a few girls in Carpinteria that I liked to go out and drink with, but I couldn't imagine becoming really close with them. They weren't up against anything, having spent their lives running between the mountains and the sea. When I complained to one of them about how difficult it was just to be a decent person, she suggested I go to the beach, listen to the ocean, and "soak up the inspiration." Southern California is a great place to soak up ethereal nouns.

But Jared suffered. He was real. He read David Foster Wallace with a dictionary, taking notes in a journal. He read the way he did everything: desperately, driven by too much need for things to be too different from what they were. He was the only person—aside from my father—whom I could talk to about the war on terror (another ethereal noun). We had feelings, not arguments—only an insane person could argue intellectually about something like torturing and jailing people for years without ever charging them with a crime—which of course made us ineffective political thinkers. Jared read the newspaper like it was a book, looking not for facts but for stories: What was happening to regular people? It's hard not to be compelled by suffering when you're suffering yourself. But if I was paralyzed by my feelings, Jared was at war with his. Alcohol was the quickest way to win.

He was the rhythm guitarist for a mediocre rockabilly band that played the local bars most weekends; he made his living selling drugs. He did drop-offs at dawn, midnight, noon. Couldn't afford to disappoint his clientele. Carpinteria was a small town with a lot of dealers. Susan was my introduction to this clientele, a few months after I'd settled down in Carp. She was petite and blond and full-bosomed, wearing red lipstick and a tight sweater, standing next to us at the bar one night, demanding that Jared buy her a drink. "I'm broke," she said, sticking out her lower lip. Jared took a twenty out of his wallet and handed it to her. I raised my eyebrows. He shrugged. We went outside and danced to the Cure, which was blasting from speakers on the back patio. Susan found us, shimmied against Jared, pulled the cigarette out of his mouth and took long, dramatic drags as she told me how far back she and Jerrie go, that she's been stealing his cigarettes at the end of a long night for years. When she went inside to get another drink, I told Jared to stop flirting with that whore, hating my stereotypically competitive tone, hating him for making me assume it.

"Suze? You're trippin'. I fucked her once. But that was years ago. Stop trippin', girl."

To Drunk Jared I was just one more needy female, as in "Woman, you are a handful" and "Girl, get off my back." He turned away from me. I turned on my heels. Pride dragged me toward home. After two blocks, I remembered that I was clacking my way to a dark apartment where I'd hiccup and sob into my pillow, trying not to wake my depressed roommate. But when I got back to the bar, Jared was gone. I searched wide-eyed, clutching the sides of my dress, forcing myself not to break into a run.

"Are you looking for the guy in the red shirt?" the bartender asked me. Yes, I was, that adorable red shirt with the bluebird over the left breast pocket. "He took off. He was really trashed. Better let him sleep it off." When Jared called me the next afternoon and asked if I wanted to meet at a diner, I told him that I would never see him again. He left a present on my windowsill every day for the next week—earrings, chocolates, flowers. Stupid things, the perfect things. Eventually I agreed to let him take me to a Wilco concert in L.A. "I'll be your designated driver," he said, and drank only Pepsi at the show. Afterward, he drove us back to his house and we jumped on his trampoline under the stars, Santa Ana winds somersaulting down the piney mountains. He fed me avocado-and-tomato sandwiches in his bed. We had sex three times and slept entangled till noon.

One night, I had two orgasms and he had none. I kept trying, desperate for proof of his attraction to me, reminding him of how he used to come so quickly, too quickly. "Because you were brand new," he said, yawning into my hair. The next day, I bought a pair of lace-up, knee-high boots for two hundred bucks. When Jared saw me wearing them, he said, "Where'd you get those boots? The Sexy Store?" I cringed; he knew I was trying to please him. The first time I wore the boots, the right heel came off in chunks on the dance floor. I left a trail of rubber everywhere I went.

And it turned out Jared didn't give a shit about my sexy boots.

He cared about seeing me from every possible angle, under the brightest lights, his nose an inch from my skin. "But—" I'd protest as he parted my legs or rolled me onto my stomach. "Come on," he'd say. "Let me see you." Attraction was access to knowledge that could not be gained from any other kind of interaction. There was nothing to hold back.

Most Friday nights, we'd split a bottle of Bushmills and ride our bikes into town. As we were walking into a bar one night, Jared put his foot out and I went straight down, too drunk to try to break my fall. Jared was laughing, but it was the laugh of not wanting the feeling that would come when the laughter ended. I raised myself onto all fours, waited for my nose to stop smarting. He put his hands under my armpits and pulled me up. "You okay?" he asked, almost scared. Something big and metal was clamped over my face. I was afraid that if I tried to talk my voice would come out funny. He moved my nose from side to side and kissed me on the cheek. "You're okay." We went into the bar. Jared ordered drinks with a series of elaborate hand gestures. He sauntered to the pool table. I went into the bathroom. While I was sitting on the toilet, I took my phone out of my purse and called my father. I told him I was in love. I wanted to give him something to be happy about. "It's three in the morning here," he said. "Why don't you get some sleep and let's talk tomorrow." The fear in my father's voice woke me up like a slap. He was normally so supportive of my adventures, encouraging me to tell him everything, he wouldn't judge.

When I left the bathroom, Jared was hitting the balls with the stick, stalking the table, scratching the crack of his ass. He was powerful and essential and doing just fine. I was in love, meaning I was addicted to a specific body; I was afraid.

~

A few days later, I tried to reassure my father—and myself—about the state of my new life in California by applying for an internship at the local paper. I had never dreamed of being a journalist, but this seemed like one way I might be able to put my feelings to use.

The newspaper office was marked by a small sign that looked like an ad for a newspaper in a children's comic book: an illustration of a typewriter spewing a page that said *Carp Weekly* in bubbly letters. The interior was a fluorescent-lit room crammed with people, desks, books, papers, phones, computers covered in Post-it notes, fax machines, mugs, stale bagels. The chaos relaxed me. The woman who interviewed me looked damaged in a way that made her dull and approachable rather than threatening. She introduced herself as Sally—no last name, no title. She was impressed with my writing samples, even more so when I told her they were papers from a high school English class. The lie I'd planned—about having dropped out of the last semester of college to care for a dying parent—felt unnecessary. In fact, Sally seemed glad to learn I hadn't gone to college, like it gave me some secret cachet. She even used the term "self-taught," which sounded pretentious, but I did read a lot and obsessively analyze my thoughts—was that being "self-taught"? I learned from the card Sally handed me at the end of the interview that she was the managing editor.

The next day, she called and offered me not the unpaid internship but an actual job. They happened to be looking for someone to run the obituary section. I suggested that I might not be qualified. "Believe me, you're overqualified," Sally said. "The job is mostly dealing with crazies." I set up an interview with the publisher, which Sally suggested was mostly a formality. Donnie asked me my favorite authors, was condescendingly impressed. Nine bucks an hour, no benefits; no wonder they were willing to overlook my inexperience. But I liked the idea of having a title: assistant editor.

They gave me a cubicle on the newsroom floor. Sally fielded my first phone call by way of training. "Thank you for your interest in *Carp Weekly*. I have to stress right off the bat that we do not publish typical obituaries. These are more like personal essays—stories rather than a rundown of events and accomplishments. If you would prefer to run a standard obituary, I am more than happy to refer you to our advertising department." She hung up the phone, showed me the coffee machine and the microwave, left me to set up my email.

As I was struggling with an Ethernet cord, a middle-aged man came out of the office next to mine, and sans intro—the kind of shorthand I soon learned to associate with him—started telling me about a woman who had been murdered by her ex-husband a few days ago. "Been divorced for twenty-five years. At least the douche bag never found anyone else to hate. Small consolation, I grant." Joe was pale and lanky with faintly humped shoulders, but his voice made him seem like he tossed pianos for fun. "She was a retired teacher, had a little house with a garden, named Effie or something like that. You get the picture." His phone rang. He returned to his desk in two strides. "Yello," he belted. "Thanks for the callback. So listen, what the fuck is up with this cat running for city council?" Less than a second elapsed between the end of his phone call and his reappearance at my desk. "So the woman's got a sister. Only kin mentioned in the daily. What I'd do, if I were you, is look up that sister." Joe carried on the conversation like this, bounding between my desk and his, sometimes picking up his thoughts mid-sentence.

I was dismayed by how easy it was to track down the sister's name and phone number. I was often nervous calling a friend to ask if she wanted to get a drink when I was alone in my house, and now I was supposed to dial a stranger and ask if she wanted to write an essay for me on her recently murdered sister, while I was surrounded by coworkers with hard, avid faces, jamming down computer keys and talking loudly into headsets (*"Carp Weekly,* Bill speaking"). I told myself I could quit tomorrow, just make the call, there was nothing riding on this. But every time I was about to press the last digit, I panicked and hung up, fidgeted with my empty Rolodex. At last, I took my purse and slipped out the back door. I made the call from the parking lot. When the sister answered, I repeated Sally's spiel about our obituaries being more like personal essays. The sister asked my name, told me how relieved she was that I called. She wanted so much for there to be an obituary about Barb but her eyesight was bad and she could no longer type. Was there any way—and please tell her if this was inexcusably rude, she was not entirely in her right mind at the moment—but perhaps, maybe, was there any way she could tell me her memories and I could type them up?

I started offering this dictation service whenever I requested an essay. I made the calls from my cubicle once I realized that everyone was too harried to notice anyone else. For a while, the work suited me in the way it suited Joe to be a reporter. He never seemed to be in conflict with himself, even when he was screaming into his phone, "You wanna hear libel? Go on and sue me and hear what this town has to say about your quote unquote *business.* You know, pal, it's never too late to stop wasting your life being an asshole." He slammed down the phone, stood in his doorway eating a doughnut, shouted at me from across the newsroom. "We gotta get something good for the Iraq vet who shot himself and his dad. Look up his girlfriend. Word of advice: Don't mention a goddamn thing about the Middle East or IEDs or PTSD. You just let her remember him—color of his cuticles, favorite license plate number, all that shit. Then she might actually open up to me when I call."

I loved being near Joe's devotion, and I liked being implicated in the socially condoned spectacle of unhinged death-grief. It made me feel less alone, a kind of selfishness I accepted in myself.

Jared would sometimes use his belt on me, never against my will. He didn't hit hard. He'd hold my arms down and place his teeth around my nipple, poised to clamp down. "Stop, stop, stop," I'd say and he'd tell me to shut up, backhanding my jaw. He'd order me to take my clothes off, but it never became more sexual than that. This wasn't about sex. It was about having power over life. Jared wanted to believe he had some and I wanted to give all mine away. I wanted bruises, empirical proof of the destructiveness of emotions. The first time he hit me too hard, I winced and put my hand to my jaw. He fell on me with a look of terror and wet my face with kisses. "Sweetie, baby, oh no, did I hurt you?"

Because yes and no were both the wrong answer, we kept pushing the limit. We wanted more—longer strangulations, redder marks, deeper and murkier troughs of shame and forgiveness. Sometimes when Jared got up to pee in the night and I watched his buttocks moving toward the toilet, exhausted and trusting, the whitest thing in the room, I felt a tenderness I could not bear without violence. It was the same feeling that kept me awake at night in junior high, scratching at my chest until I drew blood. Sometime in seventh grade, I developed a nearly constant irritation in my chest, like tiny claws scratching me from the inside. My annoyment knot, I called it, but only to myself. Some nights I'd claw at my chest until I felt warm wetness beneath my fingernails; then I'd lie awake thinking that there was something seriously wrong with me and I needed to find the right person to make it better. The knot sometimes compelled me to wear something weird to school—a flowered shower cap or jeans with one leg cut off and the other long or leotards snapped over the crotch of my jeans instead of under them. There had to be something you could do.

My dad got me the Liz Phair album when I was in high school. He thought I would like it, and I did. I blasted it every time I borrowed his car, affecting her girlish earnestness, just self-conscious enough to pretend toward irony. *I could take this in doses large enough to kill.* Jared's butt cheeks were almost repulsive in their vulnerability—disproportionately small, cuddled against each other, the skin a mottled red sprouting long, curly, brown hairs. I was entrusted with their care. When Jared gripped my neck and banged my head against his flimsy bedroom wall, my tenderness was forced out of my chest and into the world. I imagined him as a kid, sitting alone in the backyard after school, waiting for his father to get home from work, plucking a thick blade of grass and holding it taut between his thumbs. In tenth grade, he dropped out of school to go on tour with the Grateful Dead. His father gave him three hundred bucks and wished him luck. Jared hitchhiked and begged and slept in city parks for the next two years. I was the whistle the blade of grass made when his small self blew against its sharp edge.

Once I tried to explain to Jared the need to do violence to my love. Then I giggled, hoping I sounded as cavalier as Liz Phair. He was hard in an instant. He gripped my shoulders and pressed his open mouth to my collarbone and pushed inside me. For a long time, neither of us moved. In my mind, a small wave tumbled over itself to fall on dry sand, then retreated into the deep vast blue. Tumbled, retreated, tumbled again.

BRIMSFIELD

When I was seven, we moved out of the cultured, lovely town of Northampton, Massachusetts, to a shithole inhabited by cretins a few miles away because it was the only place my parents could afford the decrepit yet palacial Victorian house my mother believed she needed to live in to be happy. She was thoughtful enough to rent a post-office box so that I could, illicitly, keep going to school in Northampton, but she did not consider that since she hated to drive and my father worked during the week, living nearly an hour away from school would severely limit my ability to have friends or play sports. "Oh please, as if you were just about to take up field hockey," she said in response to my complaints. She was right: I preferred reading in bed to any other activity in the world. By moving me an hour away from the only civilization I'd known and giving me my own floor in a giant house that was always freezing since my father's intermittent videography work could not cover an exorbitant electricity bill, my mother ensured that I would rarely have to leave my comfort zone.

I was about eight when I discovered the mirror trick. I would lock myself in the downstairs bathroom, the one with a mirror that covered the whole wall above the sink. Sitting cross-legged on the cool black tiles, my knees and forehead touching the glass, I stared into my eyes. For the first few minutes, I noticed my thin lips, blue eyes, the freckles shaped in a heart next to my left nostril. I made tiny facial movements—widening my eyes, puckering my lips—to convince myself that the person I was seeing corresponded to my actual self, in real time. But gradually, as I sat and stared, my face became foreign to me, the way a particular word loses its meaning if you say it aloud over and over. The arrangement of my features looked alien, in the child's sense of the word. Later, when Magic

Eye drawings became popular, I was reminded of the exact second of the mirror feeling's arrival every time I stared at one of those computer-generated creations, and a mass of indistinguishable colored dots suddenly gave way to an intricate scene—a scientist pouring from a flask, a girl kicking a soccer ball. For a time, I was addicted to the exhilarating discomfort of seeing myself as unrecognizable. I'd always end up rolling around on the bath mat, mesmerized by this sensation that was the absence of all learned physical sensations. Of course I had none of these thoughts at the time. It was not I, but my body, that was bewildered.

My mother burst into my room one night while my father and I were playing Connect Four. She shook a woman's magazine in the air above our heads and read out loud: "Leave him after the first slap!" I had never seen my father slap my mother, but he didn't deny he had. Mostly, he seemed not to really participate in their fights—like at Thanksgiving, when she had screamed "Shit! Shit! Shit!" because the bakery ran out of her favorite kind of pie. My father read a novel on the couch through her cries. It had been his job to pick up the pie.

The kitchen table was my mother's favorite place to cry. Her sobs made me think of gasping fish, flopping about on the bottom of a ship. On the nights after their fights, my dad would read to me before bed, sitting on the floor with his back against my twin bed, his voice straining toward sweetness. After he shut out the light and left, I would roll onto my stomach with my fists pressed against my chest and imagine floating high above everyone I knew—parents, teachers, classmates—until each familiar head became an indiscriminate black dot before fading into the green-speckled earth. The trick helped, a little. I learned to hear the screaming as wordless, the sound of the space between two people, any two people, every two people.

My mother met another man and separated from my father when I was in sixth grade. I went out for dinner with my mom and her new boyfriend a few times. Rick didn't speak to me. He just looked at my mother's made-up face with this vacant urgency, as if a need that belonged to someone else had gotten lost inside him and was searching for a way out. He gave me a teddy bear for my eleventh birthday, just when I was discovering lip gloss and MTV. Rick and my mother moved to Phoenix, where one of his buddies had promised him a job "making bank"—my mom giggled when she repeated the phrase to me—as a sales rep for some popular online store. My mother invited me to move with her, but I stayed with my father, who always had time for me. He hadn't had any videography assignments in a while. He was always talking about making a documentary, but whenever he started seriously pursuing one of his ideas—doing research, contacting potential interview subjects—he decided there wasn't enough information or it had already been done or another cause was more important.

Strange, but the years after my mother left weren't so bad. I now had an excuse for how I was. I was the girl whose mother had abandoned her; it was only natural that I be eerie and withdrawn, that I show up to school in strange outfits that made people laugh nervously and give me a wide berth. It was satisfying to discomfit my peers, whom I saw as obsessed with grades and clothes and popularity. And it was nice to be free of my anger at my mother's mopiness and erratic, desperate laugh. My father was an easier person—or at least it seemed that way to me, his child, his favorite part of life. He let me cut class whenever I wanted. We'd drive around in his pickup truck, listen to loud music, blast the heat, roll down the windows, sing along with Radiohead and R.E.M., my dad tapping the beat into the dashboard—*It's been a bad day, please don't take a picture*—and my dirty blond hair flying in the icy air and catching on my tongue. Listening to tidy song feelings captured by my father's voice—*Destiny, protect me from the world*—I felt protected from everything except his thin lips and pale skin and watery blue eyes, all just like mine. Sometimes he would turn down the music and ease off the accelerator and start talking about getting whipped by his father and all the hope he'd poured into falling in love with my mother and how he felt like such a failure for never having made a film of his own, but he'd made me and that was really enough, wasn't it? I liked my father's words, their solemn import attached to my silly life of carrying a heavy backpack to and from a brick cube. I knew there was something wrong with my father's lack of restraint—a needy egotism inherent in philosophizing to one's child—but so many times, embedded in his ramblings, was some comment that soothed my inner turbulence. Every closeness is a prison. Another thing my father used to say.

Dan and I had a lot of classes together in ninth grade, but I didn't really notice him until he started calling me with questions about math homework. He wore very uncool turtlenecks and never made jokes. But he laughed a lot and said quietly smart things in class. His presence was calming. I went to his house for the first time during a hailstorm. There were about ten people from my grade there. One of the girls had an older brother with a fake ID, so we had two fifths of vodka. I had never been drunk before. After my third or fourth shot, I sat down on the bed next to Dan. "This is a new life," I said. He wrapped me in his long arms. I giggled against his chest, a little kid again, unburdened by implications: Everything happening was just what was happening. We started kissing, oblivious to the other people making out and talking around us. A shirtless girl fluttered into Dan's room. "Dan!" she cried, unhooking her bra and dangling it from her finger. She ran toward the bed. A beam from the low A-frame ceiling took her out cold. Torrents of laughter. Dan helped her up, rolling his eyes at me.

A few weeks later I was in Dan's twin bed, wearing only my underwear. He was propped up on his elbow beside me, holding my hip with one hand. "I'm not going to let you put your clothes back on," he whispered. "You're so beautiful." His were the only thoughts about my body that existed. There was a guitar on the floor beside us and I asked him to sing to me. He sat on the edge of the bed. I curled myself around his back, my head resting on his corduroys. I was still too nervous to take off his pants. He sang about ripplin' still water and free fallin'. He glanced at the Bob Marley poster above his bed and lowered his face to mine. "Is this love is this love is this love that I'm feeling?" I added my voice to his. This was the reason people did not erase themselves from the universe. Dan's parents yelled up the stairs that it would soon be dinnertime. I phoned my dad. I glided into the passenger seat of his truck. Words came out of his mouth. Short, silvered ribbons of light came out of mine.

When Dan and I lost our virginity to each other, I never considered that sex would get far better and far worse than this. "We fit together," he said. I clutched his back. My body traced the letters of the perfect sentence that was sex. A saccharine image because that's how it felt. I was fifteen. I stared out the frosted-glass windows during Spanish class and math class and while taking a history test. There was nothing else to think about.

One Friday afternoon some months later, Dan and I were lying on his bed after school. Warm air, weary from a long summer, stewed in his room. I was wearing a long, silky skirt that made me feel adulthood as a sensuous promise. He ran his fingers through my hair. I turned my lips to his. "I think we should break up," he said. "I'm just not attracted to you anymore." I rolled and jumped at the same time, landing near his doorway. It seemed then that those words had appeared suddenly in the air around our intertwined bodies, and Dan had snatched them up on a whim. But once I was alone again, trudging through the activities required to be a person, I understood that his words had been hovering over us all along.

This is the romantic advice I got from my father: "If you cut off a hen's head and then dangle it in front of a rooster, the rooster will start doing the mating dance. All it takes is a bloody gizzard. Keep that in mind when the boys ask you on dates."

But boys never asked me on dates. They invited me into closets and bathrooms at parties in dark basements. They invited me to come over when their parents were out of town. I remembered the gizzard, and if I went—I usually went—it was not because I wanted to feel special or loved or chosen. I wanted to feel good, the way I had when I was in bed with Dan.

A boy from my English class—nice enough, cute enough—invited me over to watch a movie. I said hello to his mother and younger sister, working on math homework together at the kitchen table, and followed the boy to the basement. He put on *Fight Club* and we watched the first fifteen minutes. He suggested we go into the adjoining guest room and lie down. I agreed right away; the movie was disturbing me. We kissed stiffly for a minute or two. He pulled off my shirt and inhaled my nipples. He pushed me to his waist. I never said no to their demands, stated or implied. I was there to lose control, to be surprised by another person, to share an interaction entirely unlike the dull, inane, faintly mean chatter of which most of my interactions consisted. I wanted to be roused. And the boy's moans did arouse me, so much that I could hardly wait to pull off my jeans. Maybe I'd even have sex with him that night. But arousal did not lead to pleasure. It led to millions of sperm dying in my mouth. Two minutes of dutiful cuddling. Buckling of pants. Ejecting of movie (how it enraged me to see the care with which he returned the DVD to its container). That was fun. See you around.

There were many encounters like this. They taught me a new kind of pain. In bed alone afterward, I would lie on my back with my arms clenched at my sides, heart crashing against my ribs, stupid hope pecking my skin. My body did not know to stop waiting.

You could say I was a slut. You could say the boys were assholes. You could say we were hungry people who had been led to a buffet and informed that the only way we could eat was to lie on our backs under the table, blindfolded, openmouthed. When I complained to a friend with a lumpish, flat-chested body about unsatisfying hookups, she said, "But you're so pretty! I always thought the only reason guys would treat me that way is because they found me disgusting."

A few years later, when I was living in Paris, I was bored and lonely and looking for something sexy to read on the Internet. I stumbled on a chat room of seemingly college-age boys describing the blow jobs they'd gotten. One of them described going to a girl's room to "watch a movie." The phrase was in quotes, followed by a smiley face emoticon. He got the best BJ of his life. This girl was mad skilled. She invited him to come over again the next night, but he's like set on BJs for at least a week, dude. Smiley face. He didn't even try to pick up the hot chick giving him the eye in the elevator as he left the skilled girl's dorm room. Smiley face. Instead he went straight back to his room to write about the BJ to a bunch of strangers. He was still fuckin' high on life. Exclamation point.

The girl had invited this boy over; she had lowered her head to his waist, swallowed his semen, displayed no need for reciprocation, invited him to come over again whenever he wanted. Who wouldn't take such pleasure freely offered? I got so wet reading the boy's post that I had to touch myself, imagining his perfect selfishness.

Like the girl with the mad BJ skills and the girl eyeing the satiated dude in the elevator, I kept on giving away what I wanted for myself. I wanted to come in some pretty slut's mouth. Pull up my pants. Walk home—mind clear, body light. But my body refused me this ease. When a boy got naked with me, he ejaculated. When I got naked with a boy, my body became a shapeless vibration of erotic feeling building slowly until—he grunted and rolled away and I remained frozen for hours in the wide-awake vibrating place.

The more I gave away what I wanted for myself, the hungrier I became, filled with the loud idea of sexual release, never the reality. I began insisting on my own orgasm, however perfunctory; I often had to move the boy's hand with my own. Only an orgasm dulled the anxious clamor of needs aroused and abandoned. With Dan— whose twenties whittled him into a slack-haired, overweight, jovial real estate agent whom I am glad I didn't marry—I'd had no expectations of the form my pleasure would take; every good feeling was a surprise. After Dan, orgasms were a salve. They separated my longing from the man who had aroused it. He had fulfilled his purpose; I could want him to leave and enjoy the desire for his absence.

Women who write about the failure of feminism for glossy magazines would use my experience as proof of the depravity of hookup culture, which turns girls into desperate sluts and boys into ruthless ejaculating machines. Women who write about the triumphs of feminism for glossy magazines would use my experience as proof that free love depends upon reverence for the vagina, that I was dissatisfied by my hookups because the heartless boys were degrading my inner goddess. I suppose it would be a relief to have such ethical clarity. All I have are clear memories of strong feelings. Lust, rage, lust, rage.

"But they weren't *trying* to come in two minutes and not make you feel good," Jared said when I explained this series of feelings to him. He had just come with no warning when I was most aroused, causing me to roll onto my stomach and mew into a pillow until he took me by the shoulders and told me I better explain what I was so upset about. "That's exactly what they were trying to do!" I protested. "I can only think of one guy who felt genuinely bad that he came quickly. The rest of them were so fucking relaxed afterward, it was like they weren't even in the room with me."

"Well, most guys don't care about chicks until they find the one they want," he said. He parted my legs roughly, licked me until I came and then came again. And so, gradually, my body stopped believing there was a finite amount of pleasure in the world, for which I had to fight like a wounded cat over a scrap of moldy bread, needing the scrap all the more for the knowledge that it would not heal my wounds. Jared didn't care about wounds or healing or scraps. He just gave and took. Sometimes they were the same thing, sometimes not.

CARPINTERIA

After two years of ghostwriting obituaries, I started to worry that transcribing people's sloppily expressed memories at a small-town paper would become my life. In my calm moments, I told myself to accept the job as enough—work I enjoyed; who had that? But when my days were a mess because I got to the office hours late, spent on alcohol and sex with a man I knew I could not marry, then my job felt like one more shameful thing.

One night I was running down the middle of the street, away from some bad thing Drunk Jared had done: slapping a random girl's ass; telling another girl she had porcelain skin on a night when I had a raised, sore pimple on my chin; telling me such-and-such chick was totally into some seriously kinky shit; telling me I would look hot in lipstick; buying drinks for other girls and leaving me to buy my own—any of dozens of inanities I am pained to remember not because of any inherent cruelty on Jared's part but because of my willingness to be made heartsick and livid by the same scenario played out again and again with only minor variations. I planted my high-heel sandals in one square of yellow after another. I turned back and saw that Jared was no longer following me. He was bumming a cigarette from a woman on the sidewalk. Her earrings glittered against her long neck. I was seized by full-body panic, as if I were in acute physical danger. "Can you get me a cigarette, too, my love?" I called out, fingernails digging into my scalp. "You fucking prick!" The woman laughed nervously and headed into the bar. I sat down in the middle of the street. Jared exhaled smoke in a slow, even stream and started marching toward me, enjoying the clank of his boots on the concrete. "Jesus Christ," he said. "Get out of the goddamn road, woman." I knew his face without seeing it: furrowed brow, downturned lips. He was a man in a play who is supposed to act put out and angry. One beer too many and he forgot that his actions had any effect; his only job was to distract the audience from the mediocrity unfolding. I was yelling words I didn't hear. Jared stepped off the sidewalk and walked toward me. I quieted. His hands were under my armpits, lifting me up. My breathing slowed. Tonight would be an okay night. A middle-aged couple shrunk into each other as they watched Jared pull me to a standing position. "He did this to me," I called out. "He made me this way." This wasn't untrue. But it was also true that I'd chosen him because he did this to me. He was my excuse.

I don't remember how we got back to my apartment, but once we did, his hand was around my neck and he was banging my head against the metal door. The clichéd depravity of the motion made sense to me. I liked it. He dropped his hand and walked toward the refrigerator. Despair pooled into the place in me that had opened at his touch.

"Just kill me," I said. "I'm ready to go. I'm too much of a coward to do it myself, but you could do it so easily. Do it now. Come on."

He pulled his upper body out of the fridge, took a long swig of my roommate's Miller Lite, walked toward me, his face following the stage direction: *Firm resolve tinged with sadness.*

"You're sure now?" His hand rested on my throat. "Because I will do it."

I nodded. He looked into my eyes and read out the lines, "Soon you shall suffer no more." He tightened his grip. I counted to seventeen, eighteen, nineteen. My hands flew to his. I clawed at his wrist. He let go, walked back to his beer.

"I'm serious!" I stamped one foot. "I want you to do it."

"Later," he said, and belched so loudly and for so long that we both burst out laughing.

On the mornings after our bad nights, I would wake up wet and swollen between my legs, my body begging us to fuck our way out of this dark, lonely rage. But if we reached for each other in the usual way—kissing on the mouth and grabbing each other's hips—the pattern of damage we were doing to ourselves through each other was too clear. So we had to approach each other in new ways—tonguing foreheads or pawing shoulder bones. Once we were aroused enough that arousal erased that other, all-consuming state, I came again and again, Jared giving me orgasms without seeming to notice. We had to leave each other alone with our sensations or else our personalities would rush back in.

After we had more orgasms than want or need prescribed, we went out for breakfast, locked in our private world of sex and hatred. I was afraid of the other diners, convinced they knew how we spent our time. I had been so certain the night before that my life could not bear any more contact with him. And then: We were making love and eating eggs, a little hungover, normal people raging against normalcy. "If you don't cut it out, you are not going to Melissa's party or any party, I swear to god," a father said to his daughter at the table next to us. "Now, Herb," the mother said. Jared and I were fighting because that's what humans did.

Alone in my apartment later, I would be tense and edgy, jumping at every noise, double-checking the locks on my windows and doors. There was no way to be safe.

PARIS

My year in Paris had slaughtered me. I was still trying to come back to life. I had gone to France planning to stay—go to school there or become a translator or a bilingual tour guide at some great museum. I thought I was that smart and interesting. But Paris told me I was the same nothing as everyone else, with the same stupid dream of every aimless American who goes to Paris, thinking they can make it because they've read a couple of novels in French.

After I began studying French in seventh grade, I found myself repeating the new words in my head to calm myself before sleep or bolster myself against the inevitable embarrassments of gym class. *Au-dessus* meant above and *au-dessous* meant below? The class groaned. I placed my hand over my mouth to cover my smile, in love with the clarity of this absurdity: A word's meaning could be reversed by a centimeter's pucker of the lips.

My grade's dean in high school was also a French teacher, and he took an interest in me, reading aloud from my papers during class, gifting me with books that were not on the syllabus. During the first months of my senior year, girls whom I recall (impossibly) wearing nothing but khaki pants and pastel sweaters, jumped up and down in the hallways, hugging each other and shrieking, "I got in! I got in!" Mr. Samuels invited me to his office to talk about my college plans. I had nearly perfect scores on my SATs. I had straight As. I'd sent away for applications from schools I'd heard of—Yale, Stanford, UPenn, New York University, Haverford. I completed the applications quickly, carelessly, alone: a silly word game. One by one, I received envelopes stuffed with one sheet of paper regretting to inform me. Haverford put me on their waiting list, but I'd decided by then that the very idea of college was morally reprehensible. I was going to live in Paris. I'd googled "boardinghouse Bastille," since that was the only neighborhood I knew, and found a place where I could have my own room and take my meals. My father would support me until I "figured things out." He was proud of me for doing what I wanted to do instead of what everyone else was doing. When I told my mother the plan over the phone, she said, "Have you ever actually *met* a French person? They're the worst." But she didn't try to dissuade me. She was busy with her new family by then.

When I explained my plan to Mr. Samuels, he came out from behind his desk and took the armchair next to mine. He was short and handsome. There were two photos on his desk in thin silver frames, one of Mr. Samuels and his wife hiking through fiery foliage, another of his wife in a hospital gown, beaming at the newborn in her arms. I imagined Mr. Samuels greeting his family when he got off work—giving his wife a long, close-mouthed kiss, opening his arms wide so his daughter could run into his embrace—while he talked about my potential and options and the faulty bureaucracy of college admissions offices. "I would be more than happy to write to Haverford on your behalf," he said. "I have a friend in the French department there." Did Mr. Samuels have many lovers before his wife, or was she his first? He was so small and pretty and good-natured that it was impossible to imagine his desire existing outside the careful circle of home. Was he grateful for his wife's presence every day—her mothering, her knowledge of his tastes, the constant accessibility of her body? Or did this accessibility disgust him in a way he couldn't acknowledge even to himself? "I think it's a blessing in disguise," he was saying, "that you didn't get into any of the Ivies. I can really see you at Haverford."

His office was too warm. I pressed my arms against my sides to hide the sweat marking my sweater. I had thought it through, I told Mr. Samuels. Now was the perfect time to travel. I could reapply to college next year. My voice grew loud. I would go to Paris and learn a skill and a way of life with ancient, eternal roots, not sit around trying to say smart things about Hegel to a roomful of students trying to say smart things about Hegel. As I was about to leave his office, Mr. Samuels said, "You should probably go ahead and get yourself a good French dictionary. Larousse is the best. Start using it now when you read instead of your French-English one. That's one of the best ways to really know a language." He gave me a quick, close-mouthed smile.

I got to Paris in December. A constant cold drizzle fell on the sea of fitted black peacoats that clothed the city's stern residents. The room I was renting turned out to be the maid's quarters in the attic of a boardinghouse run by the only fat woman with a mullet I saw the whole time I was in France. I never found out whether her appearance had made her bitter or if bitterness had destroyed her appearance. The room was just big enough for a twin bed and a plywood board sitting upon four sticks. The only window was a small skylight. Anytime I thought I saw a ray of light, I would climb on the desk and squeeze my shoulders through the hole in the skylight, moving my face around and hoping for the feeling of warmth to fall on it.

A few weeks after I moved in, the mildly retarded Spanish housekeeper threw away my dirty clothes because she thought they were trash. I never mentioned the incident to the boardinghouse owner and I did not replace my socks and underwear until I returned to the States. I started wearing my remaining underwear right side out one day, wrong side out the next. I couldn't face the stylish department store clerks sneering at my pronunciation—or, far worse, responding in English—when I asked where to find the *sous-vêtements*.

For the first time, my love of Baudelaire and Maupassant was made to coexist with mundane communication, and I watched, helpless, as the words that had buoyed my private self rejected me in public. I could never have imagined how terrible it would feel to be unable to communicate in a language I thought I knew. When I couldn't conjure a word or tripped over my pronunciation so that a waiter or salesclerk responded in English, I was overcome by my own worthlessness; the entire world was wearied by my presence. Waiters left my table and never returned when I insisted, with the dreadful aggressiveness that tries to mask despair, on speaking my poorly accented French instead of resorting to the English culinary phrases they had mastered. Bouncers turned me away from clubs because I didn't have the right clothes. The U.S. started bombing

Iraq and eating freedom fries with their hamburgers, and the métro was filled with anti-American graffiti that pained me all the more because I agreed with it. A man on the street grabbed my breast, then spit in my face when I gave him the finger. I ran into him again a few days later, his arm around a pretty girl's waist.

I had repeated nightmares that a naked, drooling, elfish, old man was chasing me through the boardinghouse with a knife and fork. I would make it into my bedroom and frantically shimmy up through the skylight. When I was halfway free, the cannibal caught up to me and grabbed my waist. I always woke up as he was dragging me back into my attic room, where I would be eaten alive.

The longest sustained conversation I had that year was with a lanky video-store clerk whom I met one night while drinking alone at a touristy bar in the Bastille. He asked where I was from, said he'd been to Boston once, stuck his fingers down my pants as I stood at the bar, ordering my fourth drink. The bartender poured my beer with a half smile, aware of the connection between the man pressed against my ass and the involuntary widening of my eyes. I was the slutty American girl they expected me to be. The man guided me outside and asked where I lived. It was all right to go home with him because I was drunk enough that French was easy; I'd finally be able to practice speaking. On the ride to my boardinghouse, he stared at my chest and ran his pulpy hands up and down my legs. I had no desire to have sex with him, but that didn't seem to matter particularly. There was nothing I could do with another person that would be worse than what I was doing all by myself. I clenched my jaw and blinked at the taxi's rain-streaked window. Soon afterward I was tiptoeing to my shared bathroom to wash semen off my back.

I found *Fifi* at a used bookstall along the Seine a few days later— long, lovely sentences written in a lovely foreign language, and I consumed all eight-hundred pages of them in three days without consulting a dictionary. *Fifi* was a monologue of unrequited love for cats, narrated by a forty-year-old bachelor who strolls the Parisian streets seeking out and caring for strays. The narrator's attentiveness to the vagaries of his obsession is tedious, but I found the tediousness moving. The narrator has nothing to cleave to but his feelings for small creatures who flit in and out of his life, concerned with the narrator only insofar as he furthers their survival, offering no hope of mutual understanding. It is not the cats but his feelings for them that are the narrator's only companions.

I went to the Bibliothèque Nationale, where I learned that *Fifi* was out of print and had never been translated. My aloneness suddenly had a purpose. Wrapped up in my translating project, I barely went outside for my remaining four months in Paris. I was forcing myself to stay until the following December; it would have been too shameful to run back to my father's house without spending at least a year there.

Without meaning to, I had abandoned the translation after I got back to the States. But when I woke up in a hungover panic one dawn, Jared snoring beside me, I scoured my email hoping for some distraction, and found the attachment I'd sent myself the day before I left France. I read through what I'd translated so far. Not bad. I had about two-thirds of the book left to get through. My mind fell inside the task, relieved to be put to use.

CARPINTERIA

Around the time I resumed my translation project, a lawyer representing a Guantánamo detainee came to Carpinteria to give a talk at the library. It seemed substance was conspiring to enter my life. The lawyer was short and curvy, wearing a navy pantsuit and high stilettos in which she seemed perfectly at ease as she paced before the small crowd. Her client was a young father who was sold into U.S. custody in Pakistan, a country we've never been at war with. He was fitted with sensory deprivation goggles and earmuffs, then shackled to the floor of a plane in a painful stress position for the long ride to Cuba. He was not told where he was going or why. Once at Guantánamo, he spent his days either alone in wire cages or being interrogated. His fingers were broken. His head was stuffed down a toilet. He was deprived of sleep for days. Early into his captivity, the government concluded that he represented no threat yet took no steps to free him. When the lawyer attempted to get him tried before the military commissions, they denied his petition because he was already cleared for release and so had no need of a trial. "It's like something out of Kafka," she said. This was her only bit of editorializing. She was straightforward, unpoliticized. When someone asked why she decided to represent a Guantánamo detainee, she said, "Because it's my job. Protecting the Constitution. That's what I was trained to do."

I approached the lawyer afterward and asked if she would be willing to let us publish her talk in the *Carp Weekly*, at which I implied I had more power than I did. I wasn't thinking about logistics. I was overwhelmed by love. It had been so long since I'd felt awed by another human.

I begged Donnie to run the talk as a cover story. He agreed in the manner of someone letting an underling play at power. No matter. This was the closest I'd ever come to activism. A week after the issue came out, Donnie stopped by my desk. "Very few people picked up the torture issue," he said. "We have hundreds of extras." The implication was clear: This was a failed experiment; now we'd go back to giving the people musicians and wineries and summer-camp guides. Indeed no one but Jared—and my father, ad nauseam—commented on the lawyer's article to me, to which

I'd added sidebars explaining relevant bills and Supreme Court rulings. Why was it so fucking hard for me to do one decent thing?

It seemed I needed a job that required me to be alone a lot of the time. I made lists of publishers and literary journals and began sending off sample chapters of *Fifi*.

I got most of my translating done after I broke up with Jared, which I did often, usually when I was drunk. One time, I broke my bedroom window at the same time, trying to yank it open to dump Jared's beer outside, shrieking that he was a drunk and a loser and this was the last time I was going to let him hurt me. When the window came out of its frame and crashed into the yard, crushing sixty dollars' worth of freshly planted flowers (according to my roommate's quiet, embarrassed estimate the next day), Jared laughed. I shrieked at him to get the fuck out, I was done with him, done. He was still laughing when he walked past the crushed flowers and broken glass, out onto the empty, yolky street. A Sunday, dawn. Nowhere to be, no one to answer to, Clam Shack would be serving Bloody Marys soon, the ocean was huge and the world was beautiful.

After our breakups, I would feel strong in my anger during the day, eating a lot, running a lot, laughing a lot at nothing in particular, believing that whatever flaws I had, it was Jared—discrete Jared, a real person who was not me—that had turned my life into an obscene performance of resistance.

I had one good friend in Carpinteria, a girl who worked in sales at the newspaper. She was the least analytical person I'd ever met. I could talk to Caitlin about Jared all I wanted, but the conversation would never verge on problem solving. She was interested in specific facts of human behavior—what our sex had been like the night before, whether he had slapped another girl's ass again, how

I had responded this time—but she tolerated no feeling-talk. She drank a lot of beer, which made her raunchy without being flirtatious: She'd shout in a crowded bar, "Does anyone have a tampon?," or have guys buy us drinks all night and then, just as the interaction was moving into the realm of the sexual, scare them away by saying that most women experienced more pleasure with a vibrator than an actual man or that the only man she'd ever been really attracted to was her grandfather. She was daring men to be strong enough to subdue her chaos. She made me laugh and laugh.

Caitlin was the first person I called each time I broke up with Jared, although I stopped telling her that's what I'd done after the first couple of attempts failed to last. We would go out and I'd let myself be swept along by her harmless mania. But as soon as I got in bed later and tried to sleep, I became a baby alone in a cave, freezing and starving, helpless to do anything but writhe and bite the blanket and clutch my crotch and stick my fingers into my dry pussy and into my dry mouth and sweat and get the chills and pull my hair, all the while seeing myself at the bottom of a deep, narrow hole in the ground, looking up, glimpsing a face at the top, the one who could lift me out of the hole—there, then gone. A scene from *Silence of the Lambs*: one of Hannibal's victims, kept barely alive at the bottom of a hole. I had known the movie would give me nightmares; even *Oliver Twist* gave me nightmares. But a boy named Simon (accent on the *o*, Bolivian, prematurely mustached, drawer of raunchy comics that he slipped into my desk in English class) had invited me to watch the cannibal movie, and my thoughts were always a drunken crowd clamoring for his attention in eighth grade. So I watched it and let him French kiss me and had nightmares for weeks afterward.

Hell is a state of ceaseless, fruitless relating. The effort makes you so cold and alone that you believe you will die. In fact you would like to die. But the urge for self-preservation is too strong.

So instead of dying you build a fire and hurl flaming sticks out in all directions. There is relief at first. Anger believes in itself. Anger will save you. But soon the fire consumes everything with which you had hoped to make contact, until you are alone in the center of the blaze, still unable to stop hurling sticks because the fire has consumed every other possible means of relating and all you want—the only thing you need to calm down—is to have an impact on something other than yourself. Impossible, from where you sit. You cannot exert a force on anything that is not also exerting a force on you. Newton's law, the only thing I retained from high school science. But equally impossible to stop trying. So the only hope was to exhaust myself in the effort.

A day or two after our supposed breakup, I would call Jared at bedtime and ask him ("I'm so sorry I got angry, I was just hurt, I really need to see you and talk to you") to rescue me. But he would be drunk and high on blow, an indifferent stranger for as long as this particular binge lasted. I would go on calling this indifferent stranger, praying that this time he would not answer the phone surrounded by the racket of people convincing one another they were having fun, and would not tell me I was boring the shit out of him, and would not hang up on me while I was sobbing that he was hurting me so much, I couldn't stand it any longer, please just come over and talk to me.

I lay back down, still gripping the phone. No need to be patient. Patience would not return him to me. He would be returned in the way of pain and its alleviation. This particular pain, in this particular moment of my particular life, was to be in love with an absence. It was not death, not violence, not rape. Everyone suffered, there was no reason I should be spared. I opened my mouth wide, squeezed my eyes into old, hard vaginas sewed up tight. Long, sharp, violent lines flew out of my chest, stabbing the walls and ceiling and floor, gorging the earth straight through, searching.

But the absence was hiding inside my room, my bed, my body. There was nothing I could do to force its revelation. I tilted my head back and pressed my chest toward the ceiling. Wait—the violence was golden—lines of strength come to save me. But I did not want to be saved. I wanted my love to exist outside my body. But whenever I tried, however I tried—that time he said that thing, he looked that way, I said this thing, he took it that way, I broke down, he broke—stop. I rolled onto my stomach and pressed my fists into my abdomen. If my heart and mind would only give up hoping, become so drenched in absence that they gave way . . . Morning now. A woman's voice perfectly suited to whole wheat toast and Earl Grey tea, under my window, retreating, I can't make out her last word—come back, please, no need to rush off. Stay. Chat. I won't judge you, I promise.

When I managed to get out of bed, the reflection of my naked body in the mirror stabbed me. I looked good, I liked my body. That was the thing I still had. It gave me nothing. I was relieved when the mirror caught me at an ugly angle—belly pouched; breasts pointy; thighs big and heavy, pulling my face to the floor.

When I complained about Jared to any of the girls I drank beer and complained about boys with, I liked when the word *abusive* came up. It was neat and respected and freed me of responsibility. One of the girls I knew worked at a home for battered women. During a group discussion there, a social worker asked one of the women why she had stayed with her husband. A chorus of female voices crooned, "Because she loooves him!" But I wasn't a battered woman; I didn't know what I was. Jared would always apologize and I would always let him back in. And then I had to explain to my friends that his behavior wasn't really abusive, that he just drank too much and said stupid things. Soon there was no one left to complain to.

Except for my mother. She loved to talk on the phone when Rick was at work and her new kids were at school. The person who was drunk and invulnerable to his love for me was not really Jared, she assured me; it was the disease. "But, honey, they're all addicted to something," she said. "Alcohol is better than strip clubs. Trust me." I told myself that alcohol was better than strip clubs when Sober Jared finally called and said he missed me and did I want to ride bikes to the diner? Yes, I did. I always wanted to ride bikes to the diner with Jared. Just the idea of it made life feel so decadent and generous, made me and Jared seem like the best of friends.

I could have tried to get him to stop drinking. But he was self-medicating, and if he stopped drinking, he would be overcome by an anxious depression nursed throughout a neglectful childhood and a decade of partying instead of working, and if I were the one who insisted he give up booze, I would be solely responsible for helping him cope. So after he went to a few AA meetings and pronounced it soul-deadening, I believed him when he said he wasn't really an alcoholic; he just needed to drink a little less. Some nights—many nights—he met his modest goal and we had fun. Life was fun. I liked drinking, too. And I could not help him change his life in ways he hadn't the courage to change it on his own. Or so I imagined my mother would have told me, if I had the kind of mom who said things like that.

KANDY

I did believe it was possible for a person to change. I had known other versions of myself that allowed me to hope the situation I was in would not be my life. I just couldn't leave the situation. I looooooved him.

I decided to backpack around Sri Lanka for a few months, to try to free myself of my addiction to Jared, so that something new might happen. The only thing that had changed tangibly for me since I'd moved to Carpinteria four years earlier was a two-dollar-an-hour raise. Jared thought that if I was willing to take so much time off and spend a grand on a flight, the two of us should have ourselves a delightful holiday much closer to home. "I'm trying to get over you," I said. "Good luck," he said, and rolled on top of me. We were lying in his bed on a Wednesday morning; fog pressed against the window; I dug my fingers into the flesh above his hip.

When I got home from work that night, the travel guide I'd ordered was waiting on my stoop. I looked at the charmingly cheesy photos—palm trees, sunsets over the ocean, monks kneeling before Buddha statues—and booked my ticket. I liked the idea of going to a tropical paradise that was also a recent war zone. Not long ago, the Buddhist government had won their war against the Tamil Tigers by bombing the shit out of the Tamil-populated north. In preparation for my trip, I read articles about the thousands of civilians killed, the emergency laws overriding civil rights, residential land seized by the military. I wanted to believe my attraction to other people's suffering was compassion, but more likely it was a twisted need to justify my own unhappiness. Either way, Sri Lanka was perfect.

It also appealed to me because it's a Buddhist country, and Buddhism had helped me in my childhood, although I didn't realize it was helping me at the time. I thought it was some desperate New Age nonsense my mother clung to now that her dancing career was over and she had no choice but to teach Pilates to sixty-year-old women with platinum hair. Her friend Sharon gave her some meditation tapes that she swore were totally life-changing. Throughout elementary school, I often found Mom lying on her back on the living-room rug, bound in a silk face mask, listening to a dude with an Irish accent asking her how it felt to be clothed in her particular biochemical garment at this particular moment on this particular planet. The tapes made me want to puke, and I told her so. Once when my father and I were joking and laughing in the kitchen during one of my mother's solitary séances, she marched into the kitchen and asked us to please keep it fucking down, she was fucking trying to meditate. "Just notice, just feel," the Irish dude intoned. "Free of desire, free of judgment." Mom slammed the kitchen door as she rushed back to his voice.

Part of my mother wanted to be quiet and sacred and take up as little space as possible. But her needs of the moment were always louder than her will. The quiet part of her brought me to a Buddhist temple every Sunday—a schoolhouse-like structure painted bright reds and yellows and adorned with gilded statues of beaming fat men, filled with dark-skinned people carrying fruit offerings and clutching long bead necklaces in their palms. My mother and I would sit in the back of the temple on flat, lumpy cushions while a man at the altar spoke a language we couldn't understand in a singsong hush that reminded me of *Goodnight Moon*, and the people around us—most of them wearing white—rocked slightly on their heels, their palms pressed together at their hearts. My mother was different at the temple. She never wore lipstick, she didn't laugh for no reason and touch strangers on the arm. She sat cross-legged—back straight, eyes closed. I watched her with a concentration that felt like magic. Our knees touched. Sometimes I would jiggle my leg so that I could continue feeling the contact, whose sensation had been numbed by stillness. Only by agitating my body could I feel it clearly. I didn't realize that the point of

stillness was to *stop* feeling the body and feel something else instead. Mom was so still that she didn't even tell me to cut out all
the jiggling.

After I booked my flight to Sri Lanka, my mother told me the
temple she'd brought me to was Cambodian. But what did that
matter, she was just *so* happy that I was following my inner light
and she didn't mind saying she was proud of herself for raising a
daughter with such *important* interests in shit that really matters,
not like some Wall Street asshole trying to finance his third yacht,
but anyway she had to go, she and Rick were going for a sunset
hike, there was really nowhere better in the world than Phoenix,
why didn't I visit more often? My father also thought it was terrific
I would be leaving the daily grind of America's corporate machine
to get to know myself on my own terms. He must have been secretly happy I was getting away from a boyfriend who sounded
unstable at best, but Dad rarely allowed himself to criticize my
choices.

It was almost too simple to get to Sri Lanka, nearly nine thousand
miles away. Twenty hours on two planes, during most of which I
slept away my hangover from partying with Jared right up until
my morning flight out of L.A., and then I was blinking at the
buses and cabdrivers crowding the airport exit, the men in suits
and flip-flops calling me madam and gesturing to the backs of
their taxis, the bright smell of sewage and the ocean, the tanned
backpackers and women in saris piling onto buses, one of which
had a sign that said KANDY, the Buddhist epicenter of the country,
according to my guidebook, and my first stop. I took the last free
seat and jammed my backpack under it. As the bus grumbled away
from the airport, a tiny man wearing a fanny pack walked up the
aisle, collecting fares. "Kandy," I said. He wrote 325 on a scrap of

paper and handed it to me. About three dollars for what the Lonely Planet promised to be a three-hour ride inland. The woman sitting next to me pulled a curtain over the window to close out the sun, but I caught flashes of the outside world when potholes or short stops jostled the curtain aside: piles of burning rubbish in dirt yards, women in sarongs with soapy armpits standing barefoot on rocks in muddy rivers. The driver blasted talk radio, a steady stream of chatter in a language I hadn't even heard of until a few weeks ago. An unanswered Brahms ringtone played every few minutes from the seat in front of me. At least I remember being sure at the time that it was Brahms, and thinking it was unusual for me to recognize a piece of classical music. But I just googled "Brahms ringtone" and none of them sounded like the tinny waltz I can still, for some reason, hear clearly. No one on the packed bus was doing anything but trying to stay put as we bumped along the washed-out dirt roads. I gripped the seat back to keep from tumbling into the crowded aisle. The things I'd planned to do on the bus—read my guide book, change into sandals, drink water, eat a protein bar—seemed funny now. I was ecstatic with the freedom of being unable to accomplish even the simplest task. But as the sky above the curtain darkened, I remembered the problem of my physical self. How would I know when to get off the bus? How would I get to the guesthouse? Was Kandy safe? Could I get in a rickshaw with an unknown driver after dark? Where would I get drinkable water? Was the man standing in the aisle beside me intentionally putting his crotch that close to my face? The ticket taker interrupted my boomeranging worries by tapping my shoulder. "Kandy. Here. Kandy." The bus stop throbbed with hurried people carrying baskets of pineapples and mangoes, food stalls at which sweaty men fried snacks that looked too colorful to be edible, a barefoot hunchback groaning and holding out his palm. Before I was even aware of my bewildered presence inside this scene, a smiling rickshaw driver pointed to the back of his three-wheeler. "Rose Land?" I said. "Yes, madam," he said. "Two hundred rupees only, madam." I heaved my pack onto the small bench at the back of the rickshaw and clambered in after it, relaxed in a way that reminded me of kindergarten recess, when I rarely knew the rules of a game well enough to care about winning.

I arrived at the guesthouse that my guidebook recommended just after dark and shook the gate, secured with a tiny padlock, until a middle-aged woman with a serene face and wild gray hair admitted me. The front room was large and spare, except for a snoring blond dog, a few plastic chairs, and curling posters tacked to the walls, one of a monkey eating a banana (STAY FIT!), another of cherubic white children photoshopped onto a field of sunflowers (BE A SWEET HEART). There were no available rooms at Rose Land, so the owner offered me her grandsons' upper bunk for two hundred rupees. Of course the boys wouldn't mind sharing a bed, I shouldn't be silly. She handed me a faded pink towel from the pile atop the dining room table. I felt again the odd relaxation of being beholden to circumstances, far from my phone, my car, my bed, every person who knew my face—alone in a way I never was in Paris, where the city's judgment and coldness weighed on me even in sleep. No one here seemed to care whether I knew the rules or not. I excessively thanked the owner for making room for me and asked her name. "Call me Mary," she said, and pointed to a bedroom on the other side of the courtyard.

A sunburned Norwegian, a lanky Dutch guy, a dreadlocked Italian couple, and a small, excitable Frenchman were smoking cigarettes and eating cream-filled cookies around the table outside. The Italian woman offered me a cookie. I licked lemon cream as I listened to their introductions. The Norwegian girl was traveling for a year before starting a master's program. The Dutch electrician had just phoned his boss to extend his trip for a month. The

Italian couple was stuck in Sri Lanka for two weeks because their six-month Indian visa expired. The French guy had been country-hopping for three years and would do so as long as his savings lasted. He took the cheapest bed in any given town—a mattress on the floor of a poor family's living room, a hammock in a backyard, he'd take it, he didn't mind—he only ate curry packets from the street vendors (fifty rupees fills you up for hours!) and he only traveled by bus and foot: a first world tramp on a third world vacation. One way to spend a life, no worse than most. The Norwegian girl offered me a beer. I was too exhausted to be tempted.

I propped my backpack against the bunk bed in Mary's daughter's room, which she shared with her two young sons. Sarasi was sitting on the double bed, looking over her sons' schoolwork. I thanked her for sharing her room. "It's no problem for us." She had the faintest hint of a British accent. "I just hope we won't bother you in the morning. We wake up at four thirty." I asked where she worked, rummaging through my bag in search of pajamas and a toothbrush.

"One of the best hotels in town, thanks to my English. Growing up in a guesthouse, you know." She tried to sound bored, not proud. At least I hoped she was secretly proud, which would have made my presence in her bedroom less of an intrusion. Her hair was short and gelled, unlike the long, slick braids I'd noticed the women on the bus wearing. The small radio in her room was tuned to a station that played Billy Joel, Cyndi Lauper, Michael Jackson.

A black Lab pushed through the flowered curtain covering the entrance to the room, tongue dangling. "This is my puppy," one of the boys said. "He is called Teega."

"Hi, Teega," I said.

"Careful for—" Sarasi said, just as Teega pounced on the protein bar I'd just taken out of my bag. He sprinted out the door. I lunged after him, but he was a galloping blur of black fur, swinging the square of calcium-enriched puffed rice from his mouth, running victory laps around the table in the courtyard. The Dutch guy leaped in front of him with a balletic karate chop. Teega paused, gave his stolen goods a fierce shake, and then continued his rampage, sugar-free caramel smeared over his snout. Mary stepped into the courtyard, holding a slingshot armed with a tiny pebble. She yelped, cocked her arm, and fired a warning shot onto the tin roof. Teega let the emptied bag drop to the ground. He prostrated before Mary, tiny head between overgrown paws. "Bravo, Mama," the Italian woman cried, flapping her hands together. Mary returned to her bedroom. Her daughter peered out from behind the flowered curtain.

"I'm sorry," she said. "I hope that wasn't your dinner."

"No, no," I lied, too tired to care whether I ever ate again.

Sarasi gestured me into the room and pointed to the bunk bed. "Take the bed you prefer," she said. "The boys sleep with me. At least for now." She lowered her voice. "We don't know where their father is at the moment." She looked at her short, rounded, pink fingernails. "People are so mean. They make the same mistake again and again." I didn't know whether she was talking about the boys' father or herself for forgiving him, but before I could ask her, her older son was pulling on my hand, introducing himself, telling me about his mosquito net.

"This is a new one," he said. "Best kind. You are so luck. There are many dengue fever mosquitoes. One of the boys in my class has died. I saw him before he has died. He looked like—" Tilak sucked in his cheeks and rolled his eyes to the back of his head. I grimaced. He grinned, gratified.

Sarasi's younger son was curled on his side in the double bed, his cheek resting on the back of his hand. "My brother goes to sleep so early," Tilak said as I hoisted myself into the upper bunk. "I like to be awake late in the night." He warned me to fully close the gap in the mosquito net and scanned the room to make sure no one left out a glass of water. Dengue fever mosquitoes plant their babies in the old water. They are silent, so you have no warning before they bite. They're so tiny you could kill them with one finger but still they get to you before you get to them and just like that— Tilak clapped his hands above his head—your whole body is filled with the disease and you turn purple and your blood freezes and you die.

Sarasi told Tilak to hush. She lay down next to her younger son in her jeans and T-shirt and blinked at the ceiling. *Wish it was Sunday.* After Tilak's breath grew long and deep, she pulled the sheet over his balled-up body and returned her face to the ceiling. *That's my fun day.* I tried to stay awake long enough to appreciate my cramped spine elongating against the hard mattress, '80s pop mixing with the crickets outside, the interplay of accents coming from the courtyard, the odd comfort of sharing an unknown family's home. But I'm only making up those details in retrospect. What I remember is that, just before I disappeared into dreamless sleep, I felt like nobody, far away from all the usual thoughts, both scared and safe.

I stayed at Rose Land for weeks, setting out on foot each morning to explore the temples and gardens, then coming home to eat rice and curry out of plastic bags I bought from the Muslim restaurant in town, which Sarasi told me was the cleanest. I took a trip to the seashore, as I giddily thought of the south coast, feeling like a sweet little girl in a children's book. Bikini-clad Europeans posed for sexy photos alongside Sri Lankan families—husbands gaping as they splashed with toddlers in the shallows, women in saris holding babies in one hand and umbrellas in the other, to keep their skin from turning darker in the sun. I didn't want to be reminded that I was just another white girl on vacation. So I headed back to Rose Land, where I could spend my evenings helping the boys with their English homework and letting Sarasi paint my nails. ("You have pretty hands," she said. "You should maintain.") The Italian couple had returned to India, so I took their room—two twin beds pushed together beneath a window lined with bars to keep the monkeys out, usually filled with flashes of orange robes swooshing around bare feet. There was a monastery uphill from Rose Land, and the top of the window met the very bottom of the courtyard. As I laid out my clothes on one of the beds, fully unpacking for the first time, the monks began chanting. "So beautiful," I said when Mary passed my open door. She smiled indulgently. "The government pays them to live there," she said. "Most easy job in Sri Lanka."

Still, I lay on my bed every night at sunset, listening to the oceanic crooning of unknown words, watching the square of sky deepen to black. Only someone unlovable could love aloneness this much. I didn't know whether this was a good thought or a bad thought, but I didn't much care either way.

I never used the blank moleskin notebook I'd brought with me, intending to record scenes and conversations for some future self, scavenging for the vaguely imagined article I planned to write or desperate to recall past joys. So I don't remember many specific moments or sensory details from that first trip, just that I was barreled down constantly by their combined force. The manic city streets, the koel birds crooning at dawn, the ancient stone Buddhas nestled at the base of heavy fig trees, the huge white beaches with huge green waves and huge pink sunsets and huge clouds slicing a huge sky. Sri Lanka did feel like freedom—from trying in general, if not from Jared specifically.

I met an Irish girl at Rose Land, who'd just come back from a silent meditation center in the mountains. "Most beautiful place in the world," she said, and wrote down the name of the town for me, in the back of my empty notebook.

SHIRMANI

Gongs woke us before dawn; we dressed, peed, and brushed our teeth by candlelight; followed a trail of slowly moving flames to the Buddha hall; sat still for one hour; drank tea while watching the sunrise; stretched slowly for an hour; ate porridge with dates and roasted peanuts; sat still some more; stretched; ate rice and vegetables; sat; stretched; drank tea; watched the sunset; chanted; slept. This was every day at the silent meditation center in the mountains above Kandy.

Sometimes during the morning meditations, a man at the front of the Buddha hall spoke into the darkness about ordeenearness and realeetee. He had just returned from a trip to Germany; a couple invited him to stay at their house and teach their friends about meditation. When the couple went out one night, they thought their Buddhist teacher might be amused by watching television. He flipped through the channels for hours. "More than one hundred programs," he said to the candlelit room of solitary sitters. "So many choices, all the time, night and day. This is dukkha. This is suffering." He asked us to experience instead our ordinary human forms, to feel friendly toward our ordinary human lives. What I experienced for the first few days was a barrage of thoughts demanding that I scratch my lower back, extend my legs, stand up, get the hell out of Shirmani, take a lifelong vow of silence and stay at Shirmani forever, fall in love with my breath, buy myself a new dress, burn all my clothes, become a lesbian, notice my breath without subjecting it to conceptual thinking like love, use the working meditation period to hunt down and kill that squirrel that wouldn't shut the fuck up, do something, anything, just make it better, make it better, make it better. I did not feel friendly toward this vain urgency.

"Please feel your heart," the man in white said as our candle flames disappeared into pale early light. "Please feel your heart deeply." I tried to scoff at his corny command, but the mere mention of that place brought my desperate attention there anyway and just like that my heart was feeling me, grasping at my throat from the inside, pulling taut the skin around my collarbones and neck. All those times I failed to contain my childish urges, drank too much and humiliated myself with some public display of rage or sorrow and so drank more; all the days in Paris I wasted with my misery; all the times I shrieked and punched and clutched at Jared instead of walking away; all the times I failed to take myself home. Impossible to contain the memories of the bad things I'd done, more terrible for their stupidity, for being average, repeatable badness, not even—

"Can you forgive me, heart?" said the man in white. For the first week of this question, spoken always into the gradually lightening room as the morning meditation came to an end, I did succeed in scoffing and shutting out his voice, or else becoming sensually distracted with the stream of water from my nose and eyes pooling at the hollow between my collarbones. The word "sorry" felt just as stupid as the actions that invited an apology. "Can you free the heart from the past?" His voice was slow and oddly unaccented. He repeated the question, speaking to himself. And because there was the same secret weight to his voice day after day, finally, out of solidarity, I repeated the words to my own—whatever it is, not the physical heart but the writhing tangle of remembered words and gestures underneath the wishbone center of my rib cage. After a few more days, it wasn't that I felt that place as freedom, like the man in white suggested. But at least it was no longer clamoring for my attention.

"Only silence can feel the realeetee," said the man in white at the front of the Buddha hall.

Realeetee at Shirmani was constant, various birdsong (long beaks tapping a crystal vase, a mechanical kitten crying out for a real live mama cat, the final note of a radio ad for something tasty and fattening and cheap); monkeys sitting on the roof of the kitchen hut, disdainfully gorging on stolen jackfruit; a tornado of cicadas that enveloped us in their throbbing hum each night as the sun descended; stone pathways dappled in sunlight and lizards and, one time, a frog no bigger than my pinkie nail; pastel sheets draped on a sunny laundry line; exquisitely seasoned rice and curry and spicy-sweet tea; stone benches overlooking a valley of every possibility of green rising into a sky of every possibility of white, overlaid with charcoal smudges of mountain ranges whose visibility came and went with the fog, palest blue at the horizon giving way to pure light in a measured spectrum that revealed the dome overhead; "biscuits crunching in the night," the phrase that tolled in my mind—so easy to amuse oneself when speech is outlawed—during the evening meal of what was presumably once a bread product, before it was sun-dried in a desert and then baked in a kiln, and for which, at the end of the final meditation before bedtime, we were all ravenous and gratefully consumed in the dark, under the stars, surrounded by millions of insects playing their wee violins, no match for the collective crunch our evening snack released into the reigning peace of the nighttime forest; thick, small leaves that fell from the tops of impossibly tall, thin tree trunks, twirling so quickly they seemed frozen midair at each interval of their languid descent; a saggy-breasted, elderly Sri Lankan woman who came to every evening meditation wearing an oversize T-shirt emblazoned with a steaming cup of coffee and the words CAREFUL, LADIES . . . I MAY BE HOT; a brightly dressed, exuberantly gestured young white man, either gay or Italian, who attended none of the group activities except for meals, to which he was always first in line, heaping his plate with a mound of food fit for a starving family, consuming this mound with his hands—hunched over, legs crossed, eyes intently downcast—and then re-filling his plate with such brazen greed that it seemed he earnestly believed we were at this secluded meditation center on an island in the Indian Ocean to eat as much as possible of the healthy foods harvested and prepared for us for pennies.

Mostly, there was sitting. And when I had sat still long enough that my attention was, at last, consumed by the flicker of my breath—a candle pulsing in a slight, steady breeze—and my body was so light I could only sense it as the line of contact between palm and thigh; when I felt a large insect tickle my neck and still did not move until the tickle became a shooting pain that made me reflexively flick a large caterpillar with poisonous feet off of my Adam's apple and then resume sitting still, concentrating now on the web of stinging nettles emanating from the center of my neck to the crown of my head; when I opened my eyes slightly and saw a monk's brown feet moving slowly across the floor and was overcome with a full-body sorrow for all of us meditators doing all of this sitting and slow walking and listening to the mind's harangues, for what?; when I had convinced myself that whatever I was doing in that room was irrelevant to who I should be as an individual, which was the same way I felt when I was depressed; when, snot running into my mouth and tears dripping off my chin, I kept on sitting still; when the heavy, wet sorrow of effort was suddenly, mysteriously replaced by the brightness and grati-tude of this same effort—so this is sitting; this is walking; this is breathing; this is lying; eating; shitting; seeing; drinking; feeling wind and heat and cold—and sensing finally that this was enough, to pay attention was enough; when I noticed how the tiny muscles pulsed across the top of the monk's foot with each step, like the pulse of the tiny flame of my breath, to which my whole being was, in that moment, reduced; when I felt a peace that seemed unshakable, that would surely last forever, even as the memories and plans and judgments oozed back in, because the peace-feeling understood that these thoughts came out of nowhere, or some-where unseen, like the sounds from the forest all around—outside my control, having little to do with me, unstoppable but not at all terrible; when the seemingly unshakable peace-feeling did fall away, replaced by shrieking protests from my knees and hips as my numbed lap came back to life all at once; when I extended one leg, then the other, slowly, slowly, unfurling vein and muscle and bone—ah, a new kind of perfect peace, one that quickly dispersed, replaced by the thought that all of this was just one more experi-ence and led nowhere and would give me nothing I thought that meditation ought to give me, unless I just hadn't done it enough or hadn't done it the right way—the candle flicker still there, though, the urge to come back to it still there—and on and on and on until at last, still entirely at a loss as to how to be a human being, I leaned back.

Watched. Watched myself watching. Watched the watched self being watched. So who was the watcher, ultimately? Fuck if I knew. I leaned back again. This was what meditation had given me. Not what I wanted. What I wanted was a new kind of extreme experience—freedom, bliss, transcendence. The man in white robes—he didn't seem to be a monk, but he didn't seem to be a regular person either—was actually enlightened. You saw it in the tranquil openness of his face, even though he was nearly one hundred and his feet and knees were perpetually swollen and his eyes were red and oozing. Constant comfort divorced from circumstance—a possibility I had not considered real before. But one that came from what seemed like impossible effort. The man in white spent most of every day of most of his life meditating; he had achieved enlightenment after sitting perfectly still for two full days in a row. He explained this to us during a sort of question-and-answer session one night. Bulbous feet extending from beneath the folds of his robe, he smiled out at us and waited for us to speak. People asked many questions: I have been meditating for so long and am still unhappy—what will make me happy? I was not loved as a child and now I find it difficult to love others—how can I heal? I hate my job but I need the money—should I quit and live as a pauper? The monk answered them each the same way: Be earnest. If you want to be free, do not let anything stop you. Examine every thought, desire, sensation until you fully understand its source. Expect nothing from the world. Then you will naturally wake up to your true state. Remain open and quiet. That is all you can do.

I loved the prohibition against speaking, loved waking up before dawn and falling into sleep soon after sunset, loved the signs everywhere reminding us not to read or talk or wear clothing that revealed the contours of our limbs, reminding us that we were HERE TO MEDITATE. No other reason. The only point to my life at Shirmani was to notice my thoughts and sensations as I carried out basic acts of survival. I felt a kind of happiness I'd always believed was reserved for other, simpler people.

I thought about Jared a lot, of course. But I aggressively labeled the thoughts "thinking" until they dissolved, which made me proud of myself. I was not yet up to the task of liberating myself by examining every desire. But rejecting something does not make it disappear. During one of the half hours allotted daily for right speech—timely, useful, gentle, and true—I spoke with an Australian woman who had lived at Shirmani for fifteen years. She had recently gone to renew her visa; the authorities pressed her on her reasons for staying in Sri Lanka. "They treated me like I was criminal! And I'm not! I'm not!"

"Imagine how you'd feel if the man you loved told you to get the fuck out of his face when you were crying because he had his arm around another girl," I unfortunately said out loud. Hardly timely, useful, or gentle. Silence had impaired my already feeble filtering abilities. The woman opened her mouth in a sad O. "I just mean—my boyfriend makes me feel like a criminal too. And I'm not. A criminal. So, like, I know how you feel."

After several weeks at Shirmani, I started waking up with a little prickle of fear. What was I doing with my life? It seemed that I had been HERE TO MEDITATE for long enough; wasn't I meant to experience other things, to make the best use of this trip halfway across the globe? I was in a recent war zone, assailed by humanitarian concerns. This was my chance to act on some of my depressing, lonely knowledge. I didn't know what that action would be exactly, but I was sure I shouldn't leave Sri Lanka without seeing the north, where most of the fighting had occurred. Only a couple of weeks remained before my flight home.

When I told the man in white I would be leaving for Jaffna the next day, he said, "If you are earnest, it does not matter where you go." Idealistic words, but I trusted them. It was impossible not to, after spending time in this man's presence. But how to be that single-mindedly earnest? Even the people who had been on retreat for many years—long-term meditators, they were called—

had clearly not achieved this state of constant quietness and openness, free of all expectations. Certainly they were closer than I was. But when I watched them inching along the stone pathways and taking a full minute to bring their spoons from their plates to their mouths and breaking Noble Silence only once a week to discuss the need for more toothpaste or batteries, I knew that being a long-term meditator was one more thing I was not and would probably never be. One of the long-term meditators was a Buddhist nun from England who couldn't have been more than twenty-five. She watched the sunrise in the same spot every morning, wearing the same clothes, with the same look of awe brightening her soft, round face. I envied her certainty. My personality is ill-suited to my ideals.

JAFFNA

A checkpoint marked the entrance to Sri Lanka's northernmost peninsula. My bus had to wait for me to get off and register my passport with three leering soldiers. And then we entered a kind of desolation I had never known before. Dry fields were interspersed with army barracks that looked like little boys' playthings, bags of sand painted green and brown piled before plywood huts. The bus slowed to let off a man whose lifeless right foot trailed the ground alongside him. He limped down a dirt road extending to the horizon. A rickshaw was parked outside the only store we'd seen for miles. A teenage girl crouched beside it, looking at her reflection in the tiny rearview mirror.

The dusty breeze coming through the bus's open windows began to smell of salt, which meant we were nearing the coast. We stopped at a tea shop. The passengers mobbed the counter, demanding milk tea and fish rolls. A glass container with chocolate and crackers had a sign that said FOR MILITARY ONLY. As we continued into Jaffna, street signs, buildings, and vehicles coalesced into what felt like a large, developed city. Shamefully, I was disappointed. I'd been expecting a wretched warscape. The bus deposited us at a bustling roundabout. The first rickshaw driver I flagged down didn't speak English. I opened my guidebook to the map of Jaffna and pointed out the guesthouse I'd chosen for its promise of a talkative owner "whose memories are as fascinating as they are tragic." When the rickshaw turned down a narrow road leading to the sea, the landscape shifted so dramatically that I jerked upright, my hand covering my open mouth. The fruit stands and tea shops and buses had given way to detritus: bullet-riddled walls with no roofs. A baby's cry rang out from behind an old sheet covering one of the gaping holes. A man in a plaid shirt and khakis stood in the yard of one of these bombed-out homes, talking on a mobile phone.

The guesthouse was at the end of this road, facing a dirty strip of sand before the flat sea. The words "Seaview Inn" were spray-painted on a piece of cardboard leaning against the house. The windows were boarded up. The driver cut the engine and smiled, waiting for his fare. Part of me wanted to get out and knock on the door of this decrepit house. Maybe there was someone inside; maybe his tragic stories would justify the mosquitoes and dirty sheets and fearsome bedtime aloneness. But I was too cowardly to take a risk that promised only unknown difficulties, no hope of fun or pleasure. I chose another guesthouse at random and showed it to the driver on the map.

The Purple Inn was clean and dowdy, owned by a plump family with whom I communicated through elaborate hand gestures punctuated by laughter. The only other guests were Sinhalese—

Buddhist Sri Lankans from the South—who'd come to visit the part of their country that had been off-limits for so long. Overwhelmed by the day's bustle after weeks at Shirmani, I got in bed before eight, missing the rowdy Europeans at Rose Land and the long-term meditators crunching biscuits. I pulled the sheet over my head and thought of Jared's improbably comfortable bed, a futon on top of an old box spring. How he pressed me into the hard mattress when he came. His hoarse bleating in time to the spasms of his legs. The moment afterward, when he fell on me. The helplessness of his dead weight. Jared's body unmediated by Jared. Sometimes, even if the sex was short and sudden and brought me little physical pleasure, the moment of Jared's collapse was pure love, wanting only goodness for another person, feeling only gratitude for my capacity to provide that goodness. Other times, the moment was such sadness that I never wanted to have sex again, to avoid the awful loneliness of being left behind. Jared's chest crushing my lungs and his shoulder smashed against my mouth. I rolled onto my stomach in the hard guesthouse bed, one hand on my breast and one hand between my legs. His penis falling out of me when he sighed, skin softening against my swollen opening.

It felt good to long for Jared, something accessible that also longed for me. Why couldn't I be earnest alongside him? That's what I was trying to say, in my profane way, to the long-term meditator who couldn't get a visa: Even at a silent meditation center, it's nearly impossible to feel reality, unadulterated by worries and preferences. What if I could do this in the context of intimacy—lean back again and again, return to the constancy of the breath, that other way of understanding my life? What if I could accept my helplessness every time Jared ordered one too many shots and then stayed out for days with his phone shut off? He would come back on his own, he always did. There was nothing I could do to force his return. Wouldn't I rather bear the discomfort he caused me on my own than spend days obsessing and fighting and making up about it? I could just feel his absence, like the millions of other people feeling the pain of absence at that very second. Giving one's life over to meditation explicitly was a kind of rejection, I told myself. I could have both Jared and a meditative life, I reasoned; I need not give up anything.

I spent the next morning wandering the city center, stunned by noise and motion. Auto rickshaws swerved around mangy dogs and women carrying baskets of mangoes on their heads. The bleat of truck horns offered bicyclists a second's warning to move to the side of the narrow road. Sinhalese soldiers stood on the edge of a field where Tamil boys played cricket, sweating in their leather boots, shifting their rifles from shoulder to shoulder, perking up when the white girl walked past. A pudgy-faced man with thick black curls fell into step alongside me. He asked where I was from, with whom I was traveling, what I thought of Jaffna. His flawless English disarmed me. I answered his questions, asked my own. Dhit worked as a translator for NGOs—when there were any around, he laughed. But he didn't get to meet many native English speakers. Would I like to come to his home for lunch? His mother and brother would be so happy to meet an American. I hopped on the back of his motorbike.

Dhit's parents' small brick house was shuttered and locked, the curtains backlit by the green glow of a TV. Dhit banged on the door, calling out his name. "My mother is afraid of the Tree Demon," he said, just as she opened the door. He introduced me in Tamil. She wiped flour on her skirt and took my hands. Dhit's brother clapped his hands and declared his joy to meet an American lady. Was I from Hollywood? Maari was hoping to move there someday and become a famous actor. He was large-eyed, long-limbed, twenty years old. While their mother made pittu—a steamed mash, I learned, of roasted flour and coconut—I asked Dhit and Maari what the Tree Demon was.

Maari stabbed the air with his index finger. "The slavism has come to us!" Dhit glanced through the open door and shushed his brother, but Maari continued speaking with loud insistence. The Tree Demon hid in the branches, waiting to pounce on women drawing well water or children using the outhouse. Some people said he had knives for fingers and metallic armor for skin. Dhit gestured away the horror story, saying the Tree Demon was probably just a normal person who jumped out of trees to scare people. He lowered his voice. "What is certain is that the Tree Demon is protected by the government," he said.

Maari leaned toward me so that the back legs of his chair raised off the concrete floor. "Yes, of course. There is a sentry point on every corner. How is it that the soldiers do not stop the Tree Demon from entering the villages?"

I looked out the door, trying to calm my uneasy excitement. A hairless dog sat in the road outside their house, picking at fleas. "Could you help me?" I asked Dhit. "I'd like to write about the Tree Demon for an American newspaper. Do you know people I could talk with?"

"Of course, Elsie." Dhit adjusted the collar of his shirt. He and Maari exchanged grins.

So my intention to sit for thirty minutes every morning and evening was quickly overshadowed by my pursuit of a story that was too awful—and too compelling—not to be shared; I worked for a newspaper, after all. I'd meet Dhit outside my guesthouse in the mornings. He'd take me on his motorbike to meet Tamil scholars, reporters, and friends who had heard of Tree Demon attacks. Dhit acted as translator. I tried to pay him, but he turned away from the money, seeming offended. I supposed he wanted to help a foreign journalist—"the international media is our only hope," I heard from so many people. Then I better not be the international media, I did not say out loud. But after a few days of reporting, I allowed myself to suspend my disbelief about my credentials and capacities. I simply let Dhit help me, taking me from newspaper to local government offices, going back to his house midday for lunch, once pausing to cool off in the ocean, me in my long skirt and kurta, Dhit in his jeans. At times I tried to tell myself to feel these rare moments—watching Maari shimmy up a tree in the backyard to fetch me a coconut; hurtling on Dhit's motorbike through a field of tall, dry sea grass interrupted by piles of colorful rubbish; drinking tea with reporters who had been beaten up and harassed by the police and yet kept on churning out stories in their one-room office whose only adornment was a life-size cardboard cutout of Gandhi. But I was too intent on my purpose to feel much of anything. All I did was scrawl in my notebook.

By the end of the week, I was constipated from eating nothing but fried starch, on edge from people telling me I should be careful since the security forces were probably following me, exhausted because I was kept awake at night by the sad stories and disturbing images I'd spent the day robotically transcribing, frustrated because victims of Tree Demon attacks kept refusing to be interviewed at the last minute. Yet the self-created urgency of my reporting had convinced me I couldn't give up. All that frustration and discomfort seemed to indicate that my chaotic notes might add up to something worthwhile.

My last night in Jaffna, Dhit took me to a festival at the main temple. The sandy streets leading to the structure's Gaudí-esque turrets were thronged with worshippers. Women wore heavy gold jewelry, kohl around their eyes, brilliant silk saris. Men in red dhotis clashed cymbals and beat handheld drums. Inside the temple gates, toddlers on their fathers' shoulders stared wide-eyed at the statue that had been erected for the festival, a two-story-high replica of a god whose long name I couldn't understand over the noise of the crowd, affixed with hundreds of lightbulbs. The tower of white light began to move, seeming to float through the crowd. I was light-headed with confusion until Dhit pointed out the rope, pulled by dozens of laughing, groaning boys. The tide of the crowd carried us aside to make way for the god, glowing against the red-and-orange sky. With mysterious synchronization, people occasionally raised their hands overhead and cried out, "Haro Hara!" The Tree Demon seemed like a cheesy horror movie playing in the background of a party.

As the first stars appeared, the crowd thinned and Dhit and I made our way back to his bike. On the street, we passed a truck with a makeshift wooden crane attached to the roof. A man in a loincloth hung from the crane, suspended from four thick hooks that pierced the skin of his calves and upper back. Another man stood atop the crane, pulling on a rope attached to the hooks. Somehow there was no blood, but as I watched the tents of skin expand and thin as the hooked man bounced, waving palm fronds, I grew short of breath and had to grip Dhit's arm and close my eyes. "It's okay," he said. "He is in a trance. He feels nothing." The nausea passed and I released Dhit's arm. But he stayed close to me, reaching for my hand as we continued walking. I had to pull away with some force.

It was humid and foggy. The thick, gray air was unsettling after the chaos of the temple. I gripped the seat back as Dhit swerved around potholes and stray dogs. We passed a sentry point. A soldier took a few steps into the road as we approached. He stopped and kicked the dirt with his boot. Dhit picked up speed as we passed the neighborhood of bombed-out houses lit by flickering oil lamps. I was leaving Jaffna at five the next morning, to spend my last few days at Rose Land. Shirmani seemed worlds away by now. I wished I had time to go back there before my flight home.

Dhit started to slow down. Shards of silvered light in the middle of the road resolved into stop signs held by soldiers. Dhit eased off the gas. A soldier shined a flashlight in our eyes. His gun jostled against his thigh. This is when it happens, I thought. I felt the hot space between my scalp and the hard dome of my helmet. We were just outside the entrance to my guesthouse. They had been following us. They would punish Dhit for my need to carry a tragic war story back to the States. The soldiers surrounded the bike. The man with the flashlight held out his hand. Dhit reached into his shirt pocket and handed the soldier a small plastic rectangle. The soldier glanced at the ID and gave it back. He stepped away from the bike and waved us through.

My heart was still pounding when Dhit parked the bike outside my guesthouse. "Are you okay?" I asked him.

"Fine. No problem." He took a deep breath and began a speech that sounded rehearsed. He had met many women in his life but never any woman like me, he could have many girls in his village, his mother was always making matches for him, and they were fine girls, but I was the only woman he could ever love. He took small gasps between his hurried sentences. He wanted to marry someone exactly like me. He hoped that the next time I came to Jaffna I would stay for longer, our time together was so short, he wanted to spend more time with me, much more time. Next time I came, he would arrange for me to rent my own house, and during that time he wanted to be with me—really be with me, I understood, right?—committed or not committed, it didn't matter to him.

His face was huge, light brown against the darker night. His eyes were teary. His rice belly, as he called it, pressed against the buttons of his shirt. I felt the presence of the soldiers a few feet away, with their guns and stop signs, their slight longing for the boredom to end and fear that it would.

"No, no, no," I said. "I only want to be friends with you, Dhit. Just friends." A porch light flicked on. My guesthouse owner walked out and glared in the direction of our voices.

"Maybe we can still be together. Just as friends." Dhit tried to smile but it only forced tears out of the corners of his eyes. I looked away and again offered to pay him for his translating. "No." The word was fierce, almost angry. Could he at least have a hug? I queasily submitted. He pulled me too close and pressed his mouth so firmly against my cheek that his inner lips wet my skin. I pulled back, but his grip was firm on my lower back. I pushed against Dhit's shoulders to disengage, turned my back to him and started walking away. "I can't tell you how much I've enjoyed getting to know you and your family," I said. "Please tell them thank you and goodbye." I forced myself not to run up the stairs to my rented room.

Before bed, I looked through the random collection of strangers' sorrow and rage that filled up my notebook. I told myself the fragments were meaningful.

KANDY

I was elated to be back at Rose Land, drinking tea in the courtyard, listening to the chanting at sunset, buying king coconuts and pineapples from the vendors in town. A young woman approached me as I was sitting on a bench one morning, enjoying the steady stream of families with ice cream cones and monks talking on mobile phones under the shade of umbrellas. "Oh, hi, hello. How do you do?" she said. "Can I practice English with you?" She grimaced against her nervousness. She was wide-faced and petite in too-big clothes—washed-out jeans and a pink T-shirt that said TRUE LOVE FOREVER. After weeks of being harassed by rickshaw drivers and trailed by unknown men, the relief of a girl's face close to mine made me laugh as I said "yes" and "please" too many times. "Thank you," she said. "I never risk to speak with a foreigner before." She told me her name and placed her hand around my wrist to lead me across the street. We went to an underground bakery, where Suriya ordered us chocolate ice cream and neon sugar water advertised as orange juice. She insisted on paying, even though she was only eighteen and her parents had health problems that made them unable to work and her brother, a soldier in the Sri Lankan army, used almost all of his earnings to pay for Suriya's college classes and boardinghouse rent.

I stiffened at the end of her tale of woe, waiting for her to ask me for money. Instead she leaned forward and said, "Can I do something?" Her wide cheeks were dotted with blackheads the size of freckles. She wiped ice cream off the tip of my nose and then sat back, her small breasts shaking under her loose T-shirt in time with her long, loud, illogical giggle. "My mother and father will be so happy I am speaking English with you," she said when we finished our ice cream. "I think I have the strength to talk to you because—I must change my life. It is boring."

I felt a crass almost-embarrassment for Rilke, as if he'd stolen the most famous line of his most famous sonnet from a twenty-year-old chatting with a stranger in a language she barely knew.

"What is your life like?" I asked Suriya, circling the bottom of my glass with my straw.

An endless succession of schoolwork and chores at her secluded boardinghouse, where she shared a room with the stern owner's ten-year-old daughter. In fact, she had to be going or the owner would be angry. "When you come to my parents' home, I dress you in a sari," she said as we left the restaurant. "You are so pretty, like doll." Her pupils were huge, like the perfectly circular eyes of a teddy bear. Maybe it was that openness that made her so relaxing to look at. When we said goodbye, Suriya had me write out my email three times and my phone number and my address in the United States.

CARPINTERIA

Waves of cold fear made me dizzy as I waited at the baggage claim for my filthy backpack filled with filthy clothes. Everyone around me was beautiful in a way that looked expensive and tiresome. I was immediately desperate for Jared to take me away from how much I did not want to be home.

"Baby, baby, baby," he said when I showed up at his door. We had loud, fast sex and then got drunk at our favorite bar, sharing a stool and laughing so loudly people shot us dirty looks. On the walk home, he grabbed my wrists and pulled me into the shadow of an awning. "Turn around," he said in the voice of sexual command that I never thought to disobey. Reflexive generosity, I suppose, in response to a clearly stated need. Freedom from the pause, the self-conscious gap between thought and action. Which was exactly what Shirmani had given me. Not that I was thinking about any of this at the time. I just turned around and leaned my forehead against the display window. Mannequins with spindly legs and sunken tummies grinned out of the darkness on the other side of the glass. Jared put his sweatshirt over my head and tied it at the nape of my neck, tight enough to leave a ring around my throat. My eyelashes caught against the fabric when I blinked. "This is what you get for making me miss you so much," he said. Blood rushed to my groin.

He walked me home that way, holding my wrists tightly at my back, jerking me down one silent street after another. A minivan started following us, and Jared released my hands so I could lift the sweatshirt off my head, smile, and wave to show this was all just a game. I was a child making herself invisible by covering her face with her hands. As soon as the van was gone, we started playing again.

By the time we got to his apartment, the air under the sweatshirt was hot and thin. My wrists hurt. Jared kept murmuring words I couldn't hear, ignoring my protests, fishing through his pocket for his keys with his free hand, until I cried out for him to let me go. He released my wrist and then brought his fist down on my left shoulder. As he unlocked the door to his apartment, I stuck my index finger through a hole in my panty hose and traced a tiny circle against my thigh. I had chosen wrongly in a way that made me interesting to myself. I felt I could handle the wrong choices better now, that I could live the old life in a new way.

In the morning, when I told Jared that my shoulder felt bruised where he had hit me, he said he hadn't hit me that hard, he would never hit me that hard, oh my god, he had missed me so much, was I really here, would I stay forever, did I want to hike to that swimming hole and go skinny-dipping today?

"Yes, please. But let's not bring beer."

"Okay. Whatever."

The sun-warm stone on my water-cold butt, toasting each other raunchily with cold cans of tingly beer, getting relaxed and giggly . . . "Or just two beers. One each. No more."

"Sri Lanka turned you into quite the Buddhist, huh?"

"The reason I need Buddhism is because I am a horrible Buddhist."

I tried going to a meditation group in Carpinteria. One of the girls there was wearing a halter top with no bra and a glittery bindhi stuck to her forehead. The group leader had a Buddha tattooed on the back of his neck. While we were supposed to be meditating, he would say stuff like, "Our Western culture tells us that happiness comes from material things. But all material things are impermanent. So true happiness comes from relinquishing desire. Stop thinking, stop wanting. Sit. Feel the peace." His desperation to feel the peace made it pretty hard for me to stop thinking about how much I wanted him to shut up.

I tried a yoga class called Moving Meditation. It was nice in a physical way. The teacher ended every class with the affirmation "Enlightenment is possible in this very lifetime!" A lovely idea, but one requiring a commitment—giving up everything except sitting—that neither I nor the other people who had driven to yoga for a little exercise seemed likely to pursue. It required the kind of faith, or maybe just circumstantial desperation, that made the long-term meditators at Shirmani stay there for twenty years, that made the man in white sit perfectly still for two days straight. In its classes, posters, and bookstore, the yoga studio encouraged people to love life, to honor their bodies as sacred, not to worry about the past or future. There was nothing wrong with these ideas, but I resented the grandiosity that was attached to them, the implication that feeling good led to enlightenment—as if enlightenment was just being the exact same person you were today except that you were constantly happy, as if no difficult sacrifices were required to change that profoundly. It's not as if I was making these sacrifices myself. But I didn't believe I was just one mind-blowing yoga class away from enlightenment. I just knew that meditation helped.

So I tried to sit on my own. But just assuming the posture—crossed legs, straight back, palms upturned on my lap—overwhelmed me, and I'd quickly jump up to check my phone or make a cup of coffee. Jared tried to meditate with me a few times. But it felt like one more pose—the two of us hungover, wearing only our underwear, hopped up on coffee, sneaking peeks at the clock, desperate for the fifteen minutes to be up so we could eat and talk and laugh away our shame at the money and time and energy we'd wasted the previous night. To walk away from something that has taken so much and given so little is to accept monstrous, murderous failure. It's easier to remain caught up in the unworthiness, telling oneself this is just the way life happens to be.

I got an occasional letter from Suriya, a reminder that there were other ways I could be spending my time. She took our friendship seriously, as if it were based on much more than one afternoon. In a particularly desperate mood, I bought a phone card and called her mobile phone. I couldn't understand much of what she said in her broken English over the bad connection, but the sound of her voice comforted me. I had a link, however tenuous, to something far away.

My other source of comfort was that Donnie had agreed to run my Jaffna story as a cover. It made me like myself more to think I was publishing an article about Tamil oppression, even if it was disjointed and a touch overwrought. But, week after week, my piece kept getting pushed down the line by something Donnie considered more "time-sensitive." The week before Christmas, a writer failed to turn in a story that was slated for the back of the book, and they needed something to fill the slot. The editor cut my piece in half in a matter of hours, while I argued with Donnie to make it the cover story, since the current one—"This Year, Give the Gift of Experience," which included suggestions like gift certificates to spas or movie theaters—was already short enough to run at the back of the book. "I'm sure your piece is brilliant," he said, putting his hand on my shoulder and looking me in the eye. "But people just don't want to read about depressing stuff like that during the holidays. Have a little compassion." He lowered his voice. "Don't spread this around, but I'm willing to pay you for the original word count."

I have never had a lot of gumption when faced with obstacles that feel to me unjust. Paris taught me that. I was so fragile that I'd let a few bored waiters chase me out of my potential future. And now I resolved to give up journalism for good. Poor Dhit. I had exploited his affection for nothing. After the skeleton of my original article was published, crammed between a review of a Britney Spears record and a new sushi bar, Jared comforted me with whiskey and sex. "Don't worry," he said, "one person can't make a difference."

The same week my Sri Lanka story was butchered, Jared left his email open on my computer. I read one suggestive message after another from a girl named Calypso, breathing so quickly and forcefully that my lips and hands went numb. I'd gone with Jared to a couple of drop-offs at Calypso's place. She had silicon lips and pockmarked skin caked in foundation. She worked as a pinup girl, mainly doing car ads. She was sexy in a way that made sex seem depraved and dumb. After I read her emails telling Jared she couldn't stop laughing about such-and-such a thing he said and she'd been having naughty dreams about him and missed his adorable face and would he please pretty please meet her at this party tonight, I downed three beers and texted Jared to come over after the show. His band was playing at a dive bar in Ventura. I'd decided to stay in, supposedly to work on *Fifi*.

I wasn't planning to tell Jared I'd read his email; I'd bring up fidelity some other way, open a real conversation about our future. But when we started having sex, my mind assailed me with images of his hands on other larger breasts, his mouth on other fuller lips. I pushed him off me and demanded he never see Calypso again, I knew what he was up to, that girl was such a loser, did he have any self-respect? Jared got out of bed and stepped into his pants. I jumped up and placed myself between him and the door. I felt myself yelling words I didn't hear. "Knock it off," he said, buttoning his shirt. "You're boring the shit out of me." I didn't mind what he said, as long as he was still in front of me. I wrapped myself around his legs. His leather boots were cold against my butt. Gripping his jeans, I told him Calypso was an ugly slut and I'd never see him again if he walked out the door. "You were away for months. You think I just sat around waiting for you to get back?" He peeled me from his calves and slammed the front door.

I stayed up 'til dawn looking at rooms for rent in Brooklyn, Houston, Seattle, Boston, gripping my breasts so hard I left handprints on them. I needed to be anywhere but here, anyone but me.

New York seemed like the best place to go because it was far away and close-but-not-too-close to my dad and supposedly artsy. Becoming a translator felt increasingly like my only acceptable option. I had no interest in trying to write books or stories of my own, although that would seem to be a logical vocation for me, if only a dream one, what with all my devouring of books and obsessive jotting down of thoughts. I refuse to use the word *journal*, since people started using it as a verb, as in, "Why don't you journal about your colon cancer?" Whatever it is I do in my little notebooks is more an effort to purge myself of thoughts than it is a hope to make use of them. Which is why I needed to be a translator, to use words in a way that would take me outside of myself, exploit my brain as a vehicle of someone else's expression.

I googled the name of every translator listed on my books, convincing myself that it was possible to make a living translating from home. Once I published my first book, I could reach out to museums, university presses, businesses in need of translators. It was even possible I would become one of those rare translators who made a name for herself, and I would be commissioned to translate all the works of some well-known contemporary French writer and the writer and I would become close friends and I would get one of those awards the French government likes to give foreigners whose contribution to Francophone literature is little known in their own countries. These were my actual thoughts. I found a room for rent on Craigslist and emailed applications to bookstores. That seemed like a good place to meet the right kind of people.

There were cupcakes in the conference room on my last day at *Carp Weekly*. Donnie gave me a hug that lasted too long. Sally made a speech congratulating herself for recognizing my potential. Joe approached me in the parking lot afterward. "Listen, if this is about the money," he said, "I wish you'da talked to me. Donnie is a cheap fuck but I know how to force his hand." I was embarrassed to have to shake my head no. When I told my dad I was moving to New York to become a translator, he mailed me a check for $4,000. "So that you can afford a nice apartment, not just slum it with a dozen roommates." My father didn't understand anything about New York rents, but the money would pay for my trip across the country and give me a few months to settle down.

I knew that I couldn't tell Jared I was leaving or I would never leave. So I waited until hours before my planned departure to pack up my belongings. I convinced my roommate that he was lucky to have my IKEA furniture, so he could now advertise the room as furnished. I merged onto 84 East in a Corolla filled with nothing but clothes and books.

Only when I was two-thirds of the way across country did I let myself call Jared. He started crying as soon as he heard my voice. We said almost nothing, just sobbed into our respective phones for close to an hour, when Jared finally dragged himself away. I knew exactly where he was going.

BROOKLYN

I spent my first few days in New York shaky, jumpy, and wide-eyed, like a drug addict going through detox. There were no doors in the fourth-floor walk-up I shared with a filthy kleptomaniac and her elderly, one-eyed Yorkie. Barnes and Noble was the only book-store that responded to my application.

The day before I started clerking there, I decided it was time to wear clean socks again and set out to conquer the Laundromat. I watched my wardrobe drown in murky water for a while before I realized that I hadn't put in detergent. I couldn't bring myself to ask the elderly Chinese woman punishing strangers' garments at the back of the Laundromat if she sold detergent and if it was too late in the cycle to add it. I let the wash run its course and then transferred my dirty, sopping clothes to the giant cauldron of a dryer. I pretended to read a magazine in imitation of the people around me. "Dryer number seven!" the Chinese woman bellowed at increasingly hysterical volumes before I realized she was telling me to remove my clothes from the dryer so someone else could use it.

I dropped my warm, dirty clothes on the floor of my room, decided to go to the Met, took the wrong train, ended up in Queens, walked past a group of black guys wearing Afro picks and addressing each other as "My nigga."

"Hey baby, you dropped something," one of them called to me. As I looked at the empty sidewalk around my feet, he said, "My heart at first sight of that fine body of yours."

"Why you wearin' all black, sweetie?" another boy called. "Someone die on you?"

I hadn't encountered many black people growing up in western Mass. I didn't know if the jeers were threatening or enjoyable, an innocuous thread from the land of human contact. I took the train back to the Lower East Side. It was pouring. I sprinted into the first café I passed, brightly lit and Polish and filled with tiny, empty square tables. I ordered borscht with rye bread. The waiter nodded and walked away. He met my eyes as he put down the steaming, maroon soup. "Okay?" he said.

"Okay," I said.

I picked up the bowl with both hands and gulped the salty broth. Onion and mushroom dumplings were hidden at the bottom. I ate them lovingly. I spent the next two hours in the café, drinking cup after cup of Lipton tea and watching the world outside the rain-streaked glass. A gray-haired man in soaked mesh shorts jogged past, squinting and making fists. A drunk leaned against the storefront, smearing the glass with his oversize denim jacket. A well-dressed, overweight woman held an umbrella in one hand and a phone in the other, gripping each so tightly her knuckles were white. A group of teenage girls passed by in high, high heels, walking slowly, feeling themselves walk. A man with a cane and a fedora took the table next to mine. He sipped a beer and carefully sliced his kielbasa. A white woman and a black woman shared a plate of pierogies in the front of the café, laughing loudly and eating with their hands. I could just make out Luther Vandross's voice from the rear of the restaurant, telling the cooks and dishwashers that he just didn't want to stop loving them. I had changed my life.

The next day, I woke up depressed by the thought of returning to the Chinese laundry and afraid of my comfort in the café. What if being alone doing nothing was the only way I could feel okay? I'd grow old drinking bad tea, listening to '80s R&B, and over-tipping immigrant waiters.

I met Brian a few weeks later, when we were forced to share a table at a crowded coffee shop. He had large green eyes that stared into his mug when he spoke, wire-rim glasses, carefully considered facial hair. He'd gone to UCLA for college—undergrad, he called it—and we chatted about the standard differences between the coasts. As he put on his leather jacket to head back to work, he said, "So, what's your romantic situation?"

Jared and I spoke on the phone every day, but he didn't know where I was. "I don't have a romantic situation," I said. Brian smiled and typed my phone number into his device.

He took me to a movie the following weekend, and then we shared his umbrella on the walk back to his apartment. Brian said he liked how the heroine was beautiful but was never sexualized. The comment had its intended effect. I smiled at the glistening sidewalks; it was really going to mean something when this trustworthy man sexualized me.

I could not hide my shock at how nice Brian's apartment was.

The only other New York apartments I'd seen were those of my coworkers, who shared railroad three-bedrooms in Bushwick between four people. Brian had a duplex with hardwood floors and exposed brick walls that overlooked Prospect Park. I put my hand on the spiral staircase that connected the living room to the upper bedroom and let my jaw drop. "My dad owns the building," Brian said, looking at the floor. "He's in real estate. But I pay rent." I understood his embarrassment at parental help. But it made me feel even more confused by finances. Every once in a while my father sent a check, which made me feel rich because I never bought anything, since I also felt poor. I made ten dollars an hour at Barnes and Noble, working half-time as a way to signal to myself that translation was my real work. When my coworkers worried about student loans and maxed-out credit cards, I almost wished I too had the boundary of debt to help describe my place in the world. It was lonely to be both spoiled and blue collar, just one more way I was a stranger to what most people considered the real world.

We sat on the edge of Brian's bed for a long time, staring at the wall a few feet in front of our faces. I was thrilled to feel myself blushing. It had been so long since I was nervous for a first kiss. "So, I got you back to my room," he said finally, rubbing his hands on his corduroys. I helped him tuck the hair behind my ears. And then the black bar on my roller-coaster seat snapped in place over my legs—complete freedom, nothing to do but surrender to the grip of a machine whose sole purpose was exhilaration. He didn't try to take off my underwear and eventually the ride slowed to a stop in a breezy, unmown field.

As soon as I opened my eyes the next morning, I willed myself to stay awake. My body yawned and rolled toward Brian. "Get up," I commanded it. The clock on Brian's desk told me it was seven fifteen. It was a Saturday and I had nowhere to be. I dressed silently, kissed Brian on the cheek, and slipped out his bedroom door. As I clanked home in my high-heel boots and one earring, I grimaced against the thought of the long black hair in my right nipple, which I'd forgotten to tweeze before I met Brian the night before. Maybe that was why he hadn't tried to take off my underwear. I crawled into bed when I got home, hoping to sleep off the shame of a new attachment. He wouldn't call me and I would stop liking him. I put my left hand on my breast and my right hand between my legs and slept until noon.

But he did call, and kept calling. He courted me perfectly, waiting a dependable two or three days after each of our dates before inviting me to a concert or a movie the following weekend. All that was required of me was to say yes. If he waited longer than usual to call, I felt relieved to be alone in my own bed, instead of hyperconscious in Brian's, where I waited for my new need to crash over me in the dark.

Brian and I had been dating for weeks before I let myself stay in his bed until late morning. He yawned and rolled on his side toward me. "You're still here," he said, and kissed me once just above each of my nipples. I bit my lip to keep from moaning. I wanted his sleepy lips on my breasts again and again and nothing else. I felt sad knowing I would have sex with Brian one day. Sex was the cracked, pink, mammalian tongue of a stranger who had promised me a line of coke in the bathroom of a dive bar; the pointy coarseness of the unknown cock between my legs when I woke up facedown in an unfamiliar room; the pair of hairy, pudgy thighs imprisoning my torso one cold, grainy morning on a secluded beach that had seemed exciting a few hours earlier; Jared's stern voice telling me not to move, he was almost done, he needed to be relaxed when we met his father for brunch. I wanted sex with Brian to salvage my body from memory. So the first time it happened while we were drunkenly making out, a voice in my head said, "Tell him to stop. Make this stop."

The good voice in me is always male. Not because men are wiser but because men are calming, before you get to know them. You ask a man a question, he answers. He asks you one back or doesn't. End of story. I listened to the unknown male voice telling me to make this stop until Brian said, "I'm gonna come."

"No!" I said—aloud this time, but it was too late.

"Sorry," he said. I kissed him lightly. "Sorry." I kissed him again. He sat up and reached for his tissue box. "Sorry."

"Stop saying—"

"Sorry."

I curled my chin toward the solid redness of his comforter. He asked me how I felt.

"Tired."

I was supposed to say something about having unprotected sex. That was my job as the girl. But I didn't want to make the accidental sex real by speaking about it. Brian curled his long body around me. "I don't know how you work yet," he whispered.

But he didn't ask me to show him, and I couldn't bring myself to volunteer unsexy lessons in my anatomy ("Just a little softer. Just a little higher. Here, let me show you"), complicating my easy attraction to Brian's long muscles and smooth skin and the adolescent jumpiness of his perfect penis. One wants to be free during sex, to let go completely, to feel and not think. But every time I did . . .

After Brian came, he would kiss me softly and wipe us off with tissues and fall asleep holding me. The bathroom was the only place to go. Sometimes I touched myself as I lay on his dirty bath mat, curling my toes against his cold tile wall and filling my mind with images of busty secretaries servicing CEOs or high school teachers taking advantage of their students—the kind of cliché sexual manipulation that Jared and I had enjoyed enacting. My self-inflicted release in Brian's bathroom left me small and shallow, a yellow bruise on a flat universe.

In bed afterward, empty enough to sleep, I would hate Brian's arms around me and feel an ugly satisfaction when he rolled away from me in his sleep. Finally one night, I returned from the bathroom and said his name. He was on top of me right away, smoothing my hair back from my face. "Talk to me," he said. "Please."

I didn't want to tell Brian, as I'd told many men, that I needed him to make me come if he came first. I didn't want sex to be that crass and simplistic. I did need to come, but I also needed something else. Even on the rare occasions when we came together, I'd ache for Brian as soon as sleep softened his grip on my shoulders. So I said nothing in response to his pleas, knowing any attempt to put my longing into words would depress and shame me. I let Brian kiss my eyelids, quiet my spine with his fingertips, murmur that everything was all right. My high school boyfriend told me he hoped I would never cry in front of him because people look ugly when they cry. But Brian was good enough to take on my ugliness in the middle of the night, even if he had to work for ten hours the next day.

He was a Web designer for philanthropists and human rights groups. I respected his work and liked listening to him talk about it. His good work made my aimlessness acceptable. I hadn't worked on *Fifi* since Brian and I started dating, as if I were now preparing myself for a different kind of success, one that was both easier and more successful: to marry well. It still seemed like enough, for a woman. Apparently Brian thought so, too, although I don't think either of us was conscious of the thought. He didn't seem the least bit troubled by my meager professional prospects. This probably should have concerned me, but all I felt was relief every time he laughed when I said that a mentally retarded and physically impaired monkey could do my job, which mostly involved alphabetizing and making change.

Given his family's obsession with money and success—his lawyer sister calling him at midnight to talk about a big client meeting she had the next day, his father asking Brian to look over his investment spreadsheets—it was odd that Brian found my excesses endearing. He bragged to his friends that I had lived alone in Europe instead of going to college, that I drank canned beer in bed before going to sleep, that I wanted to order pizza three nights a week. I suppose it was a relief for him to know he would never have to compete with me. He would always be the successful one, the provider, the solid man taking care of the pretty, damaged woman. It was a dynamic that appealed to me as well. I also wanted to be safe, at least in theory.

I tried to open myself to Brian. I stopped hiding in the bathroom after sex. He would hold me and tell me to take deep breaths. "What's going on?" he begged one night. I mumbled something about how everyone tries so hard in all the wrong ways. My voice was a little girl banging on a metal bed frame in the dark, refusing to go to sleep.

"What does that even mean?" He clenched his fists at his sides. "I can't stand it when you do this. I care about you so much and I have no idea what you're upset about."

My breathing slowed, my tears stopped. Here was the hidden part of Brian that I needed—some urgency, some insecurity, some sense that he did not know how everything would turn out. I let my lips fall on his cheeks, his forehead, the sharp V between his eyes. I told him I was scared. We talked about our parents' failed marriages—just because his parents were still together didn't mean they had succeeded, he said. We promised each other we would not end up like that, two people unknown to each other, forced to share a house, a blanket, a toilet. When our bodies came together after these talks, my thoughts about my life unraveled inside me like a trapeze artist's rope after the tent has folded, hanging from the sky unobserved, pulsing with the breeze.

But one night, I started to say something after Brian turned out the light and he snapped, "No talking."

"I'm not—I just wanted to tell you one thing."

"I can't take it anymore." His hands flopped around on the mattress, desperate to be calm. So these nighttime conversations, which I believed were carrying us toward a new intimacy, were a burden to him, one of the unpleasant compromises of a relationship. I never told him the one thing. I stopped crying in his bed. I asked him to make me come if he came first.

I met Brian's family for the first time over Labor Day Weekend. On the drive to their home in rural Connecticut, Brian gently coached me in what not to say to his parents—swear words, jokes about suicide or depression, anything in any way, however remotely, connected to sex. I mocked the last directive—just how sex crazed did he think I was?—until I remembered our recent weekend at my father's house. It was pouring and we'd been stuck in the house, drinking too much coffee and wine. My father told us about my mother's abortion over dinner, a story I was sick of hearing: She'd gotten pregnant again when I was only three months old. "I wanted to keep it, of course," my father said for the hundredth time. "I said we could use formula. I would do all the late-night feedings. But Elsie's mother always made her own decisions—absolutely nothing I could ever say to sway her. Hey, what kind of birth control are you guys using? The fastest way to kill a relationship is to have a baby before you're both ready, trust me." I'd tried to laugh at my father's inappropriate divulgences, teasing him for successfully scaring away my boyfriend within a matter of hours. But Brian blanched and stammered out a question about the Manny trade, hoping my father would be a Red Sox fan because he happened to live in Massachusetts.

As we pulled down a dirt driveway lined by careful stone fences, Brian said, "Oh, and don't mention you didn't go to college. I mean, just until they know you and realize how smart you are. I kind of implied you went to school in Paris, which is sort of true, right?"

"If you count drinking a bottle of wine by yourself and crying in public parks as going to school in Paris, then yes, I definitely went to school in Paris." Brian chuckled and told me not to worry, just be myself. He gripped the steering wheel with both hands and bit the insides of his cheeks as he pulled into the driveway.

I felt his parents straining to like me as we stepped out of Brian's car in front of their pastel three-story home, Brian looking at the ground and me squeezing out a smile in my hopeful sundress and sandals. His dad shook my hand with vigor and sized up my face as he called out, "Here's the brave girl at last! Come meet Elsie." Handshakes, names, more jokes about my courage. And then I felt his family—parents, sister, brother-in-law—turn away from me as we ate dinner at the picnic table outside, and I kept oohing and aahing over the pink smeared across the sky instead of entering their conversation about an eminent-domain lawsuit over one of his father's rental properties and the feasibility of adding commuter facilities to the parking garage in the Boston suburb where Brian's sister lived with her husband. I did not know how to talk about the things one must talk about; this never stopped being a painful surprise.

Brian shoveled food into his mouth like a teenager after basketball practice and refilled my wineglass with waiterly attentiveness. While the adults ate tomato pie, grilled lamb, and buttermilk rolls, Brian's nieces played in the overgrown field in front of the house, throwing crab apples and running around with a garden hose, pretending to put out fires.

"It's amazing how parents do it with the little ones," Brian's dad said.

"We did it twice. Or don't you remember?" Marianne flicked her husband's wrist with her cloth napkin. Brian's father had cheated on Marianne soon after they were married and in addition to raising two children only eleven months apart she'd had three miscarriages and one stillbirth. Brian told me that his mother "practically lived" in the clapboard shack behind the main house, where she kept the canvases and watercolors that she referred to as a hobby. Watching her slice pie and dart in and out of the kitchen for missing utensils, my breath got short and shallow the same way it did when Brian spoke confidently of our future—asking me where I'd most like to honeymoon, fantasizing about settling down in a farmhouse near his parents. When this anxiety seized me, I wanted Brian to hold me and tell me it was all right, but it seemed he might take offense if I asked him to comfort me for my fear of being bound to him.

After his family went to sleep, Brian and I stayed up late at the picnic table. He poured us generous helpings of the fancy whiskey he'd brought for his father. I was surprised and excited by Brian's carelessness. He tended to be a measured drinker, corking the bottle and clapping his hand on my knee around midnight, saying, "Bed?" I always wanted to drink more. I always told myself to be grateful for Brian's reasonableness. But tonight he kept refilling our glasses until the smoky liquor was almost gone and I was flushed and bouncy. He took my hand and led me along a creek in the backyard until we came to a tree house.

"I built this place in high school," he said. "Came out here to play guitar."

"You never told me you played guitar."

"No?" He climbed the wooden planks nailed into the tree trunk. I followed. "Thought I was going to be a musician. I designed CD covers and everything. There should be one here." He groped the planks of the tree-house floor and handed me a slip of paper. I held it outside the door to see the cover image in the moonlight: a photo of a white spiral staircase against a black background, the top step jutting into darkness, leading nowhere. A poignantly explicit image for a teenage boy. "Oh," I said, resting my fingertips on Brian's wrist.

Some weekends Brian spent two straight days on the couch. He always went through the motions of being a good boyfriend—asking what I wanted for dinner, ordering and paying for takeout, telling me he loved me and I looked so pretty in that top—but every word and gesture seemed to be a sacrifice. "I can't hear you," I'd say. "Why are you talking so quietly?" "I'm sorry," he'd say, quietly.

When I got low in the way shrinks call depressed, my lowness was aggressive, evident; Brian's was unknown to himself and therefore enraging to me because it could not be acknowledged. I wondered sometimes which was worse: to be with someone who dealt with discontent by drinking too much or by lying around. Since I was sure I knew the answer—Brian was a Web designer, not a drug dealer; a homebody, not a womanizer—I had not spoken to Jared since Brian and I started dating.

～

The next morning at his parents', Brian slept much later than usual. I'd been awake for hours, but didn't want to wake him and be forced to join the paternal pronouncements and clanking dishes coming from the kitchen adjacent to our guest room.

Around noon, Brian rubbed his eyes and reached for me under the covers. We lay on our sides, my back to his chest. I was too preoccupied by his sister's voice to feel his small, fast movements. It was nice to be needed without needing anything myself.

Preparing to join his family in the kitchen afterward, I wanted this feeling to continue. So I decided to play the role of a sweet girl who speaks only about topics that have no relevance to anyone's personal life. I put on a blouse that brought out my eyes and generalized my figure, and walked into the kitchen wearing the kind of half smile I often saw on the faces of young women speaking to their husbands in public. Brian's father had just finished reading a newspaper article aloud. He turned the paper out to Brian and me. "Just look at that bastard."

"And which bastard is this exactly?" I asked, thrilled by my boldness, my coy phrasing, my blousy blouse and self-contained smile.

Brian's father smarted as if he'd been pinched. Then he started laughing. "You know who that is," Brian said. "Honey?" He blushed and stared, willing me to retrieve the name. "Honey, you know that's John McCain." His dad was still laughing in grand, jolly gusts. "Hear that, you bastard? The youth of America don't even know who you are!"

"I know who he is," I said. I just didn't watch TV and I only read the paper online, paying no attention to pictures. I could have saved face by showing off my knowledge of McCain's hypocritical torture policy, but I was afraid I'd start crying if I tried to talk about it casually.

Brian's mother became very busy in the kitchen, humming,

discomfited by empathy, knowing my faux pas (how delighted I was, during French class in middle school, to uncover the meaning of the phrase) would guarantee her husband would never again take me seriously.

Accepting defeat, I spent most of the day reading *House of Mirth* on the couch. "Must be a real page-turner," Brian's father said, and joked that he had gotten his fill of novels after being forced to read *Ulysses* in college. The culture demands the faces of presidential candidates become second nature to us but forgives people who never listen to music or read books, who have no idea what they're feeling most of the time and no language to describe the feelings in any case.

Before we left Brian's parents', his father gave us some meat from their neighbors' farm. Brian stammered thank you several times and offered to pay his dad.

"No, no," his father said toothily. "This one's a gift."

In the car, I poked fun at the excessive formality of the exchange. Brian was not amused. "That is seriously good meat," he said. "It was really nice of my dad to just give it to us."

Brian believed that life consisted of hard work interrupted by a smattering of fun moments. He told me this later that night, lying in bed beneath his open window, shirtless and relaxed now that he was back in his grown-up home. His long lashes blinked deliberately as he spoke about the rightness of dull suffering, his face backlit by the artificial brightness of summer nights in the city. He placed his hand on top of my thigh. "Your skin is so soft it startles me every time I touch it," he said. My body responded to his words, pressing its hot skin against his, kissing his smooth cheek and prickly chin. But I felt heavy with the logic in which Brian's will was imprisoned. My hands moved over his body throughout the night, clinging to his bicep, his shoulder, his fingers, trying to feel their way out of the inertia gathering around us in the almost dark. But the morning was sunny and dry, and as Brian biked off to work, I heard him singing for the first time. *I just kept lookin' at the sight of her face in the spotlight so clear . . .*

A few nights later, he took me out for a fancy dinner, offered a short speech about how well things were going between us, asked me to move in with him, ordered a bottle of champagne when I said yes. The careful way he courted me felt like grace, like something mysterious was finally pushing my life in the right direction. I clinked glasses with his, thinking how handsome he was, marveling at his certainty that we should be together. I watched myself dipping bread in olive oil and cutting handmade pasta as if I were standing behind a plate-glass window, feeling something I couldn't quite describe while I watched people on the other side of the glass act out emotions with clear causes and correct names.

After we moved in together and Brian no longer had to ask me on dates in order to see me, I started to fear his solidity. I'd ask him to waste time with me at various bars and restaurants and concerts and he'd pull me against him and nuzzle my neck, saying he was exhausted. Weekends were documentaries from Netflix, Indian takeout, cuddling on the couch, chatting idly, sort of watching TV, Brian dozing off, me sneaking sips of the vodka we kept in the freezer, my internal organs jumping up and down on a little raft adrift within me, making me seasick. This will be my life, this will be my life, this will be . . .

But when I thought of my future without Brian, it was a dark room filled with a chemical meant to smell like rotting wood. I don't know where the image came from, but it was specific and terrible. So after Brian left for work some Monday mornings, I found myself kneeling on the floor, begging: "Do not let me be bad. Do not let me want to leave. Do not let us become a nightmare of entangled needs unmet. Do not let me kill this." The prayers came unbidden, always in the negative.

They didn't work, of course.

CARPINTERIA

I had to go back to California for my uncle's funeral. Thomas died in a one-car crash. My father was convinced it was a suicide and equally convinced he could have prevented it, had he only forgiven Thomas's boyhood meanness—smashing my father's favorite toy to bits while my father cried and pleaded; locking my father in the basement for hours; giving my father charley horses and dead legs and worse. Dad called me several times a day after Thomas died, repeating these awful stories, illogically ending each with the regret that he had not reached out to Thomas more as an adult, he could have helped him, it wasn't Thomas's fault that their parents had no idea how to take care of kids. I tried to tell my father that he was expecting too much from himself, but he spoke over me in a loud, shaky voice, telling me, not for the first time, about the one good conversation he and Thomas had had as adults, when Thomas revealed that the sound of my father's baby cries still haunted him, a small, hopeful wail escalating into a shriek of desperation that eventually exhausted my father's breath. I pictured, not for the first time, a wreckage of baby babble crashing in the air above my father's neglected crib and raining down on him, smothering him into silence. I was nauseated by love for my father, imagining him alone in the too-big house my mother had insisted on buying and then abandoning. Is there any emotion more uncomfortable than pity for one's parents? I told my father that I would borrow Brian's car and drive out to his house so we could fly to the funeral together, already dreading being a captive audience for my father's pain on the five-hour flight.

Thomas was buried on the Fourth of July in L.A., where he had spent his adult life. The funeral was my uncle's immediate family standing around the coffin, surrounded by tombstones so new they looked metallic, speaking incidental memories of Thomas as they came. The far-off cackle of store-bought firecrackers was the only music at the service. The sun was brilliant and cloying. I'd barely known my uncle. I had no memories to share with his widow or children. But being admitted to this scene of reasonably excessive suffering unhinged some badness in me. Life was too hard, it was not my fault, everyone suffered, may as well take the drug. Brian had offered to take time off work to come to the funeral with me but effused relief when I told him not to bother, to save the time off for something fun instead. I had recently resumed talking to Jared on the phone while Brian was at work; he knew I was living with somebody; I thought we could be friends. So after the funeral and the family sitting around in my uncle's house with nothing to say, I called Jared and told him I was in his neighborhood, sort of. He was at a party, but he'd leave right away. He gave me the address of his new digs and promised to be waiting outside when I got there. There is a Zen parable about a teacher who tells his student to stop obsessing over the bad things he's done, to treat his past badness as a collection to be mined for knowledge. The student takes this to mean that he can do whatever he feels like doing, and goes on adding to his collection of mistakes until it is too huge and putrid to sort through for any glint of wisdom. I told my father I was going to visit friends in my old town and drove north to Carpinteria just as the real fireworks started, littering the skies over Camarillo and Oxnard. Stupid towns—outlet malls, the smell of sulfur from factories, blimps floating in the smog. Jared was waiting outside his apartment when I got there, wearing pants that I hated. Too short, flamboyantly checkered. He hated them, too, but not enough to spend money on new clothes. And now they looked perfect to me, even manly in their disregard for appearances.

"No sex," I said as he unlocked the door to his apartment.

"Right. We're just friends."

As soon as he shut the door to his bedroom, he gathered my hair into his fist and ran his tongue from the nape of my neck to the base of my skull. I noticed the unforgiving hardness of the tips of my shiny black shoes, the overripe banana musk in his room, the crumpled newspaper by his bed. Or whatever the particular external details happened to be. What I remember clearly is that the quality of my awareness changed—Jared pushed me onto the mattress, held my arms over my head, lifted up my dress—the way water changes according to one's thirst. This could be the last time we would ever be together. The more external details I could notice, the more okay I would be. "Yes," I said again and again, until sensation wore away the meaning of the word.

BROOKLYN

The night I got home from California, Brian and I went to a German café near our apartment. We dipped hunks of rye bread into creamy tomato soup and sipped strong Manhattans. We didn't know it was movie night until fifteen minutes into our meal, when *The Princess Bride* began, projected onto the wall in front of us. I tried to continue answering Brian's questions about how my father was handling the loss of his brother, but the movie was loud. The boy asked his grandpa, who was reading him a fairy tale, "Wait, is this a kissing book? What about sports and stuff?" Brian chortled. "Sorry," he said. "I can't concentrate with this movie on."

I didn't mind. It was nice to sip my strong cocktail and watch Wesley and Buttercup brave the Fire Swamp for the sake of true love.

There was fresh snow on the sidewalk when we left the bar. I didn't notice the white branches gleaming overhead until we were at the door of our apartment, and then I did not want to go in. I wanted to stay outside, a creature walking through the world, not of it. Fortunately, Brian started kissing me as soon as we shut the door behind us. He pulled my chin down with his index finger and ogled the O my lips formed before falling on my open mouth. He led me into the bedroom and sat on the edge of the bed in front of me. In one motion, he pulled off my T-shirt, sweater, and bra. He cupped my breasts in his hands and bounced them. "I missed your boobs." He grinned. I kissed his forehead, relaxing into his delight in something that just happened to belong to me.

He yanked off his boxers and rolled my underwear down my hips. What I had done with Jared was a mistake with a clear name and a clear implication. I hadn't let myself name it while I was making the mistake; it just felt like something that was happening to me, the way Brian had happened to me. Only away from Jared could I recall what I'd done in terms of my own agency. So I listened to my boyfriend's pleasure without striving for any of my own. All I deserved was his satisfaction. When it was over, I kept my face burrowed in the pillow next to his head for as long as I could. "You're so still," he said finally.

"I'm not crying for a bad reason."

He patted my hair until I quieted.

Although Jared and I had barely slept during the two days we spent together, I was restless that first night back and lay awake for hours, telling myself I should get my book out of my suitcase.

"Your breathing is too shallow," Brian whispered to me once. "Take deeper breaths." The *S* came out in a harsh lisp, and I rolled away from him, folding my hands across my pounding chest. I awoke in the morning as he shut the door to the bedroom, having quietly dressed for work. I shot upright.

"Brian!" I wondered for one second if I could bear it if he were already gone. I ran out to the hallway, where he was zipping up his coat. "You didn't say goodbye." His leather jacket was cold against my breasts.

"I didn't want to wake you," he said. "You seem worn out." He shifted his weight from one foot to the other, one hand on the doorknob. So he had sensed my distance. Which meant he would be cold to me for a few days and then fuck me roughly, his eyes clenched, jaw set, nostrils flared. How he would have hated that image of himself. I knew that we should not use sex to release unspoken anger, like one of those stereotypical couples that terrified me so much, who would never know true closeness but would just seesaw between neediness and resentment until they died. But how could I stop him when he was bearing down on me hatefully, all muscle, no confusion? That kind of sex left me uncomfortably horny for days afterward—awful word, horny, with its harsh, adolescent hurriedness, but the misplaced need that arose from makeup sex (another juvenilely crass phrase) was awful indeed. I always wanted just one more orgasm, the one that would make all these unspoken negotiations worthwhile.

Brian wished me a good day, staring at the floor.

I called Jared a few minutes after Brian left. He yawned loudly. "I miss you, beautiful girl," he said. Just like that, this became an acceptable pattern of feelings.

〜

Brian often had several big projects due around the same time, and in the week or two before the concurrence of deadlines he was empty of himself. He would hug and kiss me, tell me he loved me, bring me flowers. But his affection was a performance he enacted while his mind was elsewhere, so industrious that he forgot to eat or shower or have sex. I took NyQuil before bed during these periods, so as not to be kept awake by desire for a body that stress had traumatized into an unfeeling mass of blood and water and flesh, dumb as a fetus. Sometimes in the early mornings, his cock would remember to need me, and Brian attacked me with a sudden, brief passion that enflamed and then abandoned me like the boys I used to meet at bars. I knew that Brian and I would have close, long-lasting, satisfying sex again as soon as he completed this latest round of websites and that I must therefore remain calm the few times he fucked me hard and fast with no thought to my own enjoyment. But precisely because I found this to be the most erotic of all sex acts—in concept—and because I could never, not once, experience this fast, violent release that I imagined to be the most perfect pleasure, I was never calm. A miniature girl in combat boots and fishnet tights stomped on my chest and shouted to me about the selfishness of all male bodies and the treachery of all female bodies, which give themselves wrongly again and again.

At breakfast—Brian both stiff and jumpy, wide-eyed with anticipation of the workday; me glaring and tense, my chest hardened against the quaking of tiny, helpless feet—I would mutter that I could pour my own cereal when he asked if I wanted Raisin Bran or Puffins, would chew with my mouth open, refuse to wipe the milk out of the corners of my mouth, turn my face away when he tried to kiss me goodbye, tell him that he was not meeting my needs and I was so unhappy and felt abandoned and was going to have a terrible day. I could behave as horribly as I wanted; it would not be long before he would want to take me again and I would want to submit. Brian would say the word "sorry" several times, pat my shoulder, back out the door, pause in the doorway to stare fearfully at my hard jaw and small eyes, tell me he would see me tonight and it would be okay. He was a good animal, plodding along the path in front of him with heavy steps, thoughtlessly following every rule of every preexisting game. And I was a ghost with an enormous belly and a tiny speck of a mouth, unable to consume enough food at one time to fill me up. The more the ghost eats, the more it is reminded of its hunger.

I would touch myself after Brian left for work, trying not to think of the sound he made just before I gave him the release for which I could not forgive him—a quickly escalating growl. Often the sound refused to leave my head and I came with little pleasure thinking of it and afterward resented Brian even more for the straightforward sound of his straightforward climax, which forced me to be always in relation to him, even when I felt most alone. We do not get what we want, biologically speaking.

After one morning like this, I got a letter from Suriya. She was now taking exams to become an English teacher, so our letters and occasional phone conversations were very important to her success, as she put it. The most uncomplicated happiness I felt in those days came from editing her letters; along with my brief, safe descriptions of life in New York (the tall buildings! the celebrities! the pizza!), I would send a list of grammatical errors she'd made and their corrections ("I have not time for fun" to: I don't have time for fun; "I miss my brother in whole my soul" to: I miss him with all my soul; "You are helpful me" to: You help me).

This letter began: "In these days, I face so many problems. Yet I still alive." ("Am still alive," I wrote at the top of my list of corrections.) In her boardinghouse, she had been assigned to share a room with a classmate who was not as smart as Suriya and jealous of her success. She hid Suriya's books and assignments just before the bus came in the morning, so Suriya had to go to school unprepared. Suriya complained to the boardinghouse owner and requested a different room so that she could keep her belongings safe. The owner scolded Suriya for being proud and thinking she deserved better than the other girls and said other bad things that Suriya did not wish to record, she wanted them out of her head so they would not harm her personality as an adult woman. Suriya decided to leave that bad place. She packed up her things in a box and left it in the corner of her room and then took the long bus ride home to her parents' house, where she lived for one week until she could find a new boardinghouse, missing classes and getting far behind in school. After she settled into a new boardinghouse and returned to the old one to fetch her belongings, the box was gone. She asked the landlady for her lost things and the lady hit her and told her to stop making problems in her house. So Suriya had to move into the new boardinghouse with only the clothes on her back. She lost her one pair of socks and one good skirt and one good pair of shoes, and she had to wear dirty sandals and dirty pants to school and the boys all laughed. She did not have books to participate in class and had to stay in the classroom during the lunch period, to study the books then. She felt as if she lost everything in a strange and outside area from her home. ("Outside area from my home" to "foreign place" or "place far away from my home," I wrote.) She called her brother, who was working in the army, also far away. He said, "Think what you have and do not think what you don't have. Once I have money, I will bring you new garments." ("Think OF," I wrote. "And we usually say clothes, not garments.") After speaking to her brother, Suriya made up her mind and hid her sadness. She studied hard and was first in all of her exams. The girl who stole her belongings made poor marks and will never have success. The boardinghouse owner who hit her has no friends because she is mean. So Suriya does not mind that they treat her poorly. They do not hurt her life. I put the letter down and was quiet and still. If I were going to concoct an inspirational tale about overcoming adversity, Suriya would probably be the star. But I didn't have to concoct anything; Suriya was real.

I made the mistake of reading the letter to Brian when he got home that night, wanting to share Suriya's sweetness and wisdom. "Sounds kind of suspicious," he said. "That's, like, a classic sob story. Seems like she's trying to get money out of you." I hadn't even considered sending Suriya money, I so rarely thought of practical solutions to anything. Partly to spite Brian's cynicism, I wired her one hundred bucks. A few weeks later, she mailed me a dozen handmade greeting cards, decorated with pressed flowers and stickers, each with a different message: Happy New Year! Happy Birthday! Merry Christmas! God Bless You! "I wish to return your money in the future," she wrote, "once I be a real teacher." ("Once I am," I wrote back.) "But until that day, you can sell these cards in a shop in New York City. They will be expensive in your country, no?"

I showed the cards to Brian, hoping he'd be as moved as I was. "Good for you," he said, as if I'd passed a test.

I started seeing Jared regularly after Brian presented me with a ring at the top of Bear Mountain and listed reasons he wanted to marry me in French, a language he didn't speak. My present recklessness was justified by the severity of the future limits I promised the sunny, windy mountaintop I would respect. Every few weeks, Jared would fly to New York and stay at a motel near our apartment. Brian worked ten-hour days. Jared and I had so much time to ourselves that I often forgot we were doing anything wrong.

I didn't need a psychologist to tell me my fear of marriage was the result of my parents' romantic misery. So I tried to ignore it. I was afraid of most normal things—talking to people, for instance. Brian was a stable, successful, attractive, loyal man who wanted to marry me. Saying yes was not an emotional question. It was a question of not ruining my life.

I took another shift at the bookstore to punish myself for neglecting *Fifi*. My favorite coworker was a gaunt older woman with spiky white hair and huge gray eyes. We sometimes got beers at the bar next door to Barnes and Noble, and she'd tell me about the sex she had in high school. She never wanted a boyfriend and she never wanted to kiss on the mouth. "No kissing!" she commanded the boys she brought home and screwed (her word) under the kitchen table while her mother snored upstairs, too muted by codeine to hear anything. She'd grip the wooden legs and close her eyes tightly and focus only on the sensation between her legs. I pictured her turning her face away when it was over, refusing to meet the boy's eyes as she told him to be sure the lock was pushed in when he let himself out. Now she was almost sixty and lived alone. She was all fucked out by the end of high school. Anyway, it wasn't worth risking AIDS and she'd rather not screw at all than get screwed by Saran wrap. While she stocked books, she sang softly to herself. She always had several novels going at the same time, one from every aisle, bookmarked and restored to their rightful place in the alphabet whenever the boss came by. She loved her morning bagel and her afternoon espresso. She wore loose, solid-colored dresses that swished around her athletic frame. No breasts.

Cancer, she told me. I wondered who had cared for her. She never talked to her parents and her brother was in rehab in Colorado. I looked for signs that she was unhappy, that her ostensible ease in the world was actually resignation to loneliness. But I never saw a chink in her social self, no glimpse of a private life hidden at great cost. So why was I scared of becoming her? I enjoyed her company, but there was always this voice in my ear—the calm, reasonable male voice—warning me that her life was empty, an embarrassment, that it was all right for me to stock books and work the register at thirty, but that a middle-aged, solitary salesclerk led a life of shame.

At Brian's office Christmas party, men and women alike congratulated me on my catch, told me how lucky I was, Brian was such a great guy. Of course they didn't have to spend a weekend with him when he was withdrawn and self-absorbed, barely registering my presence, exhausted from giving his best self to his coworkers and clients. I had these thoughts consciously—I even wrote them down in a notebook I kept hidden at the back of my desk drawer. But this thinking didn't seem like an indication that I shouldn't be with Brian specifically. Rather, the distance between the good impression Brian made on acquaintances and the disappointment he caused me at home seemed a confirmation of my belief that marriage was a secret so painful you had to keep the secret even from yourself.

Brian loved the fact that two of his friends got engaged the same month he did. I didn't like his sly pride in conforming, but it was relaxing to know he understood the business of living. And I would break down his defenses over time. He would stop protecting himself from me the way he protected himself from the world by hiding behind its rules. I would be so grateful to be the sole trustee of his full self that I would no longer desire Jared or anyone else.

When Brian and I were walking in Central Park one evening, a little girl stopped dead in her tracks in front of us. She pulled on her mother's hand and stamped one foot. "But I'm *ser*ious!" she said. The father scowled. "You're five. You're not serious about anything. You don't understand how anything works yet."

Brian chuckled as we scooted around the crying girl. "What a relief to hear a parent with some balls," he said. I swung the hand he was holding, looking at the sky, turning away from his harsh pronouncement just as I turned away from my body in the presence of his polite, hardworking mother and quietly dignified (Brian's phrase) father. I knew Brian would want kids and I hoped I would, too, someday. I liked the idea of being needed. But I could already imagine myself cringing when Brian called me "the mother of his children" with pride and bitterness, the same pride and bitterness he would feel for forgoing the chance to fuck his female underlings at work, consigning himself for life to the bombed-out ruin of my vagina and saggy, stretch-mark-riddled stomach and nipples sucked into long, inflamed, livid daggers. I begged my brain to shut up when I had thoughts like this. Brian was going to be a good husband. He put his hand on my lower back and steered us out of the park.

Since getting engaged, I'd become serious about *Fifi* again, in my way. I wanted something that was mine. On the days I wasn't working at the bookstore, I would set myself up at my desk—coffee, notebooks, giant Larousse dictionary—before Brian headed out to the office. But as soon as he closed the door behind him, I often got back in bed with a novel, giddy with the ease of being alone. An hour before he was due home from work, I would drag myself back to the desk, plow through French words without feeling them, just so I could tell my fiancé that I'd done my five hundred words for the day, and he would believe in me, in my project.

I met my friend Laney for coffee and told her I was scared of getting married. We'd gone to high school together and reconnected through Facebook. She wore crimson lipstick and platform boots that laced up to her knees. A helmet of black hair framed her taut, bluish skin. Her ripped T-shirt ended just below her pointy breasts. Sipping her large mocha soy latte with an extra shot, she told me about the guy she'd met at a party the night before. "He had this rape-and-pillage vibe going on," she said. "I knew he would be all—" She pumped her hips in the air and then made a circular tossing motion with her hands, like a sailor throwing a bag of spoiled rice overboard. "I don't think we even spoke before we got in a cab together. I just stared at him across the room and told him with my eyes: I am totally buying what you're selling." She took a long swig of her coffee and told me with her eyes that she had totally bought what he sold. Then she looked away, sighing so loudly that the sound was offensive rather than poignant. "I don't think anyone else hates men and fucks them as much as I do. Marriage couldn't be worse than that, right?"

"Yes it could," I said. "It could be that, just with less fucking."

"Oh, darling, every lady needs a husband," Laney said, affecting a British accent and smoking an imaginary cigarette. "It's our cross to bear." We played rich Brits for the rest of the morning.

Laney was always inviting me to dance parties in warehouses or burlesque shows on roofs. Brian had tried to be nice, but after we got engaged, he told me frankly that he never wanted to see her again. "She seems really damaged," he said.

"Anyone who's made it to thirty without getting damaged is barely alive," I said. "And besides, damaged people are funnier than other people." I told him that Laney had recently said to me, "I'm pretty sure the only reason I've never been date-raped is because I was always willing to do whatever the guy wanted."

"That's sad," he said.

"But it's also funny."

Brian and I started fighting nearly every weekend because I wanted to go to some concert or beer garden or friend's party, and he was working or tired from working. I liked being alone on the nights he worked late. But if I was going to be forced to be around another person, unable to lose myself in daydreams or loud music or books, I wanted to at least have fun. I erupted at him one night when he canceled our plans to go to an all-night dance party on a boat. I'd gotten us tickets weeks earlier. "I'll pay you back," he said.

"You are willfully boring," I said. We were walking home from dinner. We paused in front of the Brooklyn Museum and screamed at each other on the majestic steps. He called me vitriolic. I felt a quiver of excitement at his word choice. We exhausted ourselves and started walking toward our apartment.

"This is the same fight my parents have been having for forty years," he said as he hung up our coats.

"I don't want to have this fight for forty years."

"So let's not." He took my hand and led me to our IKEA couch. We sat side by side in the dark. The sky was pretty through our bay windows. Fluid black shapes swam through a still-blacker canvas. Brian wrapped his arm around my shoulder. He tilted my chin back with his index finger. My mouth kissed his mouth. My shoes sat beside the couch, side by side, empty, the insoles coming loose at the heels. I'd bought them for four dollars at a stoop sale one Sunday afternoon. I was so glad when I spotted them, gladder still when I asked the price. Now they stared up at me, alive with need, animals waiting to be fed. I buried my face in Brian's arm.

The next weekend, he canceled a series of Friday meetings to take me to Cape Cod. We slept a lot and drank a lot of not bad wine and walked on the beach. No one could say we were not having a nice weekend. It was April, far too cold for swimming. One night at sunset, I pulled off my clothes, ran and dove, emerged shrieking. "You're crazy," Brian said, grinning at my blue, goose-pimpled flesh in a way that looked physically taxing.

Brian didn't want to know I was cheating on him. But he was often cold to me after Jared's visits, perhaps sensing my inaccessibility as I caught up on sleep and readapted to calmer days. His coldness felt only right to me, until he failed to invite me to a party for Obama's inauguration. I learned about it on Facebook, where he posted a photo of his coworkers standing before an enormous projection of Obama's face, each raising a glass of champagne.

"You didn't tell me your office was having a party today," I said when he got home from work. "I had to watch the inauguration all alone."

Brian shook his head and dropped his bag on the couch. "Please don't start. I'm starving." I followed him into the kitchen. "What, you didn't get your fill of the champagne and hors d'oeuvres at the party? It looked really fun. Judging from all the bragging you did on Facebook."

He took a bag of Tostitos out of the cupboard and started eating from the bag. "It was really fun. Mostly because we finally have a president who cares about things that matter. But it was an *office* party."

"There were spouses in the photos. And you knew I wasn't working today. I even asked you last night if you thought you could come home early to watch the—"

"Get off my back. Today was a big day for everyone in the world. Can we please just celebrate that? All you ever think about are your own feelings." This was Brian's classic response if I complained too much about something he found trivial. It never failed to unhinge me.

"We are not fucking talking about Obama right now. Don't you fucking hide behind the first-black-president bullshit. He is half white! And if you think he's really going to change anything, you're just naïve."

This wasn't exactly what I meant to say. I was excited about seeing a black family in the White House; I was excited to have a president who spoke in eloquent paragraphs. But I was cautious. What I meant was that power shifted continually back and forth between the two parties without society changing in any concrete way, that political battles were just a distraction from actual problems facing actual humans, so that people who really wanted to be a force for good became activists, not president. I had been awash in thoughts like this all day. I would have liked someone to discuss them with.

"You are unbelievably negative," Brian said. "Finally something good happens in our country and you can't just let me be happy about it."

"I am not negative! You just don't want to accept basic facts about reality."

"I guess now you're going to tell me I could die at any time." This had become a (minor, I'd thought) point of contention between us, how frequently I urged Brian to make decisions based on the fact that this could be the last day of his life. The words were theatrical, but I was genuinely encouraging him to move away from materialist evaluations of good and bad. Which may have been just a touch self-righteous. But I wasn't evaluating myself right then; I was expressing myself.

"You are going to die, Brian. We all are. Get used to it!" He was carrying a jar of salsa and the bag of chips toward our bedroom. "You can't spend your whole life ignoring anything that makes you uncomfortable." He closed the door to the bedroom and pushed in the lock. "Like the fact that you're an incredibly selfish lover," I shouted into the closed door.

As I was walking away, the door flew open. Brian grabbed my arm. "You are a crazy bitch, Elsie. I feel really fucking sorry for you." He yanked down on my arm with each word. "You freak out when you don't have an orgasm. That's not normal. That's fucking crazy. You need to see a shrink." He released my arm and marched to our front door. "Get the fuck out. I'm sick of your shit. Just leave me the fuck alone." Stunned, I stepped into the hallway. Brian tossed my coat after me and slammed the door. A moment later, it reopened a crack. Keys flew at my feet.

I walked across the street to the snowy park and screamed. Once I was hoarse, freezing, and spent, I went home, feeling something like relief that Brian had lost it. It made the tension between us explicit. Now we would be able to really talk about it.

Brian was sleeping in the living room, his long legs draped over the end of our small couch. He would be so apologetic in the morning. Only when I got up the next day did I notice his two suitcases waiting by the front door.

He got ready for work quickly, without speaking to me. I was sitting on the couch, staring at the suitcases, asking him to please

please talk to me. The skin around my eyes was soggy and purple. Finally he took a seat on the edge of the couch, careful not to touch me. "So last night I saw a side of myself that I never want to see again." This was the first time I'd heard Brian frankly admit to an emotional struggle. I reached out to touch his face. He recoiled, hunching his shoulders. "Let me get this out. You make me feel crazy." He was speaking to the floor. "I've always been a calm person. I don't lose my temper. I'm really even keel. Everybody knows that about me."

"Honey, it's okay to—"

"And I'm not going to take a chance on that happening again. What happened last night. I cannot be with someone who makes me behave that way."

I put a hand on his thigh. He stiffened. "Honey, please, it's okay to lose your temper once in a while—it shows you care—if we could just talk about what we each did wrong—"

"That kind of thinking is exactly why I cannot be with you anymore. It's like you think we live in a war zone. Like every fucking thing matters." He closed his eyes and took a breath. "Stop. You're not going to make me angry. I'm not doing this anymore. I don't want every day to be possibly the last day of my life." He looked up and spoke to our silhouettes, reflected in the shiny black surface of his flat-screen TV. "I just want my days to be normal days." He wanted me to move out at the end of the month. He would pay for movers and a broker's fee. He would stay with a buddy until I had cleared out.

"I don't even know what a broker is," I did not say out loud, making him laugh at my worldly incompetence, because I was crying too hard.

A psychologist would call abandonment my "trigger" feeling. I begged Brian not to leave. I promised to be good. I sobbed that I couldn't live without him. I acted every bit as pathetic and desperate as I felt. But then, acting the way I felt had never endeared me to Brian. He pulled his jacket out of my grip, said he was sorry but there was absolutely no way, none at all, he was decided. I stood openmouthed at the window after he left, watching him fit his suitcases into the back of a taxi.

I moved into a cheap basement apartment I heard about through a coworker; she technically had a room there, but spent all of her time at her boyfriend's. Buddhists say shock is a helpful state: It stops the mind. I bought used furniture from sidewalk sales, unpacked my books and notebooks, hung up my thrift-store dresses. But making the bed aggressively one morning, I tore a small hole in the bottom of my fitted sheet. The ability to act without thought wore off at that moment. The hole grew larger night by night. I would wake up in the dark with my feet caught in the hole. Sometimes I told myself that I made mistakes with Brian because I was not meant for stability. Other times I imagined our reunion—Brian at last effusive, me at last calm and content. In the predawn hours, various such lies wrestled each other at the edge of a cliff, until they all fell off, tangled in each other.

In a forest in India two thousand five hundred years ago, the Buddha explained pain to a group of men who had devoted their lives to noticing what happened when they sat very still. He said something like this: "Imagine a man is pierced with an arrow. The man feels pain. The man cannot avoid this pain. Imagine this man is pierced by a second arrow. His pain increases twofold. The first arrow is inevitable but the second arrow is a choice. It is the man's hatred of the first arrow." I reread this parable on the Internet one early morning to get myself to stop pacing. My head was spinning an endless tale about how pain was the enemy attacking my heart and my head was going to be the hero vanquishing the enemy, it just had to figure out the best tactics, the right weapons, the correct configuration. But Heart's pain and Head's story communicate on different frequencies. So Head cannot help Heart, try as it might, and this trying was the clamor that made bearable pain unbearable. I understood this after I reread the parable. If this understanding helped at all—and it might have—my head was not aware of it.

I started taking a hodgepodge of counterindicated pills before bed, which permitted me to remain for hours in the desert between wakefulness and sleep. I was startled out of this state one night by the sound of a man's angry voice in my basement apartment. Seconds later, I was standing naked in the concrete backyard. My fan was on high, facing the wall—I needed the loud hum of white noise to doze off—so I couldn't hear deeper into my apartment. My purse had recently been ripped off my shoulder while I waited with a man I'd just met to get into a seedy club. The purse had held my keys and several forms of ID. I had not gotten the locks changed. I ran back inside the apartment to grab my phone off my bedside table, dialed 911, gave the dispatcher my address.

The police couldn't come in the front door because I was too afraid to walk through my apartment to unlock it. So they banged on the main entrance to the building until they woke my upstairs neighbor, a hard-bodied Japanese woman who closed her curtains whenever I stepped into the backyard. They charged through her apartment and came out her window, shining boots pouring over the sill and landing with a clack in the concrete yard where I stood naked, still gripping my phone to my ear. Red and white lights, wailing from the car on the street, chased each other on my neighbor's ceiling. The police walked down the steps to the basement in single file, guns drawn.

When I saw the guns I knew the apartment was empty. I followed the cops into my bedroom, picked up a towel off the floor,

wrapped it around my chest. I wanted them to find all of my belongings smashed to bits. I wanted a lunatic wearing blackface
and an adult diaper to leap out of my closet, shrieking and karate-
chopping the air. The cops prowled through my kitchen and bathroom, turning on lights, peering behind doors. "Is it always like
this in here?" they asked of the living room, littered with clothes
and shoes, old coffee cups, crumpled pages torn from books and
magazines. My absentee roommate's large TV, which she planned
to sell, sat on the floor in the center of the chaos. Yes, it was always
like that.

After the police left, I made a list of my potential identities.

1. *Translator*
2. *Wannabe translator living with her father*
3. *English teacher in foreign countries*
4. *Buddhist nun*
5. *Trophy wife*
6. *Patient in mental hospital*
7. *Jared's life partner (combine with option 6?)*
8. *Sex Ed teacher*
9. *Accidental mother*
10. *Drug addict*
11. *Suicide*

Only after I finished writing did I realize that I stole both the
idea and the final option from Spalding Gray. He made a similar
list in his journal, published after his death. He did kill himself,
abandoning a wife, children, success as a writer and actor, worthwhile projects that only he could complete. Whereas I had to steal
even my thoughts about my life from those who had found a form
to match their inner world—all of which argued strongly for a serious consideration of option 11.

How, though? If that really did end up being the only choice? I have no capacity for violence. I don't even kill mosquitoes. It would have to be pills. And I couldn't be cowardly about it, the way I was in high school, taking handfuls of Advil and pretending to believe that this time something truly different would happen.

I got my locks changed. But that night, I heard the man's voice again, addressing me in a singsong whisper. "Elsie. The calm before the storm. Elsie. The calm before the storm." Again, I found myself standing naked in my backyard, heart trying to break out of my chest. I knew I couldn't call the police again, but I was too afraid to go back inside. I sat on a folding chair. Rain from a late-afternoon shower soaked my bare ass. After the blackness overhead gave way to gray murk, I got back in bed, called Jared, asked if he would stay with me for a while.

"At your service, milady," he said in an overdone cockney accent at the end of another lame California night. I turned on my computer. LAX, JFK. Click. The money was just a number on a computer screen.

And then Jared and I were lying in bed together and I was no longer hearing the singsong whisper of an imaginary man. I was hearing Jared's snore. He rolled away from me but our feet remained entangled. I pictured us from above, bodies forming a vague V. A child learning to write. Odd that I didn't long to have one. How else to be of use? Why didn't I want anything that made sense? Maybe my personality—sensibility without sense—was a type that was meant to die out. My face reached for the window. The shades were drawn but light tried to crest the sill. Noonday sun, noonday sun. I repeated the phrase to make one part of my mind seem pretty to another part. Jared's anklebones crushed mine. There was no way to touch him that would allay the loneliness. Or there might have been, but I didn't want to try. I just wanted someone, anyone, to see that our faces were the tips of a child's squiggly V, woman's eyes open, mouth closed, man's eyes closed, mouth open. If only someone would take a photograph or paint a picture of the aerial view of this moment, if only my feelings belonged to a scene that had some meaning. But why would a stranger care that my face was reaching for noonday sun while my lover's ankles crushed mine? So instead I thought of the words I would use to describe the image to Jared, after he woke up, after we had sex, while we were eating cereal with the frozen blueberries I was proud of myself for keeping on hand.

"Ducks can hold their breath for a long time, but many hens still drown during peak mating season, killed by mallards during copulation. Female ducks are raped so frequently that they have evolved complicated vaginal passages, spiraled tubes with hidden pockets that allow them to store and later eject semen from unwanted partners. Most birds mate by joining their reproductive openings, positioning that requires cooperation. But ducks have penises and vaginas."

An acquaintance's Facebook status led me to the article about duck sex, which I read aloud to Jared one afternoon, crammed onto the lower side of my lopsided bed. The computer warmed my bare thighs as I wondered aloud about the mating habits of ducks—how cruel that evolution has fostered female defensiveness instead of curbing male aggression, and how wrong that my body found animals committing homicidal gang rape erotic.

Jared took the computer off my lap and pulled me down to him. "It's not wrong," he said. "You're not choosing to feel like that. Don't worry about it so much." He was propped on one elbow, his face a few inches above mine, the crevices in his cheeks footholds in a sheer cliff. I watched myself, tiny, climbing up his right cheek and resting on top of his nostril. I grazed the joints of my fisted hand over his cheek, a gesture that wanted to have meaning. "Have you been fantasizing about me?" I asked.

"All the time."

"Tell me one."

He put one hand on my neck and one hand over my eyes. "I break into your house and push you onto the bed and I rip off your pants and—" He rolled on top of me and pinned my wrists over-head, liberating me from movement. The drum-tight mound of his beer belly pressed against my abdomen. He didn't care how his torso looked; he only saw mine. I didn't care how he looked, either. My arousal came from knowing that my body aroused him, so that I got to live, briefly, alongside my body instead of inside it, my skin and breasts and armpits and cunt independent of me, giving and receiving of their own accord. Jared fucked me shallowly at first, touching my clitoris with a practiced precision that made my orgasm short and hollow, as if the tremors happened in isolation, cut off from their source. He moved his hand away and quickened the pace of his thrusts. He ejaculated with a pinched yelp, pressed his lips to my forehead, sighed. Then he began snoring, his open mouth resting on my shoulder. I looked at the ceiling, immobi-lized by satisfaction, a state that can feel a lot like despair.

Only now that there was, overtly, nothing wrong with spending time with Jared anywhere and anyhow I liked, did the appropriate sense of regret, guilt, and anxiety take shape, a black mass filled with swirls of electronic noises screeching at a frequency only I could hear, hovering over the bed where Jared snored, gripping my shoulders while I swiped credit cards at Barnes and Noble and asked customers if they wanted to join our frequent buyer's club.

Perhaps the worst part of my hellish new companion was that I could not describe the hell to Jared, the person who let me be the most unhinged. He had never acted jealous of Brian, but he had always calmly, assuredly predicted that our relationship would not last and I could not bear his calm, assured triumph now. For the first time I could remember, I felt far away from him even when he had his arms around me. I couldn't believe how much I missed watching movies on the couch with Brian, missed his laugh and long limbs and the perfect half moons of his fingernails. I had been lulled for so long by the belief that the insipid solace of his company would shape the better part of my remaining days, and now I was wide awake to immediate love for him, and all alone with it. I called him sometimes, when I was not with Jared. I left at least a dozen cheery voice mails before I gave up.

So it was I, not Jared, who bought handles of Tanqueray and Absolut, which I started drinking straight with a few slices of lemon, pretending this was an acceptable afternoon cocktail. I even drank in the late mornings before my shifts at the bookstore, hiding my dependence from Jared, who had a real alcohol problem—I told myself—while mine was temporary, a life raft to convey me to a new state of being.

Careless, I drank too much one morning and was uncharacteristically talkative at work, blabbing on while I stocked books about how I had no tether, how my only hope for an acceptable life was to complete the translation of a French novel that I'd worked on intermittently for years, that I had to get very serious about this work now that I was no longer getting married, so that I could then translate a lot of different books and maybe be a teacher or get a fellowship to travel abroad or something, but how awful that my one big hope in life now depended solely on me, I was not to be trusted, I really should answer to someone besides myself, this was a terrible setup, how to break into "society?," was I "insane?"

With my forefingers, I exaggerated the quotes around the words. I had the sense that I was being funny, but no one laughed. When it was my turn to work the register, the manager pulled me aside, said she was sorry I was having a rough time, and suggested I go home early. I walked out without saying goodbye. The last thing I needed was to be dismissed from the one place to which I was beholden.

I came home to David Bowie blasting in my living room and Jared doing lines off of my roommate's coffee table with a couple who lived upstairs, to whom I had never spoken because I rarely speak to strangers and because these particular strangers screamed curses at each other late into the night. Now, though, they both seemed to be painfully bursting with a newfound inner brilliance, which they were trying to communicate by craning their necks and opening their eyes wide and moving their tongues at break-neck speed as they told me dull details of their days—when they had moved into this building, how much their utilities cost, their favorite restaurant in the area. There is nothing worse than spending an evening being talked at by dullards on drugs. So I did a couple of lines, too, and then, because the black mass of regret was shrieking in my ear, I drank a lot of vodka, and then, because the people in my apartment were removing their clothes and applying their tongues to each other's exposed skin, I took three bong hits in the hope that marijuana would make me want to get naked and lick stuff, too.

And although the three pairs of hands roaming my skin were too insistent and hurried to give me real pleasure, the abundance of human life temporarily concerned with my life did make me feel almost good, okay enough to believe Jared had been right to invite these strangers over, that perhaps this vulgar chaos was exactly what I needed to propel myself into the new state of being. But wait—I was now being touched by only one body and that body was covered in coarse black hair that was entirely unfamiliar to me and the penis that sprang out of the hub of those unfamiliar hairs was getting encased in protective plastic.

I looked around for Jared. He was sitting on the couch, holding a pair of tits shaped like huge jester hats around his dick. My breasts are small. Jared was enthusiastically engaged in the one sex act we could not do together. The sight pained me, but I could not feel the pain through the layers of intoxicants in which my mind was suffocating. So I let the hairy, man-shaped creature put his thing in me. He was silent as he fucked me and my vagina felt nothing but a vague pressure. This lack of particularity left me all alone inside the scene, unable even to comment from inside my head on what was happening, turning the sex into a darkly comic villain who tried and tried to destroy me, but could never succeed in hurting me more than I hurt myself. My brain started pulling sounds out of the past, hearing Brian yell, "You freak out when you don't have an orgasm."

If only I could know the exact number of times Brian had fucked me and come and then stolen into sleep without offering me a word or gesture, and I had managed not to yell or beat his head with a pillow or dig my nails into his forearms (I did that only two—at most four—times, and that was after he fell asleep while he was touching me), but instead I got out of bed and took some NyQuil and read on the couch until unconsciousness took me. If I could know the exact number of times I fell asleep in that state of miserable acceptance, I would have a solid true fact that made me deserving of forgiveness. But I had no idea how many times I had done anything with Brian—two? twenty? five hundred?—and now I would never know, and I was suddenly shrieking at the man on top of me and the woman with pompom nipples to take their hideous bodies the hell out of my apartment, leave us alone, didn't they have any shame?

My next-door neighbors yanked on their clothes, calling me batshit crazy and psycho-bitchy. They slammed the door on the way out. Jared laughed. He fucked me for a long, long time since we were both too coked up to come. I awoke at dawn on the hardwood floor, toes and fingers icy, mind and heart now clear enough to feel the pain. Of seeing Jared's cock inside a stranger's tits. Of the distance between Brian and me being equal to my need to bridge it—that much space, that much need. Of knowing that if you don't treat people well, you will always have to wonder if everything wrong with life is a result of personal failure. I wriggled out from under Jared's clammy deadweight and walked to the apartment's one small window, level with the concrete backyard. The cold glass held my achy forehead. I let my eyes get small and unfocused so that the world became darkness interrupted by dazzles of artificial brightness, one of which I chose to believe was the moon. I craned my neck back and leaned my chin against the glass. But no matter how far up I could see, I was still endlessly far from all the things that matter in a day and in a life.

I left Jared sleeping on the floor and crawled into my ripped sheets, certain of one thing: I had to start working as soon as I woke up, get my mind back inside *Fifi*.

Sometime later, Jared crawled into bed with me. He was sweet and hesitant. He rubbed my back, said how glad he was that I kicked those losers out, he had no idea that dude was trying to fuck me or he would have kicked his ugly ass. "He did fuck me," I said. Jared looked away and offered to go buy coffee and bagels. I was at my desk when he got back, rereading the last passage I'd translated, begging my brain to focus.

"You know that your mailbox is overflowing?" Jared said, handing me breakfast in a paper bag. "They're leaving shit on the floor." He dumped a pile of paper in my lap—sharp corners made from tree pulp. How incomprehensible the world of objects was.

One by one, I tossed the envelopes to the floor. Credit card bills, Amnesty International needing money, a salon offering me fifteen percent off my first wax, a Thai restaurant offering fast free delivery, a thick purple envelope covered in stamps bearing an image of one of the Buddhist gods, I couldn't remember which one. Inside the purple envelope was a card on which LOVE had been written out of spices, the names of which were listed on the inside of the card, along with an invitation: "Dear El Akki, I wish you can spend Sri Lankan New Year with my family. I ask the gods for that wish. God bless you, Suriya Nangi."

Oh. Suriya. We hadn't been in touch for at least a year. And how many years had passed since I met her in Sri Lanka? Four? Five? Was the girl in that memory really me? The one with the greasy hair and the baggy salwar kameez, content to sit and watch, be nobody, go nowhere, for hours at a time—had that really been me? It must have been, because now another human was calling to the girl, practically begging her to exist. This had nothing to do with me, of course—Suriya and I barely knew each other, she just wanted to be close with an American, she probably hoped I would find her a job in the States or something—but the letter was addressed to me. Someone faraway was beckoning. Or rather some*thing*. Why not think in those terms? It helped, and it was so hard to have thoughts that helped. I reread the invitation to come to Sri Lanka as if it were an invitation from the archaic torso of Apollo. Is it even possible to quote Rilke without irony anymore? Maybe not in public, but I do it all the time in my head. Of course I would visit Suriya in Sri Lanka, help a kind stranger change her life. Which would, in turn, change me. Because I needed to be changed. I wish I were dead. A sentence I thought, wrote, spoke all throughout adolescence. A child's complaint, stated with the willingness to strike at anything, to demand anything, because nothing one wants seems possible, one is always at the mercy of people, places, words, hours, bodies larger and clearer than oneself. But the childish complaint had become real to me lately, a companion, a comfort—possible. I needed something else to comfort me. I would find it in Sri Lanka, staying with a devout Buddhist family in a remote village. I would finish my translation, I'd get really serious about meditation, I'd become involved in some important way with this poor, kind, Buddhist family—condescending, I knew, but I didn't care, so much did I need Suriya's invitation to make me better. Something big would happen to me there. Something external would claim my life. It has to. It will. I am not a bad person.

[two]

KANDY

I ignore the rickshaw drivers crowding the bus stop—"Tuk-tuk, madam? Yes, madam! Come, madam!"—and decide to carry my backpack the two miles to my guesthouse. Maybe the pain in my shoulders and sweat soaking my kurta will hurry me into the old sense of belonging. By the time I turn up the steep, narrow road to Rose Land, my legs have roasted beneath my long skirt and my sticky inner thighs grate with each step. Mary sits on the front porch, her bare feet crossed at the ankles. The calluses on the pads of her big toes are cracked and bloody. She stands and opens the gate.

"Remember me?" I ask.

"Yes, yes," she says, letting me know she meets many tourists and I am not to embarrass us both with further questions. I ask if the small room in the back is free. Mary nods and stands. Her unruly hair has been tamed into a braid. I follow her through a large, furnitureless common area to my old room abutting the monastery.

Mary gives me a tiny key, which unlocks the tiny padlock on the door to my room. Sitting on the edge of the thin, hard mattress, I untie the mosquito net hanging from the ceiling and let it fall around the bed. Lying on my back, I blink at the water-stained ceiling through blue gauze. I was a panicked mess leaving Brooklyn, moving my stuff into my old room at my dad's house, so afraid that I would end up there after all. And then as soon as I got on the plane and turned off my phone and put it away for—I don't know how long—I felt like laughing. It all seems so far away now. That wistful line in old movies. I don't feel wistful. I feel relaxed for the first time in months. Shadows of crows fly across my face. For the next twelve hours, my eyes close out the world.

I yawn and roll onto my belly. Monks patter and whoosh past my window in bare feet and maroon robes. Soon there will be chanting, followed by the ping and clank of pots, the beginning of days whittled down to the most basic decisions. It's good to be near people who have committed to being human in the simplest way, to remind myself that such a life is possible, that even I have another self who is quiet and content, aware above all of her breath. Maybe this time I will become her.

Morning at Rose Land unfurls one way only. The black Lab, no longer a puppy, steals guests' underwear out of their rooms and pulls towels off the line in the backyard. Mary bustles about in a long white skirt and tie-dyed T-shirt, cutting curry leaves off the karapincha, wringing out bedsheets faded all to the same soft beige, leaving scraps for the crows in worn metal buckets hanging from the fence in the backyard. Skinny, shaggy-haired Europeans smoke cigarettes in the courtyard at the center of the house. Breakfast is five pieces of toast with pineapple jelly, a pot of dark tea with milk powder, half of an overripe papaya. "You want more toast, you ask," Mary says, as I know she will.

I drink the pot of tea, pick dead ants out of the jelly, and eat all five pieces of toast. Then I head down to the lake, a body of unnaturally still grayness around which the town careers. A boy wearing a crisp, white school uniform follows me. Do I want to see his baby alligator? Come and see, madam, no charge. The tinny, high-pitched notes of the ice cream song trickle out of a cart pulled by a grinning, toothless man. Halfway around the lake, I pause to squint up at the Tooth Temple, which is said to hold one of the Buddha's left canines in a gilded turret piercing smog. A hurried man in flip-flops and a faded suit stops short in front of the temple gates, drops a coin in a padlocked box, and bows his forehead to his hands, pressed together in the center of his chest.

Will the coffee-colored man still be lying in the muddy grass outside the temple gates, his legs bent at the knees, his right hand mechanically swatting his forehead? Yes, here he is, his clothes the color of his hair, which is the color of his skin, which is the color of his eyes, which is the color of coffee grinds from the strongest, oiliest beans. I watch his swats for several minutes. A sick-animal smell wafts off his clothes like the vapor of all the things I have failed to do. A juvenile, narcissistic thought, but calming nonetheless. Nearby, a family of red-faced monkeys stares out of tiny, ruthless eyes.

Main street. Men hawk inflatable kitty cats and bags of pineapple covered in chili salt. A blind woman sits on a sheet of newspaper, palms open on her lap, a real kitten curled beside her. It's easy to give her a coin because she cannot see me. I don't have to make eye contact and smile, pretending to believe she'll be just fine. I pass my reflection in the black-tinted glass door of a shop advertising Internet and phone services, and push on my face to enter the store. I sit down at a computer and open the drafts folder of my email. When I told my boss at Barnes and Noble that I was quitting to focus full-time on translating *Fifi*, she encouraged me to contact a friend of hers, the publisher of a small press specializing in translations. I reread my note to the publisher: Might he be so kind as to read a sample chapter or two of this quietly brilliant magnum opus by an idiosyncratic thinker who died before reaping the recognition he deserved?

A bit florid, sure, but my humble notes never got me anywhere. I'm hopeful this time. I have a contact. My coworkers at Barnes and Noble said you *had* to have contacts, cold submissions got you *nowhere*. On the balcony across the street, a young girl hops back and forth, back and forth. Gripping my hands together over the keyboard, I press Send with my pinkie finger.

The town center is crowded with beggars and monkeys stalking roti stands and wooden tables piled with spices and men's underwear and fish doused in kerosene to keep the flies away. Auto rickshaws pull up beside me, one after the other. I flip my palm back and forth in the air, meaning no. One of them continues crawling alongside me. "I am walking," I say to the air in front of me.

"Yes, come," he says. I shake my head no and continue walking. The rickshaw coughs.

"Yes, come, you, come."

I glance toward him to say no again. His face is a large, gleaming eye. There is more activity in the area of his crotch than I suspect is necessary to operate a rickshaw.

"Yes, come. You so nice. You come."

He looks like all of them, the way I've learned to see them: soft bellies; thin, floundering arms; a tongue too quick to flick his cracked upper lip. I put up my hand to shield my eyes and quicken my pace. "Go away. Leave me alone." How have I forgotten the only Sinhala words I ever needed? The movement in his lap becomes frenzied. His voice hardens into a monotone chant. "You come. You come. You come." I shout to drown out his voice. "Go away. Leave me alone." Two women in saris pause their conversation to frown at me in either concern or irritation. I rush down a side street and lean against the wall, gritting my teeth. A gray-haired man sidles up to me. "He-llo." I march back toward the lake, eyes glued to the ground. My body is well covered in a long skirt and baggy T-shirt. My greasy hair is pulled back into a messy, low bun. The object of my rage becomes the white woman I saw in the Internet café, wearing a red spaghetti-strap dress, her breasts spilling over the gold belt tied above her waist. She's probably on vacation with a man she wants to impress and doesn't care that she may as well be prancing around buck naked as far as the locals are concerned, freely doling out erotic delight. Not that I'm usually the champion of propriety. But I don't want to be reminded of familiar social games.

A cloud of black-and-white birds blows through the trees bordering the lake, a cacophony of squawks and waste. Unlike the women around me, I have no umbrella and get shit on three times. When I pause to wipe the back of my forearm against a tree, I notice a long fish floating on its side in the smoky lake, its glassy eye reflecting the gray sky, one fin sticking up like a tiny sail. A swarm of smaller fish pecks at its underside.

What did I love about it here? Kandy is smoggy, stifling, dull, dangerous, needy, indifferent, raging with heat and noise and trash and con artists and molesters, all the while pretending to be Lord Buddha's chosen city.

A huge sound wakes me from my string of complaints. What is that? Violins? Cicadas? Siren song; siren song. The phrase marks each of my slow, heavy steps toward the temple. Tiny white birds fly in one butterfly-shaped mass from tree to tree, causing a brief, isolated tremor with each landing. The siren song blares from speakers outside the temple. Monks chanting. Pirith, I remember it's called. I cannot pronounce the word and I cannot describe this congruence of voices eddying, swooping, sinking, falling, rising, retreating, drawing near. On the lawn outside the temple, families walk and loaf. A little girl picks a jasmine flower off a bush and hands it to her baby sister. Men sit atop their briefcases with bowed heads and prayered hands and closed eyes. Here is my love for this place.

Dinner is dhal and rice out of a plastic bag. I eat in my room, mashing the spicy yellow lentils and rice into little balls with my fingers, then scooping up the balls and pushing them onto my tongue with my thumb. My hand moves quickly from the bag to my mouth. Cardamom seeds and garlic cloves and curry leaves and chilies and whole cinnamon sticks. I will sleep well again tonight, my senses exhausted.

At the hallway sink, I try to scrub the yellow out from under my nails. The guesthouse murmurs with the day's many endings— Mary's grandsons chatting in their bunk bed, the dog sighing in the courtyard, a sad German song on a radio in one of the guest's rooms. I walk back to my room and stretch out beneath my mosquito net, one hand on the soft knot of my pubic hair and one hand on my breast. My body has no context here. I've never been attracted to a Sri Lankan man. And even if I were, I wouldn't let myself feel it. Lust is forbidden to women in this country. Maybe that's partly why I came back here. An island that makes my sexual need irrelevant.

NILLAMUWE

Suriya is waiting for me at the entrance to the Tooth Temple, next to a guard shifting his rifle strap from one shoulder to the other. I wave with too much emphasis as I approach, surprised by the intensity of my discomfort. How to behave at a reunion with a near stranger? Even when I'm directly in front of Suriya, my hand worries the air between us. Her smile is oppressively genuine, sharpened by an eagerness for something I doubt I can provide.

After we say hello to excess, Suriya clarifies the plan that was vague to me in our emails: She has two months off from classes. We're going to the home of the sister of her mother, in the rural northeast. Suriya's family—cousins, uncles, and aunts—are gathering there to celebrate the New Year. They are all excited to meet me. I am to stay as long as I like. Suriya is especially glad for me to meet her brother. He has vacation time from the army. She grabs her small bag off the ground. "Bus coming!" We run down the center of the street to avoid the throngs of merchants and shoppers, hoist ourselves onto the back steps of the bus just as it picks up speed. Because I'm white, a young woman gives up her seat for us. Suriya and I wedge ourselves onto the narrow bench, me saying, "Sthoo-thiy," again and again, a word I learned from a guidebook and have never heard a Sri Lankan person use.

As we come down the mountain, the air on the bus grows so sticky and thick that it's almost soothing—nothing else to feel. It no longer matters whose bony thigh is pressing against my shoulder or whose hand is on top of mine on the metal seat back, squeezing my knuckles as we stop short for motorbikes and lurch around sharp turns. Holograms of Lord Buddha and Ganesh flash above the driver's seat. A little boy on his mother's lap blows a whistle every few seconds, then giggles. I try to explain to Suriya how angry Americans would be if a toddler were allowed to play with a whistle during a five-hour bus ride, but I grow weary with the effort of communication. Her English is much worse than I remembered, my Sinhala as nonexistent as it will always be. Why did I agree to stay with her? I could be traveling on my own, doing exactly as I pleased, speaking only if I felt like it.

We pass a roadside marketplace, an angry racket of money. Suriya taps my arm and points out the window. A throng of singing, clapping people walks alongside a ditch filled with multi-colored trash. A teenage girl in a sari blaring sunset colors leads the pack, casting backward glances at the others, sometimes worried, sometimes glad. "I think is big girl party," Suriya says.

"Big girl party?"

"When small girl becomes big girl." She smiles largely, revealing her crooked front tooth. "Have not big girl party in U.S.A.?"

"Only Jewish people do that." She stares at me. Her thick eyebrows draw together. "You don't know about Jewish people?"

"No!" The word comes out as a small yelp.

"It's a religion. You know the Holocaust, in Germany? World War II? Hitler?"

"Hitler," she repeats, emptily. The bus thumps over a pothole and we tighten our grip on the seat back.

"He was an evil, evil man. Killed millions of Jewish people. Took them out of their homes, put them in prisons, and murdered them all."

Suriya bites the inside of her cheeks and tilts her head. "Have not big girl party in U.S.A.?"

I turn to the world outside the window—decrepit advertisements plastered to the side of a high concrete wall. One of the posters is an ad for *Rambo IV*, peeling away at the top and bottom so that only Stallone's sweaty headband and sharp eyes are visible. A shopkeeper in Jaffna told me that the Tamil Tigers played *Rambo* movies for child fighters before sending them into Sinhalese villages armed with machine guns. It's good to remember that I know that fact. It makes my presence on this bus more appropriate, as if I'm here to document something important, a kind of white lie to myself. The bus comes to a rolling stop. The mass of bodies shifts frantically—bags tossed through windows, women in long skirts running and jumping onto the platform just before the bus rumbles onward.

Gradually, the storefronts and fruit carts give way to soupy rice fields and purpled lakes. Giant beehives, golden in the afternoon sun, hang from the knobby branches of ironwoods, or some other tree with a less satisfying name. A metallic rendition of "Jingle Bells" rings out from a phone behind me.

"My boarding home is so lonely," Suriya says. "Now you are here and I can share my lonely with you." She speaks to the window. Her shiny black bun is tied with an orange scrunchie at the base of her neck. "Yes," I say, grateful now for her imperfect English, familiar words arranged unfamiliarly. I unclench my fists in my lap, letting the breeze from the window pour over my sweaty palms.

"Nilla, Nilla, Nillamuwe," the ticket taker calls, leaning out the bus door into the tornado of dust stirred up by the tires. Suriya grabs my hand and pulls me through the knot of hot flesh toward the front of the bus. We jump to the side of the road as a crowd of villagers thrusts into the grumbling machine, already pulling away from the stop.

"Your bag. I think is hard for you," Suriya says as we walk down a dirt road toward her aunt's house. She reaches over and lifts up the bottom of my backpack with her hand in a vain effort to relieve some of the weight.

"I'm fine, really. I'm used to traveling like this." But I do find it hard to carry my heavy pack in this heat. Perhaps I've outgrown backpacking around third world countries. We pass one-room concrete homes with palm-leaf roofs, men in sarongs sitting on plastic chairs in dirt yards, following us with unblinking eyes. Suriya points to one of these houses. "Hashini-Mommy's home." Crotons form a fence of oblong leaves in varied shades of pink, green, and yellow. Suriya's aunt is washing metal bowls in the tap outside. She dries her hands on her dress and nods hello. Wisps of gray enliven her long dark hair. Her two front teeth protrude even when her mouth is closed, suggesting a smile that never takes shape. Speaking softly and quickly, she walks inside and pushes aside a blue curtain covering the entrance to the one bedroom. I had forgotten how people here rarely say hello or goodbye; they simply arrive and depart. Dusty sunlight passes through the small triangles carved throughout the brick wall. "Net," Hashini-Mommy proclaims, pointing to the pink gauze tied in a knot above the bed. She speaks to Suriya in Sinhala, then motions to me.

"Hashini-Mommy say this is your room. You may leave your bag and valuables. This village have not thieves."

I rifle through my pack for the small gift I brought my hosts. When I look up, Hashini is standing in the doorway, holding a tray of sweets and glass mugs of steaming tea. She motions to me to follow her and sets the tray on a folding chair in the main room. A calendar of presidential photos shows Rajapaksha's plump, beaming face superimposed over a group of cross-legged, beatific monks. Rajapaksha won the election by throwing his opponent in jail on trumped-up charges, all the while pretending to be the great protector of Buddhism. Well, apparently it worked. The president's photo is the only adornment on Hashini's walls.

I hand Hashini three foil packages of Ceylon tea, the one thing she surely has in abundance. I ought to have brought American treats—chocolate and coffee, T-shirts flaunting the Statue of Liberty—but I only remembered the necessity of gift-giving an hour before I met Suriya at the bus stop. She is so much better at people than I am. All those cards she's mailed me over the years—for the Buddha's birthday, the American New Year, the Sri Lankan New Year—decorated with stickers and pressed flowers. Hashini nods at the tea and runs her hand over the top of my head. She gestures to the sweets, oil cookies in the shape of stars. The cookies are bland and greasy, but I eat three in the hope of relaxing my hosts, who stand in silence while I munch from my post on a wooden bench covered in flowered fabric. Only when I reach for a fourth cookie do they turn to each other and exchange a soft stream of Sinhala words about the sudhu, white person.

"Hashini-Mommy ask me if you are working in the U.S.A.," Suriya says.

"I write." This is my socially appropriate shorthand for "very slowly translating the fictive diary of a lonely cat lover." I hold an imaginary pen and scrawl invisible cursive letters in the air. Hashini nods her approval. When I told a Dutch couple staying at Rose Land that I was a writer, the woman exclaimed over how lucky I was to be able to travel and work at the same time. "That's really the dream, isn't it? Sometimes I think I'll just quit my job and write a book. I already have the title. *Wonderful Wandering*." I smiled and returned my eyes to my fraudulent notebook. The only reason I was able to travel around, occasionally rendering a French sentence or two into English, was the senseless way money flowed through the world, pooling here, evaporating there. Of course I could only think of money as senseless because I'd never been forced to think of it otherwise. My father gave me a birthday check soon before I left for Sri Lanka. And why was I so smug about the woman's wonderful wandering? She seemed like a happy person.

Hashini-Mommy picks up my hands, turns them over, points to my empty ring finger, speaks hurriedly in Sinhala. "Hashini-Mommy say she worry for you," Suriya says. "No husband. Thirty, thirty-one, thirty-two!" She counts the years on her fingers and then opens her palms skyward: A woman's life evaporated once she reached her thirties.

"I was going to be married. But my boyfriend"—my eyes widen with shock as the words leave my lips—"is dead. My fiancé died."

"Oh, El." Suriya shortens my name to a single, masculine letter. "This is too sad. How does the man die?"

"He had—it was an accident. He was buying groceries, and when he was leaving the store, there was some construction in the parking lot, and a forklift, a small one—it's a machine for lifting heavy things, and it didn't see Brian walking, and so—" I stand up and mimic a claw scooping toward my face, cupping me under the chin. Snap. Beheaded by a miniature forklift in the Stop and Shop parking lot. Poor Brian. I sit down and stare into my lap, sighing, red-faced, frightened of myself. How else to justify being a grown woman with no family, no job, no permanent home?

Hashini-Mommy leaves the room and returns bearing a new plate of cookies. "So full," I say, placing my hand over my belly.

"I think the hunger leave you," Suriya says. "Because of your sad."

Brian in his boxers in the doorframe of our bedroom, tall and grinning and well-made. A sudden giddiness would come upon him at times, as if a spring inside him had been tightened and then released. He'd pin me down and tickle me and I'd squeal, "No, no, not the hook!," and he'd growl like a lion and dig his fingers into my ribs. Or he'd give me airplane rides on the bed, balancing me on his feet like a toddler. Once I fell on top of him, we'd give each other smacking kisses that vibrated our eardrums. "I need you, I need you," I said after an airplane ride, burying my face in his neck. Silent, he rested his hand on my lower back.

Suriya suggests we visit her uncle. "He will make leave your sad."

Her uncle turns out to be a neighbor sitting in his dirt yard in a plastic chair, wearing a sarong and chewing betel leaf, an expanding puddle of red spit at his feet. He stares at me as Suriya talks. Then he picks up a large carving knife and disappears into a thicket of plantain trees. His shoulders hunch up close to his ears; his upper arms are stiff and motionless, and his forearms jut out from his sides. He returns from the jungle cradling a jackfruit the size of a watermelon, axes through the bumpy green shell, and holds the sticky flesh out to me.

"For White Daughter."

I peel a gummy ribbon from the rind. "So sweet," I say, wide-eyed and sincere.

Uncle claps and exhales a low-bellied laugh. As we squat around the fruit, Uncle points to his back and explains to me, Suriya translating, that he was poisoned by Tamil Tigers. They infiltrated his air force unit, pretending to be cooks. He was lucky, Suriya tells me. The other men died, including his two brothers. Uncle escaped with partial paralysis.

"White Daughter, husband have?" he asks.

Suriya answers in Sinhala, nearly whimpering as she describes something that happened to me that seems sad even here, alongside the story of a man who lost his brothers and his freedom of movement in a war. I almost wish it were true, that I merited such compassion from strangers.

Uncle is staring at me with concern. "He ask if you know martial arts," Suriya says.

"Martial arts?"

"Ka-ra-tay?" he says.

"No. No karate." I shake my head, perplexed.

"He thinks you are scared to live alone," Suriya says.

"No, no. In the U.S.A., a woman can live alone, no problem," I say, lying again. A woman living alone has no one to keep her mind in check, to tell her not to call 911 when she hears voices in the night, to force her body not to succumb to the mental anguish that assails her at times for reasons she rarely understands and with a force that seems to have little to do with her. Pain chooses her as its vessel, makes itself at home for a while, moves on. Unable to relieve herself of this reasonless pain, she is always able to imagine the many forms relief might take, and does imagine them, endlessly. An almond croissant and a latte at her favorite coffee shop. Reading in the park. Getting a massage. Baking cookies. Sitting in a sauna at the Turkish bathhouse. So many accessible, luxurious treats, suggesting a life of such ease and privilege and contentment that she wishes she would just lose her mind once and for all and get checked into an insane asylum, so that her circumstances would, at last, match her reality.

A psychiatrist would call my bad times depression, but I prefer to call them dukkha. If I use the Sanskrit word, my periods of heavy, wet, cold malaise become a matter of enlightenment and the dozens of lifetimes I am away from it, rather than the solipsism of time passing while I wonder why I'm doing what I'm doing instead of doing something else.

The walk home from Uncle's takes us through an expanse of tall, shining, swaying grasses. Suriya points to a tree house in the middle of the sugarcane field, which protects the crops from wild elephants. Men sleep up there, and if they feel the tremor of heavy footsteps, they throw firecrackers down to scare the elephants away. She gestures to the bamboo ladder. "You want to go up?"

Inside is a rumpled cotton sheet and the smell of wet leaves and an empty bottle of arrack. A cocoon of vacant waiting. I lie on my back. Blue light dapples the palm-leaf roof where the weave has pulled loose.

The first time I felt I really loved Brian was when he made me feel better during one of my bad nights on our first winter together. "You're slumping," he said, sitting down behind me on the edge of the bed—flannel pajamas, toothpasty breath. I normally had good posture, one of the things he liked about me. He took my shoulders in his hands and pulled backward to bare my chest.

"It's happening again," I said. "I need it to stop." I kicked off my boot.

"What is it?"

"I don't know. It replaces me."

"Do you want me to hold you?"

"I think so." He pulled me against his chest. My right big toe pried the wool sock off of my left foot.

"Harder," I said. He wrapped his long legs around my waist and tightened his grip on my lower arms, crushing me into him. I love getting my blood pressure taken, always dread the pang of emptiness when the nurse presses the release button and the black cuff hisses as it returns my arm to itself.

"Think of somewhere you want to be," Brian said.

The courtyard of Shirmani just before dawn. Lying on the grass as the stars fade into the childish brightness of daybreak. I closed my eyes and felt Brian's heart beat against my back. The damp grass cooling the base of my neck and the koel birds' slow whistle, a nude teenage boy diving off a boulder into a dark lake. I turned and kissed Brian's cheek. "You made me feel better." He had reminded me of that other version of myself, the young woman who knew her purpose, knew it wasn't much, knew this smallness was something to be grateful for. "You made me remember when I was traveling in—"

Brian was so tired. Could I tell him in the morning? He was so glad I felt better. Could he please turn out the light now? I nodded against his shoulder. So many tiny failures on his part—larger ones on mine. Stop. Please. Here I am now, in the place I used to imagine myself when I needed courage to face my life in New York. Although if I had known how temporary that life would be, I suppose I wouldn't have needed so much courage.

In the sugarcane field below the tree house, a peacock mews eerily, sorrow reaching for something pretty. Suriya calls up. "El? You are sleeping?"

When we get back to Hashini's house, her husband, Rajesh, is laying red chilies on a strip of newspaper. Their shiny skins wrinkle under the harsh sun. His body is fiercely compact—the brown buds of his nipples too close together, his abdominal muscles like small stones slipped under his skin. "Jack be nimble, Jack be quick," plays in my head, deadpan. Cut it out. There is something unsettling about the mind's odd inner loops, like "Falling, falling, effortless flight," which runs, wheezing, through my head sometimes while I'm having sex. But now I'm nodding and smiling and repeating the words "hello" and "thank you." Rajesh grins back. The gap between his front teeth leaks red betel juice.

Hashini-Mommy walks through the backyard, holding her long skirt in front of her waist to make a basket. She disappears into a windowless clay hut in the backyard. The kitchen. I ask Suriya if I can see. Pockmarked pots and pans are piled against the wall. The stove is a clay cube with a cauldron resting on top of it, warmed by smoldering sticks. Hashini kneels on the dirt floor and peels potatoes, her hands a blur of unthinking strokes.

"Can I help?" Stupid question. "No!" Suriya barks, smiling.

So I sit still, resigned to aimlessness, waiting to feed off Hashini's hard work. Would it feel good to have such a clear, constant purpose, or does Hashini feel wasted on one repetitive motion after another? Suriya sifts rice in a shallow, woven basket, churning the milky kernels in search of stones, which she tosses to the woods behind the house. The first time she made rice, she tells me, it had so many stones. Every bite was— She crunches her teeth together. I ask how old Suriya was when she started cooking.

"Six years old, seven years old. Like that. I must. Because at that time my father was cruel." Her mother was afraid for Suriya and her brother to live with their father, so she sent them to live in a hut in the woods. A hut like for farmers. She brought them food at night. But one night their mother did not come. Suriya's brother said, I hungry. Suriya clutches her stomach and groans, enjoying making theater of her past. She cooked rice the way she had seen her mother cook rice. But she didn't know about stones. The rice had so many! She claps her hands to her cheeks and shakes her head side to side, as if the astonishing part of that story is that she ate poorly sifted rice. "Do you have a mother and father?" she asks.

"Yes. Sort of. They're both alive. But my mother left me when I was eleven years old." This is a sentence I've repeated so many times I no longer hear any difference between the meanings of the words. It's easy to tell the truth about easily comprehensible difficulties. People tend to find me more likable and sympathetic when I tell this story right away. It makes me pathetic in an interesting way, and then later, no matter how sordid or strange or unsettling my behavior is, they have a handy excuse. I once overheard Brian on the phone with his sister, saying, in protest, "She barely had a mother!" I stifled a groan. It's not that I don't believe my mother leaving affected me, any less or any more than my father's depression or my natural shyness. But none of these facts are an explanation for who I am. I'm still trying to find that out.

"What does it mean—left you?" Suriya asked. "She stopped to be your mother?"

"Oh no, she's still my mother. She just met another man and decided she wanted to be with him instead of my father. So she went away and I didn't see her for a long time."

"Were you angry, Akki?" Suriya asks, addressing me the same way she does her older female cousins.

"Not really. Not at the time. Nangi." I touch her wrist, proud I know the word for "little sister," happy I've earned this new intimacy. "She wanted me to move with her, and I actually felt guilty for staying with my dad."

"Dad means?"

"Father. I'm closer with my father. He's my real parent and my mother is like a fake parent."

"Did you find a new mother?"

"What do you mean?"

"A new woman to take care of you. An auntie or a lady in your village."

"No—that makes sense, I guess, but—I still have my mother. We write letters and talk on the phone. We visit each other." Actually, my mother has always insisted I visit her, that I need the vitamin D and swimming pools she seems to think are only available in Arizona. Plus, she doesn't want to leave her family. She and Rick have teenage twin boys. IVF—she wanted new babies that badly. I've met them a handful of times. Unremarkable kids. It seems only fair that I make no effort to get to know them—what my mother wanted was a shiny new family, unencumbered by my father's "negativity" and the "brutal" New England winters. And she seems genuinely happy making peanut butter sandwiches in their bright condo, wearing flip-flops year-round, drinking margaritas on the balcony with her thoughtlessly cheerful husband. It's a relief in a way that she's separate and okay. Worrying about my father is burden enough.

"And what about your father?" I ask Suriya. "Is he still cruel?"

"No." She dumps the sifted rice in a large pot and fidgets with the Buddhist protection cord on her wrist. "Now he is tired." On the road, a group of boys walk slowly past, some of the many villagers who have come to see the sudhu sitting in Hashini's yard. My existence carries weight here, effortlessly. I don't need any convenient explanations for who I am, any concrete descriptions of what I'm doing with my life.

In the days before the New Year, a loud, unremarked succession of motorbikes and auto rickshaws delivers Suriya's family members to Hashini's main room, where the TV blares holiday programming. Men in white cotton suits and women with glossy braids report in voices bright as doorbells from a manicured lawn in front of a palace. I sit outside the open door to the house, next to a teenage girl wearing a pink T-shirt that says STAR CUTIE. She stares at me and giggles, her hand over her mouth. "You good girl?" she says at last, jumps up, runs inside.

Nope, I tell the backs of her small, quick calves, irritated with these angelic Sri Lankan girls.

"My sisters so pretty, so fair," Suriya says.

"Your sisters? I thought you only had one brother."

"The daughters of Hashini-Mommy."

"Your cousins—your aunt's daughters."

"Yes. My sisters."

"Okay," I say. "Your sisters are very pretty, it's true."

"I am so dark." Suriya marks the word with a wide flick of her wrists. "My mum takes pills when she is pregnant with me."

I smile at Suriya's oddly posh diction, learned from a British textbook. "Took pills," I say.

"Took pills. To not get malaria. And it turned my skin. My father tease me—my dark daughter. Like that." She almost sings the last two words, moving her chin once left, once right.

A pity your mum didn't take pills that turned you albino. You'd be partially blind and have a reduced life expectancy, but no one could deny that you were the fairest of your cousin-sisters. "People want dark skin in the U.S.," I say. "They lie in the sun and use creams to make their skin darker. We don't think it's attractive to be fair."

"I don't believe! You too?"

"Yes, I love when I have a suntan," I admit, righteousness deflated. My hopeless reflection on a winter morning: dim pink blotches beneath my freckles. I used to try to wake up before Brian so that I could splash water on my face and put on blush before he saw me.

"In the U.S.A., I will be so pretty," Suriya says.

A motorbike pulls up, driven by a young man wearing square-shaped sunglasses, bleached jeans, and a worn T-shirt nestled against his soft belly. "Ayya!" The second syllable flattens itself against Suriya's tongue. "My elder brother," she tells me. He removes his helmet and stares, seeming unable to reconcile what he knows about his aunt's yard with the sight of a blue-eyed American woman. He and Suriya speak for a while with careless intimacy— quickly and softly, not looking at each other. I sometimes think I would be normal if I had a sibling. A real one. The IVF twins don't count.

When Ayya goes inside, Suriya explains that her parents will not be coming for the family gathering this year. Her mum is in poor health and cannot travel. In a few days, we will visit her parents at their home. Ayya will drive us on his motorbike. He has four weeks' leave from the army.

"What's he doing now that the war is over?" I ask.

"He works at a sentry point. Still there is much need for safety. Soldiers are working so hard in these days to make the country strong."

I look away and tell her that's great—an American word I

loathe. "Did I ever tell you that I visited Jaffna the first time I came here?" I ask Suriya.

"Oh, El, were you afraid? My brother was in Jaffna for a time. I had so fear for him. In those days, I made water offerings to Lord Buddha two times per day."

"I loved Jaffna. Some of the kindest, most intelligent people I've ever met."

Suriya purses her lips. "Well, you are tourist. So they are kind to you."

"Did you hear about the Tree Demon that was attacking people up there?"

"Yes, we have heard that story. But the government has shown it is false. So we do not think on that." She speaks quickly, walking toward the house. "And now my brother is in Colombo. Is better. You have hungry, Akki?"

Steamy bowls are laid out on the table inside. Hashini gestures to me with a spoon. She dumps a mound of rice in the center of a metal plate and surrounds it with curries. Suriya gives words to each thwack of the spoon: Jackfruit. Potato. Dhal. Aubergine. Hashini hands me the plate and motions to me to sit on the one chair in the room. Suriya frowns. "I think chair is—I don't know the word." She shakes the chair back to show me how loose it is. "Take care, Akki." She bends her knees gingerly in demonstration.

The family stands around me, silent, waiting. "Aren't you going to eat, too?" I ask Suriya. Jared is the only person I've ever been comfortable eating around. He always sits next to me at restaurants, not across, so he can keep one hand on my thigh while we eat. When he slid in the booth beside me for the first time, I told him it was embarrassing to be so intimate in public, people would think we were rude. "Who cares?" he said. "People think all kinds of things." He tucked the hair behind my ears and kissed me on the mouth as the waitress walked up to take our order. I shied away and softly asked for huevos rancheros. And when they came, I struggled to cut the fried tortillas into bite-size pieces, my eyes fixed to my plate, until he took the fork from me, broke off a piece of tortilla with his bare hands, smothered it in salsa and cheese, and brought it to my lips.

But now I am a guest of honor surrounded by eager witnesses. Strips of fried eggplant cling to my fingers as I try to work the curries into a ball. A piece of potato falls to the floor as I lift the ball. Rice coats my chin as I place the ball on my tongue. My fingers have vertigo; they know they're being watched.

"Is it taste, Akki?" Suriya whispers the question, reminding me of a Sinhala word she taught me while we ate ice cream cones the day we met.

"Rasai," I say. "Delicious." An explosion of laughter—the kindness inside our respective insecurities unloosed. I take another bite. The crisped exterior of a strip of eggplant gives way to a creamy mix of cinnamon, cumin, coriander, and green chili. The well-being of others is so contingent on my displays of well-being that it is necessary for me to be well. Hashini nods, satisfied, and heads toward the kitchen as the others fill their plates and then sprawl across the room, crowding onto the couch and sitting cross-legged on the floor.

"Hashini-Mommy will not eat with us?" I ask Suriya.

"She eats when she cooks. She has more works. So many people."

Suriya mashes her curries and rice into a perfect ball and then opens her mouth wide, her tongue drooping over her lower lip. I imitate her wide mouth and eager tongue. It's fun to eat. As soon as one of my curries gets low, Suriya balances her plate on her hip and dishes me more with her clean left hand.

The family kneads their leftovers into pasty balls that they drop in the dirt yard. A pack of dogs gathers around the food, snarling and wagging their tails. One of them has a gouged-out eye socket from which dangles a filthy string of something I don't want to believe is excess eyeball. He runs and growls and gorges like the other dogs. I stand behind Suriya's cousin at the pump, waiting to rinse off my plate, but Suriya slides it from my hand. "No, Akki. You are guest." A twenty-one-year-old—or is she twenty-two now?—treating me like a child. I ought to be looking after her. But I'd be terrible at that, even if we were in the States.

I grip the back of my neck, watching Hashini carry curry bowls back and forth from the house to the cooking hut. "Hashini is always working," I say.

"Yes. She does the mother's situation very well." Suriya dries my plate on her T-shirt. Her placid praise frightens me. But maybe Hashini is happy doing the mother's situation. Why do I want only inconvenient things?

I've decided not to use my iodine tablets, to force my body to adjust to the well water. I'm grateful for my headlamp during my second trip to the outhouse that night. Squatting over the hole, my long nightshirt gathered up in my right hand, I'm reaching for the blue plastic bowl floating in the water bucket, preparing to splash myself clean, when I hear something moving on the dirt yard, close to the outhouse. I pause, shirt in one hand, bowl in the other. It could be any number of tiny, harmless animals—I tell myself—but then I hear the movement again, too delicate to belong to an animal. The sound of a human trying not to be heard.

Calm your breath. It's probably just Suriya or Hashini, making sure I'm okay out here.

I crane my neck to the side of the outhouse, where the noise came from. My headlamp catches two disembodied gleaming orbs, pressed against a slat in the boards. Illogically, impulsively, I return my eyes to the ground, fully illuminating my naked lower half. Fuck. I switch off my headlamp and sit on my heels in the dark, heart pounding, gripping the bowl of water like a weapon.

Please God, let those eyes belong to a pervy uncle. Do not let them belong to someone from the village lying in wait for me. How awful that a pervy uncle would not be so bad, compared to—no. Calm down. My bent knees start to ache. Mechanically, I wash myself, pull up my underpants, and stand. I can't stay in this outhouse forever. I can scream if I need to. I turn my headlamp back on and flash the side wall. The eyes withdraw. That sound again: calculated delicacy. I hold my breath to hear the direction into which it retreats—a sure path to Hashini's house.

So it was a family pervert. Fear gives way to disgust. Ayya of course. It couldn't be Rajesh. He's old and timid and sweet. And Sri Lankan soldiers are notorious sexual predators—the awful thing in Haiti, how the soldiers who went to help after the earthquake had to be sent home for having sex with underage girls, people in Jaffna telling me women were forced to give sexual favors in exchange for seeing their husbands or sons in political prisons. Suriya rolls onto her back when I return to our room. "Okay, Akki?" she whispers. How blind she is to all this.

"Okay, Nangi. Go back to sleep."

The next afternoon, I work on my translation while Suriya watches cartoons with her cousins. I can't bring myself to tell her that her brother is a Peeping Tom. She would be crushed—disillusioned.

The permanent kind. I'm sure she's not even capable of imagining
sexual deviance, let alone associating it with her brother. And in
daylight the whole thing seems more pathetic than nefarious: Ayya
is so desperate for sexual contact he's willing to spy on his sister's
friend squatting over a shit-smeared hole.

So I smother the thought and become a ludicrous foreigner with
a giant dictionary on my lap, seeking the right word for *fougue* in
the context of a man comforting himself over a lost cat by attrib-
uting it to the creature's *fougue*. I love the French word because I
can't explain it precisely in English. Any potential equivalent (vi-
tality, chutzpah, pizzazz, spirit) is too colloquial by comparison—
because, of course, French is never colloquial for me. I've barely
spoken the language since my year in Paris more than a decade
ago. I lean back in my chair. Sweat gathers under the heavy dictionary on my lap. There's something sad to me about the act of
translating. To fit the book into my language destroys what I origi-
nally loved about it—the French sounds like instruments lending
nuance to coarse song lyrics, manipulating emotion into shapes
as gaudy outside the body as they felt inside; the subtle, unconscious work required to make literal sense of words not native to
me replacing the subtle, unconscious criticism I bring to English
sentences. *La musique sonne mieux quand on n'a rien d'autre à
aimer.* Music sounds better when one has nothing else to love. Or
maybe: You feel music most strongly when it's the only thing you
love. Hideous. Is the original sentence pretentious and self-pitying,
rather than the blunt expression of strong, simple feeling I took
it to be when I first read it in French? Or am I just a bad translator? On the cartoon inside, female characters giggle and gasp in
response to a man's bravado monologue. Suriya laughs. Maybe the
publisher will be interested in *Fifi*. Then it won't matter how I feel
about translating. I'll just do it.

Ayya returns on his motorbike. He's been out most of the day, visiting friends in the neighborhood. He offers me a brief smile as he walks to the house. I lower my narrowed eyes to my book. A tuk-tuk hurls itself into Hashini's yard. A tall, soft-bellied man who seems very conscious of the beauty of his hair spills out of his tiny, open-air car, shirtless, the top button of his trousers undone. His wife follows, sweaty and plump in the annoyingly forgivable way of full-time mothers, a naked baby on her hip. "Puta!" Rajesh kisses the man on both cheeks. Puta means son, Suriya tells me. Or sometimes daughter, if favorite daughter. This is the family of Hashini's eldest son, visiting from Colombo. Suriya coos at the baby.

Within minutes, Puta has distributed plastic cups of Sprite, spiked his and his father's with Johnnie Walker, handed me a guava and Suriya the gold bangles off his wife's wrist, held his baby's feet straight upward in a worrisome handstand, and put on a CD so loudly the family has to shout to be heard over it. Suriya picks up the baby and starts dancing—small, precise jumps in rhythm with the sitar blasting from the stereo. I take the baby's other hand and bounce along. Suriya mashes his cheek with her lips and tries to hand him to me. I back away, still bouncing. I like babies, but they make me uncomfortable. I would like to just observe their barbaric humanness—the intense, mercurial parade of facial expressions and sounds that overtake their bodies—but people always expect you to reach out for them, grinning and cooing.

"A baby is only heart. No head!" Suriya shouts over the music. I shout back my agreement, delighting in the chaos Puta has wrought, delighting in my sober delight. When the sitar album comes to an end, Suriya hands the baby to his mother. "I think you want to make shower before bed, El," she says. My toes are caked in dirt, the hair around my ears matted with dried sweat, my shirt plastered to my back. I am so grateful for my perceptive host! I follow her into the bedroom. "Open shower, so we must cover," she says, and shows me how to knot a sarong tightly over my breasts.

We pad out to the backyard. The showerhead protrudes from the outhouse. Suriya watches me, saying, "Is okay, Akki? Is okay?" I am so irritated by my overeager host! I just want to feel the cold water soaking my hair and sarong, look up at the cloud masses combing the purpled sky and the loud, tiny birds dipping in and out of fluffy, persimmon-colored flowers blooming atop lanky trees. Yes, Nangi, is okay.

When we return to the house in our sopping sarongs, Hashini is preparing pallets on the living room floor. The drunk cousin snores on the couch. They have offered me the one bed. "I can sleep out here, Nangi," I say. "The older people should have the bed." But Suriya laughs and tells me again that I am guest. Guiltily, I follow her into the bedroom. We change, facing away from each other, into loose pants and T-shirts that will dry too quickly in the parched air. I want to stretch out naked and savor these brief moments of coolness. Impossible. Suriya showers clothed, changes into oversize pajamas without exposing herself, sleeps in a room covered by a translucent cloth into which her family members peer unhindered. She is almost never alone with her body. I clutch my stomach against that imagined deprivation. I need my closeness to my body partly because it makes me feel close to my own death, that empty space inside me that none of my words or behaviors can touch.

"You must loose your hair for sleep," Suriya says, brushing her knee-length black mane, resting one swath at a time over her forearm. "To make long your hair."

I leave my hair in a messy topknot, exasperated by Suriya's preening. She's always smoothing out my shirts, brushing imaginary dust off my shoulders, asking if she can braid my hair. As if I need even more unwanted attention from men like Ayya. "I'm traveling," I say. "I'm not trying to impress anyone."

"But we must always look our best, no?" Suriya says. "For Sri

Lankan peoples, if you dress a dirty shirt or messy hair, it is like a beggar. You understand?"

"Yes." It's wrong of me to insist on my right to comfortable slovenliness. But Suriya's obsessive grooming makes me think of photos of my mother dressed like a little woman in the second grade, with her starched dress and permanent. Her mother made her sleep in rollers every night, just because that's what one did then, even if one was six years old and tossed and turned all night because the rollers were too tight. To make a child suffer discomfort in order to appear a certain way: a mild form of barbarism. Now that children are free to dress however they want, they begin gleefully objectifying themselves in elementary school, courting power through miniskirts and high heels. I dressed that way, too. Freedom and power are not the same thing. It's always refreshing to see a little girl haphazardly clothed, her hair messy, her eyes distracted by a million things besides how she looks. I feel like that girl in Sri Lanka, the one I should have been when I was eight. I understand this is a privilege denied to Suriya, and I know that I am exploiting it when I tell her I could care less how long my hair grows, I'm just trying not to die of heatstroke. She laughs. I love when she gets my jokes.

She combs her shiny hair through her fingers, staring at something I can't see, her lips parted. "One time I brushed my boyfriend's hair with my fingers," she says. "He said, So gently. Your hands move so gently." Her voice moves far away from the snoring cousin and the sloppy American visitor. "I was just thinking about that."

I used to have those thoughts. It stings to remember that there was a time when I lay awake at night worrying about what bra to wear the next time I went to my boyfriend's house.

"Do you still have that same boyfriend?" I ask. "The one you wrote me about?"

"Of course! I only love one."

"Is he still working in Qatar?" When I met Suriya, he had just finished university and taken a computer-ish job abroad.

She nods. "I miss him more."

"You haven't seen him this whole time?"

"No. But we write letters. Sometime we talk on the phone." The loose ends of Suriya's straw mat grate across the concrete floor as she settles into bed. I roll onto my back. A spider disappears into a brick cave at the top of the wall. I wonder if Suriya's calm goodness will survive her first contact with sex. Maybe it will. The first time will be with her husband, and it will hurt as it's supposed to and she will be relieved when he finishes. Maybe she will never have orgasms and never miss them. She will never know why the snore of a man who has just climaxed inside you is the loneliest sound there is.

Suriya yawns. I raise myself on one elbow and whisper down. "You realize I've had sex before, right?"

She bolts upright. Her hair spills into the basket of her crossed legs. "You have done the sex?"

We stay up late, whispering over the snores and stirrings coming from the main room. I tell her about losing my virginity to my high school boyfriend, how happy I was during and afterward, and how I told my father and he brought me to the gynecologist and paid for my birth control pills. I explain birth control pills and condoms and IUDs. I tell Suriya that I love having sex. "I know your words are true," she says. "But I cannot believe."

Just as it is hard for me to believe that Suriya has never kissed her boyfriend on the lips because she is afraid it will lead to pregnancy; that there will be a white sheet on her wedding night and if there is no blood on it, her husband can demand an immediate divorce; that her married cousins all brag about being pure on their wedding night; that she knows it's perfectly normal for some virgins not to bleed at all and her only feeling about sex since her big girl celebration is fear that she will be one of these godforsaken girls; that she thinks some boys in Sri Lanka do the self . . . (she grimaces, unable to complete the phrase), but girls would never, ever do the self . . . because they have too much fear for their wedding night; that she has a friend who had love for an older man and that man tricked her and made her to have sex and the girl became pregnant and the man's family made him marry the girl and now she is nineteen and she has two kids and her husband is drunk and mean and angry that he is made to marry this poor girl; that where that girl went is a hell and Suriya will not go to that hell; that her boyfriend never tries to French kiss her or touch her body because he is protecting her until marriage, when she will be his forever and ever. She runs her hand down the side of her neck and kneads her collarbone.

In the middle of the night, I shake Suriya awake and ask her to come with me to the outhouse, saying I'm afraid of the dark. It's not a lie. No longer surrounded by Suriya's bustling family and oppressive sunshine, Ayya feels like a real threat.

I have been promised a lake. Ayya and Suriya walk on either side of me, our towels tied around our waists. I have no swimming costume—the long-sleeved bodysuit and knee-length skirt that Suriya wears over her bra and underwear—so I've covered up my bikini with running shorts and a T-shirt emblazoned with a map of the U.S., something I'd never wear at home. My sandal straps dig into my feet, puffy from the heat. Furry grasses form an arc over the narrow entrance to the lake. Women scrub saris with large brushes and take turns washing themselves under their sarongs, resting the bar of sun-colored soap on a rock when they're finished. Their hands still as Suriya, Ayya, and I drape our towels over a tree branch. I hurry into the water to hide my Nike shorts, which I fear look ridiculous to the women and sexy to Ayya.

The shallows are frothy with laundry detergent and soap. But as the mouth of the passageway yawns into the open lake, the water becomes cool and clear. Tiny waves lap so rapidly against my chest that it feels like the same wave in endless dialogue with itself. *Where? Here. Where? Here.*

Suriya turns to me as the water covers my shoulders. "Akki, this lake very danger, okay? Have crocodile, okay?"

"Right now?" I splash wildly, hopping toward shore.

"Not now. Sometimes have. It's okay. My brother knows crocodile mantra." She smiles and gestures me into the body of the lake, where the stares that had felt hostile as I waded in become curious and open. I dive and place my palms on the sandy bottom. Sun washes my pointed toes. When I emerge, Ayya is grinning, wide-eyed. "Married?" he asks, the first time he's addressed me directly. I say no curtly and turn toward Suriya, floating on her back nearby. Surely he already knows from Suriya that I'm not married; this is just the come-on line that all Sri Lankan men use, usually followed by, "You come with me, madam." Instead, Ayya shouts, "Single rocks forever," the first English sentence I've heard him speak. My surprise makes me laugh. He imitates my handstand, his feet paddling the air. I wish I could relax and be friendly toward him. But he's made it impossible. I swim away. Water tickles my wrists. I lean backward, squint at the sky, go under.

Trust games were the only gym activity I was any good at when I was a kid. One time I let my partner walk so far behind me that the teacher came running, hands raised. "Whoa, whoa. That is a bit too trusting!" The whole class looked over at my partner, several feet behind me, poised to catch my shoulders just above the ground, and burst into the raucous group laughter of children, a rote response to anything out of sync with the rhythms of the world they've memorized so far. My cheeks burned even though I didn't understand yet what was wrong with trusting the body to be okay.

I kneel on the muddy bottom of the lake, letting the air out in small bubbles every few seconds. My hands come together, fingertips touching, thumbs at my chest, like Suriya pausing in front of a Buddha statue or bodhi tree. My impulse is to resist the explicitness of the gesture, but instead I bow my head. It feels good, I don't care why. When I come up, Suriya is moving through the water toward me with small, bouncing steps. Her hair is piled in a soapy mess atop her head, a stray tendril spilling shampoo into her eyebrow.

"Is fun, no? I think you love."

Yes. I do love.

"Slowly, slowly, you become happy again."

Heat presses against the walls of my chest. My eyes hold Suriya's eyes.

Oh. Fuck. She is thinking that slowly, slowly I will recover from the death of my beloved. My lower belly hardens. Why must I concoct events to explain my feelings? Why is being alive not sufficient justification for feeling lost and in pain?

New Year's Day begins at dawn, firecrackers raging through the village. Suriya and I brush our teeth at the pump in the yard while Ayya slices coconuts, holding the hairy spheres above his head and whacking them down the center with a long, curved knife. The milk chutes into a pot at his feet. Straddling a bench with a serrated blade on one end, he furiously scrapes the inside of the coconut. A bowl beneath the bench catches the baby-white pulp. Rajesh emerges from the woods dragging a stalk of bamboo as thick as his wrist and a banana leaf twice his height. He slices the leaf into four pieces and folds one of them into a cone. He separates the top of the bamboo stick into three even sections, which he peels back to make a container for the leaf cone.

How delightful it is to be inside this scene to which I will never belong. Until I become aware of my delight, and another, stronger part of my brain steals the simple enjoyment from me, characterizing the scene as an exotic spectacle worthy of noting, to be used later as a way to prove something about myself—that I'm interesting, brave, unusual. I am a parasite of my own experience.

Ayya lights a pile of sticks in the center of the stones. Rajesh places the pot of coconut milk on the fire, adds copious amounts of rice and sugar, and seals the pot with one section of the banana leaf. Fathers throughout Sri Lanka are doing the exact same thing at this very moment. The chronology of New Year's Day never changes, the beginning of each activity marked by a racket of firecrackers blaring from television and the street. "Do you have a New Year ritual in the U.S.A.?" Suriya asks me. Yes, we do. We stress out for weeks about where we're going to get drunk. When the pyrotechnic cacophony signals that it's time for everyone in the country to eat khir bhat, Rajesh removes the pot from the fire and places a bit of the steaming, sweet rice inside the leaf cone, around which he's arranged small cards bearing cartoonish images of Lord Buddha, Ganesh, and Shiva. Shiva rides atop a bull, in full command of his great sexual power. The cross-legged Buddha touches one hand to the ground, asking the earth for strength to resist the images of naked women clouding his mind, urging him to abandon his seat just as he's on the verge of enlightenment. My mother had a print of this image on her dresser. As a kid, I thought it was as ridiculous as the Irish dude intoning about inner peace. It was only on my first trip to Sri Lanka that I learned what the image represented—the courage to reject conventional ideas of pleasure and pain—and I found it moving. But imagining such an object in my parents' old bedroom makes it seem desperate, like covering over a rotted, moldy wall with a fresh coat of paint.

Rajesh scatters khir bhat on the ground in front of the images. Suriya points to the cone of rice: "For the gods." Then to the ground: "For the demons."

There are invisible beings around us all the time. Suriya knows this is true because she feels that when she is alone, there is always someone with her. And one time she had a ghost attached to her, an old man who breathed down her neck when she tried to sleep. The monks told her he was comforted by her long hair and taught her a mantra to make him go away. Gods and demons can protect us and help us, but some people use demons to hurt their enemies. That happened to Suriya's father when she was little. He got very weak and could not remember anything about the past. So he went to the hospital for two months and got electric shock treatments to make his mind work again. Suriya and her mother visited him; he did not remember them. The doctors said that they could not find his sick. So Suriya and her mother went to a Buddhist priest, and the priest talked with demons in her father's mind, who told the priest that one of Suriya's neighbors was jealous of her father's successful business and wished him to be poor. So he bound— "B-I-N-D," Suriya says, "is this the right word?"—two dead people and one devil to Suriya's father. The priest told Suriya's mother to do offerings to the demons and to Lord Buddha to free her father. And then her father remembered his life and left the hospital and went home.

"So the monks here have magical powers?" I ask.

"Not all. Some. White magic."

"Do they ever meditate?"

"Not all. Some. That is how they reach the magical powers."

"Do you ever meditate?"

"Oh no, El. Meditating is too difficult for regular people."

"Anyone can meditate. I meditate all the time. You just sit still."

Suriya clamps down on a smile. I am a silly American girl. "Maybe there is a different kind of meditating in U.S.A. But in Sri Lanka only advanced people meditate. Regular people go to temple for chanting and offerings."

Rajesh carries the steaming khir bhat inside. Everyone dips their hands into the pot, scoops out gooey palmfuls of sweet coconut rice, and feeds one another. I open my mouth wide whenever a cousin or parent or grandparent or niece approaches me. Their fingers touch my tongue. The porridge is warm and good. When the pot is empty, people begin kneeling and touching one another's feet. The standing person touches the kneeling person's head. The toddler touches my feet, I tickle the down on his head and kneel to touch his feet. An eruption of laughter. "El!" Suriya says. "You are big girl. You must not worship baby." Hashini comes out of the cooking hut to worship her husband. I prepare to feel angry, but anger does not come. Rajesh runs his hand over her head. She smiles up. He takes a big breath and cups her ears in his cracked hands. What do I know about their life together?

When the firecrackers announce that it's time to visit friends and relatives, I splash water on my face and change into a long skirt and baggy T-shirt. The road throbs with the desperate joy of arrack. Glassy-eyed men clap and sing as they stumble past, arms slung around each other's shoulders. They look grossly disheveled and unmoored, but still I envy their temporary madness, the longing for wild nights such a strong reflex of my personality, even though I know by now that wildness is a luxury in concept only. The monk at Shirmani explained what the Buddha meant by austerity. I jotted it down in my notebook: "Once you have gone through an experience, to not need it again."

Our first Halloween together, Jared and I dressed up as Sid and Nancy. He scrawled "God Save the Queen" across a ripped T-shirt and squeezed into a pair of my jeans. I rented a platinum wig and wore a see-through black dress with red stilettos so high I couldn't walk. Jared had to carry me on his back from my apartment to the bar, and then, once inside, walk me to a chair and plant me there while he ordered drinks. We ran into some friends of his, and they started a game of pool. I couldn't even hit the white ball. I crossed my legs on my corner stool. "She's like Kate Moss, Jared," one of the girls said, motioning to me with her cue. "Supermodel thin." She glowered at me as she enunciated each syllable of the dumb thing girls were supposed to want to be. But I felt better to be sitting alone in my fishnets and silver bra now that I was supermodel thin. A stupid feeling. It was a relief to be comforted by stupidity.

After the bar closed, we piled into a stupid graffiti-covered van and drove back to Jared's, where his roommate was throwing a party. I wanted Jared to come to bed and fuck me in my red stilettos, but it was impossible. He was belting out Sex Pistols songs and making everyone laugh with his perfect British accent. I took off my shoes and had a vodka tonic. Then I went in his bedroom and puked out his window. Sometime later, he was pulling me to a sitting position. "Come here, beautiful girl. I drew us a bath." I could tell right away that he was high on blow, as he taught me to call it. His navy comforter was mottled with early-morning light falling through the pines outside his window. I let him lead me to the mildewy bathtub, my eyes trained on my shuffling feet. I was mad not because he'd left me alone to vomit in his bedroom but because he let me sleep through sunrise instead of sharing his drugs with me. We faced each other in the lukewarm water.

"You look melancholy," he said. "I'm sorry I make you melancholy." He turned away and slapped his palm on the surface of the water. "Stop being sad! Why can't you be fucking happy?"

Brian used to ask me the same thing. It killed me. I think of myself as someone with an unusually high capacity for happiness, just not from the right things. I feel it here, inside these days of sitting and eating with such singleness of purpose—parsing the garlic from the cumin from the cinnamon, watching earth-size clouds dissolve into hot white space—that I feel sure sitting and eating in this village is as worthwhile an activity as any. But when I'm bloated and sleepy after the noonday meal and doze off facedown on the bed, my filthy feet dangling off the end, terror jerks me awake a few minutes later: What have I been doing all this time? Shouldn't I be doing something else? Like jogging or knitting or finding a husband or going back to school? Instead, I'm wiping my ass with my left hand and eating fried vegetables smeared in chili paste with my right. Which makes me much happier than it should.

To try to assuage the should-feeling one afternoon, I ask Suriya if she ever goes running. She looks at me strangely. "I must. If I am late."

"That makes sense." I settle back in my lawn chair to watch the evening's first pink-tinged clouds take shape.

Until I met Brian, I'd been averse to the gym—all those people exerting all that effort for nothing. They didn't need their flat stomachs and bulging biceps to carry well water or dig ditches or climb coconut trees. But when I grew quiet and sedentary in the middle of our second winter together, Brian got us a joint membership and insisted I try it. I went to a class called Total Surrender. An inverted triangle with a human head made me surrender to a series of sit-ups, push-ups, squats, and leg lifts while hip-hop music blared and he shouted, "Six, five, four—let's go! Higher! Three, two—aaaand new count! Ten, nine, eight . . ." Across the street, a fast-food restaurant advertised a free soda with any weekday lunch special. The storefront was decorated with paper hearts for

Valentine's Day. When a chubby woman tried to leave, the instructor bounded to the door. One arm shot out from his body like the limb on a Lego policeman. "Back on your mat! No one is leaving!"

"You're an animal," the woman groaned. She sounded idolatrous.

During the last set of crunches, I grunted at the same time as the woman next to me. Our eyes locked and we smiled at our misery reflected in the other's face. It feels productive to suffer. Without desperation, what momentum would there be to my days? If I were to tell my life as a story, surely the listener would be more interested in my sordid shenanigans with Jared than in my eventless days in this foreign village. Yet I feel *good* here. What does that say about goodness? Or about the human brain—mine in particular? All those concerned parties in Barbara Pym's *Excellent Women* pity the unmarried thirty-year-old, who reads and goes to church and has lots of friends, because she does not have a "full life in the accepted sense." The part of me that believes in that kind of fullness is comforted by drama. With Jared, my life felt full. Too full to worry over whether I was eating or sleeping or meditating. Even from here, the memory of that chaos doesn't seem all bad: the crying and the sex and the ostensible meaning in every street sign and song lyric. It felt like I was doing something important—feeling all that.

What I have now—swimming in the lake, eating rice and curry out of lotus leaves, sleeping nine hours a night, waking to Pali chants at dawn, sipping sweet tea, chatting with Suriya until I fall asleep—is joy, not tiny, bleating, toy-human fun. But part of me still wants the toy-human fun. I have to fight upsurges of resentment against Suriya's family for their groundedness, their lack of ambitions and judgments, their ignorance of the giddiness I felt when I downed cans of beer while trying on clothes and dancing alone to fast, bright songs that everyone knows before heading out to a bar, stupidly hoping that this night of all nights would be worth it. "Abandon hope": something a Buddhist nun said at a talk in Carpinteria, which I taped over my desk at home. But it feels good to be stupid.

In the afternoons, Suriya sits in the yard with a giant binder filled with vocabulary lists, verb conjugations, and summaries of books and plays, studying for the first round of exams to become an English teacher. I test her on vocabulary and ask her to repeat sentences in various tenses. I'm surprised when we get to the literature section: She is expected to be familiar with writers like Dickens and Shakespeare. "You've read Shakespeare?" I ask.

"Just some small parts. The play is about Romeo and Juliet. Until my teacher explains, I did not understand one word."

"Well, that's all right. Most American students can't understand it without help, either. So," I say, reading a question from her binder, "what is one of the main themes in Shakespeare's play *Romeo and Juliet*?"

Suriya bites the tip of her index finger. "The theme of karma?"

I ask how she would explain that on an exam. "The families of Romeo and Juliet," she says, "they create bad karma by their fighting and their anger. And then the children suffer for the bad karma of the parents."

"In English we would say this is fate or destiny. Do you know those words?"

"Yes! My teacher has said the word fate. But I do not understand."

"It's that Romeo and Juliet's love is doomed to fail. There's nothing anyone can do to save it. It's what the stars want."

"I do not understand. Why do the stars want that children suffer?" Suriya's cousin comes out of the house with the baby, feeding him sips of tea out of a glass cup.

"Well, they suffer because they don't accept their fate. No one can fight the stars."

Suriya widens her eyes and tilts her head, as if I'm being intentionally ridiculous. "Some nights it is bright and I say, 'Look at the stars!' But this is not making me suffer and die."

"But you ask Lord Buddha for things—good health and protection and stuff."

"But Lord Buddha is not stars. He is a person."

"But now he's dead."

"He is not dead. He has got nibbana."

"Well, wherever he is, don't you think asking him for things is kind of like believing the stars have power over your life?"

Suriya shakes her head emphatically side to side. "When we ask Lord Buddha, we must remember him. And remember that he acted in a good manner and became like a god. That is karma."

"And you think this is the main theme of *Romeo and Juliet*?"

"Yes. For me." She settles back in her chair and runs the end of her braid through her fingernails.

GAMBAWELLA

The rush of air on the motorbike is like the spritz of mist from the spray bottle that kept me company on hot summer nights in junior high. I'd stretch out in my underwear, listening to the Violent Femmes and Radiohead and Nirvana, making myself wait between squirts until the heat gathered at the white tufts of baby hair along my forehead, then crept downward and rouged my cheeks, prettily, I hoped. I am sitting on the motorbike between Ayya and Suriya, on our way to their parents' home in a neighboring village. Suriya insisted I ride in the middle, lest I fall off the back on a fast turn. I take care to sit up straight, gripping the side of the bike, although Suriya keeps shouting over the wind, "El, you must hold to Ayya!" This seems such an intimate position to be in with a Sri Lankan boy that I worry Suriya may be pushing me toward her brother, fantasizing about a romance between us, her brother mar- rying an American girl, bringing instant success to her family. But the bike is fast and loud and unsteady, and it soon jostles away my concerns about other people's imagined imaginings.

This is poya, full moon day, and so we stop at an ancient cave temple on our way. The entrance is crowded with pilgrims dressed in airy white skirts and sarongs. Suriya hands me a five-rupee coin to feed to a green-faced wooden man. I place the coin on his thick, curled tongue and watch it roll down his throat into a padlocked box. I try to laugh with Suriya and Ayya, but it's hard to watch them spend money on gimmicks at a well-endowed temple. We add our sandals to the heap of flip-flops just inside ornate iron gates. The stone pathway is scorching. We run on the balls of our feet toward the gaping mouth of a cave. Women with slack, twiggy arms crowd our faces with lotus flowers to offer inside the temple. Ayya buys us each one. The seller peels back the outer leaves of the thick bud, making a star of deep purple petals.

The statues inside this cave that has been a place of worship for thousands of years remind me of *Simpsons* characters, their beatific smiles sardonic imitations of beatific smiles. Suriya stops short before a potbellied blue man, covered in coarse gray hair, with fangs like daggers. In one hand, he holds a scythe; in the other, the thin arm of a sexy, bare-chested woman with huge, black teardrops painted on her cheeks—an adulterous woman reborn in the hell realms, at the mercy of this hairy demon about whom Suriya used to have nightmares after she came here to worship with her parents when she was young. Her girlhood fear reminds me of my mother's stories of growing up Southern Baptist—lying awake at night worrying that she had accidentally committed the Unforgivable Sin of blasphemy and was already doomed to eternal torment. Or worrying that she hadn't committed any unforgivable sins and was doomed to be herself forever and ever, floating on a cloud in the sky, no escape. For my mother, Buddhism was the escape. She'll be disappointed when I tell her how the religion is practiced in an actual Buddhist country, rather than by hippies and "recovering Christians," as my mother likes to call herself. She mostly uses spiritual practices to fortify her desperate grip on "bliss experiences"—she actually calls them that—rather than to challenge her narrow idea of what she needs to be okay. Not that I'm finding many fruitful challenges in this cave myself. Suriya offers her flower to a fat, happy, cartoon Buddha, lovingly removing the stem and bowing her head as she lays the fanned-out petals in the Buddha's lap. I try to imitate her, but I pull too hard on the stem and the lotus flies out of my hands, landing at a startled pilgrim's feet. Suriya scoops it up and tosses it in the bucket of discarded stems. "Cannot give to Lord Buddha," she whispers.

I'm glad when we are returned to the bright, dry day. Suriya asks if I like to climb mountains. I do, very much. We walk to the base of the mountain towering above the cave. A trail leads up through lichen-covered boulders under a canopy of waxy little leaves dancing and shimmering. "This is the sky palace," Suriya says. "Okay, Akki?" Okay, Nangi. Ayya removes his shirt and shoes, and carries his water bottle in a backpack he's fashioned out of string. He shows me how to put the straps of my sandals over my wrists so we can use our toes and fingers to clamber up the rocks. "We go," Ayya cries and darts upward. "You are pig!" Suriya yells up at him. He pauses and grins down from a sheer-faced boulder.

"You are noodle!"

The two English sentences I've heard Ayya speak: *Single rocks forever* and *You are noodle*. This strangeness almost endears him to me.

For a long time, we climb in silence. The boulders are warm on my feet, the dirt cool. Suriya's loud exhalations are a beat longer than mine. A green-and-purple bird swoops in front of us, pausing midflight to chirp and stare. I am lost in the spiritual joy I could not find in the temple. I once made the mistake of mentioning "spiritual joy" on a first date with an attractive bartender/musician and he replied, "Spiritual joy, huh? I think that phrase is the reason my brother started doing heroin." But most purely good things sound sappy in description—a kind of punishment, maybe, for insisting on confining goodness in words. The bartender/musician begged me to marry him while we were having sex and then never called me again.

It's late afternoon when we resume our journey. The triumphant drone of the bike's engine dies in a yard filled with decaying blue and pink plastic bags that seem more real than the dirt they rest on. Suriya's home is two-story and concrete, one of the few large houses we've passed on the two-hour ride from Hashini's. Aside from a few tenacious yellow patches, the building has shed its paint. A metal sign that says BODHI BAKEHOUSE is propped against the side of the building, spilling its advertisement into a pile of crushed water bottles. A sliding glass door cracked into a jagged web of prisms opens to a large, barren room on the ground floor. The only furniture is an old swivel chair with a dangerously tilted seat.

"Your home is big," I say.

"So big, yes. But now it is broken." Suriya's voice is loud and quick. "You know about eye poison, Akki?" Suriya's family used to run a bakery and restaurant that made them sort of rich. Their neighbors had eye poison, the unconscious ability to cause harm through envy. The restaurant started to lose money, then collapsed completely. Suriya thanks god for her brother's army job, but still it is very difficult; the money is not enough for so many people. "I have more works," she says, and leads me up the stone staircase on the outside of her house. "My mum is sick so she must not clean."

Two rooms open onto the upper balcony. One of them contains a bed piled to the ceiling with linens and saris and T-shirts. The light switch makes a hollow cluck when Suriya flicks it. A young man flicks a light switch on and off with the tip of his tongue to improve his oral sex technique in that "Self-Improvement" poem by Tony Someone, which my dad gave me when I was just old enough to be disturbed by my father's placing thoughts of oral sex in close proximity to my own. But still I liked what my father suspected I would like—that the girlfriend dumped the boy after demanding he school himself in pleasure, that what he was really practicing was how to suffer. Tiny claws scurry across the floor. "I think rats make home," Suriya says, and flicks the switch once more. A rowdy snore responds. A man is nestled between the wall and the mountain of multicolored cloth, his cracked hands resting on his stupendous belly. "My father," Suriya whispers. Her voice tries not to apologize. "Come to put your bag in my room."

Her room is large and empty save for another sheetless mattress. The small square window frames the top of a palm tree wilting in the late-day sun. "Hide your valuables," Suriya says, and leaves me to order my things. I paw through my bag until my hand lands on my small stuffed whale, lopsided and covered in smiling frogs, sewn for my first birthday by my grandmother, two years before she died. The consolation of losing Brian has been sleeping with Whaley again. I'd shoved him under the bed the first time Brian slept over, and then could never find a way to casually reintroduce him. Of course many young women have worn teddy bears on their beds. I guess the bow ties and missing glass eyes add an appealing irony to the moments before a one-night stand. But there is nothing ironic to me about Whaley's threadbare flippers or loose seams, revealing thin strips of crayon yellow, the color he was before my fitful sleep wore him into countless shades of beige. I hid Whaley from Brian because I still believe he's real, meaning that when I wake up in the dark, panicked and lonely, a reject of my own thoughts, the half-moon of Whaley's polyester body is always right there, smooth and cool and ready to receive my cheek.

When I was six, my mother took me on a whale watch in Boston Harbor. I brought Whaley with me, excited to show him where he came from. But as soon as we were on the open sea, I became afraid of holding him, imagining his tiny fins consumed by the opaque, frothy water. I didn't trust myself not to throw him overboard. I did bad stuff sometimes, like opening the car door on the highway; I'd just imagined pulling the lever and then the door was flying open and Dad was screaming and swerving into the breakdown lane. I clutched Whaley with both hands as I peered over the ship's guardrail. "Let's reconnoiter the top deck, shall we?" Mom said as the ship moved farther offshore. Reconnoiter was one of my mother's pet fancy words. Rec and oyder, rec and oyder. I sang the phrase to myself as I handed Whaley to my mom, so she could order him among her belongings while we went to wreck the deck of the ship.

Sitting on the edge of Suriya's lumpy mattress, I wrap my passport in a skirt and rest Whaley on the pillow. Suriya will think he's cute. Women here play with dolls and stuffed animals well into their twenties.

~

Downstairs, a woman sits with her legs outstretched, her silver-streaked black hair matted against the wall behind her. Ayya's head rests on her thigh. The woman's fingers are long and slender and play through Ayya's hair. Suriya sits on the other side of the woman, her head resting on her shoulder. "Amma," she says to me. The tenderness is almost obscene. "Hello," I offer. A loud cough sounds above us, followed by the guttural yank of phlegm. Glistening spittle lands in the dirt yard.

Suriya stands. "I must cook."

The kitchen is a vast chaos of cookery—empty display cases, a pile of bamboo spoons, rusted baking sheets. Suriya opens tall plastic containers until she finds rice, an onion, some dried chilies, a head of garlic sprouting long, green curlicues. She speaks to Ayya, menacingly. He hands her some coins.

In the store across the street, Suriya points to buckets filled with beans and vegetables. "Meka keeyada?" she asks. When no price allows her to relax her face, I insist on paying. We leave the store carrying dried garbanzo beans, coconuts, and mango. She makes me promise I will not tell her family that my money paid for this meal. "So many secrets to keep love, no?" She circles my wrist with her hand as we cross the street.

For the next several hours, Suriya chops and sifts and sautés on a single-burner hot plate. She walks back and forth from the well to the kitchen with a large jug resting on her hip, forcing her upper body nearly parallel to the ground. Ayya darts in and out of the kitchen, stealing handfuls of chickpeas and slices of mango. Suriya lunges toward him as he does a backward skip out the door, dangling the stolen food like a prize. "He not know how to work," she says. "He only know how to play." Which is true—her laughter or my rage?

Useless in the kitchen, I work on my translation, meaning that I read one paragraph several times and pity the sentences the undue anxiety of their current reader, who tries to say the word *tournure* aloud several times, distressed each time by her inability to create the sound she can hear in her head, telling herself that her French has not improved since junior high and she'd better give up on ever saying *tournure* or any other French word correctly because right now she sounds like a mentally ill gorilla trying to communicate with her zookeeper. I ought to just be translating. But I'm finding *Fifi* increasingly boring. A man takes in stray cats. He describes the color of their fur, their eating habits, their sleeping positions, the reasons for their names, the photographs he takes of them. A maliciously boring account, as if the narrator were exacting revenge on the world for refusing to accept him. And I undertook the translation with similar malice, set on distinguishing myself from the concretely productive masses. With my purposeless virtue, the line from the book that first made me fall in love with it: *Il a atteint l'hésitation.* Well, I perfected the art of hesitation, too. But at least now I know better than to congratulate myself for analyzing instead of acting. So stop analyzing *Fifi*; just translate it. If I give up on this, what will I have? I'll hit my mid-thirties without one thing to show for myself. My breath grows ragged at that thought. I sludge through the next two pages.

Suriya's father walks downstairs, nods sharply at me, and points toward his daughter, who is placing a bamboo spoon in a steaming bowl. "English," he says. "English." He stares at me as a metal chain of unknown words clangs from his mouth. I feel like I have three nostrils or a missing eye, some deformity against which he must harden himself in order to bear looking at me.

Like Hashini, Suriya does not eat with us. She serves me a plate heaped with coconut sambol, rice, chickpea and mango curries, and then hovers over my plate with a spoon as I eat, replacing the curries with a flamboyant dollop as soon as I make a dent in one. I should play my part, saying how *rasai* everything is, this is the best curry I've ever tasted, just one more helping, how could I refuse? But I disrespect the stakes of the game too much. When Suriya tries to give me a third spoonful of mango, I stop her with my palm. "That's enough. Really."

She suspends the spoon a few inches from my eye. "At Hashini's, you ate more."

"It's not hospitality to force-feed your guests," I want to yell. "I'm just full," I say.

Her father's eyes weigh on me as she returns the bowl to the kitchen. Suriya serves tea after the meal, heating the water with a metal coil attached to an electrical cord. I take small sips of the sugar-thick liquid. The wrinkles in her father's forehead knot between his eyes. He raises himself off the floor and walks as if in imitation of an angry man marching. Amma stands up also, glides into the kitchen. The soft splash of water by the tank, where Suriya is washing dishes, stops. I wince every time I hear the words *sudhu* and *Amereeca* in her father's eerily calm speech. A crash of water, a gasp. His footsteps punish the stairs. I find Suriya wiping her face with her shirt, her spine arched into a flat C to keep from exposing her stomach. "Did he just—was that tea? Are you okay? Are you burned?"

"No, Akki. No burn."

"Is this about the food?"

"Do not worry for that, El."

"Can you please tell him that I love your food? And I didn't come visit you just to eat curry?"

"I think he not hear that." She shakes her head impatiently, as if trying to reason with a child. "He is a madman. Sometime." She lathers bar soap on the plates, speaking quietly and hurriedly. If she came in second or third on a test when she was younger, her father would heat up the metal coil and hold it against her stomach and back, where the marks wouldn't show. She has been the top student in her class since she was nine.

"What about your brother?"

"He hates to study. And now he is a soldier. The soldier's life is so hard. So when he has vacation time he must do as he wants." She tilts the water jug onto the sudsy plate.

"Your life is hard, too, Nangi."

She sets the jug upright and faces me. "If you are not here, I am all alone." I touch her wrist. Suriya lives with her family; she knows everyone in her village; she is always busy with schoolwork and chores. Maybe separateness is not a person's fault; maybe some people just come into the world that way.

Suriya swirls the water at the center of the plate. Then she giggles. "My father say, You feed sudhu garbage!" She imitates his voice in a deep, robotic whisper. "He say, She will never get you job in America if you—" She claps her hand over her mouth. "That's not why you're my friend, El—but—for my father—"

"No, no, of course, I understand." Confused and embarrassed, neither of us notices when I start helping Suriya wash the dishes. I haven't considered the roots of her family's excessive desire to please me. I figured they were simply bored. Just as I was. But every bored person hopes.

I dread using Suriya's parents' shower—a cold-water spigot and a bucket inside the outhouse—but there is no way I can sleep without freeing myself from the day's grime and sweat. I latch the door behind me, hang up my sarong, and bend down to fill the bucket, facing away from the shit-smeared hole. I could be staying in a well-appointed guesthouse for less than ten dollars a night. Why am I still here? A sense of obligation to Suriya, a sense that my presence is making her feel more alive or something. Maybe I'm flattering myself. In any case, I will be out of here soon. I miss solitude, living by my own daily rhythms. And Jared. He's probably upset I've been out of touch so long. I don't want to think of how he might be distracting himself.

The shock of cold water crashing over my head stops my thoughts. How instantly it erases the heat and the dirt, so that I find myself in a new state—cool, private, immediate. After I've lathered myself in bar soap, I fill up another bucket. As I'm lifting it overhead, a gleam of light through the outhouse slats catches in the corner of my eye. My throat constricts. I turn my head to the side just in time to glimpse two dark eyes retreating. Disgusted and outraged, I dump the bucket over me and cover up with the sarong, not even bothering to rinse the soap off my legs. I want to chase Ayya down and shout insults, shaming him in front of his family. But for all I know, it's perfectly acceptable for young men to spy on naked women here. Maybe Suriya's father has implied that Ayya should make a pass at the American girl. And of course, Ayya could simply deny it and make me seem crazy. Causing a scene would only humiliate me.

How wily of him to put me in a position where I have no way to fight back against his violations. I want to talk to Jared, touch the dimple in his chin as he pulls me toward him and tells me not to worry. Sharp ache. How different helplessness feels when imposed by someone you don't care for. With Jared, the helplessness hurts, yes, but there is a kind of relief in how he makes me hate him one moment and forgive him the next, as if he's freed me of the responsibility to protect myself.

~

I once asked a boy I was fucking to pretend to rape me. The fucking bored me and the boy bored me, but I didn't realize that at the time. I thought I was bored of life. So I told the boy—I don't remember his name—that I often fantasized about coercive sex. His eyes widened. Would I really let him fake-rape me? With a stocking covering his face and everything? Sure. I would love it, in fact, if he liberated us of his face. I was living with my father after my year in Paris, and I gave the boy keys to our house one Friday night when Dad was away for the weekend, shooting a cereal commercial in Philadelphia. The boy could "break in" anytime he chose. The moments leading to the fake-rape had a limpid fineness—closing my eyes in the shower, leaning into the refrigerator for a jar of peanut butter, turning the handle of my bedroom door, my heart pounding, demanding I be exactly where I was.

But once the boy was really there—he slipped, predictably, into my room just after I turned out the light—I was aware of myself acting, trying to make him feel tough and scary. He gagged my mouth with a stocking, but I could have shouted through it if I wanted. I twisted left and right as he held my arms over my head, but the power in the motion was all mine. I knew how I looked as I writhed, naked from the waist down. I could have kneed him in the testicles, shaken off my gag and captured the tip of his nose in my teeth. Instead I stared up with cartoon fear at the reflective surface of his masked face, and let him hold my hips still with one hand. I made breathy protest moans into the stocking. It took him too long to come and I had to twist and moan ever more histrionically to distract him from his failure at brutality. At last, he extracted himself, told me I'd better not tell a fucking soul about this if I knew what was good for me, whispered that he'd call me tomorrow, maybe we could get a drink. I didn't even feel like touching myself when I was alone. All I felt was the stupidity of finding even pretend rape erotic. The unsocialized abandon I fantasized about had nothing to do with actual coercion.

The boy called and texted for weeks afterward. I felt guilty every time I saw his name on my phone. Even as my rapist, he couldn't make me feel more than indifference. Whereas my outrage for Ayya's real, calculated transgressions keeps me awake long after Suriya drifts off that night, my arms crossed over my squirming chest.

The words Ayya is yelling seem like they're trying to strangle him. His nostrils flare out of his crimson face, his skin stretched tight around his protruding jaw. Or at least that's how I see him when I enter the kitchen, picturing him in a lookout tower above a Tamil town where the Tigers have killed a prominent monk or taken off one of his friend's legs with a hand grenade. Ayya's actual demeanor is more pouty than maniacal. Suriya sets down her knife to pat his hand, speaking quietly. After he stalks out of the kitchen, she explains that one thousand rupees—about ten bucks—are missing from his room. Karma's a bitch, I do not say out loud.

Suriya flattens garlic cloves with the wide blade of her knife to loosen their skins. "My brother is so sad. He works hard for this money. But I cannot do for him. I can only look at him." There is a woman thief in this village, she explains. One time, she stole the chairs out of Suriya's yard. They would walk past her house and see her sitting in them.

"Why didn't you take them back?"

"We don't want fighting with her. Maybe we get back our chairs, but it makes anger in us. This woman thief, also she is a"—Suriya rests her knife on the cutting board and searches the ceiling for the word—"a depraved. Mens come to her home. She says, he is my brother, he is my uncle. And we laugh because she has no brother and no uncle."

"So she's a prostitute? She has sex with men for money?"

"Yes. She is so greedy."

"What about the men who go to her? Aren't they the ones who are greedy?" Sarasi from Rose Land told me that widows are considered used goods, ineligible for marriage and fair game for sex. If the widow had children to raise and no family to support her, she might become a sort of informal prostitute, temporarily kept by one man after another.

"Why isn't the woman married?" I ask Suriya.

"Her husband dies in a fire."

"Suriya, that is so sad. The woman probably has no other way to make money."

"But many women are poor and they do not become a depraved. This woman love money. My mother tells me that." She crushes garlic with the flat edge of a knife, her forehead creased. "Why do you say it's sad, El?"

She has not yet known the moment just before a man ejaculates, when his whole self is on the surface of his body. They all make different noises or guard different silences and they each have a different way of clutching your body as the semen rushes to the tip of the cock, and his openness widens you so much that you would do anything to safeguard the release he needs, for that instant, more than anything else in the world and which, for that instant, you alone can give him. And then he groans and empties himself of this need and rolls away and wipes himself off and stands up and clothes his body and the loneliness that rushes in as a yawn escapes his limp face is the worst pain I have known in my life, a full-body longing that has sometimes felt so unbearable I would rather have been raped, to at least have the clarity of being the victim of exploitation and cruelty instead of the confusing, self-loathing knowledge that I chose to be the receptacle for the sticky, cloying, arrogant goo the man needed to be rid of. A lot of women who have sex for money would laugh at the stupidity of that. They would laugh at me for talking about the man's whole self being on the surface of his body, for thinking about his ejaculate long enough to personify it. But they need the money to live.

I try to explain a tame version of this thinking to Suriya. "You know something, El?" she says, scooping the crunchy shells of garlic cloves into her palm and tossing them out the window. "You are a kind lady."

The cousins from Hashini's are crowded into the living room, stopping by on their drive back to Colombo. Suriya hops from foot to foot as she sets out dishes and plates. "Are your legs okay?" I ask when she hands me my lunch.

"I have to make toilet. No time yet today." It is noon. She rubs her temples, still hopping. "Is your head okay?" I ask.

"It is paining."

"You have a headache? Do you want pills? I have good pills with me."

She looks stricken. "No pills."

"Can I bring you some water at least? You're probably dehydrated."

"Please, Akki, sit, eat." So I sit and eat, knowing what she wants is to feel her suffering has been put to use. Her relatives' fingers are covered in the food she prepared. Her father has seconds and thirds. He murmurs to Suriya as he hands her his plate to wash. She meets his eyes. His smile is brittle, awkward. He turns toward me, saying, "English. Daughter. English."

"Her English is very good," I tell him. "She is very smart."

He nods once and walks toward the outhouse.

~

After Suriya's relatives have eaten another meal and then slipped inside their loud vehicles without saying goodbye, I ask Suriya where I can go to use the Internet. She taps her nose with her index finger. "Why do you need a computer, Akki?"

Well, if I get to a computer, it's theoretically possible that I'll read emails from Jared claiming to have given up drinking and dealing, begging me to come back and marry him; or telling me he fell off a roof when he was drunk and is paralyzed from the waist down and I need to move back to California and care for him. Or I'll have an email from a publisher offering me a generous contract for my translation, or telling me this book is crap and my translation is not much better and did I know how easy it is to self-publish on Amazon? Or Brian will have found life unbearable without me and beg me to give it another try. Or my mother will have found her calling as the proprietor of a gluten-free escort service, and would I like in on the enterprise?

"I might have some important letters," I say. I haven't checked my email since I left Kandy. It's nice to be unmoored, but I can't just float here forever. Suriya retrieves a rusty, heavy bicycle from the field behind their house. I sit on the handlebars, holding my legs out in front of me. My tailbone wobbles on the metal bar. "The wind tastes sweet on my arms," Suriya says. Her breath tastes sweet on my ear.

We pass a motorbike going the other way. The driver does a U-turn and pulls up in front of our bicycle, blocking the way. The boy is small and unsmiling. He and Suriya chat in soft, withholding tones.

"That boy is my school friend," she says when we bike away. "He asked me about love one time."

"He wanted to be your boyfriend?"

"To marry." She leans over my shoulder to press her weight on the pedals. "Many boys asked me about love in the money season. But when my father lose—losed?"

"Lost."

"When my father lost his business, the boys all stopped speaking to me. So I hate them." I smile. Suriya is quietly fierce.

"Do you have any friends who are girls?"

Girls in school say they are her friends. They act in a nice manner to each other. But she doesn't trust them. They are jealous because she gets good marks in school and she has a boyfriend working abroad. They joke and say her boyfriend is ugly. And one time, her friends told her a lie that their exam was canceled. So she did not study and she did poorly.

"I don't have many close friends, either," I say. I've always had women I could call up and go out with. I enjoy these interactions, but it would make me sad to characterize them as friendship—unless a given social activity was going to involve drugs or alcohol, I usually preferred to be alone.

My turn to pedal. I love the whir inside my body as the blood rushes to keep up with my legs. "So fast," Suriya calls over my shoulder. "Fun!" We pass a still, green lake lined with feathery grasses. A duck walks through sticky, black mud toward the water, which makes grace of its clumsy waddle.

Suriya yells to stop and hops off the handlebars as the bike slows. The family that has a computer with Internet is not at home. Someone must have died, Suriya says. The only place they could possibly have gone is a funeral. It takes a few tries to explain to Suriya why I find that funny. Her laugh jostles her whole body. It's good to be alone with her. I no longer have the urge to flee her village, put on my pack and wait in the dust for a bus to come by, going elsewhere. If I leave, when will we see each other again? And it's nice to be able to simply imagine Jared's expressions of raunchy love piling up in my inbox, along with, perhaps, even a kind note about *Fifi*.

I wake up in the night with the sense that someone has entered our room. I blink at the darkness above my head, willing my eyes to adjust to the dark, then press my chin to my chest. A silhouette is just visible in the doorless doorway. Masculine, threatening. The vigor of my heartbeats drowns out my thoughts. I stay very still, waiting for the figure to make a move, waiting for my brain to wake up. He takes a step forward, into the moonlight. I still can't see his face, but the floppy hair and wide chest clearly belong to Ayya. Suriya is sleeping on the floor beside me, my frantic mind reminds itself. If he advances, I will scream.

But after staring at my bed for a while, he simply walks away. Fear gives way to rage. This has gone too far. If he's willing to approach me in the middle of the night, while I'm sleeping beside his sister, what would he do if he found me alone somewhere? I must stop this. I'm up and walking before I have any sense of how to do that.

Ayya is on the stairway leading to the ground floor. He turns at the sound of my footsteps. I tower over him from the top of the stairs. The half-moon reveals his face, surprised and open. "Leave me alone." The harsh whisper grates my throat. "Stop spying on me. I'm here for your sister, not for you. I'm going to tell her what you're trying to do."

Ayya knots his hands at the center of his chest and wrinkles his face. "El Akki." The whisper barely reaches me. "Hello. Sleeping." He's probably hoping I'm about to follow him to his bedroom. My anger reminds me of a phrase from my guidebook, which I used to say to men who harassed me on the street. "Palayan yanna!" Get lost!

I wait outside the bedroom for my breathing to calm. I'll tell Suriya in the morning. I don't want to disturb her few precious hours of rest.

I sleep late the next day and awake too hot to think. I have been reduced to the need for water on my face. The tank outside is almost cool, shaded by shaggy coconut trees. Frangipani petals are scattered on the ground, their Club Med loveliness smeared into a beige bruise on the dirt. I splash water on my face and begin to gargle the fuzz off my teeth. Suriya runs up. "Don't use the water, Akki! Pig rat died in the tank." The swirl of water over my tongue stills. "I bring you well water." She hurries toward the overgrown backyard. I spit. I do not ask what a pig rat is.

Suriya returns with a metal urn and stands with me as I wash. "El, can I ask you something?" Her voice is quiet and serious. Ayya must have spoken to her first. "Do you have some problem in the night?"

I pat dry my face and look up. "Yes. I wanted to talk to you about it. But I don't want to upset you. It's about Ayya."

"Ayya, yes, he tell me—"

"Told me."

"Told me he saw you in the night. You were angry or worried."

"He was peering into our bedroom, Suriya. Staring at me. It woke me up."

She puts her hand on my arm. "Does he scare you? Do not worry for that, El. Ayya walks in the night. Because in the army, he is a night guard. You understand? So he has the habit of not sleeping."

I sigh, not wanting to hurt Suriya, hating Ayya for forcing me into this uncomfortable position. "I think he was lying, Nangi. Because he has also been spying on me in the outhouse, when I'm using the toilet or taking a shower." Blanched, Suriya withdraws her hand. "I know this must be upsetting to hear about your brother," I continue, "but it's probably just being a soldier has made him—"

"Akki, I need to speak with you. In a lonely area. Okay?"

"A private place," I say, following her into the backyard, past the outhouse, into an overgrown mess of bamboo. She sits down on a log in a clearing. I take the opposite end, facing her. "El Akki. That was not Ayya looking at you. What was your word? Sie?"

"Spy."

"Ayya does not spy." She takes a deep breath and closes her eyes. "I hope you will forgive me, Akki. I have spy you."

"Have spied on you." I repeat the words mechanically, awaiting an explanation.

"Yes. It is me." She speaks quickly, keeping her eyes closed. "The first time, in the night at Hashini-Mommy's house, I want to make sure you are okay. But then your lamp in the outhouse is so bright and I thought I can see inside without that I disturb you. Then I am *more* interested because I see only little bit—"

"What did you want to see?"

"Oh, El, I am embarrassed." Suriya still has not opened her eyes. "I want to see white girl naked."

Suriya is wearing her hair in perfect braided pigtails; her baggy dress comes to just above her ankles. Yet she sounds like she's about to hit up a strip club in Bangkok. I reach out and grip her hand. She opens her eyes, but keeps them cast downward. "Nangi," I say, "it's okay. Honestly, that makes me like you even more."

Suriya lifts her chin. "You have not angry?"

"Not at all. But you could have just asked me. I'm not shy about stuff like that."

"But I am shy! I never dare to ask you."

"Did you see what you were looking for?"

"Yes." Suriya looks at her feet. "I want to know if you have hair. Because one time boys in my class have shown this photo of a naked lady. Some bad thing from the Internet. And one boy say me, 'Ooh, do you look like that?' And another boy say, 'No, I think she is hairy!' And the boys laugh. The lady in the photo has no hair! Just on her head. And I am worried that it is bad to have hair—in that place. But then I think, maybe it is only white girls who have no hair."

"I guess I answered your question." Suriya blushes. I laugh and jostle her shoulder. "Come on. I don't mind at all. Really."

She faces me, biting her lip. "But how do girls become like that?"

I explain waxing and shaving and the gross American infantilization of women and sexualization of children. I want to make the practice seem as absurd as possible, to be the role model of a woman who is comfortable with her body just as it is. But if Suriya had been spying on me a few weeks earlier, when Jared was staying with me in New York, she might have remained confused. It is oddly unthinkable to me that I would go to the beach or on a date without undergoing uncomfortable, gratuitous hair removal.

Sometimes when I got a bikini wax, I would begin to imagine that the strips of hot wax were being applied and yanked against my will and I didn't know when it would stop, if ever, and I thought of the secret CIA prisons and Abu Ghraib and Guantánamo and Bagram and the so-called stress positions into which prisoners were shackled for hours and days until their shoulders dislocated and their legs broke, and all the other forms of torture happening all around the world at that very moment that were infinitely worse than forced genital waxing—which was, after all, not nearly painful enough to even exist as a form of torture outside my mind—and my lips and hands grew numb and I had to take long, deep breaths and the Russian lady would ask if I was okay, it was almost over, sweetie, just one more little strip.

A tiny purple bird lands on the log between Suriya and me, but flitters off when I turn to look at it. "You know," I say, "I had a similar thing one time. With a boyfriend." I haven't told Suriya about Jared, wanting her to think of me as a heartbroken woman slowly recovering with no one's help but her own. "He wanted me to look like the women on the Internet."

Near the beginning of our relationship, when Jared and I were lying in bed after sex, he asked if he could wax my asshole. I was satiated and dreamy and openhearted. "Maybe," I said. "Is it the hot wax part that turns you on, or—"

"I don't mean like that. Not as a sex act."

I stiffened. "You mean you want to wax my asshole to make it *look* better?"

"I just think it looks hot when it's all bare."

"And where have you seen all these bare assholes?" A thin, steel question.

"Relax, baby, I'm not thinking of other girls. I've just seen it in porn, I guess."

I jumped out of bed. "Do you have any clue how much it hurts to rip out your hair by the goddamn follicle from the most tender area of your body?"

I glared at the floor as I pulled on my clothes. Jared sat up and reached an arm out to me. "I don't get it. You said I could when you thought it would turn me on."

"I didn't realize I'd have to become your private porn star to turn you on."

I repeat this line to Suriya, offering a chaste explanation of a porn star. "That is good, El," she says. "So you did not see the boy again?"

Amma yells Suriya's name three times. I am saved from having to lie. We find Suriya's mother in the yard, looking alarmed. Suriya hugs her and speaks reassuringly. "She believe I am lost," she tells me.

Amma is feeling well today and will be able to prepare lunch. So Suriya is free to study for her exams. She sits in the yard with her giant binder, trying to memorize a few paragraphs she must recite for the exam. I haven't changed my underwear in a couple of days and resolve myself to the necessity of laundry. As soon as I drop the matted knot of my clothes into a bucket, the soapy water turns opaque gray. I squeeze my orange T-shirt into a ball and rinse it out under the tap. It drips on the laundry line stretched between two squat palmyra trees. As I start to repeat the process, Suriya's mother comes up and pats my arm. She takes my shirt off the line and returns it to the bucket, into which she dumps much more detergent. With glad violence, she repeatedly dunks my shirt, beats it against a rock, scrubs it with a coarse brush, twists it into a tight coil, and wrings out the coil inch by inch. The cloth is nearly dry when she hangs it on the line. She smiles at me and gestures to the bucket. I imitate her with slow awkwardness. She presses the back of her hand against my cheek.

Suriya walks over and holds her mother around the waist. "She teaches you to be a good Sri Lankan girl," Suriya says.

"She can try," I say. I used to participate in psychology experiments to make an easy fifty bucks. The questionnaires asked me to rate from zero to ten how strongly I identified with certain feelings, such as *Think frequently about how I look* or *Feel certain that other people are talking about me behind my back.* I always circled ten for *Believe I should be punished for my sins.* I am the voracious girl in the legend that mothers tell as a warning to their daughters.

To be good is to bear repetition and dissatisfaction without complaint, or only inner ones that affect no one but yourself.

Ayya runs toward us, dips his hands in the dirty water, flicks it on his sister, bounds away, shrieking, "Iyeeeee!" Suriya shouts after him and shakes her fist. Still smiling, Amma walks toward the kitchen. Her equanimity feels like a shield or reproach. It reminds me unpleasantly of Brian's family, the implicit pressure to maintain a state of perfectly reasonable happiness. My eyes reach for Suriya's. "Has Ayya ever told you anything about being in the war?" I ask, wanting to pierce the bubble of equanimity. "The kinds of things he saw or did?"

"Oh no. He does not tell me that. That is like code. Secret code for soldiers."

"I'm sure your brother is a good soldier. But not all the soldiers are good. I heard a lot of things from Tamil people while I was traveling—that thousands of innocent people were killed and tortured and raped and lost their homes at the end of the war. And even now they have very little freedom."

Suriya takes a skirt from the bucket and beats it against a rock. "Why do you not ask Ayya these things?"

"He doesn't speak English, does he?"

With subtle sarcasm, Suriya widens her eyes and points to her enormous English binder. "Of course. You can translate," I say, more nervous than relieved. Suriya calls out for her brother. He emerges from the kitchen, eating a banana. My throat grows dry as he approaches. I haven't spoken to him since I told him to get lost last night. "I'm sorry—" I begin, but Suriya shakes her head no and addresses Ayya in Sinhala. "I explain it is my fault you are confused in the night," she says. "Do not worry for that."

I offer Ayya a wide, close-lipped smile, the same one I used to give the camera when I was a child, doing my best imitation of an acceptable photographic face. But now the very desire to be genuine makes me come across as aloof. Suriya explains to Ayya that I have traveled in Jaffna and am sad for the Tamil people. Ayya meets my eyes. His voice is tight and matter-of-fact. I should not feel bad for the Tamils. They are so rich. So many Tamils are living abroad and sending money back. They are luckier than the Sinhala people.

"There are only Tamils living abroad because they've been displaced," I say. "A lot of people lost their homes or had to escape from the fighting. I heard about one man who swam all the way to India."

Ayya believes that I met some kind people in Jaffna—caught up in my argument, I don't register how well Suriya is translating— but the Tamils are not all kind. Can he tell me a story? He takes Suriya's chair and speaks for several minutes, the English binder in his lap. Suriya stands nearby, watching him closely. She looks at the ground when he falls silent, her face muddled. "This is hard to explain," she says. "There is a girl in Jaffna when my brother was there. Twelve years old, thirteen, like that. She is the daughter of the man who has a good restaurant. Favorite restaurant of the soldiers." This girl is kind and speaks Sinhala well. The soldiers have to communicate with most Tamil people in English. They are impressed that this young girl knows Sinhala so well and enjoy talking to her. One of Ayya's friends wants to teach her to write Sinhala characters. So they sit together sometimes after lunch and practice writing in a notebook. One day Ayya and his friend go to the restaurant to take their lunch and there is a new family there. Slowly, the soldiers learn what has happened to this girl. Some people in her village started talking about her, saying she has a Sinhala boyfriend. Of course she is not supposed to have a boyfriend at all until she marries. And to have a Sinhala one is very, very bad. The people in the village say that the girl is so upset by what people are thinking of her that she committed suicide. But Ayya doesn't believe. The story is that the girl took off all her clothes and tied herself to a tree and set herself on fire. That seems not even possible. Ayya believes the men in the village raped her and burned her alive. Suriya's voice is quiet, coaxing the unwilling words to leave her throat.

"I'm sorry," I say, without knowing why. Does it help anyone for me to know these things? For Suriya to know these things?

"But is it possible—weren't a lot of the Sri Lankan soldiers raping Tamil girls?" My voice is small, embarrassed by the words, the pretension that this story has any use as a political lesson. It takes Suriya a long time to explain Ayya's response. She keeps pausing, searching even for words she knows well. Most soldiers would not hurt a woman. There are only some bad soldiers, yes, who use the women. But the Tamil men do the same. Ayya heard of one girl, she was raped by a soldier. That is very bad, yes. But Ayya says something happened to her even worse. Men in her village learn she has been raped and so they raped her too. More than one hundred men. Because she is already ruined. That is how the men think.

Ayya traces circles in the dirt with his big toe while Suriya speaks. I have an urge to stamp out the delicacy of the motion, make him look at me. What is it that we were supposed to be arguing about? "Did you know these stories?" I ask Suriya.

"Stories like this, yes. We all hear bad things from Jaffna during wartime. But we must not think on these things."

A young father I spoke to in Jaffna told me he didn't care whether the Sinhalese soldiers or the Tamil Tigers ruled in Jaffna—"Fifty-fifty badness," he called it—so long as there was no more fighting. He mentioned some videos on the Internet of Tamil prisoners being tortured, which he assumed some good soldier had posted as a kind of anonymous protest. The father hoped these videos would be destroyed, that the war crimes would be forgotten. "These things just make Tamils want to fight. And we cannot fight. We will not win." Running around researching an article I believed would open Americans' eyes to Tamil oppression, I heard the comment as pathetic, the words of someone who has been cowed into silence. Now I have no way to interpret it, no sense of the words beyond the literal.

Ayya tosses his banana peel into the bamboo grove and begins walking toward the house. "Thank you for speaking with me," I try to call after him, but my voice stays close to my chest.

I spend the rest of the day on my translation, plowing through two chapters with little thought to their meaning.

That evening, Suriya suggests the three of us go to a nearby temple to make a water offering. We fill up small plastic bowls from the tap at the entrance and carry them in cupped hands while we walk in circles around the Buddha statue in the courtyard. "Eight circles," Suriya says. "Lord Buddha's magic number." It feels silly to be counting laps with this plastic bowl of tap water, but then pirith begins playing from inside the small temple—a long, one-story structure that looks more like a stable than a house of worship. A monk walks into the courtyard and stands still with his hands clasped behind his back, watching us or the sunset or both. Hard to believe it was the monks who agitated the most for violence against the Tamils, sometimes even leading mobs in ransacking businesses or putting kerosene-doused tires around Tamils' necks and setting them on fire. Please stop. Just focus on one real, immediate thing. Smooth, warm tiles meet the soles of my feet. There is nothing damaging about this activity, no reason to hold myself aloof and analytical.

On the ride home, a flash of light behind the clouds turns the sky into a sheet of pale pink construction paper stenciled with elaborate branches. "Oh," Suriya murmurs behind me. Heat lightning. A wall of rain moves across the field toward our bike. We are soaked to the skin. Ayya drives slowly the rest of the way home. Rain eclipses our senses. Impossible to worry about the state of the world when you are moving through black, dense water on a vehicle over which you have no control.

Suriya's house is dark and silent. Her father is sleeping and her mother is at an Ayurvedic hospital to get medicine for the health problem that Suriya has explained to me only by pointing to her chest. She flicks a light switch in the kitchen. "Have not current." She tries to open the tap on the side of the house. "Have not water." Her voice is mischievous and happy. She is freed from cooking and cleaning. Nothing to do but lie on our beds inside the watery air.

"I feel happy with the dark," Suriya says. On the street, a man makes a kissing noise, the sound men use to attract each other's attention.

"It's peaceful, yes." I stretch out on the bed as Suriya begins her ritual hair brushing. "Nangi," I say, "you were never hoping that Ayya and I—you know . . ."

I wait for her to absolve me of the need to go further. "Please explain, El," she says, putting down her brush.

"Were you ever hoping that Ayya and I would get married?"

She rests her hairbrush on her knee, looking so stunned I'm almost offended. "No, no, El. To Ayya, you are Akki. Big sister. American sister."

"Oh, good. I only want to be his American sister."

Suriya resumes tenderizing her hair. "And Ayya is not looking for wife now. He is too sad. He had a girlfriend for some years. He loves her more. But this girl marries another boy while Ayya is away. I told him when he comes home to visit. Oh, Akki, he cried more." I can't bring myself to correct Suriya's emphatic misuse of "more"; it sounds so grave and endless.

Suriya does her best not to ever cry, because if she starts she cannot stop. When I ask how she manages not to cry when hard things happen in her life all the time, she says, "Patience and activeness."

"You are very smart. But I do think it's all right to cry from time to time." I hear a song my mother used to play for me when I was four or five, sometimes singing along in a manner that came across as unhinged and desperate even to a child. *It's all right to cry . . . Raindrops from your eyes. It's gonna make you feel better!* I was already well aware that tears were acceptable in my family, given how many times I walked into the living room and found my mother lying on the rug with cucumbers over her eyes and a mound of used tissues beside her, blasting Joni Mitchell, in the dry-heaves stage of a long weeping. Or watched my father emerge from the bedroom at noon, eyes red, face slack. There is such a thing as being too permissive with the expression of emotions.

I reach out and touch Suriya's knee. "Nangi, tell me about your mother's illness. Is she going to be okay?"

Suriya shakes her head and looks into her lap. "I must not talk about that. I only pray."

My brain knows this is a sad thing to say. But instead of compassion, I feel defensive and irritated, as if listening to someone complain about something she has no right to be upset about. Suriya's mom might die, I say to myself, scoldingly. But the appropriate feeling does not come.

We swim in the lake most evenings. Sometimes a teenage boy who lost his legs to a land mine bathes with us. His father pushes him to the lake's edge in his wheelchair and then carries him into the soapy shallows, holding him under the armpits as the boy lathers his face and chest. Once, as we drop our sandals and towels on the sand, we see the boy floating on his back, his father's palms supporting him underwater. The boy's closed eyes and upturned lips and sinewy arms stretched wide halt us. "Oh," Suriya murmurs, intertwining her thin fingers with mine.

Ayya will go back to his sentry point in Colombo in two days. This fact rudely alerts me to the passage of time, something I do my best not to keep track of. I've been with Suriya for more than a month, the length of time I was hoping it would take me to complete my translation. Five long chapters remain. I need to find a quiet hostel somewhere, sequester myself, and do nothing but work. But first Ayya and Suriya are eager to take me to a festival that is coming to their village. It will be Ayya's last day of fun before he goes back to work. And Suriya has had so many chores and she fears that her chores became my chores. But tomorrow we will go to a festival and have fun!

She spends an hour braiding her hair with the help of a plastic pocket mirror on the big day, undoing and redoing every strand that betrays the minutest of bumps. Ayya's motorbike delivers us to a large swath of shadeless sand, imprinted with the crosshatched trails of ice cream carts and the footprints of barefoot kids. Intercoms blare aggressive male voices. Ayya abandons us to join a group of boys who are trying to climb a statue covered in grease, atop of which is a small box that Suriya tells me is filled with money. The boys' faces flush crimson as they cling to crevices in the stone man's giant body—the crook of his bent arm, a fold in his robe. They grimace and curse as their fingers slide downward. Those who make it up highest shove at their competitors, some laughing, some horribly serious, punching as if to kill. Ayya is one of the serious boys. He runs and hurls himself as high up the statue as he can, never pausing long enough to let his fingers lose their grip, keeping his gaze fixed on the box atop the statue. He avoids the other boys unless they go for him, and then he is ruthless. When he shoves a younger boy in the forehead, the boy's neck snaps back as he falls. I cry out as he lands on his butt with his hands behind him. But he raises his fist in the air and shouts at Ayya, grinning.

"Ayya is so strong. Sometime it makes me afraid to see that," Suriya says. "He wants the money for my family. I hope he will get it."

"I hope he lives. This seems dangerous."

"Very danger, yes. Boys have crazy games. You want to see the lady games?" She leads me to a group of women furiously weaving palm fronds into large, tight squares, sweating, grimacing, licking their lips. A fat woman in a white cotton dress finishes first, shoots her hand into the air. A man blows into a whistle. He inspects her work, pulling at the corners, turning it over to check for holes in the weave. The woman stands aside, panting, beaming, hands on hips, chin high. Her pride breaks my heart. Condescension, yes, but the sorrow is real. All I can know of this woman's life is what I can imagine.

"You need ice cream?" Suriya asks me.

"No, thanks. I'm not hungry."

"Small one," she says, and orders vanilla cones from the metal box passing by. She allows me to pay. We stand still, licking balls of sugary ice atop cardboardy cones.

A group of boys walks past, holding hands in a tight chain, whispering. "Boys from my school," Suriya says.

"Hello," I say, loud, bright, hoping to make a good impression for Suriya.

"Hello," one of the boys mocks me. "Hello, hello," the others echo, loud, bright. They skirt away, cackling.

"Stupid boys," Suriya says. "I think this festival is boring for you."

"Is it boring for you?"

"Yes." She laughs. "I did not know the festival is boring until I bring—bringed—

"Brought."

"Thank you, El. Until I brought you here. There are some rides."

"I love rides!" This is true, but mostly I want Suriya to believe we are having the good time she needed us to have.

The Ferris wheel is powered by teenage boys in flip-flops and blue jeans, who run around like hamsters on a wheel, jumping into the air to grip the metal spokes and pull the giant wheel down to earth, then heaving themselves up and over the bar just before it skirts the ground, riding the spoke to the top, then dangling to pull the tiny cars filled with shrieking families earthward once again, jumping to the ground, grabbing a new spoke, beginning again, cheering one another on, moving faster and faster. A girl of about twelve or thirteen is crying when she gets off, gripping her father's hand and wailing without apology.

Our turn. I shriek as we whoosh toward the ground. Suriya crushes my hand in hers. At the top, we can see the whole sandy field, crawling with crude human colors and noises and bodies. We spin around and around, propelled by skinny boys in sandals.

When the ride ends, Suriya leads me to a tall, cylindrical tower. I give a man two hundred rupees and we climb a staircase about twice as high as the Ferris wheel. At the top is a doughnut-shaped platform; in the center, a hole with plywood walls; at the bottom of the hole, a man and a motorbike. "What will happen?" I ask Suriya.

The man will ride his motorbike to the top. The plywood walls are perpendicular to the ground. The man looks up at the people crowded around the fence at the top of the hole. His face is a blur. He starts clapping his hands, loud and slow at first, then fast, hard, frantic, psyching himself up to risk his life for a few dollars. I grow nervous and hateful of fairs, spectacles, people crammed into small spaces, trying to have fun. "I don't want to see this," I say. But the platform is packed with spectators whistling and clapping, peering over the fence around the top of the hole, watching the man mount his bike. He revs the engine twice, three times, four times. How is it even physically possible to scale these walls with that heavy machine? I'm sickened that my money has supported this wasteful risk.

He starts riding circles on the ground, building speed, taking the walls with his front tire and then crashing back to earth. He rides around the bottom for so long that the crowd jeers. At last, the bike grips the wall and keeps going, making a blurred circle of the man's body, his head a child's toy top in the center of the hole. No helmet. He stays low, a few feet off the ground, until the crowd once again taunts and whistles. In a nasty act of the will, he shoots all the way to the top of the fence. Suriya grabs my hand. A teenage girl cries out. Her boyfriend puts his arm over her shoulder and laughs. The man on the motorbike spins and spins below our transfixed faces, moving so fast he has to raise himself up on his legs and grip the hateful machine between his thighs, the wind pushing his lips out in a gummy rectangle around his gritted teeth. His eyes are huge and unblinking. No thoughts—just action, will, wordless prayer. How will he get back to earth, three stories below? He begins spiraling downward, slowing with each revolution. His body knows the exact speed that will maintain friction, yet give him enough time to slam on the brakes when his tires touch ground again, stopping just short of the opposite wall, just short of toppling this entire makeshift structure, killing us all. He dismounts and raises a hand in the air, looking at the ground. We clap. People toss bills and coins into the hole. A grinning father holds his toddler over the abyss. The child's small hand releases a fifty-rupee note. It takes the money a long time to float to the sand below.

"Do you like, El?" Suriya asks, which is when I realize that my jaw is clenched, my sphincter contracted heart-ward. "It made me scared," I say. "People should not risk their life for a trick." As if I know what people should do.

"Let's leave this place," Suriya says. But when we try to make our way to the stairs we are pushed back by an opposing force. The stairs are packed with families, talking, shoving. Suriya learns that a woman rider is up next. People are thrilled to see a lady risk her life on a motorbike. Suriya and I are mashed against the back rim of the platform, along with fathers holding children on their shoulders. A young man at the front of the crowd points to me and beckons, inviting the sudhu to join him at the edge of the hole. "Come and see, come and see." I turn away. Menacing words blare out of loudspeakers. The crowd settles and quiets.

A wail pierces the hush. At the base of the stairs leading up to the platform, a small boy is shrieking and beating the thighs of the ticket collector, who blocks the stairs with his wide stance. "Poor boy," Suriya says. "There is no room for him." But then a couple comes by and hands the ticket collector a bill. As he moves aside to let the customers pass, the little boy ducks under his arm and bounds up the stairs. He reaches the top just as the crowd starts clapping and cheering.

The woman rider—chunky and short, wearing a solid maroon salwar kameez—has entered the arena. The boy resumes wailing, pushing his way through the crowd. "Amma," he shrieks, "Amma."

"My god," Suriya says. "That is the son of the woman on the motorbike."

Strangers reach out to him, murmur gently, or grin and offer to lift him, probably drunk and glad to be involved in anything that seems to matter at all. The boy slaps the hands away, pushing to the front of the platform as the woman below revs the engine. His eyes are red slits. Suriya moans quietly. "I have fear for that boy." I grip her hand. How stupid this drama is. I could pay that woman right now more than she'll make for this stunt, spare her son this terror.

The woman rides circles around the perimeter of the sandy hole, speeding up much more quickly than the man before her. Within a minute, she is suspended from a machine whose tires grip a vertical surface, churning the woman in circles so fast I get dizzy watching. The boy is silent now at the front of the platform, gripping the top of the fence. I can't see his face, just the skin stretched taut over his knuckles, his greasy brown hair smoothed down the back of his head. A woman next to him murmurs and tries to remove his hands from the flimsy barricade, tries to lift him up. He grips and stares. The woman doesn't want to miss the show, either, and gasps with the rest of us as the rider traces a large figure eight across the walls, zooming down dangerously close to the ground, reversing direction at the last second and speeding upward until her front tire is inches from the spectators' waists. She is wearing a helmet. Scant reassurance. Her body is alarmingly calm. She doesn't grip the machine with her legs as the man did. She moves too casually, almost pausing at the end of each of her trips earthward. On one of her trips up, she stops just below the little boy. "Amma!" he cries. She cranes her neck back to see his face. Her front tires leave the wall. She returns her eyes to the bike, revs, revs, revs. Too late. The tires paw the air. She seems poised for a long moment before gravity takes her. I lose sight of her before she hits the ground. The thud is not as loud as it should be.

Her son shrieks and leans out over the tower. A man behind him grabs his T-shirt and swoops him up. The boy kicks and punches until the man passes him to another stranger, all talking, all trying to get at the boy or get off the platform. Suriya juts her hand in the air and repeats a loud, clear sentence until a pathway clears for her. She kneels before the wailing boy, then takes his

hand and leads him toward the stairs. Does she know him? I follow a few paces behind. The crowd is thick. I have to wait for
minutes like years on each step before moving to the lower one. I
lose sight of Suriya. It doesn't matter. Nothing I do matters at all.

At the base of the stairs, Suriya is speaking to the ticket collector, still clutching his tickets in one hand, the other hand empty,
open, resting on the banister. If I don't move, the hands are thinking, I will not exist. If I stay very still, waiting, something else will
happen. The door to the arena is opened. A clot of men with their
hands in their pockets, one of them silently weeping, obscures the
view of the mother. Suriya feels me beside her, turns. Her face is
soft, contourless, merging with the sweet, greasy air, as if she has
abandoned herself in order to be present inside this hell. "I do not
know this boy, but I tell the people I am his auntie," she whispers, answering the questions I cannot formulate. "He needs one
grown-up, not all the grown-ups."

She lifts the boy on her hip and moves toward the open door of
the plywood hole. No longer crying, close enough to his mother to
see her, the boy becomes afraid and burrows into Suriya's shoulder.
I don't want to see, either. A man emerges from the crowd as we
approach and gestures Suriya back outside. They whisper. Suriya
addresses the boy, beams, jostles his leg. "Mother is alive," she tells
me. "But she is not awake. We do not want the boy to see her and
believe she is dead."

"That's great," I say, barely registering my own idiocy.

For a long time, nothing seems to change. Then a white truck
approaches, honking its way across the sand, scattering the frozen onlookers. It parks just outside the arena. Men—no, these
are boys—jump out of the truck, open its back doors, pull out a
stretcher. Everyone begins moving at once then—the crowd on the
stairs surging downward, the people on the outskirts of the field
closing in around the tower. And here is Ayya, pale, out of breath,

nodding harshly in response to Suriya's questions. He begins walking away from the tower, against the crowd closing in. Suriya follows him. I follow Suriya. She murmurs something to the little boy. A friend of Ayya's will drive us to the hospital in his truck. Why are we at the center of this drama? How does Suriya know exactly what to do?

We wedge ourselves onto the front seat of the truck, my thigh mashed against Suriya's, the boy's weight shared between us. His leg pours heat into mine. He's probably about five. His hair smells like fried food, not unpleasantly. I have the urge to wrap my arm around his waist, cuddle him to me. But I make myself follow Suriya's example: committed but distant.

The hospital is a sunny building with open-air corridors and stairs that wrap around the outside of cavernous rooms. The waiting area is made of stone, one wall open to the bright, smoggy air outside. A young woman brings us tea and cookies on a plastic tray. The boy looks away from the food. Suriya presses cookies on me. They taste good. I reach for another. Suriya tries to play with the boy, hiding behind the chair and hoping he'll find her, pointing at me and saying, "America" and "New York." He watches Suriya closely, expressionless.

Sometime later, a middle-age doctor with reassuringly severe cheekbones joins us. Suriya hops up and smooths back her hair. "The mother is okay," Suriya tells me after the doctor leaves. "Broken hip and broken leg. But her head is okay because she dressed a helmet." This seems like a miracle to me, and I tell Suriya so. "Lord Buddha helped her," she says. "So she can take care for her child." The boy's body is light and motile now. He hops from one foot to the next, biting down on his thumbs.

Now that he has relaxed, Suriya kneels down and asks him serious questions. He answers seriously: "Rajith. Ha. Ne. Ha. Ha. Ne." Rajith is six years old. His father is a bus driver so he is not at home very much. An auntie in his village takes care of him when his mum is busy, so he can stay with her while his mother recovers in the hospital. "We must visit him in his auntie's home," Suriya says to me. "He will be sad without his amma."

Suriya does not lie awake at night wondering whether or not her life has a purpose.

The boy peers out a window, turns his head side to side, sings. Suriya translates his song for me: "Trucks trucks TRUCKS trucks trucks TRUCKS . . ."

After we have a meal in town, we are permitted to see Rajith's mother. Suriya and I stand outside, letting Rajith enter alone. The sounds of their reunion are stifled and unsatisfying—a surfeit of feeling trapped in timidity and weakness. A doctor pokes her head out the door and gestures us in with aggressive hand movements. Rajith's mother is prone on a stretcher, her right leg in a cast from toes to hip. Rajith kneels at the top of the bed, leaning over his mother's face, pointing to Suriya and me, bouncing lightly on his bent calves. "She must not sit up," Suriya tells me, "so we must come near to her face."

We stand over her. Her eyes look queerly small and bewildered, just as they did before the motorbike lost its grip on the wall. She stares at us, unblinking, then turns to her son, says a short sentence about the sudhu. Rajith lowers himself off the bed—slowly, slowly, lest he disturb his mother. He kneels in front of me and touches my feet. "He worships you because you help to save his mum," Suriya says.

"But it was you who helped. I didn't do anything." I would never get involved in a stranger's problem. I might cry over it, but I would not take action. I stare at my clasped hands.

"Yes, you helped, El," Suriya says. "Rajith waits for you to touch his head." I smooth my hand over his head just so that he'll stand up, worship Suriya too, return to his mother's side. But the doctors are standing before me now as well, thanking me again and again in English. "You are the hero of today," one of them says, long spaces between each of her words.

"Suriya did everything," I say. "I didn't do anything. Suriya deserves the praise, not me." But they don't understand me and Suriya is content to stand silently beside the American witness to her goodness.

Before we leave, she writes down Rajith's address and mobile number. Rajith will stay at the hospital with his mother tonight. In the morning, he will go back to his village to stay with his neighbor until his father comes back from work or his mother gets out of the hospital. "Rajith will be all alone," Suriya says. "So I promise that we will visit him and play."

Only once we're on the bus back to Suriya's house does she voice the thought that's been a wordless hum in my head all day, one I've been struggling not to hear. "A mother must not have a danger job. A mother must stay with her child in the home."

Even Suriya sleeps late the next morning. I'm awake when she rolls up her mat and begins sweeping, but I keep my eyes shut until she leaves the room. I need aloneness. The day has the obligatory tone of a winter morning in New York, I don't know why. It's as if I were standing for a long time with my hand on the doorknob before heading out to work my shift at the bookstore. Wind, people, cars, bikes, rats, ice, trains, hats, horns, beggars, trash, millions of tiny

movements required to get from A to B and back again; no reasons, just thoughts and steps, thoughts and steps. I have to wait for
the oddly conflicting strands of my personality to braid into a generic staunchness—weary, then stiff. I have become a part, apart.
A breeze crests the windowsill and I lift my sticky shirt up to my
collarbone. I long for Jared, as I always do when I feel this way—
the strength of his desires steamrolling the productive world, his
loud commitment to squashing immediate suffering by any means
at hand, even those that will make him suffer more later.

I don't want to be a part of Suriya's world anymore, this village where the only action available to me is to eat food prepared
by poor people. I need to get to a computer—see if the publisher
wrote me back, look up other publishers if she didn't, write to
Jared, plan my next move. But I cannot leave without some gesture
of real thanks.

I find Suriya sweeping the dirt yard, making a pile of dead
leaves and trash. "I've been thinking," I say, "that it's getting to be
time for me to leave. Travel around a bit and then head back to the
U.S."

Suriya rubs her lips together, distracting her mouth from forming unbecoming sounds. "Oh, El, but you can wait to go back to
Kandy with me, no? My school starts in two weeks only. We can
go back together then, okay?"

Giving a set quantity of time to these days of being nothing but
an American witness to Suriya's life of chores and worship panics
me. I have to do something.

"I thought maybe you'd like to travel with me, before I go
back." Suriya looks at me hard, her lips downturned. "I'll take you
on vacation."

"I take vacation with you?"

"Sure. Why not? You want to stay at a fancy hotel and swim in
a pool and meet lots of Europeans?"

Suriya grins, eyebrows raised. "I will take a vacation in my own country!"

"Yes, I will take you. Let's get your things together. You don't need much. I can lend you clothes. Or we can buy you new ones." I'm holding her hands, bending my knees as if preparing to jump, as if it's the scene in the musical where the crippled boy learns to walk or the prostitute finds true love and gives up the smack and finds a cure for AIDS.

Suriya drops my hand and looks toward the kitchen. "We need to bring food for our trip. How will we take our meals?"

I take my toothbrush off the ledge of the water tank. "At restaurants. I'll pay. You won't have to cook." I spit toothpaste into the cakey dirt. "Your father will let you go, right? You'll only be gone a few days."

Suriya's father is snoring on a cot in the room of rats and abandoned clothes. "Just tell Ayya," I whisper to her. Ayya is in his room, staring into a half-filled duffel bag open on his bed. I stand beside Suriya while she explains our plan, adding encouraging phrases now and then—"So much practice with English!" "Very nice hotel!" Ayya looks from Suriya's face to mine. "Go with your friend," he says in English, adding Sinhala that Suriya translates for me: Do not worry for our father. I will make him not be angry. Have fun.

Suriya puts a couple of skirts and T-shirts in a bag. "This one, El? Or maybe the blue is better?"

"The blue one," I say without looking, wanting to get on the road before her father wakes up, giddy now that I'm finally making something happen.

She stands in the center of the room, sighing and serious in the way of a final goodbye. What exactly does she believe I'm offering her? "El Akki?" she says. "I promised Rajith we would visit today. He will be lonely without his mother."

"Let's take him with us! By the time we get back, his mom will be better."

Suriya laughs. "You are serious?"

She makes a pot of rice and prepares three plates for her father—food she made for breakfast this morning and dinner last night. She leaves the day's meals in a neat row on the table, covered by a plastic dome to keep the flies away. Although I insist it's unnecessary, she wraps up a couple of leftover curries to take with us, in case we get hungry on the bus. She splashes water from the tin jug onto the food-spattered kitchen floor. The water breaks into tiny beads as it hits concrete.

Rajith's home is a one-room cube with an old sari for a front door. Suriya calls out. No one comes. We peer inside. Dusty floor. A table topped by plastic bowls abuzz with flies, drunk on the stench of congealed coconut milk and rotting vegetables. Suriya calls out again. A woman responds from the yard. She wears a long skirt and faded sari blouse, holds a baby in one arm and Rajith's hand in the other. Rajith points at us, his eyes wide, his hoarse voice urgent.

The woman smiles and draws near. Suriya holds out her hands and takes the baby, who starts crying as soon as his mama releases him. Suriya bounces him forcefully until he quiets. She is so much more confident than I am. Still bouncing, she explains why we've come. The woman steps back, stares hard, asks a question full of doubt. Suriya insists. The woman laughs and claps her hands together. She addresses Rajith, who nods his head with dangerous vigor.

THE ROYAL RESORT

Suriya chooses our lodging. I ask if there's anywhere she's ever wanted to visit and she names a fancy hotel a few towns away, pronouncing the word as if it's a disagreeable question. I look it up in my guidebook: a resort and spa in the mountains, seemingly the only tourist attraction in the area. The rooms are six times the price I'd pay for myself. But this is a gift.

At sunset a bus deposits us at the base of a primitive mountain road. Barefoot children and hunched elderly women with broken teeth mill around a small sign advertising THE ROYAL RESORT in pink cursive, their palms extended. A tuk-tuk driver pulls up in front of me and gestures to the back of his car. "Royal Resort, yes, madam? Come, madam." He looks disappointed when Suriya crowds into the back with me, Rajith on her lap. "Keeyada?" she asks. He answers sullenly, forced to give the local price.

We crawl up the stony mountainside, listing from side to side to avoid the largest troughs and spikiest rocks. Rajith beats his hand on his lap, thumpety-thump-thump. Suriya watches the orange sky rushing over billions of sea-green tea leaves, her back straight and lips pursed, affecting an air of sophistication that makes me nervous. I purposefully fall into Rajith at the largest bumps, making him laugh, trying to put Suriya at ease.

The hotel entrance is a white arbor encircled by tiny, aggressive jasmine flowers. While I pay the tuk-tuk driver, Suriya takes out her handkerchief and pocket mirror, dabs her face, smooths back her hair. Her real self and her reflection compete for solemnity. As we walk into the lobby, brown bodies buttoned into white uniforms pause to look at us, then hurry on, unsure how to address our unusual trio. The man behind the desk looks only at me as I book a double room.

A Sri Lankan woman with enormous eyes and breasts takes us up. Suriya grips Rajith's hand as we step inside the elevator, whispering fiercely. "They are your friends?" the pretty hotel clerk asks me just before she leaves us. I wish Suriya would answer in Sinhala, but she just stands still and serious, waiting to be identified.

"Yes." My voice is loud and ugly, feigning comfort. "They are my friends."

Once we're alone in our room, Suriya begins to relax. She sits on the edge of the bed and bounces the mattress, looks out the window at the now purpled sky and darkening hills below. "Wow, El," she says. "Wow." Rajith burrows under the covers headfirst. Suriya tickles his feet, resting on the pillow, ankles splayed. Then she makes him get up and scrub his feet in the bathroom. She removes the case his feet touched and fluffs the pillow. Clean-toed, Rajith returns to his den and giggles from under the covers. I ask Suriya if she would like to take a bath before dinner.

"Sit in that bowl of water?"

"Yes. Hot water."

"No, Akki. That is not necessary." But she spends a long time getting ready. She leaves the bathroom door open at first, knotting a towel around her chest like a sarong. "I'll take care of Rajith," I say. "You can have privacy." I pull the door closed before she can protest.

I lift up the covers from the foot of the bed where Rajith is burrowed and—peekaboo! He laughs. Suriya turns on the shower. I feel agreeably new to myself—motherly, accommodating—as the minutes pass and Suriya remains alone in a room with a closed door, naked, a continuous stream of hot water raining down on her, steam to draw out her private thoughts, enough time and space for the thoughts to exist without scrutiny. A few Sinhala words interrupt the white noise of falling water—soft words caressing and dissolving. Or so I want them to be. Words like rose petals melting on Suriya's eyelids. I feel so good.

Rajith chatters away on the walk to the hotel restaurant but grows shy once we step inside the enormous room. Plastic gargoyles menace the diners from its four high corners. Rajith reaches his arms up to Suriya, but she refuses to carry him, takes his hand instead. I lead us to a table near the buffet. Suriya stands behind her chair, staring at the place settings, stricken. One large plate surrounded by cutlery: two knives, two forks, two spoons. "El," she whispers. "I cannot eat with a fork."

"Why would you? We're in your country." But as we fill our plates at the buffet, I notice that even the Sri Lankan families— men in ties, children in bejeweled salwar kameez and kurtas—are eating with utensils. So what. Who cares what people think? We are here to have fun, to be free. I speak these words aloud as we settle back at our table, my voice sharp and clear, as if I'm addressing the whole room, making a statement. About what? For whose benefit?

Rajith digs in first, loudly crumbling his papadum over his goat curry, mashing it into balls and shoveling the balls down. Suriya pours us water from the pitcher at the table with absurd care, back erect, forehead clenched. The water falls in a frustrated trickle. I must eat with my hands to put her at ease. But my fingers remain poised over my plate, refusing to dirty themselves in this room of Western eaters. I can't help myself, I'm hungry, this meal will probably cost me more than all of my previous Sri Lankan meals combined. I pick up my fork and mix the aubergine and fried bitter gourd with moist, spicy sambhol. Yum. Suriya takes the large spoon, wipes it across her plate until it's full, opens her mouth so wide I can see her tonsils, ducks her chin down to her plate, closes her mouth around the spoon, swallows with the utensil still in her mouth. Pitying, embarrassed, made thoughtless by discomfort, I take the forkful of food I'm about to consume and dump it into my other hand, then pop the handful into my mouth. Suriya watches my hands and mouth in astonishment. With a small sigh, she picks up her own fork and also begins using it as a miniature shovel. My movements grow mechanical and frenzied. Fork, hand, mouth, repeat, fork, hand, mouth, repeat. Suriya's forehead is dotted with sweat as she tries to keep up with me. I had wanted so much to give her a decadent, relaxing meal. Now I just want this awkwardness to end as quickly as possible.

Rajith watches us and laughs. He begins using all three pieces of cutlery at once, dumping food from his spoon onto his knife and catapulting the knife toward his open mouth, spraying coconut milk and goat bits. A waiter approaches to ask if we'd like anything to drink. I have a fork in one hand and a palmful of curry in the other. Food coats my chin. "I would love a Coca-Cola, thank you." I hate soda and have never ordered a Coke in my life. "Suriya? Rajith?" I ask brightly. "Yes, please," Suriya says, rice kernels coating her large, purple lips, green sauce dripping from her chin.

"Coca-Colas for everyone," I say.

"Yes, madam." The waiter—teenaged, pimpled, self-consciously tall—hurries away. When he returns with our Cokes on a plastic tray covered in flaking gold paint, Suriya sits up straighter and enacts my ridiculous amalgam of eating techniques with painstaking care.

A long, unabashed laugh enlivens the dining room. Several waiters are crowded in the doorway to the kitchen, staring at our table. One is doubled over with loud guffaws. Another shushes him, just as loudly, staring and grinning. Rajith is beside himself with delight, plowing his food into a mound at the center of his plate, mashing it down with a thwack of his spoon, giggling, shoving handfuls into his mouth, destroying and rebuilding his mountain of fancy curries. The waiter stands erect over us. Would madam care for anything more?

I would not, thank you, please just charge the meal to my room. Suriya's face is tight and red, as if she's not breathing. She commands Rajith harshly and wipes her face with her napkin. "Why are we eating in this manner, El?" she asks.

"Because I got confused." I'm not used to being the madam, to charging meals to my room. I wouldn't know how to behave even if I were alone. "I'm so sorry."

We don't speak on the walk back to our room. Suriya scrubs Rajith's face with a washcloth, his eyes falling shut then snapping open. She carries him to bed and curls up next to him, not even brushing her hair. I want her to sleep with me, her purple pajama pants and loud, slow breaths reassurance that she is okay, still herself in this strange place. "You can sleep alone if you like," I say. "I'm happy to share with Rajith."

"No, no, El," she murmurs. "The bed is good. Comfortable fun for my body."

I apologize again for the mess I made of dinner.

"Do not worry for that, Akki." Her voice sinks into the short, sweet pause of sleep.

Room service for breakfast the next morning: a large basket whose contents—jam and bread—seem to disappoint Rajith. No matter. The swimming pool will fix that. I offer to lend Suriya a bathing suit but she looks at me like I've lost my mind. She does ask shyly if she can wear my running shorts on the bottom, instead of the knee-length pleated skirt she normally swims in. "Wow," she says to her mostly bare legs in the mirror. "I dress like this in my room sometime but never outside before." She cups her knees and swings them side to side, examining her thighs from all angles. Legs of such a beautiful shape and color that I have a pang of absurd envy: No one will ever see her legs except her husband.

I have to keep myself from breaking into a run as we approach the pool, whose far end spills over the edge of a cliff overlooking endless hills of tea leaves, lapping at each other, folding in on themselves, bursting out in exuberant summits. The sky is barely blue, barely there at all—emptiness, space. "Oh," I say. "Wow," Suriya says. She remembers Rajith and grabs for his hand, lest he propel himself into the rectangle of cool water, made teal by the porcelain tiles. Long, oiled white limbs are sprawled on lounge chairs. A Sri Lankan girl in a ruffled one-piece and goggles is in the pool with her large-bellied father, who is trying to teach her the breath pattern for the crawl stroke. I ask the pool attendant—leaning back in a plastic chair, surveying the sky—for three towels.

Partly to cover my nudity, which feels grotesque beside Suriya's suggestive modesty, I walk straight to the deep end and dive in, pump my legs and arms through velvety water until I run out of breath. I beckon to Suriya and Rajith. Suriya pulls off Rajith's T-shirt, speaking excitedly. He hops from foot to foot, belly protruding, eyes big. In a rush that seems like a surge of courage, Suriya pulls off her drawstring pants, exposing the small running shorts beneath. She takes Rajith's hand and leads him to the pool stairs, pauses on the second step, smiles at the water lapping her calves. The pool attendant marches up on long, fast strides. "You must not swim with a shirt," he says. "Proper attire, please."

"It's not a shirt." The words drop out of my mouth like bricks. "It is a swim costume."

"Proper attire, please," he says.

"It is proper attire. It is a Sri Lankan swimming costume and we are in Sri Lanka." I enunciate loudly, hoping the other Sri Lankans at the pool will hear this absurd interaction and come to

Suriya's defense. But they're all wearing Western swim trunks and sleeveless bathing suits. I wait for Suriya at least to speak to the man in Sinhala, but she's already removed her feet from the water. "We did not know this rule," she tells the attendant in slow, perfect English, her arms crossed over her chest. "Thank you."

"You can borrow one of my bathing suits," I say, joining Suriya on the pool deck. "Let's just go back to the room and change."

"A bathing suit like you dress? No. Maybe in your country, I dress that. But in a place with Sri Lankans—no no no. You swim with Rajith."

But as soon as Suriya pulls her pants back on and settles on a lounge chair in the shade, Rajith walks up to her and pulls her hand. She explains, gestures toward the pool, smiles, urges. He shakes his head. She leads him forcefully to the water's edge, places his hand in mine. He looks up at me, his face waiting to know how to feel. "The water is good," I say. He probably understands some English. "Come and swim." With each step down, his grip on my hand tightens. On the last step, he stops and says, "Ne." Of course. He must not know how to swim. So we stay on the bottom stair, hopping lightly, water up to his chest. I long, shamefully, to be alone here, swimming laps, floating on my back, ordering a piña colada, stretching out in the sun and letting the contents of my mind dissipate. Soon Rajith, too, longs for something different. He walks to Suriya. They decide to go back to the room for a little while.

"Should I come with you?" I offer. "We don't need to stay at the pool."

"No, El, you stay here," Suriya says. "Enjoy your swim. We will be back soon."

Relieved and guilty, I float on my back and then stretch out on a lounge chair. A middle-aged Sri Lankan woman wearing rhinestone sunglasses approaches me. "Are you a sponsor?" she asks.

"A sponsor? Of what?"

"The young woman and her child. My husband and I were noticing you and we would like to offer our congratulations. You are so brave. We also sponsor poor children, but only in our home."

"They are my friends."

"It is so kind of you to take them here."

"Believe me, I'm no one's sponsor."

She fakes a laugh to cover her confusion and bids me a good day.

Suriya returns to the pool carrying both Rajith and the newspaper packet filled with curry that she made yesterday morning. Oh no. She cannot be planning to eat that here. "Rajith needs to take a meal," she says.

"Me too." I hurriedly pack my things. "Let's check out that café over there."

"The restaurant is so much money, El. I think it is waste. We have our food." She sounds tired. I brought her here so that she could finally rest.

"Don't worry about the money. Let me treat you. That's what a vacation is for." My voice is bright-eyed and bushy-tailed, the long-ago sound of my mother urging my father out of bed on his bad days. I take Suriya's hand and steer us to the café next to the tennis courts.

Inside are several patio tables, two of which are occupied by single men drinking beer; a chubby-faced bartender chatting with a white couple sitting on barstools and drinking an icy blue beverage out of long, bright straws; Christmas lights flashing over three rows of liquors.

"No," Suriya says, standing in the doorway.

"Hello, madam!" the bartender calls out. "Come in, please."

"Do you serve food?"

"Of course, madam, whatever you like."

"No," Suriya repeats, holding the door open, refusing to take one step inside.

"Don't you want to see the menu?"

"No."

So I follow her back out. "What is wrong with that café?"

"For my whole life, if someone asks me 'Have you been inside a bar?,' I must answer no."

"That wasn't really a bar. It was also a restaurant."

"El. There are people inside that room sitting and drinking beer. They are committing no other activity." She shakes her head, lips pursed. "I cannot eat in that place."

Rajith is growing fussy, complaining, tugging at Suriya's hand. I give up.

I follow Suriya back to the lounge chairs by the pool. She unwraps tepid two-day-old curries whose stench overpowers the wafts of chlorine and sunscreen. Rajith takes eager handfuls of Suriya's cooking. She drops a large ball of food onto her tongue and then gestures to the pool attendant with her dirty hand. "Now he will tell me I cannot eat in this place," she says. But he just watches us with the same disdain he reserved earlier for the domed, cloudless sky. I'm hungry and dig in, too. An enormous white man wearing a Speedo that sprouts long, curly, blond hairs dives into the pool. A small girl in a party dress complains to her mother in French that it's too hot outside. A hummingbird dips in and out of the arbor marking the entrance to the bathhouse. The Sri Lankan girl in goggles performs a perfect crawl stroke from one end of the pool to the other. Out of soggy newspaper, we eat handfuls of sticky red rice and fatty curries. I can't stop eating, even though my stomach contracts around each bite of the old food, grown viscous and clumpy on our travels.

~

Suriya takes a long shower again that afternoon, emerges with rouged cheeks, wearing the towel like a sarong, her knee-length black hair soaking the rug. I invite her to sit on the edge of the bed with me. Her face is open and easeful, until she sees the tightness in mine. "What is it, El?"

"I've decided that I need to travel on my own." Terrible phrasing. "I mean that I need to spend some time alone now. It's been so good to be with you here, but I just—" I pause and wait for her to help me. She stares. "I am not really good at being with people. I wanted to show you a vacation. But now I need to be alone and quiet. Go somewhere and meditate, I think. And work on my translation. My French works."

"So Rajith and I go home. No problem. Thank you for showing me a vacation. You are so kind. I understand it is difficult for you." She stands up and rummages through her bag with her back to me.

Carrying clothes folded into perfect squares, she returns to the bathroom. I watch her narrow, downy calves until they disappear behind the closed door. I actually allowed myself to believe Suriya and I were changing each other's lives. The angelic, impoverished Sri Lankan and the privileged, self-destructive American join forces and set their small worlds to rights. A heartwarming tale.

At the foot of the small mountain that supports the Royal Resort, we wait for buses going in opposite directions. Rajith is bouncy and talkative, taking my hand and telling me things I have no hope of understanding. I thought I would have time at the bus stop to properly thank Suriya for being such a good host, to explain how much her friendship means to me and how impressed I am by the way she moves through the world, tell her I'll miss her and will try to come back soon. But my bus comes right away. My skinny arms enclose her skinnier frame. Her body is hot and stiff. I step back and hold out two ten-thousand-rupee notes. "I can give you more if you need." She shakes her head side to side, takes the bills, puts them in the breast pocket of her dress, bites down on her lip. I hug her again. Her arms remain limp at her sides.

I heave my pack onto one shoulder and fumble for the other strap, feeling a pang of such emptiness that I cannot wait to be alone on the bus, just another tourist. "Nangi, please tell your brother and your parents thank you for me. And Nangi, I can't tell you how—" The bus starts to pull away. "Go, go." Suriya gestures frantically. I leap onto the bottom rung of the steps, practically shouting, "Colombo? Colombo?" An adolescent boy wearing bleached jeans and a gaudy necklace meets my eye and nods. I push my way through the thick mass of flesh in search of a place to stow my bag. The bus lurches into a pothole. I swing backward and nearly crush an infant with my pack. The mother presses the baby to her bosom, her hand clamped over its head. "Sorry, so sorry," I say. There is no Sinhala word for sorry. She looks at me steadily through narrowed eyes. I should not be traveling in her country for the equivalent of a handful of pennies. I have been blessed with birth in America. If I can afford a plane ticket to this country, it is my duty to pay for a private driver. But I'd rather stay home than watch Sri Lanka pass by through tinted glass. I don't care how many babies I have to take out in the process. No, no. I *do* hope your son's head is okay. And I'm so glad you don't know English. Or telepathy. "Sorry," I say again, aloud, sincere, heavy with the weight of myself now that Suriya is gone, now that I've sent her away.

Ducking under arms, swinging from one seat back to another, I make my way to the front of the bus and deposit my bag under the driver's seat. A young woman holding a baby and sitting beside a small boy points at me and nods her head toward the few inches of space next to her older son until I sit down. The musculature of the woman's face seems to have wasted away around its frame, displaying her gums and teeth like the plaster model of a mouth in a dentist's office. Her cheekbones press into her skin, half-moons extending from her temples to her nostrils. Her sari is tied in the Indian manner, bunched and stretched in a thin strip over her shoulder for ease in traveling. Her torso is a small, hard cylinder. The baby lies across her lap, his thick eyelashes pressed together and his tiny tongue falling to the side of his mouth. The mother couldn't be much older than twenty. She reaches into the purse sitting on her older son's lap and takes out two pieces of dull yellow candy. She hands one to the boy and the other to me. I open my mouth wide and dramatically place the candy on my tongue. The child imitates me with slow precision. The baby gurgles and paddles its feet against his mother's concave stomach. She puts him over her shoulder and pats his back, but it's too late. He is wide awake and suffering and his suffering must end now. He pulls at his mother's sari blouse, pushing his feet into her stomach and trying to scale her upper body. The mother pulls—gently, gently—his hands from her blouse buttons. She puts her index finger in his mouth. He cranes his neck back and bites down. Her eyebrows wince lazily. He spits out her finger and resumes his wail. She holds him against her chest, rocking methodically, her face blank with exhaustion. Motherhood: the greatest gift of all time, according to Suriya and government posters pasted throughout Sri Lanka. The little boy sits with his hands on his knees, leaning forward to see out the window past his mother's shoulder. The baby's wail claws at my throat.

When I was a little girl, I had the usual fantasy of feeling the baby kick in my stomach, singing it to sleep, nourishing it through my breasts, my body existing only as sustenance for another creature. The fantasy began ebbing in adolescence, as I retreated further and further from my peers, lusting after vagueness. I have little respect for the maternal instinct now, the hope for self-fulfillment through the most obvious pathway of the body, the dumb ease of a woman with a baby, their bodies so perfectly suited to each other it's as if they're already dead and appearing in an album of old family photographs. At what used to be called childbearing age, Virginia Woolf wrote in her diary about the devils that plagued her, "heavy black ones," devils of failure—a twenty-nine-year-old woman, unmarried, childless. Twenty years later, she wrote to herself that children were nothing compared to writing. But of course I am no Virginia Woolf. I am a modern evolutionary casualty, a woman capable of bearing children but deprived of the will to do so; a woman endowed with the will for meaningful work but constitutionally incapable of pursuing it. I am the type of human who will die out.

[three]

COLOMBO

Outside the train station, vendors are building pyramids out of watermelons, papayas, and wood apples. They shake out their legs, down clay cups of tea, yawn, hack, spit. "I give you good price, madam," a man says, holding out a watermelon to me. I'm carrying a water bottle in one hand and a coconut roti in the other. The straps of my backpack dig into my shoulders. Heat surges through the veins in my face. I look down at the watermelon and shake my head, scowling.

"But you can balance on your head, no, madam?"

Peals of laughter from the vendors.

A man covered in warts and fist-size moles shuffles his bare feet along the pavement, hand outstretched, repeating a Sinhalese plea in a monotone. I put a coin in his hand as we pass each other. He scowls at his palm. He expects paper money from tourists.

I was relieved the first time I heard the anti-panhandling announcements on the subway in New York. *We ask you NOT to give. Please help us maintain an orderly subway.* There was a gray-haired black man who kept showing up in my subway car. His tiny eyes blinked under thick brows as he shook the coins at the bottom of his battered twenty-ounce Pepsi cup, intoning, "If you can spare anything in the category of a few dollars or a few cents. If you can spare anything in the category of a few dollars or a few cents . . ." The vain, stubborn care of the word *category* was a fist around my heart. The authoritative voice on the intercom required me to ignore it. I tried to explain the sadness of this relief to Brian. "But it doesn't help anyone to collect a handful of coins on the train," he said.

"But that might be the only way some people can make money," I said.

"You can't really believe that."

So many times a day I loathed him. Why does it still feel terrible to be exiled from the "normal days" he promised?

I walk into the train station and buy a ticket south. I want to find a sleepy beach town to finish my translation, stare at the ocean, reckon with the state of my life. When the train arrives, I heave my pack through the window to reserve an open seat and then clamber aboard after my belongings. I lean back against the sticky leather seat and close my eyes. My favorite fact of traveling: so many hours in which it is impossible to do anything at all. The train grumbles and lurches. I rest my elbow on the ledge of the open window. The wind tastes sweet on my arms. Suriya will be alone in the kitchen tonight. The image is a lump in my throat. But I don't wish I were there with her.

We chug through the hysteria of Colombo's sounds and smells and competing needs until we are riding the spine of a high, narrow mountain, alongside a river gilded with mineral silt. Fragments of artificial color dot the hillside—the saris of Tamil tea pickers plucking rough leaves by the handful and dropping them in giant sacks tied to their backs. Water buffalo crawl antlike in the paddy fields below layers of mountains, the closest ones feathery with giant pines, the farthest purpled silhouettes.

We stop at a town that has set precarious roots in the hillside just below the tracks. A pudgy woman gets on the train and sits next to me, a toddler on her lap. The girl wears a red tank top on which sequins form the words HEARTS HEARTS HEARTS!!! She eats cookies out of her mother's purse and beats a rhythm on her knees. "Butalay, butalay, boom boom!" Men walk up and down the aisles, hawking fried fish and dhal balls, calling "Swaray, swaray!" Sunlight spears the tip of my elbow. Metallic claps coming from the floorboards between cars keep time with the jolting of my seat. As pictures outside the window flash and disappear—waves hurling themselves at shore, women weaving palm fronds into roofs in their front yards—I feel myself inside a small, sparse room. Curtainless. Bright. White walls, heavy furniture with peeling white paint. A bed covered only in a white sheet, always mussed. Clean but untidy. Objects lie about, living inside their discrete functions. A mew of contentment presses against my closed lips. For a short while I am so relaxed that where I imagine myself to be is the same place as where I am. The train picks up speed and jostles the room out of my hands.

Hours pass. I sit. The mother and toddler are replaced by a man with a small, deeply creased face. He nods at me in greeting, picks up an English-language newspaper that has been abandoned in the aisle, shakes it open and laughs. I glance at the headlines: President Lowers Rice Prices! President De-mines Northern Region! President Opens State-of-Art Cinema!

"Were you reading this?" he asks.

"No."

"Good. All lies."

"Is that a government paper?"

"Indeed. Garbage. You are from the U.S.A.?"

"Yes, I am. How can you tell?"

"My elder brother has lived in Chicago for many years. I recognize the American manner."

"What is the American manner, exactly?"

"Friendly but cautious. Wary."

"Your English is better than most Americans'." I offer a smile that I hope distinguishes my friendliness from that of my wary compatriots.

His family used to be quite cozy with the British, he tells me. He spent most of his childhood on a golf course, in neat little suits and bow ties. His laugh is raucous and long. His uncle served in parliament and his parents were some kind of government administrators. The British loved the Tamils. Divide and conquer! Well, the Sinhalese have certainly put us back in our place. "Nimal." He holds out his hand.

"Elsie. So what happened to your family after independence?"

They had to leave Colombo after Black July, the month of riots in retaliation for the Tigers' first big attack, which killed thirteen Sri Lankan soldiers. Colombo raged for weeks afterward, with Sinhalese mobs setting fire to Tamil homes, businesses, and people. A mob nearly killed Nimal. His perfect Sinhalese accent saved his life. "Death to Tamils," he shouted, until the mob was convinced he was one of them. But his family could not stay in Colombo after Black July. Sinhalese his parents had been close with cut off all ties, afraid of being branded collaborators. Nimal's best friend bid him farewell after school one day. "I must not look you in the face again in this life," he said, and turned his back. After the riots, Nimal's uncle quit parliament. He had stayed even when his party was forced to support the Sinhalese-only language policy, even when they gave up the fight against the law requiring Tamils to get better marks than Sinhalese to enter university. But after the government-supported pogrom, Nimal's parents and uncle had to accept the gravity of anti-Tamil feeling. Their family name would not protect them from a mob armed with machetes and kerosene. They moved to Vavuniya, Tiger country. Those were the golden years for Prabhakaran, who had prepared himself to lead the Tamil

Tigers by torturing insects and sticking pins in his fingernails to inure himself to pain. He demanded every family give one child to the LTTE. Nimal had only one sister. The Tigers loved female fighters—bombs could easily be hidden under the dresses of seemingly expectant mothers—but Nimal would never have sent his sister to war. So Nimal joined the Tigers. When they said jump, you jumped. Anyway, he didn't mind joining, after what the Sinhalese did to his cousin. Crucified him in the road. Nailed his hands to the pavement. Left him there to be stampeded. Nimal thought Prabhakaran was a lunatic, but this lunatic was the Tamils' only hope. The Tigers used to put up posters that showed two different Tamil girls: One going to school with pigtails and a neat dress, then ending up dead in the bushes, her skirt pushed up past her waist; Sri Lankan soldiers smirked nearby. The other girl stood tall and proud in camouflage pants, staring down the barrel of a rifle. This was not only propaganda. Nimal's sister did not join the Tigers and she was raped by the Indians, the supposed peacekeeping force that came to help end the war. India sent the most brutal men they had—from backward tribes, no inkling of civilization—and gave them no direction. Nimal told his sister never to tell anyone that she'd been raped so she would be able to get married later. Which she did, to a carpenter who was forced to build bunkers for the Tigers. They had four kids. The whole family is dead now. Killed during the last months of the war. Rajapaksha knows how to win a war, you have to hand it to the man. Jail the journalists and bomb, bomb, bomb.

Or so goes my fantasy of the story Nimal might tell me, a tidy, personalized illustration of the Sri Lankan horror stories I've read about.

What actually happens is that Nimal crumples the newspaper and chucks it out the window, asks me what city I live in, tells me he was in New York once, asks what I think of my country's first black president. I try to get him to talk about how his family fared during the war, mentioning the Black July riots to let him know I'm informed, but he just laughs more, tells me I know my history, am I sure I'm American?

I turn my face into the breeze from the window, strong enough to justify closing my eyes, Dieu merci. I spend a lot of time reading alone while others are sitting in traffic on their way to a desk, and I tell myself this makes me better than other Americans, with their slavishness to their computers and SUVs and houses with two guest bathrooms. But what do I have? I have a full, active mind that brings me neither peace nor love nor contentment nor purpose. If I were a character in a novel, I would be the quintessential twenty-first-century narrator: characterized by the aimless bustle of the sharp mind, revealed through thoughts about my inner torment rather than events that explain the torment. There was a blog post about this on some literary site one time. I read it in my pajamas after Brian left for work, drinking coffee, eating instant oatmeal. My mental activity both sustains and paralyzes me! Exactly! I finished my oatmeal, sat at the table. The obvious paradox was that there was nothing I could do with the realization. I was not some dynamic character out of, say, Dickens or George Eliot or, um . . . I grip my fist in front of my mouth, deeply ashamed, even in the theater of my mind peopled only with other thoughts, to be unable to recall a single other nineteenth-century novelist. As if quick recall of canonical writers would lead to inner peace.

But now something is happening that shuts my brain up. We are hurtling through a darkness so complete its texture is the total absence of texture. There is no boundary between self and air. My hand, inches from my eyes, is an indistinguishable part of the mass of black particles careering about me, interrupted here and there by thin wisps of light. Near the end of the tunnel, the white threads spin together. The light becomes shapes. The shapes become objects, disappointing in their familiarity.

Nimal claps his hands on his thighs. He looks past my shoulder at a train station, barren except for a man in a sarong, picking his teeth on a shady bench. "I exit at the next stop," he says. "Would you like to come with me?"

I cross my arms over my chest and stare at the seat back in front of me. "I am married," I lie.

"I wish you and your family happiness and good health." He retrieves his bag from the overhead rack and explodes in laughter by way of goodbye.

So long, stranger.

And now we come to the land of infinite plywood shacks with plastic tarps for roofs. The only visible earth is a small rectangle of dirt in the center of every four shacks. In one of these tiny yards a dog lies on its side, unblinking. In others, kids chase one another and shout. The train continues past a mound of garbage several stories high. I block my nose against the stench. Scavengers walk atop the compressed mass of refuse: insects crawling atop a mountain of colored sand. Nearby, barefoot kids play cricket in a field.

A family gets on the packed train and settles in the passageway between cars. The mother and three children immediately fall asleep, draped over one another. The father remains awake, sitting in the open doorway with bent legs to keep his family from falling to the tracks below. As they near their destination, the parents wake the kids with chocolate cookies, which the baby laughingly smears in her sister's hair until the older girl cries. The father takes the baby while the mother fixes the toddler's ponytail, murmuring in her ear. A family. The most natural thing in the world, for some.

MIRIGALLE

I get off the train in a beach town whose name appeals to me. On the street outside the station, well-dressed men fall into step alongside me, offering me the best room in town, very good price, special price just for me, come and see, they drive, no problem. I find an unaggressive rickshaw driver, fit my bag into the back of the tiny three-wheeler, and ask him to take me to the Retired Peacock, a guesthouse recommended to me by a pimply older man just before I got off the train—"Italian lady owner. You say Tharaka sent you." The driver barrels past vans and flatbed trucks piled with timber, then turns down a narrow coastal road. The air is alive— vapor exhaled by leaves after a rainstorm. Or something. Droplets of sunlight flirt with the surface of the ocean. It's pretty, is what I mean. Boys in torn shorts stand on fishing stilts in the shallows. A pile of rocks covered in wire separates the road from the sand, protection against another tsunami, more hopeful than actual.

We turn down a dirt path. I am all alone in the back of this rickshaw on this unknown road under a pale pink sky, just visible through the gaps in the silly palm trees. My freedom is huge and it adores me. The driver honks at a cow blocking our path. The beast moos in protest before ambling into the woods. Rebar juts out of crumbling pastel walls, the remains of houses decimated by the tsunami. The driver stops in front of a white picket fence. "Welcome" is written in English, Italian, and Sinhala in small, neat, golden letters. As I step out of the rickshaw, a pack of dogs bounds toward the gate, leaping and growling.

"Dogs okay," the driver tells me, extending his palm to collect the fare.

"You don't scare me," I lie to the dogs as I walk through a yard of patchy grass and unpainted stone huts. A lanky boy lugging a dead palm leaf stops short when he hears my footsteps. He looks terrified, like I did that time in Paris when two giggling girls passed me as I was walking in the Jardin des Plantes and I shrieked and dropped my book. I spent so much time alone then—raking the dead leaves of my thoughts, staring at the piles and hoping a pattern would emerge—that the intrusion of laughter frightened me.

"Do you have any rooms?" I ask the startled boy.

"I get Manuela." He walks to a stone patio attached to a house. Fluffy blue cushions are scattered on the ground. A solid stone coffee table and bench seem fashioned directly out of the earth, an ancient boulder resigning itself to the quaint human need for furniture. A woman rises off the bench and sets her book on the ground. She wears a yellow linen skirt and a loose tank top, no bra. Her hips are wide, her arm muscles conspicuous, her hair long and dry and white, tied in a ponytail slung over one shoulder. "You want a room? You did not phone?"

"No. I just—someone on the train told me about this place. Tharaka? He said he knew you."

"This is a resort. This is not a backpacker hangout. Really, you should have called. You should not trust a stranger on the train." She stares out of pale, pale blue eyes.

"How much are your rooms?"

"We have private cabanas. They start at three thousand rupees."

"Oh. Shit."

"How much were you hoping to spend?"

"More like six hundred." I have thousands of dollars in the bank. Still, it feels true that I could not afford to pay thirty dollars a night for a private hut on the beach. I'm so accustomed to frugality, never having counted on myself for a steady income. That's partly why it felt like I was doing something really good when I brought Suriya and Rajith to a fancy hotel. But it was just another idea from which I wanted too much.

"I can't open up one of the cabanas for six hundred rupees," Manuela says. "I'm sorry to turn you away. I'll have one of the boys take you back to town at least. I was about to send him to the market anyway." She has the indeterminate accent of a nonnative English speaker who's been speaking English for many years in a country of nonnative English speakers. "Might as well take off your pack and have a drink before you go." She walks into the main house and returns with a lopsided hand-blown glass filled with ice water. She sits down cross-legged in front of the bench and rolls a cigarette. I walk to the edge of the patio, which extends to a cove. Upturned canoes lie on the sand. Hammocks link palm trees. Manuela coughs.

"How long have you been here?" I ask.

"Twelve years."

"And you stay here year-round?"

She nods inside whorls of smoke.

"You never go back to—"

"To Italy? No." She smiles with abrupt tenderness.

"Do you mind if I walk down to the beach?"

"Please."

The wet sand mirrors the sunset. I raise my skirt above my knees. Warm water pools around my ankles. "Oh," I say out loud, and cup my hands over my smile. Could I ever love anything more than the ocean? A huge wave rears up. I run backward, but the water crashes down on my legs and knocks me off my feet.

Manuela calls out from the patio. "Why don't you just stay here? I don't have any reservations for a while. Eight hundred rupees?"

My cabana is a hollowed-out stone containing only a white bed frame—high off the ground and net-free, since there are screens

on the many circular windows. We eat bread and bananas for dinner. Manuela eats with one hand and reads with the other, sitting cross-legged with her back against the stone bench. I float in
a chair swing. Cicadas fill the gaps between the crash of waves.
Manuela offers me a glass of wine. I hesitate for a moment, afraid
of my excitement at the prospect of breaking the alcohol fast my
body has been relishing since I got to Sri Lanka. "I'd love some
wine. Just one glass."

"I wasn't offering more than a glass."

She walks toward the kitchen. Acne covers the surface of her
back, pustules so tiny and white they are almost pretty on her
leathery skin. She returns with two glasses half full of lovely maroon liquid. A dog sighs and rests its chin on its paw. The ceiling
lights are dim, their fixtures clogged with dead insects.

"For a resort, this place doesn't seem all that hedonistic," I say.
"It's more like a monastery."

"Or a prison. A voluntary prison."

"Why did you put yourself in prison?"

Manuela's laugh is like a glass half full of lovely maroon liquid. Convenient metaphor that happens to be accurate. When she
first came to Asia, she tells me, she had all these ideas of changing her life. She had been trying to party her way out of misery
for most of her adulthood. She spent two years at a monastery
in Bodh Gaya, the place where the Buddha attained enlightenment. Although she never actually took the vow, Manuela lived as
a nun—celibate, no eating after noon, barely speaking. And then
she realized that for her being a nun was just another extreme,
another way to avoid herself. She got to know an Italian couple
staying in Bodh Gaya—nouveau Buddhist fanatics who were in
the process of divesting themselves of their worldly goods, one of
which was a large property on the Sri Lankan coast. They offered
it to Manuela dirt cheap when it seemed like the war would never

end. Manuela never ("nev-er," she repeats, separating the syllables) thought she'd be the kind of person who would operate a resort, but it's ended up being perfect for her. As soon as she started hiring local boys to build the cabanas, she felt immense relief, as if the vague inner demand she had spent all her life trying to ignore suddenly shut the hell up.

"And now you're helping people. Giving them a place to get that same kind of relaxation."

Manuela shrugs. "Everyone wants something different from this place."

I push off the ground and swing toward the far wall, where drawings hang suspended from a wire with clothespins. Several of them feature Christmas trees of increasing precision, neon green and covered in sparkles. *"Buon Natale!"* is written in red and green block letters. I ask who drew them.

"Emil. My son." Manuela stands and tucks her book under her arm. "Take care walking to your cabana. I don't have the ground lights on." From the darkness beyond the patio, she asks me to forgive her, she never asked my name.

I dream of a middle-age man wearing a dirty sweat suit, carrying a cane. His belly droops over the exhausted stumps of his legs. His few hairs are slicked against his sweaty scalp. I'm lying on the edge of a bare mattress. His wide hips hold my knees apart. He puts the unlit end of a candle inside me. Even my dreaming self is ashamed for conjuring this cliché grotesquery. But once he moves my underwear to the side and sticks his thing in me, I no longer see the man. I think only of his thoughtless, greedy enjoyment. I come in my sleep, my legs clenched around my hand.

Immateriality gives way to the material—the soft sheet sticking to my sweaty shoulder, roosters crowing outside, interrupting the susurration of broom on stone. It's soothing to have a grotesque fantasy in a sweet setting. Maybe the particulars of my desire don't matter much at all. Maybe it's not so bad that all of my fantasies involve women being degraded. It would be less morally confusing, of course, if another kind of sexiness were possible, but I don't think it is, not for me. To express love explicitly through the physical—hands clutched overhead, eyes locked, murmured "I love you's," mutual orgasms in which I felt like a sweet little bird soaring over a waterfall—how unerotic it seems. I used to worry that I'd been broken by bad casual sex and online porn, which I started watching during the gray, gray Paris winter, alone in my tiny maid's room on the attic floor with a two-euro bottle of wine and a couple of chocolate croissants, convinced the world owed me whatever inkling of pleasure I could wring from it. I would cover the worn, fake-tanned faces of the girls on my computer screen so I wouldn't have to see the way their eyes and mouths floated, detached and vacant, in the midst of the fucking. I just wanted to see fucking, humans making themselves feel so good they lost all control. But the guys went on talking and talking, calmly planning to make their sex partners drink gallons of cum or stretch out their assholes or destroy their pussies with their huge cocks. The scenes made me queasy and upset but they also got me wet (a self-protective evolutionary adaptation, I told myself later), so I'd go from video to video in search of something I could conscionably get off to. Finally I'd just stick my hand down my pants and start coming almost instantly and the orgasm was hard and tiny like a pebble and then I was all alone with the gross porn thing that had made me come, feeling now that its eroticism was really rage at the inaccessible things we could not keep ourselves from wanting and the unreasonable demands the grown-up world placed on us. Some of the girls seemed genuinely turned on by the violence done to their orifices—"Pound that pussy! Stretch that asshole!"—as if their bodies belonged to some hateful stranger. Every ejaculation would only increase their willingness to be used like this again and again, just as my porn-inflicted orgasms felt good only insofar as they briefly relieved an incessant itch. The videos are addictive because they do not satisfy; each offers only the shallowest consolation for the inaccessibility of satisfaction.

A man gives orders to a girl on her knees, speaking as if he were ordering a hamburger. "Look at the camera. Open your mouth wide." He jerks off and ejaculates without sound or expression, the dumb enactment of an image—man's semen, woman's face. I once heard a radio interview with a porn star promoting her memoir. Her advice to the numerous male callers who wanted to get involved in the industry: If you can masturbate in a crowded room and stay hard for an hour and then ejaculate the instant someone tells you to, congratulations; you've got what it takes. And that's the classy, official stuff. The free, amateur videos have no rules at all: A woman being asphyxiated and whipped while her asshole is simultaneously fisted and fucked. Vaginas being electrocuted. *REAL LIVE RAPES captured on film!* A black woman in a hotel room into which more and more white men keep entering, laughing, wagging their cocks in her wide-eyed face, their own faces obscured to protect their identities, the woman turning in circles like a cat cornered by coyotes. A group of blobby, laughing men fucking a woman with a champagne bottle. If it broke, it would puncture her organs, her bowels would stop functioning, she would need a colostomy bag for life like that character in that David Foster Wallace story—stop, please stop. These are a few of the scenes I stumbled on while trying to find a video of two people fucking. How to forgive myself for being an ordinary human? How to forgive the world that ordinary humans made?

I tried watching feminist porn a few times, but it only left me unsettled. The loving looks, the tonguey kissing, the focus on cun-

"My son will be here in a few weeks," Manuela says one night. We're drinking hot water with ginger. "He spends the summers here."

"Where does he live the rest of the time?"

She stands up and straightens one of his Christmas cards, talking with her back to me. Emil's father left when he found out Manuela was pregnant. They were crazy about each other but he didn't want to be a parent and Manuela just could not have an abortion. The blond dog runs onto the patio and flops at Manuela's feet. She bends down to scratch his ears. Motherhood made her lose her mind. She could not bear the love she felt for Emil, how that one attachment eclipsed all the other ways she used to be a person. It took her hours to decide whether she should put a coat on him before they went out for a walk and months to decide whether he should sleep with his bedroom door opened or closed—stuff like that, every second of every day, all alone obsessing about tiny details. So Emil has lived with his aunt and uncle and their two kids since he was five. He loves his family. He seems okay.

I fish the ginger out of the bottom of my mug. Before he became the Buddha, Shakyamuni named his son Rahula, meaning fetter. The nun who gave the talk about abandoning hope also said that her family accused her of neglecting her children when she started studying Buddhism. I feel lucky, for a moment, to be unfettered. The only impediments to getting to know myself completely are fear and desire, dragging me toward this and away from that, searching and searching for what can't be found.

Manuela stands up and picks a notebook off the table. "Tell me if this is too personal," I say, "but I just—being here all alone for so many years—has it been hard—I mean—not being with anyone—"

"You're wondering about sex?"

Yes. I'm always wondering about sex. It's the main question of

nilingus (depressing that the clinical Latin term is less unappealing than the slang—carpet-munching, muff-diving—which I cannot even write without laughing). I should have desired these images but did not. Jared told me to stop worrying about it. "You're not blowing some fat fuck on camera because your daddy didn't love you," he said. "You're blowing me." He took my jaw in his hand and pulled my lips apart. I reached for his belt buckle. We had sex and I came twice, imagining a group of overweight men ejaculating into the various orifices of an underage ballerina. Or some other scenario that I pray never happens to anyone in real life.

A therapist might say that my fantasies are a sublimation of my distress over the pervasive portrait of sex as ruthless masculine aggression, the way a rape survivor may fantasize about rape to reclaim the experience, make it a means to sexual pleasure instead of an obstruction. The therapist would probably be right, and maybe I would be a more balanced person if I had agreed to see one, as Brian wanted me to. But I don't want to subject my mind to someone else's idea of a good life. I want to do my own research. God knows I have the time.

I have barred myself from checking email until I finish the translation. A kind of superstition: If I pretend that the publisher wants to buy it, he will buy it. I force myself to work for two hours before lunch, *efficace et machinal*, waiting for my real day to begin.

Every meal at Manuela's is mango and bananas and spicy cashews and dhal and thick slabs of coarse bread. In the afternoons, we drink tea and then read, cocooned inside hammocks. I borrow books from the shelf on the patio. A few are in French, romantic and frivolous. It's good to engage with French besides my translation. I adopt Manuela's easy dress—tank top, loose skirt, no bra. I cover myself when the boys come to clear palm leaves or fix the plumbing in one of the cabanas, but they hardly seem to register my presence. In the late afternoons, I walk on the beach, clambering over rock embankments that separate one cove from the next. The dogs are giddy companions, sprinting and digging and burrowing and wiping their sandy snouts against my skirt. I stand atop the rocks and watch the coming waves. Their whitecaps mist and froth as they gather force and speed until they lose control of their own momentum, hurl themselves against the rocks, explode upward like geysers, spritzing me in saltwater.

There is no point to my life. The sentence appears in my head several times a day. If I said the words out loud, it would sound like a lament. But kept to myself, it's the best thought I've ever had.

I sit on my bed in the mornings and evenings, remaining still for long enough that I become attuned to my body's involuntary movements—abdomen filling and deflating, air rustling my nose hairs, pressure building and easing in my guts, itchy pressure at the center of my chest that gradually grows into the sensation I used to call my annoyment knot. If I can sit still and endure the knot for what seems like a long time, the feeling of agitation gives way to the nearly pleasant pins-and-needles tingling that arises when a numb body part regains sensation, and my heart and groin begin vibrating and floating like those curlicues of light that drift through bright skies, and the only thought I know is a line from a song—*oh my little love*—which plays in the head of a character in one of my favorite stories when he has sex with his wife. The shift is like opening the door to a gas station restroom and finding a deserted beach. Sky sand ocean stop sky sand ocean stop sky . . . Only after hours of listening to inner monologues—"Can you see the line of my underwear through these pants? Where did I buy these pants again? And when was that exactly? And what was I wearing that

day? I am such a loser for never having read Thomas Hardy. I Manuela knew that I have no idea how much I weigh. Is thi going to make a noise? What about this one?"—do I believe the monk at Shirmani was not just making a cute philosop metaphor when he compared the mind to a mug with a hole i bottom. The entire Indian Ocean could never fill the mug. do not need to fill the mug. The mind provides exactly wha mind needs. I just sit; I'm free.

As a narrative experience, it sounds like New Age bunk. A actual experience, it is enough to live for.

I imagine how my meditating form would appear from outside—jaw unhinged, tongue wadded against my lower t eyes opened just wide enough to let in shapeless light; lower puffed and rounded, as if a baby animal has burrowed into warmth at my center. Why does it feel obscene to be this relax

In the hottest part of the day, I sit on the wet sand and b in the waves' runoff, then rinse my salt-crusted legs with the in Manuela's yard and lie in the hammock in wet clothes. Du the brief, violent rainstorms, I sit on the rocks and watch the w lose its edges. Suriya is back in her boardinghouse hell, staying late doing schoolwork, waking up early to sweep the house. I her, but I don't miss sharing her life. There is only one pur that could justify the privilege of my remove from society, there is no word for it that does not make me seem like a won who drinks a potion of cat urine and wasabi root on harvest m nights: egolessness, superconsciousness, truth. If I use my fr dom for any purpose other than cultivating constant awareness the reality outside my mind, I should die now. The earth shou sneeze while I am atop this boulder and feed me to the roarin frothing wave mouth below.

my life. You could call me shamefully privileged, but my privilege is not the part that I'm ashamed about. I was not born a blind, furry, transsexual orphan. I can accept that about myself. What upsets me is the cliché of my privileged concern. When I was working at Barnes and Noble, it seemed like every other week I was charged with making a conspicuous display of a new book by a woman who claimed to have found a spiritual solution to the problem of sex. Gang bangs heal the wounds of a traumatic childhood! Casual sex is a soul-destroying addiction! Sex is power for women who ignore their emotions! Worship your vagina like the goddess she is! Expert blow jobs are the secret to a happy marriage! Anal sex is the key to women's liberation! The books reminded me of Sally from *Carp Weekly,* who would complain when her husband stayed out late. "He is so in the doghouse. No nookie-nookie for him!" As if sex is only a way to get something that has nothing to do with sex.

"I had beautiful sex with Emil's father," Manuela says. "So I've had that experience. I don't feel like I need to keep having it over and over until I die."

I wonder aloud what she means by beautiful.

"I mean that I could relax completely. After we'd been together a little while, of course. I made him feel good; he made me feel good. We didn't have to talk about it. It was easy."

I've had sex like that a few times, unhurried pleasure given and received of its own accord, no striving. That kind of sex made it feel like all my other encounters, experiments, fantasies were just consolation for the lack of this basic need simply met. Maybe it would be enough to be able to count on sex like that for a sustained period of time; I'd be free to worry about something else.

Still, the first few years here were hard sometimes, Manuela tells me. She's looking through the bookshelf, her crisp, pale ponytail facing me. "This book helped," she says, and hands me a thick volume with a smiling Indian man in white on the cover, one hand over his heart: The kind of hippie book my mother would own. *I Am That*, it's called. Manuela says good night and joins the darkness beyond the patio.

In bed later, I glimpse my reflection in the window as I reach up to pull the cord of the overhead light. My legs, tan and bare and covered in blond down, seem very far away. I run my hands up my calves, massage the sides of my kneecaps, rest my thumbs in the nook between thigh and groin. I willfully conjure the image of Jared inside me. Part of his body moved in and out of part of my body thousands and thousands of times—probably more times than I've done any other activity involving another human being. And yet it seems dizzyingly extreme to think of it now, like jumping off a bridge into a pitch-black lake.

Jared and I both liked having anal sex. I felt relaxed and protected, lying on my stomach with my face hidden, his mouth so close to my ear that I felt the tiniest shifts of his breath, the sound of his need for me; his movements small and slow, so precise that I could imagine my way into Jared's experience of them. I was all alone, with someone else. Once we were having sex that way in the early morning, when I was still dreamy and calm. Every time Jared pulled back he left me completely and waited for a few seconds before pushing back inside, so that every time he entered me it was like the first time, and I was counting the first times with animal concentration and there were no worries about what I was giving myself up to. I just gave. It was all right. I pressed my pelvis against the mattress. A groan vibrated in my throat. Jared stopped moving. He raised himself off my back. He jumped out of bed and ran into the bathroom. I reached behind me and touched between my legs. Very wet, very brown. I felt myself tumbling into a well, the sound of rushing blackness. After I cleaned myself and put on lace panties and a silk nightgown, I lay down on the very edge of the bed, as far as possible from Jared, terrified of his thoughts about my body. I wanted to let the moment disappear, but my voice intruded, dry and loud. "I feel disgusting."

Nothing I say aloud is what I really want to be saying.

What I meant was, Is it necessary for me to feel disgusting? For us to be distant and ashamed because a sex act didn't go the way we wanted it to? Must we pretend my ass exists solely as an erotic portal?

In the lady's sex book about surrendering to anal sex, one chapter was devoted to hygiene, another to attire. It was easy for me to mock the writer as I consumed her small, punchy treatise during my lunch breaks. (So you're telling me female liberation requires anal douching and silk thongs and stilettos? And why exactly should I hope to liberate womankind with my sex life anyway? I don't know about you, toots, but I have sex to feel good.) Yet I also eroticize ideas of myself. I never fantasize about receiving pleasure. I always come at the instant of the imagined man's climax. But I am not a man, so my own orgasm abruptly splits away from the fantasy I've been lost in. I want to feel as Jared seemed to during anal sex, so consumed by the actual sensation of the actual moment that he could not help but release. Whereas I can only come when imagining something different from the current moment, even if the current moment later becomes what I imagine.

One time was different. Jared was licking me and the usual imagery came to mind—man's penis, woman's mouth, he was going to come so hard—and then I was back in the room and it was me, not an imaginary brute, who was going to come so hard. I felt the sensation in my groin pulsing outward through my body, until I was clutching the headboard, every muscle tensed, engaged, ready to release all claims to itself, and then the sensation barreled me down and I was gone for a little while, aware only of the complete release of complete contraction, instead of the sensation just being something that happened to me while I thought about something else. A pure moment. I want it back. I want it now.

I flip through the book Manuela gave me until I come to an underlined passage, which I read with a shock of recognition, as if someone has made sense of years of thoughts I didn't realize I was having. "It is not desire that is wrong, but its narrowness and smallness. Increase and widen your desires until nothing but reality can fulfill them. Transform desire into love. All you want is to be happy." Before he became the Buddha, Prince Siddhartha lived in a palace filled with concubines at his beck and call. Some teachers say it was the experience of orgasm that opened him to the possibility of living that freedom in every moment. But he left the palace and sat in a cave for eight years because he understood that the desire to ejaculate inside a different woman every night is the very essence of suffering. He wanted to receive all of life with that openness, that presence. Of course I'm using the Buddha to stand in for my own ideals. I've never had an experience of sexual pleasure that compares to the expansiveness I've felt at times during meditation. Which does not mean I'm about to give up sex. But it helps to be reminded of what I want more.

An hour after translating the final sentence of *Fifi*, I'm sitting in front of a computer at an empty Internet café, shouting *nervous nervous nervous* in my head. My father once told me that if you know how you feel, your body calms down. He also told me to manifest what I want—picture myself having it, trust that I will get it, feel grateful for having it even before it arrives. So I visualize the content of the publisher's email before I open it. *Dear Ms. Elsie*

Shore, it will read. *We would be honored and delighted to publish your translation of* Fifi.

Deep breath. Click.

"We greatly appreciate the opportunity to consider your work. We're afraid *Fifi* is not a good fit for us . . . happy to consider more work in the future . . . best of luck . . ." I wipe my hands on my skirt, close my eyes until I can feel the pause between heartbeats.

Well, it's only one publisher. I should look up other publishers and literary journals, go back to submitting cold, tossing pebbles at a wall in the hope that it might crumble. But how dull *Fifi* has become to me, in the course of translating it. So then I should translate another book, a better one. But even if I work quickly, that's a years-long undertaking, and then I'd have to go through the dismal submissions process again and even if by some miracle I were able to get one book translated, what then? I don't want to spend another decade just hoping to become this particular thing. If I stop imagining the way my life looks from the outside, I don't even care about being a translator.

The rest of my inbox is filled with Jared's name, offering email after mercifully distracting email of pornographic yearning ("i love how you're this smart and well read and independent woman and then i get you in bed and you become my trembling fawn. come back, beautiful girl. i need your pussy around my cock"), words Jared created by jamming down computer keys with his index fingers, typing as he walked and ate and spoke: with ludicrous insistence, a hedge against the suspicion of weakness.

"got in some trouble baby," Jared wrote me seven hours ago. "some assholes from the city of angels my face is pitch fucking black it hurts so bad i feel like such a loser gonna give this work up for real a buddy says he can hook me up with a job at the firehouse don't even have to take the emt test come back i'll be good for you if you come back you're my dream girl i need you." I run my fingers over my lips. Longing rears. Anger strangles it. How has this become my life? That my most appealing future prospect is to live with a philandering, alcoholic drug dealer-cum-fraudulent fireman?

The phrase would make Jared laugh. It would be so good to hear his laugh right now.

I ask the Internet owner if I can use his phone to make an international call. He rises from his desk, gestures to the giant phone atop it, and goes outside to smoke a cigarette. I punch digits. The phone rings against my ear. How easy it is to reach him, all the way from here.

"Mornin'. Jared Desiderius Hart speaking." This is his given name, spoken in his social voice, surrounded by the din of many disparate conversations.

"Jared. It's me."

"Well, hell. Say that again, beautiful girl."

"Jared. It's me."

"Damn. That sounds good."

"Are you okay? You sound like you've been crying."

"Nah. Been too busy. I was up 'til dawn this morning talking to this dude about super-massive black holes, which I'm now a follower of. Because they have such a strong gravitational force. I don't *really* want to have this conversation all over again, to be perfectly honest. Coffee and a Mexican omelet, please, darlin'. Extra jalapeños. If you would."

"Are you drunk?"

"A little bit I guess."

"What time is it there?"

"Morning. So the black hole at the center of our galaxy is our physical god. It means we have a chance to know we exist. Which is all we can hope for, right? The super-massive black hole is not going to grant wishes. It doesn't give a fuck."

"You wrote me that you were going to stop drinking."

"I will. I've been really pretty good. And you're not giving me much incentive to follow the straight and narrow, being in a different hemisphere and all." His old-fashioned expressions, gleaned from the crate of paperback classics he keeps by his bed—they surprise me still, soften me. He slurps coffee. "What are you doing there anyway? You're safe, right? You're not calling because you're in any trouble?"

"No, I'm not in trouble. I love it here."

"You sure you're all right, beautiful girl? You sound sad."

Something in need of unhinging comes unhinged. I speak quickly, about Suriya and Manuela, the violence of the waves, the purity test on wedding nights, the endless fucking curries. Jared exclaims and laughs. I see his open mouth—craggy tongue, crooked front tooth.

"I miss you crazy much," he says. "Thank you kindly, gorgeous. Just some hot sauce, if you would. Mind if I eat?"

"I should go anyway. This is getting expensive. But I need to ask you something."

"You have my undivided," he says through a full mouth.

"I think I want to move back to California. Maybe we could live together. I want to try living with you."

"You're not shitting me?" He swallows, clears his throat. "You wanna move in together?"

"I think so. Are you still going to get a new job? That thing at the firehouse?"

"Yeah, yeah, I'm trying. Why didn't you write me earlier? You said you would write me when you got there. You said you would email me a lot."

It's always a relief when Jared identifies something I've done wrong, some clear way I've been inconsiderate. We're both screwed up, we've both let each other down, we're both trying. I guess it's the same relief that makes all those girls in books and TV shows and movies eager confessors of their own faults. They date guys who mistreat them, sure, but that's only to be expected, given that the girls are, like, total wrecks themselves. They drink too much and sleep around and probably deep down they're afraid of commitment and they have no friggin' clue how to cook anything but spaghetti. But if they can just get it together, then maybe the boys will get it together, too, and stop treating them badly, and they'll all live happily ever after, except that they don't even want to live happily ever after, they just want to have sex with the same dude a few times a week, you know?

"I'm calling you now," I say, hopeful as the well-dressed girls on TV. "I want to live with you."

"I want to live with you, too. Get your perfect ass back here. We'll figure it all out." Jared smacks his lips against the receiver.

When I hang up, I email Joe at *Carp Weekly* and remind him of our conversation in the parking lot on my last day of work, how he said that he wished I'd spoken to him before I left, he would have argued for a promotion for me. I barely notice the words I write, only the eagerness of the keys rising back after I press them, happy to be the same letter again and again.

Manuela has been busy getting Emil's cottage ready for his stay. Although she doesn't say so, I know it's time for me to leave, give her some time alone before her son arrives. I feel good about moving on. I feel good in general, a little light-headed when I remember Jared's voice on the phone and think about being near him again soon. He's been the one constant, the one thing that's held my interest all these years. Time to accept that. When I was younger, I didn't want to be the one who was strong enough to be steadily open, even when he hurt me, even when all I wanted was to be left alone. I wanted to be the damaged one who was healed. But I've been trying to get what I want for so long now, steering my life away from this image, manipulating it into that shape, and it has felt mostly like mitigating failure all alone. If I give myself to this relationship completely—I don't know. But something different will have to happen.

NAVANTHISSA

The bus is fast, airy, almost empty. A garland of fake magenta flowers jiggles over the rearview window. My feet rest on my backpack, divested of the Larousse, which sits now on Manuela's bookshelf. She laughed for a long time over my lugging it around as if it were the guarantor of my days. Two girls in white school uniforms get on the bus. They stare at me, whispering and giggling.

A gap in the trees lining the road contains a girl in a bikini walking along a wide beach. She's tall and thin and tan, a fine brown slice through the white air, a sure sign that the next stop on the bus belongs to me: a town of private cabanas equipped with boogie boards and outdoor showers and hammocks slung between palm trees, where white girls can walk in bikinis without getting harassed by gawking boys and have cocktails in hollowed-out coconuts delivered to their lounge chairs. On my first trip to Sri Lanka, I stayed on the beach for only two days. The paradise was like a math formula with no conceivable application. I could plug in the numbers and get the right answer, but I didn't know what it meant. Now, though, even the metaphor irritates me. I am a person going to a place. End of story.

I check into a large motel on the beach. A group of twenty-somethings chat on the sand out front, bottles of arrack scattered around their chairs. I change into my bathing suit and take high-kneed hops across the scorched sand to the water's edge. A wave rears up before me. I raise my arms and dive into its ferocious tunnel, frightened and happy.

When I return to the beach, a Sri Lankan man wearing basketball shorts and several gold necklaces is standing next to my towel. He looks like a skinny man wearing a fat suit for comedic effect—preternaturally round belly, twiggy limbs. He smiles as I hurry to cover myself with my towel, glaring just past his face. "Welcome," he says. "You just arrived?"

"Hm-hum."

"You picked a good hotel. Have you tried the rum punch here yet?"

I turn my back to him.

"Let me order you one." His accent is barely discernible.

"I came here to read and relax and I just want to be left alone."

"Sure. No problem." But he stands nearby until his phone rings. He answers in Sinhala, and his loud voice retreats down the beach.

I stretch out on the sand and close my eyes. The sun is so bright I can see the backs of my eyelids, a mess of slithering red threads.

"Take my chair if you want. I'm not using it." A young man with sandy curls and bright eyes is standing over me. His large aureoles sag agreeably.

Lievin is from Holland, traveling around on PhD money while he supposedly works on his dissertation. He introduces me to the rest of his group. A Belgian girl—dyed-orange halo of curls, Minnie Mouse T-shirt—is reading on a lounge chair. The Israeli boy is as lovely and boring as an ad in a glossy magazine—green eyes, thick lashes, dark silk skin snuggled against small muscles. "Your rings are good," he says, looking at my fingers. "This one means:

I'm pretty. This one means: I'm weird." He sits down cross-legged on the sand, his chin resting in his hands. "I'm glad you're here."

"I'm glad I'm here, too."

"Do you want a rum and coconut water? I'm going to get another one." The yellow flecks in his eyes flash out a code that grants access to nothing.

I surprise myself by declining. I don't want to turn the beach into a wavering backdrop for my somersaulting thoughts. "I'll take one," says the girl from Wales, drawing circles in the sand with her unpainted toe. She's attractive in the way I normally envy—tall and large-breasted with uncomplicated, well-defined facial features. But right now I have blood in my veins and organs carrying out their discrete functions without complaint and muscles that carry me wherever I want to go. There is no problem with my body.

The Belgian girl puts down her book—a novel by a French writer I like—and asks me what I think of my president.

Confidence is the most important component to mastering a language, and now would be a fun time to have some. But I am far too shy to address the French-speaking girl in French. Like everyone else here, she speaks nearly flawless English. I feel cheated to be from the one country whose language, culture, and politics everyone else knows. Even after spending thirty hours alone on a plane, I cannot escape the place I grew up. Except when I was with Suriya. Her village is the only place I've ever felt truly displaced, free of context.

A group of Sinhalese teenage boys comes running down the sand and the Israeli jogs out to meet them. They laugh and high-five and do handstands and backflips in the shallow water. Nearby, local women dip their toes in the waves' frothy wake, wetting the ends of their carefully pleated saris.

I spend the afternoon under the fan in my room, reading a

pleasant food memoir borrowed from the guesthouse library—a lonely white girl, a wise black maid, biscuit dough and blackberry cobbler. At sunset, I return to the beach, empty now of families. Blue-green waves froth and crest like a whale's open mouth, inhaling the sea and spitting it back out. Vigorous winds lift the saltwater into a tickly mist. I walk past the tourist strip, where couples sit with beers and surfers rinse off their boards. Around the bend past the surf break, the wind demands all the space in my head. The beach stretches endlessly, beige sand the wind has whipped into hundreds of small peaks topped by tiny, opalesque seashells. Sea grass clings to the steep slopes of the dunes and the waves are murderously huge and broad strokes of mauve and fuchsia are smeared across the high, flat sky. I want to walk on and on and on. But I don't know if it's safe. I turn back toward the surf break. I can just make out a tourist couple sitting on a towel. A man in a dhoti is walking in my direction, a brown smudge on blue air. I begin to walk back toward the tourists, taking my sarong out of my bag to cover up my bathing suit. The wind and waves are so loud that I must not really matter, there must not be any hurry. The wind whips the sarong above my head and plasters it against my face. I pull it back down and tie it around my chest. When I look up, the man is walking so quickly and purposefully toward me that I am suddenly running, my eyes fixed on the tourists, trying not to see the man who is growing larger and larger. I feel small and warm, not quite afraid. I reach the couple and plant my feet in the sand in front of them and feel the man behind me disappear.

Later, I ask an Australian woman who's lived in this town for years if it's safe to walk alone past the surf break.

"Definitely not."

"Even during the day?"

"Never go there alone."

"Et vous?" I ask, happy now and a little drunk and utterly free
f concern about what this stranger thinks of me. "Vous habitez en
elgique?"

No, he lives in Paris. He motions back to the café. "Juste un
erre?"

He pulls out a chair for me at the first table we come to. I
uggest we sit closer to the café, where two white girls sway to no
nusic. One wears a spandex skirt that ends a few inches below her
ss. "Comme vous voulez," Claude says, and follows me to a table
aught in a cone of mustardy light cast by a bulb hanging from the
afé ceiling.

Claude was born in Colombo, but his father is French. He orders
s two glasses of arrack. He went to university in Paris and decided
o stay. He comes back to Sri Lanka a few times a year for business.
He buys and sells hotels, here and in southern France. He asks me
f I like Sri Lanka, saying "my country" in English with an over-
lone Sinhalese accent. Yes, I adore his country.

I try to tell him about my first trip here, how I met Suriya
nd then came back to stay with her family. The neglected French
ounds cling to my tongue, piling up inside my mouth. I push
hem out into the warm, dark air, where they hover close to my
ace, needy and insecure. I hear everything I'm saying too clearly—
he way my mouth refuses to form the right shapes, the pauses be-
ween phrases, the emptiness of their meaning. In English, I can
ide behind hurried, excessive phraseology. But there is sufficient
lifficulty in speaking and understanding French that I'm forced to
otice how traumatized I am by the simple act of talking. Inside
he space between how I experience life alone and how I experi-
nce it among others are the vital mysteries of myself, impervious
o cynicism or jokes or plans, unable to handle the external world

"Have bad things happened?"

"I've heard of men trying stuff, yes. They hide in the dunes
and watch for women walking alone. It's not that they are bad
men necessarily. It's—our Western ways. Our insistence on always
being so free."

Silly woman, romanticizing the East, villainizing the West. But
how lazy I felt as I wrestled with my sarong in the wind, and how
good, and how free.

Lievin invites me to join his group for dinner. We fill up a long
table at an outdoor café, ebullient with the nonsense of strangers
pretending to be family. A young boy runs back and forth from
our table to the kitchen, carrying copper pots so large we have to
stand up to fill our plates. Whenever a curry is nearly depleted,
the boy exclaims, "No more! All finished!," explodes into laughter,
runs back to the kitchen to fetch another steaming pot. We tell the
boy again and again how delicious everything is, we just can't stop
eating, please can we have a little more chili paste. We're proud of
our hunger for a world not our own.

After dinner, we walk to a café that has promised dancing. My
Kingfisher beer comes in a twenty-two-ounce bottle. The waiters
are teenage boys with red eyes, saggy grins, Bob Marley sweat-
bands. Lievin points out some cloth signs tied to masts of drift-
wood and spray-painted with the words "Dance! Drums! Fire!
Beer!"—remnants of last weekend's festival.

The Welsh girl tells me I was lucky to have missed it. "It was
hell. The whole point of the festival was for Sri Lankan boys to
grab white girls' butts. The second we tried to dance, we were surrounded and accosted."

"It was pretty gross," Lievin agrees. "There was something in the boys' eyes. Like they were crazed. Compelled by some demon to grab the girls' butts." I look more closely at Lievin as he continues. He has a little sympathy for the boys. Most of them had probably never gone to a real party before, let alone seen girls in short skirts. Lievin has been coming here for years and he's never heard of a festival like this one; the locals' idea of a crazy party typically involves ice cream cones and human-powered roller coasters, like the festival that came to Suriya's village. But there will probably be a lot more drunken debauchery, now that the country has been rebuilt and tourism is picking up so much. The Welsh girl pulls me out of my chair. She's singing along with Michael Jackson. My limbs are loose from the beer. I kick off my sandals and dance in my tiptoed, buoyant way, like I'm trying to take off and fly, as Brian once said. The Welsh girl rolls her body like an upright snake. "Let's swim," she says in my ear. We sprint down the beach until the tiki torch flames are orange sparks, pull off our clothes, and dive into liquid blackness. Ocean skinny-dipping: I've become just another drunken, debauched tourist. Shards of lightning gouge open a tiny purple wound of sky. Don't worry; just be grateful.

We dry ourselves by jumping and flapping our arms, get dressed and walk back to the party. A large-bellied Sri Lankan man is standing next to our table, legs wide and knees bent as if preparing to lift something heavy. It takes me a minute to place him as the man who offered me a rum punch earlier. Avoiding his eyes, I take my bag off the back of the chair, where I've stupidly left it, and join the mess of bodies flinging themselves about with self-forgetful exuberance.

My friends for the evening get tired and decide to go back to the motel. I shout good night over the music, still hopping. Lievin lets his smile linger on me. I wave and turn into the music. Once the other tourists begin to wander off, I pick up my bag and shoes,

bow to the orange moon being slowly flattened betwee of endless darkness, and head off down the beach. Th with the bling runs after me.

"Already leaving?"

"Yes." I walk without looking up. He follows a hind.

"Can I buy you a drink before you go?"

"No."

"Good night then." When I'm several yards away "Attendez, vous êtes belge?"

I stop and turn. The music is wordless now, a tin the murmur of low waves. "Non, je suis américaine. français."

He thought there was something French about time he saw me. His smile is palpable in the darkn I've relaxed toward him. But I'm too preoccupied wit he's speaking French and that I understand it to wo lewd hopes.

One day during my senior year of high school, came up to me in the hall to tell me that my French ise Labé was so brilliant he wished he had written made copies of my essay and distributed them to hi was the last thing I'd done that I was really proud of. years since, reading Proust or Flaubert or Stendhal only thing I could rely on to make me feel okay wit have avoided speaking French since Paris, where my of worthiness was scrutinized and scorned by unst and clerks who insisted on addressing me in clip glish as soon as they heard my accent. Strange, but I French even more now that I've given up on *Fifi*. I w I still have the language as a friend, a source of enjo hasn't all been a waste.

even in its gentlest form. I'm sitting squarely in that space now, giddy with vulnerability.

Claude finishes half his drink in two swallows. His upper body is backlit by the café lights, a snowman's silhouette: one smaller lump atop a larger one. He thinks Sri Lanka is a good place for a vacation. But he couldn't stand living here. He got out as soon as he could. Because of the war? I wonder.

"Non. Pas du tout." He turns toward the café light and begins to roll a cigarette on his knee. Where he lived, the war didn't matter at all. He left because the people here are stupid. Like his parents. Their servants once found some pieces of human flesh in their backyard, probably dropped there by some birds.

"Quelqu'un qui est mort dans la guerre?" I ask with tasteless eagerness, thrilled that he's speaking about the war, proud that I understand him.

Claude lights his cigarette and turns back to me. The person probably died in the war. How the hell would he know? I stiffen. He takes hurried drags on his thick cigarette. What disgusted him about the whole thing was that his parents seemed *embarrassed*, as if it were *impolite* to have human flesh in the backyard. His mother asked the servants to get rid of the corpse in this terrible, soft, ashamed voice. Claude shakes the ice in his drink. She had no clue what the war was even about. People here don't give a damn about politics. They just want to kill or be killed. Not that Claude blames them. Anything is better than politics. His laugh is a baritone rush of hot air against my face. I turn toward the café, now empty. The waiters are probably in the back, smoking hash. I cross my ankles under my chair and turn my body toward the darkness, away from Claude's loud hiss. I ask him why he comes back to Sri Lanka for vacation if he hates the country so much.

"Comment?" He pronounces the word with the harsh impatience I got used to hearing in Paris, when people either could not understand my accent or simply wanted to shame me for it. I try to repeat my question slowly and clearly, but self-consciousness makes me stumble over simple words, the guttural beginning of *retournez* sticking in my throat for so long that I blush and cringe.

"Ah! For vacation, Sri Lanka is wonderful. Luxury hotels for practically pennies." He's speaking in English now. My French is unacceptable. I am unacceptable. "And I do miss a decent curry when I'm in France. The French are such fanatics about their food, but a well-done chicken curry is much more interesting than foie gras. Tomorrow I'll bring you to a local restaurant. You won't have food like this anywhere else on the island, believe me. You have—" He reaches over and takes a piece of lint from my hair. My chin curls to my chest. "I like you," he says. "I never like Sri Lankan girls. My mother is always arranging meetings for me with local girls. They're pretty. But they don't excite me at all. Sri Lankan women hate sex." He turns his chair toward me and rolls up the sleeves of his T-shirt, exposing flabby upper arms as wide as my thigh. "I bet you don't hate sex."

Claude believes he can have me, even though he is short and fat and the only thing he knows about me is that I am an American girl traveling in Sri Lanka. He is rich and used to getting whatever he wants. The thought judders me out of the stupor of failure into which I have plunged. Why am I sitting alone late at night, exhausted, with a stranger whose bearing disgusts me, instead of sleeping in the cocoon of my mosquito net so that I can wake up early, meditate to the pirith coming from the temple down the street, jump in the ocean, drink tea, eat fresh papaya and mango?

"I have a boyfriend," I tell Claude.

"Then what are you doing here with me?"

"I just wanted to speak with you." My voice drags like the tired feet of a small girl. If only I had become obsessed with any other language. Italian, Spanish, Hindi, Arabic—a happy language that encouraged foreigners in any attempt to speak it. I felt uncomfortable around every single person I met in Paris. Why did I take this as my fault, a barrier formed of my own incapacity, an incapacity I needed to remedy if I ever wanted to belong to anything worthwhile? Whatever made me so convinced that the only hope for my life was to prove my connection to a country in which I hated being myself? French was like an abusive lover—not so abusive that I was fearing for my physical safety and contemplating pressing charges, just abusive enough to keep me interested, to make me feel special when he treated me well, to make me hope.

"I have to go to bed," I tell Claude. "I'm exhausted."

"You're exhausted? Or you're afraid I'm going to rape you?"

I jerk back, raising the front legs of my chair off the sand.

"I'm kidding," Claude says. "Une blague française."

"It's not funny. It's terrifying."

He leans toward me and grins, more at ease now that I'm afraid.

"Thank you for the drink. Good night." I stand up. He stands up, too, so abruptly he upends his chair. He takes my hands in his and squeezes until my knuckles grind against each other. He pulls down on my arms until I sit back down. The lights in the café have gone off. The tiki torches have burned out. The blackened windows of the nearest hotel glisten when the moon shines through the cloud cover. I no longer feel unacceptable. I feel like a word I'm trying not to hear.

"I don't have to leave quite yet," I say. "We can talk a little more."

Claude moves his patio chair directly opposite mine. His knees grip my knees.

"I'd like your opinion on something, actually," I say. "I'm sort of obsessed with the war. That's partly why I came to Sri Lanka in the first place." Claude tilts his head and fixes his eyes on me. His silence is reassuring. "It seems really fucked up to be obsessed with a war in this kind of voyeuristic way, but then when I think about Abu Ghraib and Guantánamo and how it suddenly became normal to talk about torture with strangers at a bar, holding people's heads underwater and hanging them from the ceiling until their shoulders dislocate and they lose consciousness—this became just something our country does sometimes, like all the other countries. And then there are these games on the Internet where you can torture people for fun. Free games, anyone can use them. Take a photo of your enemy, click a button, and jam nails in his face, move the mouse over his foot and saw off his toes. I see teenagers playing this game on the subway. Casual entertainment. This is the world, right? And all I'm doing is crying over boys. But I can't help it, the feelings are true, they don't stop, I can't help it. So I guess I thought that maybe if I could just really understand—if it could be not just some sad news story to me, but if I could really understand what it has been to live through this war in Sri Lanka, from the point of view of the people who have suffered the most, then I would—um. You know." Claude is gradually closing the distance between our faces. His fleshy hand opens and closes on his knee. I speak faster, staring at and not seeing the ripples so small and gentle they seem frozen on the surface of the ocean. "I've always known I have no right to be as fucked up as I am. So I'm obsessed with people who have the right. It's a kind of narcissism. Of course I know that. I wish I could be like Suriya. She's my friend in Kandy. Or else be an activist. Be like Suriya or be an activist. Or maybe I can just be ca—"

"Are your eyes blue or green?" Claude leans in so that my knees press into his belly.

"Oh, that really depends on so many things. On the light and what I'm wearing and if the person looking at me has some tiny bit of color blindness. Maybe not even diagnosed." I look at my hands, upturned in my lap. When I called my father after Brian kicked me out of our apartment, Dad said, "Go for a walk around the block. Have a glass of water. Sit still and notice the way your hands look in your lap." I tried to do all of those things. I couldn't do any of them. I bought Jared a plane ticket to New York.

My hand is in Claude's hand now, his palm sweating on my cold, stiff fingers. He pulls my hand to his chest and presses it against his saggy left breast. His heartbeat is rapid and faint. For an instant, it's soothing to be reminded of the efficiency and independence of bodies, each reduced to the same basic urges. But then Claude clears his throat and spits on the ground by my feet. His saliva makes a tiny glistening pond in the sand. A specific pond on the verge of specifically disappearing. Not a thought at all.

In ninth grade, the boys in my classes started fighting in the soccer field after school. The violence was taken for granted, a foregone conclusion. I felt dizzy whenever a kid with a black eye and swollen cheeks passed me in the hall. Someone had done that to him. He had felt that being done to him. "I'm telling you, don't mess with him, holmes," I heard one kid telling another in the cafeteria. "I pissed blood for a week. I thought I was gonna die." When I went to a Take Back the Night march a few years later, and held a candle while I listened to girls—some crying, some stone-faced—telling stories I wished I didn't have to hear, I remembered that small-nosed teenager. Is one kind of violence worse than another? Or is the idea of rape as a violation of the most inviolate part of self—one's soul or essence or purity, or whatever you call it— the unnecessary second arrow of suffering, intensifying the energy of an experience whose horror might be limited to the physical and temporal? Is the perceived power inherent in inflicting that psychic violation part of what incites rapists to rape? These thoughts come to me as shapes and textures. I sense what my mind is trying to say, but I can't yet hear the words it's using.

Claude holds my chin between his thumb and index finger

and leans toward me. The insides of his large lips wet my closed mouth. He pulls down on my chin and presses his tongue against my tongue. Without meaning to, I bite down. Claude sits back and slaps me with halfhearted aggression that matches mine. He kisses me again. I let his tongue circle the dead weight of my own. He stands up and walks behind my chair, squeezes and releases my shoulders, kneads my collarbone, moves his fingers to the hollow at the base of my throat and presses hard. I can't breathe for a moment. He releases his hand. I cough. He places his palm over my forehead and pulls me back against the base of his belly. His penis hardens against my neck. For a moment, my body opens to the familiarity of the touch. Then there's a sound like strings breaking in an orchestra in some windowless school auditorium in a little town filled with mostly empty parking lots. I fall into that other frequency, far below the clamoring moment, sorrow great enough to forgive me. Claude kneels in front of me and touches my face and smears the tears against his thigh. "I need sleep," I say.

He lifts me out of the chair and puts his arm around my waist. I hiccup as he walks me back to the motel.

At the door to my room, I mumble, "Bonne nuit," but Claude takes the key from my hand. I stand in the doorway as he reties my mosquito net over my bed and fumbles with the light switches until he finds the one for the fan. He returns his arm to my waist and walks me to the bed. He won't hurt me, not really. This will be the kind of badness that I can't help but recover from. He cups my shoulders and lowers me onto my back. He wheezes as he wrestles with my pants, still damp and clingy with saltwater. Sitting upright on the edge of the bed, he jams his fingers inside me. I put my hand on his wrist and tell him to get a condom out of the toiletry bag in the bathroom.

As he walks back to the bed, I think of a scene in a movie that shows only boot-clad feet, that kind of cheap foreboding. I like the thought, and nestle into it as Claude parts my legs with his knees. He lowers himself onto his elbows, depressing the mattress on both sides of my head. Raising himself onto straight arms, he pushes in. His hips move in a slow, rolling motion that makes me feel nothing. Here I am, all grown up. This is not rape, not sex, not life, not death, not right, not wrong. Unwanted, but here. I have succeeded. I have rid sex of its vanity. I have stripped myself of my ego. I have lost all concern for my circumstances. This is enlightenment, for a regular person (Suriya's phrase) who is not close to ready for enlightenment, who skipped the part about circumambulating the temple with my head bowed, begging Lord Buddha—or whatever you call it—for absolutely nothing. Without the humility required to make some sacrifice, however simple, all the spiritual insights in the world still add up to nothing. A drop of Claude's sweat falls onto my face. I turn my head and wipe my cheek against the sheet.

With no warning, he pulls out and walks into the bathroom. I am too tired to speak or move, which is not the worst postcoital feeling I've ever had.

Minutes or hours later, large hands pull me into a sitting position. "I will come to get you at noon, okay?" Claude says. "My driver will take us to lunch at a resort in the mountains. Bring your swimming suit. You will love it." I nod. He pats my foot and stands up.

After he leaves, I get out of bed and draw the lock across the door. I glance at my stuff, scattered on the floor around the room: a bottle of Rite Aid sunscreen, a faded blue bikini hanging from the doorknob, hiking sandals caked in dirt. "I'm glad Claude didn't beat me to death," I tell my things. I wish they could laugh.

~

I always made sure I had at least two blankets on my bed when I was a child, so they could keep each other company while I was at school. If I realized that one hand towel in the bathroom was getting used more than the other because it was closer to the sink, I switched the towels to give them equal affection. I broke down sobbing at my fifth birthday party when my mom suggested my friends and I take a plastic baseball bat to the piñata she had stuffed with my favorite candy. My care for objects was rewarded. Pillows, towels, markers, socks comforted me, offering themselves up with infinite friendliness. Then I entered junior high and learned that my behavior was acceptable only as a literary technique. But there was nothing poetic about the consciousness I attributed to things. I was possibly psychotic. This was one of many indications that it would not be wise for me to speak my true thoughts aloud.

At some point during one of my meaningless sexual encounters in Paris or during the barhopping years afterward or at several points during several such encounters, I had the thought that if I had been able to maintain that easy mutual love for things, I would have been always filled with love. People-oriented attachment and desire would not have been able to control me. Even if there were some truth to this thinking, the truth could not shift anything in me because, at the moment in which I was thinking this way, I was only exploiting the thought to feel something other than the reality of two bored people trying to feel a tiny bit good. It was a comforting distraction to conceptualize the sex as existentially sad, and my desire for it as existentially pathetic, because I could not then bear what I now know the sex truly was: banal, affectless, *rien du tout*.

"Protect this vow, even at the risk of your life."

I am lying at the coincidence of two infinitudes—black air

above, black water below. I had to swim far out, past the lines where the huge waves break, to be able to float on my back. I take refuge in the Buddha, I take refuge in his teachings, I take refuge in the people who abide them. That is the vow the Tibetan saying asks me to protect with my life. The water is wide awake and warm. I am terrified of sharks and sea snakes, one of which crawled out of the water and hissed at a group of drunken tourists the other day. I take refuge in the Bu— Stop.

I rise and fall along the crest of waves about to break. One sucks me under, tumbles me, releases me. There is no hope of refuge, no chance of being saved.

This man saved me. This job saved me. This exercise routine saved me. This religion saved me. This house saved me. This child saved me. This book saved me. This vitamin saved me. This parakeet saved me. This country saved me. Enough.

It takes a long time to swim back to shore. Afraid, okay, afraid, okay.

Afraid? Okay.

My English teacher in high school used to tell us that suicide was never an option in fiction. So this is what he meant. Of course people kill themselves in novels. But first the plot must be entrenched in such an eensy-weensy, immovable, rock-hard crevice that suicide becomes the only inevitability. In real life, suicide is always just one of infinite options, as avid and useless as any other fantasy.

KANDY

Loudspeakers crackle to life before blasting recorded pirith. The smell of the ocean is spicy and proud, not yet overpowered by frying rotis and burning trash. The bus stop is in front of a fancy hotel enclosed by a tall brick wall, which I lean against to relieve the weight of my pack. I don't have to wait long before the bus barrels toward me, the loud complaints of its engine stirring up a gust of butterflies from a patch of grass on the other side of the road. Their bright, motile mass disappears into a palmyra grove, and I climb up the back steps of the bus, shouting "Kandy? Kandy?" to no one in particular.

An elderly man nods. "Kandy, yes. Long trip."

I push through thickets of flesh in search of a place to stow my bag. The bus is packed with children in white school uniforms, businessmen in suits, businesswomen in saris. I tighten my abdomen and widen my stance to keep from falling when my sweaty hand loses its grip on the seat back.

Relief. We're all just a person on a bus.

When I called 911 soon after Brian and I broke up, I knew, the instant the police filed in—guns drawn, backs to the wall—that there was no intruder. It was just me in a towel and two police officers whose jaws were set against the terror of being surprised by an armed lunatic. After they left, I walked over to the antique mirror Brian and I had carried home from a flea market one late-summer day, fallen leaves cartwheeling at our feet as the sun turned our noses pink. It was the only piece of furniture I'd taken when I moved out of his apartment. I sat down cross-legged in front of the mirror and met my own eyes. For the first time, I was glad Brian was gone. He would have been horrified that I'd mistakenly called the police, would have made me promise not to mention the incident to his parents, so ashamed he often was of my odd transgressions against decorum.

But this is also what drew him to me. He loved to watch me devour ice cream or tear up at the first threat of sadness in a movie. "You're so susceptible," he said once. "To everything." And he laughed in a way that relieved me of the obligation to respond.

That first morning in our newly shared apartment: drinking mimosas, singing along to Neil Young, making pancakes filled with strawberries. We were so hopeful. He insisted we not get dressed. I sat on his lap and ate pancakes with my hands. At first, I kept my feet on the ground to take some of my weight off his lap. But as we both kept eating and drinking, I forgot to hold myself up and I let his thighs support me. An overly explicit metaphor. It was always like that with him, crystal clear, no surprises—like even our best times were part of a script that had been written long before we met. The bus hits a pothole and I'm jostled into an older woman. I almost grab her hand. Brian's arm around my waist as we walked down an icy sidewalk: This is what I imagined love was, when I was a child. But they were only moments. We did not share the world that surrounded them.

At the other end of the bus, a pimply middle-aged man is waving at me and pointing to the empty seat in front of him. "Ne, ne," I say. But the people in the aisle all stare at me while he gestures, so I make my way to the front. Best just to accept the kindness. The driver hands me a plantain. "Sthoo-thiy," I say. Thank you, Brian, I think. For making me leave. The driver beams at the road before him. It's not so difficult, really, to share moments of love with others.

As we near downtown Kandy, I hop off the bus at a storefront advertising international calls. A skinny boy in a Yankees shirt leads me to a curtained phone booth in the back. I start dialing before he pulls the curtain closed. The space between each muted ring is too long. On the other side of the curtain, the boy shifts in his squeaky chair. My chin curls toward my chest. No one home. Click. A man clears his throat.

"Bueno. Dime."

"Jared? Why are you speaking Spanish?"

"520 Clark."

"What? Jared, it's me."

"I know, come over. It's not a party 'til you're here, doll."

"Jared. It's Elsie. I am in Sri Lanka." The words are slow and heavy, trying to stave off panic.

"Elsie? Oh, hey baby. I didn't recognize you."

No, no, not this voice—sloppy, affectedly deep, unchanging in tone and quality no matter what I do or say. He cannot be in that state now. He cannot be unreachable now.

"I really need to talk to you." I clutch the curtain in my free hand, twisting it round and round my fist.

"Now's not great. I'm having this thing." Girls cackle near him. A stereo blasts anthemic rock. Talking to Jared is impossible right now. I should not try. I should hang up.

"What thing?" I say.

"We're starting an S&M club. Come over, baby." These words are not Jared's. They are spoken in a woman's high-pitched bravado, the voice of a sexual aggressor who never gets her needs met. I smell her sticky red lipstick as she leans against Jared's cheek, stealing our conversation with his consent.

"Jared," I say, "if you don't leave that room right now and find a quiet place to talk to me—"

"Jesus Christ. You are always mad at me. I'm hanging up. Good luck out there, Elsie."

"Please, Jared, please, please." I'm whining, digging my fingers into my cheeks, about to lose myself. I see it happening, cannot stop it.

"Jesus H. What is it now?" He sounds like an overworked CEO who has just been screwed out of millions of dollars. Alcohol, parties: This is his confidence.

"I need you right now. Please leave the party and talk to me."

"I will be back imminently," he announces to everyone but me. "Apparently I am needed."

ool singing a lady's love song they probably didn't even know
s written by men?

How gross it is that I am still thinking about this stuff. Men
d women, how a penis erect transforms a man, how a woman is
de to receive this transformation, what parts of herself take him
what parts she withholds, what she has the power to withhold.
w to protect herself without cutting herself off, how to be gen-
us without being self-deprecating, how to be detached without
ng cold, how to be attached without being obsessed, how to
her own needs met without being demanding, how to meet
needs without being sacrificial, how to be gentle without being
ushover, how to be firm without being bitchy, how to be calm
hout being lifeless, how to be passionate without being enraged,
y to be independent without feeling alone, how to be dependent
hout feeling alone, how sick I am of it all.

I would lose anything to be free.

at I need is food. I need to consume all the spices and grains
vegetables and oils in the world.

march into town, order five curries, have three large bites, let
fourth fall out of my mouth. Gasp. Pay for my meal. Am walk-
slowly now, noticing every sight and sound and smell around
but I won't be bothered to put them into words.

cannot see him again. I will not.

There is no possible way to imagine myself into the small house
were going to share by the beach. His breath on my neck as he
s us home from a bar. The sweet pudginess of his large arm
cles going slack as we fall into bed. My lips against his neck in
morning, puckering against his loose skin until he says, "Cut
t, that tickles," and rolls on top of me, his belly warm and
y against mine. The relief of his body beside me, after the

"I need you here, Jared!" the S&M woman trills.

"Get away from that bitch," I say. "I need to talk to you."

He sighs grandly, but I feel him walking outside. Silence over-
comes the background hum. I can breathe again.

"Hi, love." My voice is desperately sweet. "Thanks for leaving
so we can talk. I hope you're not sleeping with that awful woman."

"Look. Just stop it. I am not going to waste another night hack-
ing out your insecurities. It is so goddamn boring it makes me
want to cut off my dick. You are always mad at me. Stop being
mad at me. Just don't ever call me again if you're gonna pull this
shit, judging me for every goddamn thing. I can't take it anymore.
Just don't call me again. Leave me alone. Déjame en paz." He
laughs at his lisping Spanish.

My organs are losing their contours, melting, dripping, laughing at me as they ooze to the floor. Hard to hold the phone. "Oh
no. Dear God." I'm in a small, black room, cold, no windows, no
doorknobs. "Please, God."

"Are you praying?"

"Please, God."

"Jesus Christ, what are you praying for?"

Someone to talk to, someone to say something that could
change, even just barely, even imperceptibly, the landscape inside
my head. "I cannot believe you're speaking to me like this right
now." My voice is a stale whisper. "This can't be happening. I
can't—I got raped."

The lie is a relief for as long as it takes the three words to leave
my lips. Then it is evil, the hopelessness of connection given language.

"Hey man," Jared is saying. "Yeah, go in, I'll be right there. Are
you shitting me, Elsie?"

"Not really."

"Not really. Jesus Christ. Did you or did you not get raped?"

"Not. I did not. I mean I did. I did get raped. I raped myself."

"Okay, that's it. You think you can say whatever the fuck you feel whenever you feel like it. I'm hanging up, Elsie. I told you this was not a good time and then you went ahead—"

"I wanted to talk to you about what happened!"

"—and say all this intense shit and I am really needed inside right now. You are not going to ruin my night. It's not exactly easy to get this many cool people together in the same room. I'm finally feeling good and then you call me and say whatever the fuck you feel like saying and I'm hanging up now, good night, goodbye, I love you, be safe." Click.

I am too weak to be involved. That is what I know, lying in this bed below the window with the wooden bars, two missing, a space large enough to admit clever monkeys and feral cats. But no life comes through. The lace curtain is yellow and frayed at the edges, sticking to the hot breeze. How many days has it been since I even imagined a human noise? The crying—treacherous, jagged icicles cutting my throat. Sucking my thumb again, even. I would be ashamed to recall that, except it was my only comfort. How did I think I could calmly withstand this pain, see it as just a temporary combination of thoughts, feelings, sensations—notice them, accept them, this too shall pass? The shock every time—of being hurt, turning to Jared (who else to turn to?) to soothe me, finding only more pain. How could he do this to me. God, I mean. Questions like that—old and dumb—barreling me down. Clutching my chest, hyperventilating on purpose in the hope that I might faint, hearing the dry heaves of my sobs as if they were coming from someone else, a child stuck on a movie screen, someone I cannot help. For days I have been reduced to that noise. There is no one else at this guesthouse, which is just a house with a sign in

the yard that says ROOM FOR RENT. The owner th
brings me plain white rice and tea, which I eat
grabbing handfuls from the bowl on the floor b
tea into my open mouth, catching some of the li
before it spills out the other side and soaks the
nice. Sugar and plants.

Once there is nothing else to do, no other h
this room, I fold my stained pillow in half and j
My fingers are in my mouth, my spine curved,
heavy, waste fluids pouring over my fist and cl
rock, rock, rock until it is no longer I but my
the space between my breasts, the soft tissue ir
ing me forward and back. The movement re
until I can't stand it any longer. Jump up, beat
fists, toss the pillow on the floor, sit on the edge
head in my hands. My best effort is not enoug

Show him that you care just for him. Do th
to do. Some popular girls performed "Wishin'
talent show in tenth grade. It was supposed to
nist girls with nose rings and perfect GPAs wea
their ponytails and blue eye shadow and hug
they were making fun of their mothers and g
ing the idea that "true love" is a woman who
her man. But the fantasy hasn't much change
violent in speech and dress and behavior, but
ing their ugly, rebellious complexity to get to
relationship that works because the girl make
power. Once I've given my life over to helping
I make my relationship my full-time job, the
me. He just needs to be accepted exactly as he
stop being so angry. Once I fully commit, h
Isn't that what I'm hoping for, just like the

nights when I won't know where he is or what he's doing: all the dumb, tiny soldiers inside me dropping their guns and drifting off to sleep.

If I went through my life in a meditative state—observing instead of reacting—I could live that way. Or if I were normal, more desensitized to the vagaries of sex and connection. Some people feel the pain of love's disappointment, and then do something else with their time. I cannot move, cannot think, can barely breathe. Passion. What a lie. The way I love gives up everything.

I'm sitting in front of a computer at an Internet café. I'm not sure why I brought myself here. Seven emails from Jared. I guess that's what my brain was hoping for. He thinks I called him last night, he hopes he wasn't out of line, he'd had a little to drink, please can I call him again, he misses me so much, he's so sorry if he was out of line, he's gonna stop as soon as I get home, he can't wait for me to get home. Of course. He always asks for my forgiveness in a way that allows me, effortlessly, to grant it. The morning he came to my apartment with a bouquet of handpicked flowers in a handblown vase his mother made for him before she fell in love with a woman and moved to Europe, how the flesh softened around his bones when I opened the door, our foreheads touching and our snot and tears all mixed up.

"Please don't close your heart to me," he said. "You are the best friend I've ever had."

And the night when the spider woke me up in some motel bed I was sharing with Jared. At first, the skin on my arm felt something like wonder at how wide apart the creature's legs were, how many there were, how slowly they walked in perfect concert with one another, creeping, trying not to disturb me. And then it was at my throat and I was wide awake and shrieking. "Get it off! Get it off!" Jared thrashed out of bed and turned on the light. I jammed my finger in the direction of the black body escaping across my pillow on long, strong, gauzy legs, one of which Jared grabbed between his thumb and forefinger. The spider dangled, its free legs pawing the air and its fuzzy head stiff and protracted, while Jared's wide eyes darted about, landing on the glass of water beside the bed. Into the water Jared flicked the creature. Stillness. He sat on the edge of the bed, his back to me, peering into the glass. Remnants of disgust and outrage at the sensation of the spider's legs on my throat competed inside my chest with shame at the frivolousness of my outrage. Jared's shoulders began to shake, his head bent forward, he sputtered and opened his mouth wide, did nothing to stifle his sobs. "He tried so hard," he said. "He was trying so hard but the water was too much for him. He wanted to live so bad. He just wanted to live. He was trying so hard but the water—" He kept talking as I took the glass from his hand, pulled him down to me, held him, murmured it wasn't his fault, he had done nothing wrong, I was sorry, I was so sorry, I didn't know how to not be always freaking out, how did a person stop always freaking out, I didn't know, I was sorry. He slept and I held him and then sometime in the early morning I became the sleeper, he the holder.

No. Must not think of that. Must choose memories that harden not soften me, must tell myself a story in which he is simple and bad. Fierce determination to get to a place of steadiness. I do not get to keep my love for him.

The tinny ice cream cart song trickles past. Suriya's name is in my inbox, too. She has written me three notes, all saying the same thing: "Elsie Akki, my mother has died. Can you come to my home please? I hope you are receiving this mail. God bless."

GAMBAWELLA

My mother had a manuscript of unpublished poems written by a friend of hers in college. She would get them out when she was in one of her moods, lay the pages on the kitchen table and pick them up at random, silently mouthing the words with a deliberateness I found annoyingly melodramatic. One time I snatched the page out of her hands. "My father took me at the same time every day," I read aloud.

"Her father raped her, that's what 'took' means there." My mother fidgeted with the edge of the tablecloth. "There was Satan worship. A cult. Anne is complicated. A bird—a large bird of prey—slaughtered over her. The blood dripping on her. She was naked, a little girl. Something happened to her, some thought, something kind of good for the first time. Darlene, too, she has a master's degree, she is *very* smart, she never could understand Anne's poems. Some kind of Satan worship, a large bird of prey. The men wore hoods. But there was this good thing."

My mother often told stories in fragments like this. When you asked for clarification, she would respond in more fragments. I dropped the piece of paper back on the table and poured myself a glass of orange juice.

When my mother moved across the country with Rick, she brought the box of Anne's poems with her. I saw it on the backseat before they drove off, Rick gripping the wheel in one hand and a plastic travel mug that said "Dunkin' Donuts" in bubble letters in the other, my mother's hair pulled back into a diamond-studded barrette, tears rolling down her cheeks and catching in the thin ring of excess skin around the base of her neck, her biggest insecurity.

Not long ago, I asked my mother if she still had the poems.

"Oh yes." She started to repeat her fragmentary take on Anne, how complicated she was, even Darlene did not really get her, the bird of prey, the Satan worship, the little girl with blood—

"Do you still talk to Anne?" I asked.

"God no. Not since college."

"Why do you care about her poems so much?"

"I wouldn't say I care about them *so much*. You just don't throw away something like that."

I want my mother to be a deep person, to matter in some way aside from having pushed babies out of her womb. But she doesn't want to be deep; she wants to be happy. She answers the phone when I call. And she did bring me on those whale watches and to that Cambodian temple. She cannot be more than she is. Of course I've had this thought many times before. It's Psych 101 stuff. But now, riding the bus to Amma's funeral, *god bless, god bless* tolling in my mind, I feel the thought rather than think it.

Ayya is waiting for me at the bus stop. He raises one hand. "We happy you come here," he says, enunciating too deliberately. It's clear he's been saving these words. He takes my backpack and I follow him across the street to Suriya's house. There is a coffin in the empty front room attached to the kitchen. As Ayya carries my bag upstairs, I walk to the edge of the box. Suriya's mother has been dressed in a white sari and gold jewelry. Her face is made up with kohl around her eyes, cakey whitening powder, red lipstick. Her lips are upturned, but the smile belongs to the living; Suriya's mother is nowhere near this room. I'm permitted the preciousness of the thought because I have no attachment to Amma's specific body.

"Come," Ayya says, and leads me to his neighbor's house, where it seems the whole village is gathered in the front yard, laughing and talking and squatting over plates of food. Children chase each other, running figure eights around the grown-ups' legs and shrieking when they get caught. I find myself smiling as I enter the yard. But then I see Suriya's face, an island in the chaos of limbs and voices and consumption. Making eye contact with her is like staring at a blinding light. "El," she says, and takes my hands in hers. "This is my auntie's house. We must come here for meals. During funeral days, we cannot eat in our home. Or we will become sick. One time there was a woman in our village who fed her child during a funeral. All the people told her no, but she said, I don't believe old stories, baby is hungry, and she gave some rice milk. And then that baby becomes so sick. He must live in the hospital. So we cannot take meals at our home until the funeral is finish, okay, El? Very important." She speaks quickly, tonelessly. Her English seems better than ever. "Okay, El?"

"Yes, okay. I'm happy to see you. I'm so sorry." Pause. Silence. Try again. "There are so many people here."

"Yes, there are many. Because my mother is kind."

I look away from the wounded gape of Suriya's eyes. "Where is your father?"

"He is in the bed. Like baby. In these days, I must do everything for him. I give him to eat and wash his face. He is not moving. When we learned she has died—the sound that came from his mouth, El. It eats my heart."

A short woman with wide, flat nostrils gives Suriya a plate of oil cookies. Suriya stares down at the cookies as the woman speaks to her in Sinhala, gently at first, then more emphatically. At last the woman takes the plate from Suriya's hands and walks toward the kitchen. "I don't know what that woman is saying to me. I am to do something with those cookies. I think." Suriya's mouth barely moves as she speaks. I want to pull her toward me, but my body offers no assistance. I stare at the dirt clinging to my swollen toes.

"What happened, Nangi?" I ask. "How did she die?"

"She had a tomb in her womb. And she had blood coming from her breast. Like milk. Except blood instead."

"Did she have cancer?"

Suriya closes her eyes, her thumbs pressed against her temples. "My head is a ghost's garage."

We dress in white on the day of the funeral. Suriya irons the family's clothes on the upstairs patio, holding each item of pristine cloth to the light and turning it about in search of creases. As I start to tie my hair back in my usual haphazard bun, she looks at me in alarm. "Akki? Shall I fix your hair?" Her mundane concern makes me giddy with relief.

Three monks from the village temple come for the service. They stand in front of the casket in worn robes, eyes softly unfocused, hands clasped before them, a little too poised. The oldest one speaks for a short, dreary while. When he stops, Suriya's father raises a golden pitcher into the air. Suriya and Ayya place their hands atop his, and together they tip the pitcher downward, letting the water it contains fall into the dry earth below Amma's coffin. A willingness to give up the most precious thing, maybe. Allow the heart to break because that's how the heart survives.

Suriya's spine curls toward the ground, an unseen weight pulling her down. Her wail reminds me of the time my auto-rickshaw driver ran over a puppy in Colombo and then laughed at my anguish over such trivial suffering. Ayya takes Suriya by the armpits and pulls her upright. His chest absorbs her howl. I don't realize the service has ended until people begin to crowd around us, patting Suriya and murmuring words that are probably trite but necessary before heading into the cloudy day. Suriya's father and brother stand on either side of her and pull her up the stairs to her room.

Hashini and her husband walk over to me. I put my hands in front of my chest and bow. Hashini smooths down my hair. Rajesh grins and nods vigorously. Suriya's wails continue from her bedroom. Ayya comes down the stairs and hurries to me, pointing down the road to the eating house. "Take a meal," he says. "Please."

"I go to Suriya," I say, accidentally mimicking her English.

I find her lying on her side, clutching at the sheet, her mouth opened wide, shrieking soundlessly. How much of my adult life I have passed in this position, for reasons that seem so wasteful now. I lie beside her, my butt falling off the small bed. I take her hand in mine and press our clasped hands against her chest. Her heart pounds through her back. I can admit to myself now—in feeling, if not in words—why I was irritated when Suriya spoke of her mother's illness. It seemed almost sweet to die, compared to choosing to leave. I had no idea; I still don't. I breathe loudly and slowly. I can't think of anything else to do. Only after it grows too dark to watch the large, slow bounce of palm leaves through the window does Suriya quiet. I loosen my grip on her hand as her cry loosens into a thin, slow wheeze.

When my eyes open many hours later, Suriya's back is still pressed against my chest. The white pit of the sun fills the window. Suriya yawns and fidgets her way to wakefulness.

"I want tea," she says. "Okay, Akki?"

After she leaves, I cross my legs under me and sit still for a while, waiting for the ache to become nothing more than an ache.

The front yard is empty, the tent and casket gone. Suriya is in the kitchen, ladling thin, beige batter into a small pan on the electric burner. The batter hardens into a bowl-shaped crepe. "Do you like hoppers, El?" she asks, handing me a full plate.

I love. I bite into the thick, spongy center, soaked with spicy coconut sauce. I ask Suriya to tell me how to make these, for when I'm back in the States.

"So easy," she says, swirling the pan to even out another spoonful of batter. "Rice flour, coconut milk, one egg. Or two eggs. Or no egg, if you don't have. Salt. Little oil. Hopper dust."

"Hopper dust?"

"Yes," she says evenly. I miss her usual exclamatory inflection. "Mix in a bowl and cook in a hopper pan."

Suriya's father walks in, wearing the same clothes he wore at the funeral. She straightens her spine. Her voice is too cheery as she tries to hand him a plate of hoppers. He scrunches his small nose as if smelling something rotten, turns his back to us, addresses the doorway. The words march in a slow, loose line, following orders out of habit.

"My father is angry with me," Suriya says when his hunched shoulders disappear through the door.

"Why is he angry this time?"

"Because my mother loved to make hopper meals. He says to me, 'Everywhere I see her remembers and her moments.' This is my father's sad. But I need her remembers and her moments." She stirs up the batter, which I will clearly not be able to reconstruct at home. "You know the parable about the woman with a baby that died, El? And she ask Lord Buddha to make that baby live again?" The Buddha told her he could make a special medicine if she brought him mustard seeds from a house in which no one had ever died. The mother went from house to house, clutching her dead baby, begging for the seeds, receiving instead story after story of loss. Finally she buried her son in the woods, sad and okay. A miracle of acceptance. "I need to think of my mother's small things, to remember them all," Suriya says. "But I must balance small things with big ones. Do you understand?"

Yes. No. I look at her closely.

"What are you thinking, Akki?" She slides a hopper onto my plate.

That your goodness is not make-believe, not part of any machine.

"What a good cook you are," I say.

"You only say that because you are my friend. I have so much to learn." She nibbles the crisp lip of a hopper. "Can I ask you for a help, Akki?"

"Of course."

"I would like to talk to my boyfriend. He wrote me that we can talk with the Skype. You can help?"

At the house with a computer, I check my email while Suriya plays with the owners' baby. Joe from *Carp Weekly* has written back. He has cancer—"of the goddamned tongue! What a fuckin' wanker God is"—and he's taking time off from work. The good news is that Donnie will do pretty much whatever Joe asks—"you don't cross a cancer patient"—and Joe was happy to call in a favor for me. As usual, the paper is in dire need of good editors. Donnie would be glad to have me back on staff, and I'd be salaried. Starting at $40,000 with benefits, a number that sounds to me like success. I'll have to edit the What's Hot? section in addition to the In Memoriams—"ladies' handbags and cocktail recipes and the like. At least that's what it is now. Let's just say, there is ample room for improvement." I hear the words in Joe's determined, self-contained tenor. So. That's what I'll do.

But—Jared. I cannot live in his town. I would never escape my thoughts about him. Anyway, I ought to be teaching impoverished children how to farm or trying to make plastic out of recycled fingernail clippings or becoming the first Buddhist nun who is also a sex educator or biking across the U.S. to raise awareness about Tamil oppression. I wish I would do any one of those things, I really do. But I won't. Maybe I could move to Montreal, finally get good at speaking French, work at a bookstore or coffee shop or something. My forehead drops into my hand. Enough ideas. Do what is before you. Take the newspaper job, but don't live in Carpinteria, live in a nearby town—maybe that tiny, gorgeous one with brightly colored cottages and vegetable gardens in the yards and cheap rents because the cliff above it is inching year by year closer to landslide. Return to the work you had when you were twenty-two, knowing now that no greater life is beckoning from afar. I've always been right here.

After I set up a Skype account for Suriya, I sit outside with the owner of the Internet café, as Suriya calls this house with a computer. He has a large, silly chin. "Your name?" he asks me.

"Elsie."

"Your country?"

"U.S.A."

Time passes. Whorls of dust agitate the pale sky.

"Your name?" he says.

"Elsie."

"Your country?"

"U.S.A."

I am an ordinary person with an ordinary life. Even my acceptance of ordinariness is ordinary, the undercurrent of so many "big books." *Madame Bovary, War and Peace, Freedom.* The mistake is always the same: trying to live the life one has in one's head instead of the life before one, which is endlessly generous if you humble yourself to it as the only possible means of fulfillment. But isn't there something condescending about being told by great artists that ordinariness leads to happiness? Those who create art that preserves their lives from the dull, repetitive labors to which the masses are confined tell these same masses to labor joyfully. Plato's Noble Lie, retold endlessly. But that kind of ordinariness is not what the man in white robes was talking about in the meditation center in the mountains as the candles flickered and the insects sang and my ass went numb on a thin, hard, overused cushion. What was he talking about? Stopping. Wondering. What am I doing right now. Is it necessary. He was not talking about doing any particular thing. I could stay at the newspaper until I'm old and gray, or come back to Sri Lanka and teach English, or write a novel about a totally imaginary person who has nothing to do with me, or translate a French book that even a non-suicidal person might enjoy. The point is to pay attention to what's real, not to my imagination. To remember that it's enough just to sit on a train, seeing, hearing, bouncing, dozing, thinking, letting the mind go blank. That's love, too, a kind of love. It seems possible to love like that all the time, but then—Suriya walks out of the house. I stand and ask if she was able to reach her boyfriend. Seeming not to hear, she loosens the bun at the nape of her neck to let her hair fall down to her knees, shakes her head, reins the stringy, black mane back in. I offer to bike home and she barely nods, just hops onto the handlebars, the same way I glided into my dad's car after spending the afternoon in Dan's attic in high school, when he sang me radio love songs and made me believe I was the most beautiful girl in the world.

Suriya leans over my shoulder as we bike past the swampy lake. "El, that is the first time I have seen my boyfriend in two years. And I will see his real face soon. He is coming back to Sri Lanka. In six months or one year. We will be married."

I backpedal to a stop in Suriya's yard. "And you are sure he will be a good husband?" As if that question has an answer. Suriya walks the bike to the back of the house. She cannot know everything of her husband until they marry. But she knows some things. She runs her hand down the side of her face and lets it rest on her neck. She takes the broom leaning against the house and starts sweeping trash and dead frangipani flowers toward the street. Ayya pulls up on his motorbike and throws anxious words at Suriya. The machine coughs dust around our ankles as he roars off.

"The funeral takes Ayya's money," Suriya says. "So he goes to find money in the village. One man, he owes my father money from some years ago. Maybe Ayya can find that man." Suriya stares at the crosshatched line Ayya's bike leaves in its wake. His military leave was extended for the funeral. It will be awhile before he returns to his sentry point in Colombo and gets a paycheck.

"Ayya is such a kind person," I say, following Suriya to the backyard. "Does he ever feel bad supporting—" Stop this right now, says a calm, male voice in my head. Suriya's mother just died. "I mean, ruling over the Tamils, helping to keep them down?"

"The soldiers must rule." She sounds bored. "LTTE was so bad. We cannot let them come again."

"The way to stop the LTTE from beginning again is to give equal rights. Treat the Tamils well. Your president has done the opposite." Suriya's father is sitting alone on a pink lawn chair, a plate of untouched food resting on his lap.

"Maybe you are right, El. I cannot say. The rulers have the power. We cannot fight our ruler. We do not have this power." In my head, a chorus of imaginary activists groans, "Speak truth to power! Fight the good fight! Don't give in to injustice!" But Suriya is not an activist; she is something else. She takes the plate from her father's lap. "Why did you come to Sri Lanka, El."

She says it as if it's an answer she understands for the first time and she feels sorry for me. There is no particular person or event I'm running from, no tidy past tragedy to justify my current des-peration. I am a confused American who came to a land of poor, dark-skinned, war-scarred people hoping to learn how to be simple and happy. I am aware of the cliché of my journey and so have di-minished in the retelling of it even the parts that did truly change so Ayya can understand my meaning through cadence. "I love it here." He smiles, reassured, and heads up the stairs. "But, Nangi, I do need to leave soon."

"I know. You must go back to your country and make a family." Suriya taps an imaginary watch on her wrist.

"No, no." I shake my head vigorously.

"El. I am joking."

I squeeze her hand. "You have to go back to Kandy soon, anyway, right? How long can you take off school?"

Suriya gives me the look of condescending surprise that means I have failed to grasp some obvious fact of her life. "I will not go back to school. I must stay here and care for my father."

I drop her hand. "Suriya. Please. Your father is a grown man. You can't give up your studies. You've worked so hard."

"I do not give up my studies. My success with school gives me power and it makes me brave. Like the first time I spoke to you in Kandy."

"That's exactly why you have to finish school. Get a good job."

"My boyfriend is here soon," she says, as if I haven't spoken at all.

"Will be here soon," I say.

"Will be." She walks toward the kitchen.

I email my father: I'll be home in a week. I'm coming to stay with him for a little while, before I move back to California. Can he pick me up at the airport? He writes back within minutes. He can't believe how perfectly I timed my email. He had *just* been sitting down to write me. He misses me so much, can't wait to see me, how long will I stay? Just a warning: His accountant has told him that the inheritance money is getting low and the remainder needs to be invested, blah blah blah (my father's words), he's not going to

me—if change means relinquishing the habitual markers by which one measures the progress of one's life—because I am loathe to turn the real goodness I felt in the lake, in the sky palace above the cave temple, on the handlebars of Suriya's bike, into a self-congratulatory moral, yet another way to manipulate the minute smudge of my personality. So if I ever do manage to make anything out of these notes, it will be the story not of who I am but of who I fear I am.

"I don't know," I say. "I don't know why I came here." For half of an instant, I become the person I feel myself to be late at night when I can't sleep and I'm all alone with the minutes passing, and I'm wide awake with thoughts I want to force the minutes to understand, but the seconds are too fast, they pass and pass, and then pass again. I take Suriya's hands, cool and pliable, all those necessary, tiny bones. "I love you, Nangi. I love how you are."

"Okay. I love you also. You have hungry, Akki?"

We take bouncing steps through frothy brown water, where women are bathing and washing clothes. They smile and nod, smile and nod. Suriya is the girl who just lost her mother and I am her friend all the way from America. I'm no longer embarrassed by my U.S.A. T-shirt and Nike running shorts. I walk through the soapy canal and then dive beneath opaque stillness, keeping my eyes open. The underwater world is a blue lace curtain billowing over a bright window. When I surface, two women about my age are talking excitedly, pointing to the far edge of the lake, where a small circle of sky rains on green, green paddy fields.

Suriya swims over and stands beside me. She whispers my name. I crane my neck upward: an untroubled pastel dome. "There must be a rainbow," I say, just as the women nearby smile hugely and point to the other side of the lake. "I never—" I shut my mouth.

A thick band of colored light is climbing slowly over our heads, forming a perfect arc that touches down at last on the tall grasses near the mouth of the canal.

A young father carries his baby into the water. The infant gurgles and smacks the surface of the lake with her small palm. The sky takes a huge breath, sucking the heat from the air. Suriya cups her ear. "Heard you that noise?" she says, English failing her. "It's coming, oh, it's coming." And then we are engulfed in raindrops so huge and fast and loud that it feels like my skin is leather stretched taut over the surface of a drum. I shield the rain from my eyes, while everyone around me cups their hands over their ears. Even physical discomfort is cultural. We turn in slow circles, watching drops bounce off the mirrored lake. Suriya hops lightly. The lake water is hot on my thighs. Cool rain pelts my shoulders. "Disaster wind," she says, beaming, wide-eyed, enjoying her fear. She puts her arm around my waist under the water. Distant thunder grows closer. Gilded daggers cut jags out of the slate sky. "We should get out of the water," I say. "You can die."

"Oh no!" But Suriya moves deeper into the lake. She floats on her back, her mouth opened wide. She swims back to me and takes my hand. We hop together back to shore. The sun comes out on the walk home, raising steam from the rain-soaked earth.

The next morning, I tell Suriya that I would like to take her to America with me. She's hanging freshly washed sheets and towels on the line, wearing her purple pajama pants and True Love Forever T-shirt. "Before you get married," I say. "We can stay with my father. He has a very big house. And travel around."

She lets the sheet she's rinsing fall back in the bucket. "I go to U.S.A.?" She lowers herself to the ground, rests her elbows on her

crossed legs and her chin in her hands. She looks up at the space between her first two fingers. "Akki, this i But I never risk to ask you." I finish rinsing the sheet that we'll need to go to Colombo to get her a passpor forms for a visa. We can travel all around the East Co Statue of Liberty. Go to the beach in Florida.

"In your country, I can wear a bikini?"

"Of course. You can wear whatever you want."

"Wow," she tells her lap.

But as we're brushing our teeth at the water pum she says that she has been thinking about the trip to she has decided that she must not go. Before she met thought about leaving her country. Lanka is enough is the best way. She begs me not to have angry with make her dream come true. But she cannot go to Am

So instead of booking plane tickets and waiting air-conditioned offices in Colombo, we spend days le soothe our senses. After the storms exhaust themselv the yard and watch the spidery watermarks on Su house get slowly erased by the sun. I didn't really a Miami beach with Suriya in a bikini. I just want something.

"Are you lazy, El Akki?" Suriya asks me one a resting my head on the chair back, my legs stretch me. I sit upright. Ayya and Suriya stand in front of ing at me expectantly. "Lazy?" I say. My head gro hot. Ayya raises his arms as far as he can above his wide V, and then yawns dramatically. "You. Lazy. H

"You mean bored?"

"Lazy?" Ayya says.

"Sitting. Eating. Talking. Gazing." I pause af

worry about it, he's never agonized over money in his life and he's never gone hungry. He's started working as an electrician again, like he used to when he was practically still a kid—I knew that, didn't I? (I didn't.) He likes it better than film work, really. No ego. And pretty fucking good pay, considering.

Suriya bikes us home from the house with a computer. Too fast, perfect fast.

Suriya insists we visit a highly revered cave temple, to make a fruit offering to the gods in exchange for protecting me on my trip home. We make the two-hour trek by bus on a Saturday. The temple gates are frenzied with pilgrims buying lotus flowers, candles, and fruit platters. Suriya requests the largest platter and asks the harried fruit seller to fill it with rose apples, mangoes, bananas, pineapples. As the young woman deftly slices a pineapple and fans the pieces into floral arrangements, I wish I were buying this food as an offering to Suriya. Her family needs a beautiful plate of fresh produce much more than this famous temple that enjoys the government's showy patronage. And it seems highly unlikely that any god will concern himself with my personal safety in exchange for a banana in the shape of a tulip.

At the top of the craggy pathway leading to the temple, Suriya and I join a long line of weary worshippers, also bearing elaborate fruit and flower offerings. At first, the people at the back of the line join their hands in prayer when the chanting from inside the cave drifts back to us. But after some time in this sticky mass of bodies shuffling toward the cave's narrow passage, waiting becomes just something to get through. Two teenage girls lean against each other's backs, making ineffectual fans out of their hands. A tiny elderly woman elbows past me, and I nearly elbow her back.

At last it is our turn to duck inside the mouth of the cave, which opens to a candlelit hotbox too small to stand up in. The altar is a mess of coins, flower petals, and melted wax. An infant wearing gold earrings and glass bangles shrieks against the dark and the heat. The shirtless, round-bellied priest makes a signal and we all kneel, our thighs pressed against one another's and our knees mashing the toes of the person in front of us. The baby keeps wailing and the priest starts chanting in a monotone, wiping sweat from his forehead. Why the hell are we waiting to drop a coin or a pineapple or a wilted flower on this overfull altar so that the exhausted priest will tie a protection string on our wrists with limp fingers while intoning some words he has memorized? Suriya brings her hands together and bows her forehead to her fingertips. I imitate the gesture. Because we want to live well and we don't know how. I peel my hands apart and let them fall open at my chest, two empty cups.

When I wake up the day before my flight, Suriya has already folded her mat and swept our room. I'm going to take an early bus to Colombo and stay in a hostel near the airport. I get dressed, shove my pajamas in the top of my backpack, snap it shut. Then I lie down on the bed like a starfish. An arm of light reaches for my throat and chin. I open my mouth to taste sun. I force myself to stand, carry my packed bag downstairs. A small gray cat sits on the foot of the stairs, a patch of fur missing on his back.

I walk into the kitchen and lean my bag against the doorway. "I make you small eats, for your trip," Suriya says, aggressively stirring a pot of red rice.

"Oh, Nangi. You are so sweet. I can't thank you enough for—there's no way to explain—what you've given me—I don't—"

"No, El." She begins wrapping the meal in a torn plastic bag and newspaper. She turns her back to me. "Now you leave and I am a frog in a well." The words tiptoe across a tightrope. She folds each side of the newspaper into a triangle.

I put my hand on her shoulder and try to turn her toward me. "You'll be okay." She folds the newspaper into a neat package. "I still think you should go back to school. You could just take some time off, help your—"

"I think my mother was sick because she works too much. So much worries and all the time fighting with my father. And she did it all because of me. She said, I cannot leave your father because you are little, and later, when she was sick the first time, she said, I cannot stop working because you must go to school. But she is always calm and happy. Everyone love her more."

"Suriya, she would want you to keep studying, become a teacher." My eyes reach for hers, but she turns her face away.

"No, El. I must not do everything. My mother does everything and she becomes sick."

"What about money? Can you live off Ayya's salary?"

"Until my boyfriend comes, I can do something—sell fruits at the bus stand or something. I don't know. When I look the future, it is like a stone over my head."

"Look at the future." I speak to the table, where Suriya has piled up stones she's sifted out of rice.

"Look at the future," she repeats in a whisper. "So I must not look at it."

I hand her an envelope I've filled with thousand-rupee notes. She shakes her head and shuts her eyes tight. "Thank you, Akki. Please go now."

"You know I'm always here for you, right? If you need money or you decide you want to go back to school or you want to visit me, you write me, okay? I'll help."

She presses her lips together to steady them. "I know about you, El."

I spin my ring in circles on my index finger, starting to panic. There must be something I can do. I pull the ring off my finger, lay it on my palm, hold it out to Suriya. "I want you to have this." She is violently shaking her head, backing away from my outstretched hand.

"Please, it's no big deal, just something to remember me by."

But to me the offering is difficult, meaningful. I bought the ring for ten bucks at a flea market, but it's the only piece of jewelry that I've had for years and wear every day. A selfish sacrifice that only emphasizes the distance between us. As if I believe Suriya will be thrilled to have this cheap jewelry that she has never commented on or expressed interest in, just because it's from America. The Israeli boy on the beach was right to call the ring weird—golden sticks of various lengths piled up inside a ball of resin. Probably Suriya doesn't even like it and now will have to wear it out of obligation. A selfish gift, not at all demanded of the situation. What is called for is a display of sorrow. But I cannot feel sad, not yet. I am still buoyed by the contentment that comes from easy love, hinging on nothing, expecting nothing. I leave the ring on the table next to the pot of rice and wrap my arms around Suriya. "Thank you," she whispers. She hands me the package of food and tells me I must go, Colombo bus coming. "Yes, bus coming," I say and heave my pack onto my shoulders.

NEGOMBO

The bus stop, about a mile from the airport entrance, is crowded with tuk-tuk drivers waiting for an easy fare. "Yes, madam, come, madam." They nod and gesture to the backs of their rickshaws, which quickly fill up with luggage and tanned limbs. "I walk," I say, pointing to the block of concrete in the distance. "It's just right there."

The street to the airport is a one-lane highway of speeding vans, tour buses, and rickshaws. There is no sidewalk. Barbed-wire fences rise on both sides of the road. The sun quickly turns my clothes heavy, as if I'm draped in blankets drenched in hot water. I slip my hands under the shoulders of my pack to relieve the pressure of the straps. I'm plodding along with my elbows jutting out from my sides like chicken wings and sweat dotting my forehead and upper lip when a soldier in a watchtower calls down to me, "Hello. What happened?"

I stop walking and squint up at him. His camouflaged suit billows around his thin arms. "I guess I'm walking to the airport," I call up.

The teenage soldier in the watchtower on the other side of the road leans over his own guardrail. "Why you are walking, madam?" I hear the grin in his voice.

"Because I thought I should. Because I'm silly."

"Walking madam," the soldiers call after me as I continue toward the airport. "Silly madam." Their laughter jostles the rifles on their shoulders. Easy camaraderie borne of intractable boundaries. That time I passed a temple with Suriya and the Hindu holy man came toward us, chanting and waving incense about our faces and then smearing red paint on our foreheads with his thumb. When we passed a monk later that day, he peered out at me from under his umbrella and laughed so hard he had to wipe tears from his eyes, pointing at me and tapping his forehead. "White girl with red dot," Suriya said. "Is funny for monk." I basked in his inscrutable laughter as Suriya took my wrist in her fingers and continued leading me down the street. My love for Suriya wants nothing more than her presence. But now here I am, walking—without—my

God—my Goad, as Suriya says. Her smooth fingers, her huge
laugh—stop. Already my memory is turning her into a trinket.
Waking up to her tea every morning, falling asleep beside her
every night. Oh yes: the problem of sleep. The first time I came
back from Sri Lanka, I did not properly lose consciousness for
weeks, spent all day in a waking sleep, could barely wait until dusk
so that I could get in bed and pass out, which I did, and then woke
up two hours later and lay awake until dawn, almost hearing the
koel birds and the pirith, almost seeing the enormous, flat, still
clouds—holes in the sky whose periphery a person with scissor-
feet spent one good, long life walking—almost smelling the curry
leaves and jasmine plants, almost feeling the bumpety-bump of
the train seat against my back, almost hearing the wide, exuberant Sinhala vowels, almost hearing strangers ask me my country,
madam, my name, madam, welcoming me, oppressing me, taking
me away from the parts of myself that can't seem to stop betraying
the other parts. The sensual sterility of the U.S.—keep it quiet,
don't talk to strangers, don't give money to beggars, don't make
eye contact, don't invade personal space. How lonely. No wonder I
need so much sex.

Why can't I stay here?

It's not my home.

Inside the airport, a scratchy Muzak rendition of "Take Me
Home, Country Roads" hovers over the heads of tired-looking
people pushing silver carts piled with luggage. I almost give in to
the generic yearning. But my bangs are matted to my forehead
and my pants are cleaved to my thighs and I will not be able to
shower or change for the next twenty-four hours. I close myself in
a bathroom stall, strip to my underwear, wash myself off with the
toilet hose, mop the dirty residue off my lower back and thighs
with wads of toilet paper, put my clothes back on, splash water on

my face, pin my hair back with a barrette that is mercifully close to the top of my bag.

At my gate, Sri Lankan men in business suits and Teva-clad Europeans stand in line, waiting to walk out to the small plane that will take us to Delhi. A young man wearing a suit that's too big for him stands at the door, checking passports. When I hand him mine, he glances down at the startled twenty-six-year-old pictured there, and cries, "U.S.A.!" Clapping the passport shut, he belts out, "He was a buffalo soldier! In the heart of America! Stolen from Africa!" He beams and waves his hands back and forth in rhythm with the words. I join my voice to his, even though it's grating and off-key, even though I hate this song. It's only polite to sing along.

"When will you return to Sri Lanka?" he asks.

"I have no idea."

"You won't even remember me." He hands me my passport, looking to the passenger behind me, eager for the next round of jokes.

I walk onto the tarmac. The heat-softened asphalt makes a soft sucking sound with each step. Off-white clouds are pasted against the smoggy sky. There will be turbulence on the plane—maybe as we pass over Nepal, whose mountains I used to think I'd cross one day with a man I loved, the intensity of our sex life marking the distance we'd put between ourselves and the worldly—and as the plane shivers, I'll cross my legs and tighten my groin and close my eyes and feel almost really good; I always get wet when we hit a rough patch of air. A woman wearing an orange vest motions to me with small flicks of the wrist. I am meant to join a group of passengers standing between two planes. Not so long ago sleet was falling against the window of the bedroom I shared with the man I meant to marry, the ping of ice on glass punctuating my pleas—I want you to do everything to me, everything, everything. A roar bursts from the engine of the plane behind me, almost overwhelming the husky whir of the propeller in front of me. My hair flies upward into the space where one huge sound rests against another. Standing in this glut of white noise, I wait for someone in a uniform to motion me forward.

Acknowledgments

Wreck and Order benefited from early readings by Christine Small-wood, Alex Chee, and Russ Spencer. My agent, Jin Auh, saw with quick brilliance what worked and what didn't in my first draft; her guidance was invaluable. Alexis Washam is the editor I never dared to hope for. Her hard work, precise suggestions, and insight-ful questions made *Wreck and Order* the book it wanted to be. I'm grateful also to Jessica Friedman at the Wiley Agency, as well as Sarah Bedingfield, Dyana Messina, Kayleigh George, and every-one else at Hogarth: My book is blessed to have landed in such passionate, competent hands.

For wise words that informed this book directly and indirectly, I am indebted to Upul Nishantha Gamage, Munindra-ji, Kevin Courtney, and—most of all—Eddie Ellner. In addition to filling my head with zany, helpful ideas about the world, Eddie intro-duced me to Sri Nisargadatta Maharaj, whose transcribed talks figure heavily in this book.

Mom, Dad, and Corina: Your love, encouragement, and humor sustained me throughout the highly uncertain process of writing a first novel. Thank you all for being there no matter what.

Lanka Ekanayake: It's easy enough to thank you for practical help with Sinhala language and customs, but impossible to put into words my gratitude for your friendship.

Wyatt Alexander Mason: I feel lucky every day that I get to

spend my life exploring the limits of words with you. Thank you for being my champion, kicking my ass, reading every sentence of every draft with love and care, showing me how it feels to be understood.

I am also grateful to the following pieces of writing, which are referenced in *Wreck and Order*:

"Head, Heart" by Lydia Davis

When Things Fall Apart by Pema Chödrön

Brief Interviews with Hideous Men by David Foster Wallace

The Journals of Spalding Gray

"Archaic Torso of Apollo" by Rainer Maria Rilke

I Am That: Talks with Sri Nisargadatta Maharaj

"Sonnet IV" by Edna St. Vincent Millay

The Myth of Freedom by Chögyam Trungpa

"Self-Improvement" by Tony Hoagland

"The Chattering Mind" by Tim Parks

"The Arms and Legs of the Lake" by Mary Gaitskill

"On Not Being a Victim" by Mary Gaitskill

About the Author

HANNAH TENNANT-MOORE's work has appeared in the *New York Times, The New Republic, n+1, Tin House, Salon,* and the *Los Angeles Review of Books* and has twice been included in *The Best Buddhist Writing.* She lives in the Hudson Valley.